GRAD NIGHT

CARVER PIKE

DEDICATION AND AUTHOR'S NOTE

This book is dedicated to all the educators out there trying to navigate uncharted waters. It's a new world. Cell phones are practically as useful as a student's right hand, meaning it's not even feasible to take them away most of the time. Gone are the days of encyclopedias, dictionaries, and thesauruses. Why visit the library and flip through the card catalogue and understand the Dewey Decimal System when all the information a kid needs is right at his or her fingertips? We've replaced chalkboards with white boards and traded those for smart boards. Discipline has gone from beatings and dunce caps to hand-written warnings to a pleasant talking to.

Real teachers understand the struggle; they're trying to adapt, and in the end will succeed with a lot of patience and a whole lot of persistence. Protect yourselves with professionalism, arm yourselves with knowledge, prepare yourselves with practice, and be open to using technology in the classrooms. Many of you are like a second parent to these kids. Sometimes you're the only constant in their lives. You may not feel it all the time, but I do believe *most* of them value you, trust in you, learn from you, and will strive to be you... if you show them someone honorable to follow. Keep your head up. You really are a hero.

THANK YOU

I want to say a special thank you to the ladies who helped me get this book ready for publication. You always help me catch the little snafus along the way. Thank you to Joan W., Stephanie A., Kaye B., Mary H., Chriss P., Autumn S., and Fran for reading through this one for me.

I want to also say thank you to a few others. To Joan for championing my cause on the other side of the world. I know you're working your ass off to help me get my name out there. Not every day is a great day, but you never let that stop you. You'll never know how much that means to me.

To Faith Gibson for taking time out of your writing schedule to always read my books and give me such valuable feedback. You know I adore you.

To Kendall for being my wingman as we navigate these horror-filled waters.

To Autumn L., thank you for leading the charge and rounding up people interested in reading and reviewing my work.

To Tasha H. for looking for new promo opportunities.

I have such great friends in the book world, and I really appreciate all you do for me. You don't owe me anything, but you're always ready and willing to lend a helping hand.

As always, I have to thank my family. My daughters listen to me bounce my crazy-ass ideas off them. Especially when it came to this book lol. My sons always ask me about my books, pray for better sales, and not-so-happily give up the WiFi when I need to do interviews and live feeds. My wife sits side-by-side with me as she works on her college homework and I punch out these stories. She works her ass off, and I'm glad I get to be next to her while she does it.

Thank you to the readers. If you weren't here, I'd be telling stories to myself. That, my dear friends, would make me crazy.

1

MR. ROWEN

"Aww, you son of a bitch," Mr. Samuel Rowen cursed under his breath as his keys bounced off his kneecap and clattered against the cement hallway floor, sending a shrill echo that filled the dark, empty corridor like jingle bells on an evening long before Christmas Eve.

The self-proclaimed 'Mr. Scrooge' of Darrius Sawyer High School had chosen this classroom five years ago because he wanted to be far removed from the other teachers. Nobody would dare take it from him now. It was like he'd staked his claim in the Great Oklahoma Land Rush of 1889. The thought made him laugh. He sure felt like he'd been around that long.

He'd been at the school longer than anyone else. Even longer than the principal and Mrs. Grainger, the librarian. At one time, he was considered *Top Dog* around here. Now, he supposed, he was more like the annoying yapping little Chihuahua. If the Chihuahua were on the last leg of its journey.

Mr. Rowen couldn't stop his hands from shaking. His knees bothered him too much to stand for long periods of time, and his back ached constantly. He'd gotten his ass kicked mentally and spiritually. His mind was close to its breaking point. Physically, his body was trying to catch up, and it nearly had. He was worn out.

You're definitely not the man you once were.

He remembered being a student back when he thought himself invincible. Before the war, before marriage, and before the funeral. When he was in high school, he offered to carry his teachers' bags if they needed it, he held doors for his female classmates, and he stomped on bullies. Things were so different these days. Not only had the students changed, the teachers had too.

For many years, it was normal for teachers to stay late to grade papers or to prepare exams or to put true effort into their planning. All that had gone to shit, which was what led him to his current situation. It was late, and all of his colleagues had already fled the campus, excited to get away from their students and back into the safety of their homes.

The safety of their homes.

School should have never become synonymous with danger, but that's exactly what it was now. Students had become violent, with each other and with the staff. Teachers and administrators had been attacked. Nothing as severe as the school shootings that occurred on other campuses in the U.S., but this wasn't a rare situation here either. It didn't revolve around one child wanting revenge on the rest of the student body. It involved *most* of the students wanting payback against *everyone.*

Something far worse than teenage rage lurked in the DS High corridors. Everyone could sense it. Teachers hinted about it. They spoke in hushed tones, told stories about odd occurrences in their classrooms, and traveled in numbers as they made their way to their cars after school. Yet, nothing was done about it, so the sinister presence putting constant pressure on everyone who entered the campus remained.

Evil walked the hallways and Samuel knew its name.

James Bender.

He wished he hadn't stayed behind to grade papers. The truth was, he dreaded being home even more than he did being here at school. Ever since his wife, Martha, passed away, Samuel didn't feel right at home. It was too quiet. Too lonely.

Now, alone in the dark, he wished his classroom were on the

indoor side of the school instead of over here where only the shop, art, and music classrooms were located. The outdoor wing was reserved for the artsy electives. His math classes had no business out here, but he couldn't stand the stuffiness of the classrooms in the other wing.

With that freedom came something else. What it was, Mr. Rowan couldn't quite put his finger on, but he felt a chill run through his body as he looked down at his keys still resting on the ground. He needed to bend over and pick them up, but he was reluctant to turn his back for too long.

Turn your back on what, you old coot?

Nothing, of course. Nothing was behind him but the school court-yard. Wind passed through the trees at that exact moment and seemed to carry with it a strange hum. No, not a hum, but a growl, like the deep throaty sound a dog makes when it's trying to decide whether or not to pounce.

Maybe a nearby construction crew. Or a generator. It's nothing.

His internal voice wasn't very convincing. He was certain the sound wasn't man-made. As he turned and glanced out at the court-yard, his eyes scanned potential hiding spots and found nothing and nobody.

The small green area, barely even that hue anymore – it had turned from once vibrant and lively to mostly dull brown – was another of the reasons he'd picked this class. In many ways, he felt like a prisoner to the school, to these students, and this was his chance to have his cell located in an area where he could actually see the outdoors. Yet, at this moment, he wasn't too fond of the courtyard. There were too many places to hide.

Who would be hiding though, you old fart?

James Bender. That's who. The kid who wasn't in any of his classes and had never actually threatened him – had never spoken a word to him at all. Not a single one. He always walked with his head down and his hood pulled over it, covering his face. He was a strange boy who'd shown up halfway through the school year yet made friends with all the other students instantly. Friends was too soft a word. It was more like the others flocked to him, hovered around him, maybe even protected him.

Samuel didn't like James Bender. The kid gave him the creeps. It was by accident that he'd spoken to the boy in the first place. A group of kids, boys and girls, had been standing outside one of the bathrooms long after the bell rang signaling the start of the hour.

No students should have been outside the classrooms, and he knew many of the seniors had taken to skipping class in favor of other prohibited activities, like smoking in the bathrooms. Some had even been caught performing sexual acts in there. Teachers were supposed to issue detentions for any students found outside their classrooms without a hall pass. But Samuel didn't want to take it that far. He only cared to make sure the kids were safely in their classrooms and not doing anything that would get them in trouble.

"Hey, you kids know you should be in class," he'd yelled at them at the highest volume his aged vocal cords could handle. "You better get there before I send you all to after-school detention!"

The students parted like the Red Sea, divided right down the middle until Samuel could see *that* evil boy, James Bender, standing right at their center.

At the core of this class-skipping committee, he faced the old man with his head down and his shoulders hunched. He slowly raised one arm and what slid out from his sleeve still gave Samuel nightmares. His skin was dark, charcoal-black and was cracked, flaky, like pieces of it might chip off and fall to the ground. His arm looked like a charred tree root. The fingers that stretched from its opening fist were long and bony with aged and jagged nails. They clacked as they extended in stuttered jerky movements.

The other kids looked back at the old man with blank expressions, like they weren't even in the hallway witnessing this. It was how they looked when he tried to relay a complicated mathematical formula they couldn't quite grasp.

Samuel never saw the boy's face. It always stayed hidden in the shadows of his hood. The kid didn't even speak, but the warning was clear. Without uttering a single word, James Bender told him to mind his own business and keep his mouth shut. There were worse things than being reprimanded by the principal.

A series of visions flashed before his eyes, and the old man grabbed hold of the wall next to him to steady himself as he saw his wife's bony corpse exploding from its grass covered plot at Bakersfield Cemetery. Her skeletal face peered back at him, its jaw open, worms crawling out. Cockroach antennae flicked at her nostrils. A centipede traversed her forehead.

Her body rattled from within. He thought it was her lungs fighting for breath, but they'd long since decayed, and he realized it wasn't her body making that noise. Out of her opened jaw shot the head of a snake, its clear eyes and bared fangs coming straight at him. He screamed and thought the sound might have emitted from him in real life too, not only in this nightmare state.

The vision changed. He saw testicles with a drawstring tied above them, squeezing them so tight they turned pink, then cherry red, then deep purple. He traveled up the naked body and saw that it was himself. It was his scrotum being cinched. He chomped down on his own bottom lip until his dentures bit through and gnashed at it. Blood leaked down his chin along with the shredded, gummy remnants of his tattered lip.

His testicles exploded in a burst of blood and he screamed. With his face twisted in pain, he begged for the agony to end and his voice came out so loud he knew James Bender must be able to hear his plea.

A sharp, jagged fingernail slit open his belly, and a black, charred hand reached in to pull out his intestines, draping them over his chest as he watched in horror. His gut hurt in real life. The pain was unbearable, and he felt himself shitting his pants.

Then he was bloody and naked lying atop his wife's skeleton inside her coffin, suffering even in death. The snake wrapped around his neck, the centipede crawled into his ear, and the worms and cockroaches pushed at his lips, wriggling between them, trying to barge their way into their new home until he could no longer hold them back and they trod over his tongue and clogged his throat.

When the visions finally stopped, Samuel felt shit running down his leg. His khaki pants wouldn't hide it for long. The kids surrounding James Bender laughed. They jabbed fingers at Samuel and cackled with merriment. The teacher with the highest tenure in the school was knocked down to kindergarten level as he watched the schoolhouse bullies poke fun at him until he turned and fled as quickly as his arthritic legs would allow.

He rushed straight home, sat in the shower, watched the trail of crap run down the drain, and sobbed as he remembered the visions and thought of his wife suffering in her grave… alone.

Sick leave gave him the rest of the week off, and he considered leaving the school altogether, but he wasn't one to give up so easily, and even *he* couldn't fully believe what had occurred. He was old. What if it was a figment of his imagination? The more time that passed, the less he believed it had happened at all.

At one point, he had considered telling the principal about the incident, but he was terrified of the boy and the retaliation that might come as a result of it. So, he simply slipped an anonymous note into the principal's mail bin. All it said was the student James Bender should be looked at carefully. That there was something wrong with the boy.

Since that situation in the hallway, Samuel avoided the boy at all costs. He walked the long way to his classroom to make sure he'd never run into him by accident. He arrived early to work and left later than necessary – all to evade a student he didn't believe was a student at all. Yet, who would believe him if he said he thought the boy was a demon? They would call him crazy. Best case, they would convince him to retire. Samuel knew when the day came to call it quits, he would die soon after. Without a reason for living, he would readily accept his passing.

James Bender has no reason to punish you.

With his eyes still on the courtyard, he found it odd that he'd thought of the word *punish*. What would the boy punish him for? He hadn't done anything. Or had he?

What if he found out about the note to the principal?

Surely, he would have retaliated by now. Yet, that didn't set his mind at ease. James Bender was here at the school for a reason. Punishing Samuel could very well be a part of it.

You're not afraid of that idiot boy.

He could talk himself up all he wanted to, but Samuel knew the truth. He was way past his prime, and if that boy and his hoodlum friends wanted to hurt him, this would be the perfect opportunity to do it. But that would have meant they'd stuck around and waited for him all these hours.

Or they've driven by and noticed your car in the parking lot.

Branches cracked in the trees around him as a gust of wind whooshed through them again. The low murmur, that constant growl played at his ears causing him to tense up and wince.

"What is that?" he asked aloud, instantly wishing he hadn't because any answer he received would mean he definitely wasn't alone.

Every sound seemed amplified at this late hour, when only one security guard was still on campus. Who knew where that son of a bitch hid at this hour? The guy was a youngin' which meant he was probably somewhere tinkering with his phone.

A security guard who secures absolutely squat.

Samuel hated phones. He had nobody to call on the things and nobody to call him. His fingers couldn't move quickly enough to play games and his eyes were too tired to stare at a bright screen and laugh at dumb videos all day long. He preferred his books and crossword puzzles. That was all he needed in life.

It was time to go. Even if he returned to his house late, he still had a routine to follow. He'd go home, change into his pajamas, cook himself a steak, heat up frozen green beans, and then sit in front of the television and watch whatever was on at this hour while he ate his dinner and enjoyed exactly one cold beer. Then he would go to bed and read until he forgot that Martha wasn't lying next to him. When he switched off the light, he'd whisper, "Good night, sweet girl." Like he had every night since they got married over fifty years ago.

The only thing standing in the way of his routine was that damn set of keys on the ground. He stood six feet in his younger years. Now, in his constantly crouched manner, five inches could be subtracted from that. As hard as it was for him to bend over, the distance to the floor might as well have been a mile.

"Oh boy," he said aloud as he squatted ever so slightly.

His knees screamed at him, *"What are you doing old man? Are you fucking crazy putting us through this?"*

He pushed them past their comfort zone and lowered his back until his fingers swung from side to side like the wire clothes hanger he used to pop open his car door that time he'd accidentally locked his keys inside. His fingertips were so close to that damn keyring. They brushed it.

The growl behind him caused him to pause with his forehead pressed against the wall. If anyone saw him now, they'd have a story to tell tomorrow.

I must look like a complete jackass.

The growl grew louder, thrumming in his ears with a buzz that almost sounded like an otherworldly whisper.

"Who... who's there?" he asked.

Nobody answered. Only that hum that reverberated through the air. That angry dog ready to pounce.

Your mind is playing tricks on you. Just grab the keys and go, you old bastard.

He commonly used nicknames for himself that Martha used to call him whenever she was teasing him. Old coot, old fart, and old bastard were her favorites. Sometimes she'd add crotchety in there somewhere for emphasis.

Another inch and you've got them.

He lowered his forehead, which in turn brought down his back and his knees. His entire body right now was acting like some kind of machine. Turn the lever this way, activate the pulley, which will pull the belt and kick those five digits into gear. The human pulley system worked, and his fingers moved at the right moment.

Got 'em.

He snatched up the keyring, retrieved his briefcase from the ground, and lifted his body way too quickly. A wave of numbness crashed over him that almost knocked him on his ass. He gripped the wall and waited out the head rush that had become so common. He knew better than to push himself like this, but he didn't like that growl, and he wanted to hurry out of the school.

Because James Bender is near.

He wasn't. That was all in his mind. He had the keys and now he could go home.

No more late nights for you, you crotchety old bastard.

The dull lights in the corridor teased him. They provided only enough illumination that Samuel could have been underground and making his way out of a coal mine. Each lamp had so many dead bugs inside its fixture that its yellow glow barely seeped out.

Alone and feeling unusually spooked, Samuel walked toward the parking lot as quickly as he could. His levers started his pulleys, which turned his belts and got his body moving forward. He heel-toed it one step at a time.

He wished he had a weapon, but he held only a briefcase, the old-fashioned kind teachers used to use before they became such pansies. Today's teachers looked no different from the students. Some didn't even wear button-up shirts anymore and slung backpacks over their shoulders. He'd even heard the chorus of silly chimes from smartphone games flowing from inside the teachers' lounge bathroom stall.

For Christ's sake, take a shit and let that be that. Do your business and be done with it.

None of that mattered to him anymore. Soon, Samuel would be gone from this world. He figured he probably had another ten years left at most, and then he'd kick the bucket and be with Martha again. They'd been good enough people, so they'd both go to heaven where people took silent shits, wiped their asses, and moved on. *That* and long walks in the park.

A door slammed somewhere behind him, and Samuel almost hurt himself he turned around so quickly.

"Goddamn it," he cursed under his breath.

The hallway was empty. The courtyard appeared to be too. Branches swayed, shadows danced, but no person moved behind him.

"No good son of a bitch," Samuel said softly as he thought about the security guard letting a door slam behind him somewhere on campus.

"Trying to give me a damn heart attack."

His blood pressure was at an all-time high. He knew it. He was getting way too worked up for his own good.

Seeing nobody behind him, the old man turned toward the parking lot and kept moving. It was Friday night and he wasn't sure how he felt about that. He never knew what to do on the weekends. Sometimes he would sit on his front porch and do nothing at all. Regardless of what he'd choose to do later, he needed to get out of the school. It wasn't healthy to spend so much time around all these adolescent brats and the crap work they left behind. Most of them couldn't even get their own damn name and the date right.

Most of all, it did him no good to spend so many hours in a constant state of unease. The only certainty in his job was the crappy paycheck he'd receive. Everything else about it now seemed to keep him inches away from a full-blown panic attack. Or, at his age, a heart attack.

Halfway to the parking lot, Samuel became acutely aware of the sound of his feet tapping against the concrete. The *clip-clop* echoed off the wall to his left and seemed to dance around the courtyard trees before coming back to him like a boomerang of unsettling sound. The keys, which were now tucked snugly in his pocket, also jingled with each step.

The old man grabbed hold of the outside of his pocket and squeezed his keys tightly while at the same time softening his foot-steps. He was unsure why he did these things, but he felt the over-whelming need to be quiet. Like this was his chance to sneak away from the school unnoticed by anyone who might want to do him harm.

It's James Bender who might do you harm.

The sidewalk began to descend ever so slightly into a handicap ramp on its way to joining the blacktop parking lot.

That's when he saw them. Out there.

Beyond the parking lot was the baseball field, and for security reasons, one of the stadium lights was kept on at night to illuminate the school's exterior. This was a safety measure started several months before, after one of the local gangs robbed a teacher in the parking lot.

Now, that light exposed a new threat. Silhouettes of three figures stood side by side, watching him from the baseball diamond. They didn't move. They only watched.

Samuel froze in place and squinted to try to get a better look, but it was of no use. The blinding light behind them made the figures nothing more than dark, menacing shadows.

The old man looked behind him and back toward the school. He scanned the corridor, hoping to see the security guard somewhere in the distance. Even if he was there, Samuel's voice never raised to a volume loud enough to be considered a yell. He couldn't cry for help even if he wanted to. And if he could, he knew that guard wouldn't accomplish much. If he made it here on time, he'd fall victim just as quickly as Samuel would. Armed with nothing more than a baton and a walkie talkie, the guard was more of a deterrent than anything else.

Turning back toward the parking lot, it looked as if the three figures had moved closer. They were now halfway across the baseball diamond. The shadows had extended and now he could see the long end of what looked like a baseball bat resting against one of the silhouette's shoulders. A chain dangled from the fist of another. The guy in the middle could have been holding anything, for his weapon was hidden in the darkness.

Walk tall, Mr. Rowan. Don't let these little shits spook you.

Samuel was a proud man. He'd served time in the military and had been in a brawl or two over the course of his life. Once a scrappy young man and now a fragile older one, he wouldn't allow himself to cower in fear. Supernatural threats frightened him. But mere men couldn't cause him to quiver. No, he would walk to his car, get in, and drive home. These assholes in the shadows could go fuck themselves.

"Go scare someone else," he said barely above a whisper as he stepped toward his car.

The throaty growl filled the parking lot and Samuel's heart sank. These weren't regular hoodlums. Out of the corner of his eye, he saw the figures walk slowly the rest of the way across the baseball field, pass through the open gate, and move into the parking lot. And he knew James Bender was the boy in the middle.

Samuel's mind raced.

His hand shook again as he reached into his pocket.

The tough exterior he tried to carry melted there in the darkness. He was more afraid than he'd ever admit.

He'd known there was something *off* about this night.

With his key in hand, he reached his car, the only one in the parking lot, and wished he'd gotten the little remote thingamajig fixed. He'd always thought himself fully capable of sticking the key in the lock and turning it. He hadn't felt the need to push a button and have his door unlock for him. It was pure laziness. It was one of the things wrong with the world today.

When he tried to stick his key in the door, his hand shook so much the rest of them jangled, and his keys dropped to the ground.

Then the vision hit him, and he fell to his knees.

Martha stood in front of him, her old naked form as beautiful to him now as her younger one was back in the day. Her breasts were large, no longer firm, but that never mattered to him. Her hair was curled, nicely taken care of the way it always was. She smelled of lemon, like her favorite tea. Her arms reached out to him, offering for him to stand up, so he did, and he let her comfort him in her warm embrace.

But then she transformed. First, the lemon scent changed to that of rotten eggs. Her skin lost its rosy luster and faded to a greenish pallor. He pulled back to see her face and, with his movement, yanked patches of thin, brittle skin from her shoulders. Both his fists were clenched around crumbling chunks of Martha's flesh. Her eyeballs sunk into her skull, disappearing into dark voids. Her chin lowered and those pitch-black pits peered back at him. Her pretty hairdo fell in clumps that dropped to the ground in heavy thumps, the pieces of her scalp damp with gooey blood the consistency of mud.

Her arms extended, her hands reached for him, and her nails dug into his arms as she pulled him back to her chest. He couldn't fight her. He loved her. "Hell is nice this time of year," she said, her voice not her own, but coming out on that wave of deep growl he'd heard all night.

Then he was back in the parking lot, and the figures were close enough that he could hear their footsteps coming around from both sides of him.

"No," he whispered, refusing to look at them. They'd never see how terrified he was. Yet, he understood he'd taken too long getting to his car.

It was too late.

They weren't here to scare him. If they were, they would have yelled something at him, taunted him, and waited for him to beg for his life. They'd said nothing. He had nothing worth stealing, so it wasn't a robbery.

This was punishment. It was revenge or possibly a show of force.

It's James Bender. He warned you, but you had to put that note in the principal's mail slot. The demon's here to collect.

Footsteps moved slowly across the parking lot. Something dragged against the ground, and as one of the figures drew closer, Samuel saw that it was the heavy chain. Metal scraped the pavement.

"Oh, Mr. Rowen," a calm voice sang softly. "Oh, there you are, Mr. Rowen."

It was one of the boys with James.

The demon, himself, would have a different voice. It was why he never spoke, for when he did, it would mean the end of things. The end of life. Samuel understood that now and hoped the boy wouldn't speak. He pressed the palms of both hands against his ears to make sure he wouldn't hear it even if he did.

The demon's face remained hidden in the darkness of his hood.

"James," Samuel said as he decided to leave the keys on the ground and stand up to face the creature.

Through the pitch-black void at the boy's face, yellow orbs floated where his eyes should have been, and Samuel knew he was staring face to face with pure evil. Moonlight shone only enough to shimmer on the demon's shattered, serrated, saliva-drenched teeth.

Samuel tried to straighten his arched back. He wanted to appear strong and fearless, but his body betrayed him, and the pain reminded him he was a soldier no more. The light from the baseball field glinted off the metallic chain as one of the boy's whipped it through the air and brought it down against the old man's head.

It hit him with a thwack. A crunch sounded off inside his skull and bright lights lit up behind his eyelids as immense pain pierced his brave façade and sent him crashing to the ground. He was a useless heap holding onto only the hope of reaching his beloved in heaven.

There was a crack as the chain came back around.

Heat. Searing pain at his wrist, his forearm, his ribcage.

Flesh ripped from his forehead down his cheek and chin as the chain's shoddy soldering grabbed hold of his skin and peeled it from his face.

Then so much pain he couldn't identify any of it anymore.

He was on the ground, his body a spasming pile of broken bone and bloody parts.

The bat came down hard.

Then the chain again.

James Bender carried nothing.

The last thing Samuel Rowan saw before his heavy, bobbing eyelids closed forever was the glowing orbs shining down on him, saliva dripping from the drawstrings of the boy's hood, and that long-clawed finger pointing at him.

2

CHARLIE

"Did you see that motherfucker? Punk ass bitch thinks he's hard. I should show his ass who's hard."

"You're always trying to show off your hardness."

"Fuck you, man."

Charles "Mr. Charlie" Evans stood outside the bathroom door, listening to the conversation on the other side. The boys were angry about something. They usually were. It seemed his students were always finding something to bitch about.

Modern-day kids were different from those Charlie had grown up around. He supposed every teacher thought that way when comparing the youth of the past with the students of the present. To him, they were today's version of 70s Vietnam War protestors grabbing hold of society's current beliefs and wringing them out like someone's wet laundry. Only, instead of marching in the streets, they posted memes and vague statements from the comforts of their homes.

If it made people stop and listen, they'd do it, no matter the cost. Some were online bullies, many were violent in their ways; however, Charlie still believed that deep down in their roots, the majority of his students were good people.

For this reason, Charlie often found himself making excuses for the wicked shit he saw on campus. When other teachers wrote them off, he searched for ways to identify with them. He played devil's advocate more often than he cared to, but it kept him sane. He refused to believe his students were any more devious or sinister than those of yesteryear. They were victims of their environments.

They're just trying to get attention from parents who'd rather remain plugged in to a social media existence than check on their children.

Homelife conversations had gone from, "Come here and sit down. Tell Mama about your day," to, "Hold that thought. Come here and take a selfie with Mama."

It wasn't *all* the parents' fault, and regardless of his beliefs in the overall good of his students, he couldn't deny that he'd seen and heard some wild shit this year.

A video had been passed around to all the students at Darrius Sawyer High, often called DS High, and it was one filmed at the back of a classroom. A girl was on her knees sucking a classmate's cock while their colleagues created a crescent-shape shield to block the cameras positioned at the back corner of the room. When the video made its rounds, the participants weren't mortified like one might think, but did their part in making sure it went viral.

First of all, there was no denying that they were wrong. It wasn't okay. Charlie's excuse for them? It was what they understood of the world today. It was how many of their role models found their way. Famous socialites, musicians, and actors "accidentally" leaked sex videos and found their fast track to fame. Not one, not two, but many more.

Add that to the oversexed media they viewed, the explicit lyrics to most songs topping the charts, and the belief that sex is not bad but is a wonderful way for two people to connect, and you've got a recipe for youthful mistakes caught on camera.

Years from now, he knew they'd regret their decision to do it, but right now they were stars because of it, even if only on a local level. Their names spread across the social media universe like wildfire.

This is what they want right now. It's the modern-day equivalent of running off to join the circus.

But then there were the violent attacks. One of the teachers, only a week earlier, got stabbed by a pencil. It went straight through her hand. Why? Because she asked a female student to leave her class for arriving twenty minutes late without a written excuse. Charlie couldn't come up with any justification for that one.

Another teacher, this one an old man who'd been at the school half his life, was beaten to death in the school parking lot. It happened on a Friday night, and if not for the school security guard finding the body, the kids would have arrived Monday morning to the sight. Rumor was the old man's body had been torn up so badly he was only identifiable from the car his remains rested beside.

It was chalked up to a gang beating, but Charlie had his suspicions. He hated to think any of the students would be involved in something so heinous, but he wasn't confident enough in their innocence to put all his faith in the gang theory. It would be naïve to think some of the students weren't rotten fruit. One only had to follow the flies to find the source of the stench. It seemed local police decided to ignore the foul odor altogether.

True, local gangs, especially ones whose members once attended the school, seemed to like using the campus for their initiation practices. This was the reason teachers were no longer allowed to stay after hours, and a police squad car was always stationed in the parking lot each morning before students and teachers arrived and would return each afternoon and stay until the kids and facilitators evacuated the premises.

Charlie had taught rambunctious teens in the past. Some were spoiled rotten and knew nothing of going without. Some were the exact opposite and lived rough, harsh lives. Both of these groups had a few students who were plain mean. What if the old man's murderer wasn't out on the streets spray painting bridges and doing drive-bys? What if he or she was already here on campus, answering the morning roll call and getting school lunch discounts?

Would I see that kind of psychopath written in the eyes of my students?

Handling immaturity was one thing, but dealing with kids who were downright cruel was something else entirely. Childishness wore on the nerves, but the vileness of pure evil wore on a teacher's hope for humanity, and Charlie encountered both at DS High. Sometimes distinguishing one from the other was the real task of the teacher, and that was what ruined most of the newbies who came into the career strong with compassion and vision and left downtrodden and destroyed.

It broke his heart each time he saw it happen, and it helped him realize the ones who remained were real warriors.

Charlie was exhausted, and nearly defeated, but he was not yet done. He held onto hope but imagined it like cheese stretching off a piping hot pizza. At some point, it would snap, and he'd let it fall how it would. Only then would he truly see which of his students actually gave a damn. They needed to prove him right before he realized he was wrong.

Outside the school's walls, things were twice as bad. The police were outmanned and outgunned. They were so busy playing defense they couldn't figure out how to strike first. The poor neighborhoods were on their own and the rich ones walled everything up to make sure none of the riffraff outside made its way in.

Big city riots were so routine some of the citizens started calling them annual festivals like the Bastards of Baltimore Festival, the Mayhem in Miami Festival, and the Outrage in Oakland Festival. Charlie figured they were only a few violent crimes away from the country adopting the plan laid out by the movie *The Purge*.

The fact that kids even attended schools anymore was a shocker with so much real-world drama going on all around them. Maybe he was expecting too much of them by hoping they'd do more than simply show up for class. So many of them didn't even do that anymore.

For those who did show up, Charlie would be here. If he could reach even a few of them, then he'd consider himself a success.

Standing outside the bathroom door, Charlie listened to the rest of the boys' conversation, waiting for the moment that would help him decide whether to walk away or barge right in.

"Mr. Lafferty's always tryin' to make an example of me, dawg," the first boy said.

"Then do it, bro," the second replied. "Kick that motherfucker's ass. Bet he don't do that shit no more after that."

And this was precisely the moment Charlie dreaded. At what point are teenagers making idle threats and when should it be considered serious? In this school, this year anyway, every threat might be real. Now, the decision at hand was, should he report the boys? And if he did, would he be putting himself in harm's way? Or should he pass this off as teenage frustration and leave well enough alone?

Mr. Lafferty, the teacher these boys were referencing, taught grammar. He was, indeed, quite the asshole. Charlie prided himself in being the *cool* teacher. He got along with some of the kids, loathed most of the teachers, and tried his best to spruce up his literature classes with technology, interactive workshops, and games. He hoped livening up the experience would help some of what he was teaching sink in.

Teachers like Mr. Lafferty did the opposite. Some of them seemed to get-off on forcing kids to open their books, read, and answer the textbook questions. And when the kids tried to challenge them, mostly because they were bored, teachers like Mr. Lafferty would belittle them, embarrass them, and be downright rude to them.

They were right. Mr. Lafferty was a punk-ass bitch. Yet, he was a colleague and it was now Charlie's responsibility to make sure he was in no real danger.

Charlie pushed through the bathroom door and waved thick steam-like smoke away from his face. The boys were vaping. They leaned against the counter and one quickly hid something behind his back.

Fuck. Challenge number two. First, are they a threat? Second, should you deal with the smoking issue?

Being the *cool* teacher came with its disadvantages. It was like walking a tightrope above a burning city with a few of the people below shooting darts at you, doing their best to knock you down. One wrong step and he would no longer be the guy some of them looked up to. They would cease telling him things. He would lose their trust.

The air wreaked of chocolate. The problem with these e-cigarettes or vape pens was kids sucked on them like candy and believed they were as harmless.

Even sweet things give you diabetes.

"We're all going to die someday." That seemed to be their belief when asked about it. Like kids' sudden fascination with the devil. TV shows and books and video games made people stop and consider that Lucifer might be a good dude. Kids liked to say things like, "Guess I'll see you in hell." Or, "Hell will have better parties."

Risking it all to be funny.

Charlie didn't pretend to know the truth about everlasting life or eternal damnation, but he wasn't willing to roll the dice and find out. He figured he might as well be a good person and see where that landed him.

"Gentlemen," Charlie said as he stopped in front of the two boys.

The one who'd hidden the device behind his back was a senior at the school. Drew Dryer. He'd been an all-star on the basketball team before his grades fell below eligibility level and he was removed from the team. His coach made a huge fuss when it happened. The boy's parents did too. They all claimed he was being ridden too hard by his teachers and that none of it was fair. It had been fair. Completely. Drew rarely came to class, and when he did, he slept through it.

"Drew," Charlie said, as he looked the boy up and down, mentally warring with himself over whether or not it was worth it to ask the boy what was hidden behind his back.

He knew he should. It was his duty to prevent the kids from engaging in prohibited activities on school grounds. Smoking was definitely forbidden. Even doing it in the parking lot could get him expelled. Yet, Charlie knew it wouldn't change anything. Plus, Drew was only a week away from graduation. This was their "skate week" as in they would skate right through it because no teacher wanted to grade more papers when these teenagers already had one foot out the door.

Drew would graduate... barely.

"Roth," Charlie said as he turned his attention to the other boy.

Milton Rothmeyer, better known as Roth, was one of the spoiled kids. Yet, he dressed and acted like he'd been suffering through life. Having grown up in extreme poverty for most of his childhood and knowing the difficulties that came with it, Charlie couldn't help despising the boy. The punk walked around like he lived a neglected life.

Charlie knew the truth because he'd witnessed the boy's lavish lifestyle when he tutored him in ninth grade. Mr. Rothmeyer was a very wealthy lawyer who made it home in time for dinner every night. Meals cooked by a maid. Mrs. Rothmeyer was there waiting by the door every day when Roth arrived from school. Young Roth probably hadn't had a difficult day in his life, yet he strutted around campus like King Dick, bullying the younger kids and throwing up gang signs for gangs Charlie doubted even existed.

Even now, the asshole's smug expression made Charlie's temperature boil. He wanted to turn Roth in, but he kind of liked Drew. The boy was lazy, but he was looked up to on campus. Every time he doubted Drew, he remembered the time he introduced *The Count of Monte Cristo* to class, and even though Charlie had warned them it was a heavy book, Drew liked the description of it and convinced his class they could handle it.

They couldn't, but Drew tried even if only for a week or so. That meant he wasn't beyond reach. He wasn't nearly as awful as Roth.

"Yo, what's up, Mr. Charlie?" Roth replied.

Charlie slid between the two so he could get to the sink. "Stinks in here."

"Yeah, I know," Drew said. "Some punk was in here before us—"

"—and I told him he better get out of our faces with that nasty chocolate vape shit," Roth interrupted. "Vape stuff. Sorry. No disrespect."

"It is shit," Charlie agreed.

Both boys laughed.

"You're alright, Mr. Charlie," Roth said.

Charlie moved past them to grab a paper towel. "You boys ready to graduate?"

"Oh, hell yeah," Drew said. "You know it."

"I heard you a second ago," Charlie said, deciding to do his best to smother this situation before it boiled over and caused anyone real arm, "about Mr. Lafferty."

Both boys slumped over and went silent.

"You're almost out of here," Charlie reminded them. "Stay out of trouble. Mr. Lafferty isn't worth it, guys. Nobody is. I've taught you for how many years now?"

"Several," Roth said with a snicker.

Charlie couldn't trust that he'd listen, but he got the feeling he could reach Drew.

"Can I tell you a secret?" he asked them both.

They nodded.

"I don't like that mean ol' bastard either," Charlie admitted, breaking the teacher code and siding with the students. It was never okay to badmouth one of your own, but he felt this was the only way to reach them without ratting them out. "He's been mean a long time, and he'll go on being mean long after you graduate. We've had enough violence on and off campus. Just let it go. Graduate and move on, guys."

They were both silent for a few seconds and then Drew nodded. Roth laughed. Then Drew joined him in laughter.

"You thought we were serious?" Drew asked.

"We ain't gonna hurt nobody," Roth said.

"Promise?" Charlie asked.

"Yeah, man," Drew said, but the way he looked away made Charlie nervous.

"Drew?" he asked.

Drew looked him in the eye again. "I promise, Mr. Charlie. Come on, man."

"Roth?" Charlie asked.

The sleaze ball nodded and grinned. It was the best he would get from these boys. He knew that, so he didn't press any further.

"You're almost finished," Charlie said again as he threw his paper towel into the garbage can. As he walked out of the bathroom, he added over his shoulder, "And I expect to see you both in class next hour."

When the door closed behind him, he heard Roth say, "Fuck him, dawg. I ain't goin' to his lame fuckin' class."

Charlie stopped in his tracks, clenching his fists as he contemplated going back in there to confront the boy.

"Shut up, man," he heard Drew stick up for him. "Mr. Charlie's a cool-ass dude. The only motherfucker in this school that actually gives a shit."

Charlie's mouth turned up into a smile and he walked back to his classroom, glad he didn't barge back into that bathroom and haul that wannabe gangster out of it.

3

CHARLIE

Being a younger teacher, only thirty-five years old, made keeping control of his temper difficult. He was a good teacher. He'd done his best to always stay level-headed and do well by his students.

Have you, though? You've been pretty worn out these last couple of years. You're losing patience. You're losing your desire to teach.

It was true. He'd started the job with so much fire to turn these kids around and help them have fun with learning, but after witnessing all the cheating, hearing all the complaints, sitting through all the parent-teacher meetings where parents stuck up for their children and placed all the blame on him, and facing that brick wall every time he tried to get his students to study or try hard… yeah, it was kicking his ass.

He even cursed around the kids sometimes now. The first time he did it, it was purely out of frustration. He lost it. He yelled, "I'm sick of this shit. Just sit down and shut up."

And they listened. They actually heard him. He could have said *it*. He could have yelled, "I'm sick of it!" But they wouldn't have stopped, stared, and then sat down quietly.

Why?

Because it was *their* language. He'd always thought curse words were simply a form of expression, and he'd discovered that now, they were action words. They meant something. They meant their teacher wasn't afraid to speak to them like adults. He wasn't fearful of retaliation. He wasn't putting himself on a pedestal. Like them, he'd lost his cool.

As Charlie sat down at his desk and surveyed his empty classroom, he wondered how many more years of this he had in him. The pay was shit. Everyone knew that.

What would you do if you could leave?

He'd be a bartender. Not because he knew anything about mixing drinks, but because he could do it and go home at the end of his shift. He couldn't cause any permanent damage by incorrectly influencing one of America's youth. He would pour drinks, hear sad tales about love and loss, he'd listen to music – some good and some horrid – and then he'd go home at the end of his shift and sleep.

No grading papers. No planning classes. No creating tests. No fear that today might be the day he pisses off a student who feels like he has nothing to lose and strikes back in a violent way.

That's the real harsh truth, isn't it?

The good kids held his heart, but the bad ones could shove a cold blade through it at any moment. Charlie had become afraid of them. Not because they were stronger than he was. He could handle himself well enough. But they were prone to making stupid decisions.

Even the school security guard wasn't safe. He'd gotten his leg slashed open by a broken piece of pottery when he tried to break up a fight between two boys.

This year was the worst. Minor incidents seemed to happen at least once per month, and most seemed to be the result of students flipping out due to "too much stress" as the school principal put it. As usual, teachers were to blame. After all, it was their job to control not only the lessons taught in the classrooms, but to help clear the emotional storms brewing in all the angsty teenage students.

Some weren't *just* angsty though. One kid creeped him out. James Bender. The boy who walked through the school with his hood pulled down so low his face was never seen. If Charlie taught him, he'd make him remove it in class, but he'd never had the displeasure of teaching him. For that, he was thankful. The interesting thing was, the kid had never done anything wrong to Charlie, but he seemed... *off*. The way a lot of the others rallied around him was strange.

He'd been surprised to see the yearbook and not find James Bender listed on the senior superlatives page as Most Popular or Friendliest or even Mr. Personality. The kids definitely treated him like royalty. Charlie wondered how he behaved in class and imagined he probably put his head down and slept through most of it. With his cult-like following, maybe he'd even order the teacher to sit down and listen as he stood at the head of the class, spread out his arms, and preached a sermon.

You really do need to get out of your head, man.

The next time he spoke with Mrs. Laymon, the school guidance counselor, he decided he would ask her about the boy. For curiosity's sake. There was a good chance she'd know nothing about him either since it seemed she did very little counseling. The few students of his interested enough in their futures to inquire about college only scoffed when he told them they should speak to their guidance counselor. One actually replied, "We have a guidance counselor?"

"Hey, Mr. Charlie!" came the voice of one of his favorite students, interrupting him from unpleasant thoughts about a kid he knew absolutely nothing about.

Of course, teachers weren't supposed to have favorites, but he did. Just like he had the ones he hated. Sure, he believed in the overall good of the kids, but some were mean-spirited assholes. He and his best friend at the school, music teacher Joel Mendez, often spoke about the students. It was their way of blowing off steam. Joel would ask, "Which student, of all the students, would you love to punch in the face if you ever had the chance?" "Easy," Charlie would answer. "Rothmeyer. Rothmeyer or Cupo."

Liz Cupo was one of the meanest bitches in the school. Charlie didn't teach her this year, and he was so grateful for that. He thought he was going to lose it last year when he got stuck with her in his homeroom class. Her dad was some kind of mob boss, connected enough to make everyone afraid to piss him off, which made everyone afraid of Liz, too. She was as ruthless as her father, maybe nastier. And she was Senior Class President.

Go figure.

Of course, Charlie would never punch a girl. He'd never punch a student at all. It was nothing more than a long-running joke between friends, and sometimes it took a bit of witty banter to take the edge off. It was either that or sip from a flask, and that, too, was something Charlie would never do. He suspected a couple of the other teachers might indulge in a stiff drink between classes. A few seemed half-drunk most of the time.

"Mr. Charlie?" He'd gotten tangled up in his thoughts and forgot to answer her. The voice belonged to Josie Simmons, a twelfth grader who didn't seem to carry the same hateful baggage as some of her classmates. She was quiet, kept to herself mostly, but she was always pleasant. She would graduate with honors, and she completely deserved it.

Josie was cute, had short brown hair barely long enough to pull back into a ponytail, which was how she always wore it, and would have fallen into the nerdy-kid classification if she hadn't also excelled at dancing. So, while she maintained a high grade point average, she was also quite popular since she was a member of the cheer team and dance squad, alternating between the two depending on the sports season.

"Hey, Josie," Charlie said, with genuine happiness to see her. She was a prime example of the good kids he knew still existed in a world gone mad. "Sorry, lost in my thoughts."

He noticed she had a book tucked under her arm. That excited him more than anything. Seeing a kid with a novel, one he hadn't assigned to them, was almost as mythical as finding the pot of gold at the end of the rainbow or seeing a unicorn strutting through the school halls. Charlie actually chuckled with glee.

"Whatcha reading?" he asked, trying hard to hide his surprise.

"Oh, nothing," she replied, stopping to look at him and then cocking her head to the side and squinting her eyes. "What is it?"

"What do you mean?" he replied.

"You're grinning. Do we have a pop quiz?"

"No," he said, followed by a laugh.

Can't a teacher be ecstatic to see his student reading?

She blew out a breath and continued to her desk. "Ooookay."

He stood from his desk and approached hers. She was already digging through her backpack, pulling out everything she needed for class. He glanced down at the novel on her desk.

"*The Maddening,*" he read aloud. "By T.K. Tantrum. Hmm. Never heard of him. Or her. Or whomever…"

"Him," Josie assured him. "It's a horror book. Really twisted too. It's been making the rounds. You know how kids are. When one of us finds something worth reading, seeing, or doing, everyone else wants in on it. The ol' if she jumped off a bridge, would you jump?"

"Got it," he said.

Like vaping. A handful do it, post pics on social media, and suddenly it spreads like a virus.

He made a mental note of the title and author. He'd have to look this up later. If it was interesting enough to get his kids reading, it might be worth bringing into the classroom officially.

"Hi Mr. Charlie," another voice he knew all too well sang.

He looked over his shoulder to see Valerie Kemper strutting into the room. As usual, her skirt was entirely too short, and her shirt was much the same. The dress code at DS High was strictly enforced. Some of the teachers took great pride in busting the students refusing to follow the rules, but Charlie wasn't dumb enough to set himself up for that kind of failure.

Valerie was the typical hot blonde, the one most of the guys drooled over, most of the football players passed around – or at least that's what he'd overheard, but rumors could be nothing more than rumors – and most of the teachers disliked her. She got by mostly because her parents owned half the town.

How easy would it be for the situation to be twisted around if he said to her, "Young lady, don't you think your skirt is a little too short?" He'd taught her long enough to know her response would be something like, "I see you've been checking me out." And that would be that. No more Mr. Charlie at this school. Probably no more Mr. Charlie at any school.

As he glanced over at her, Valerie tossed her backpack onto her chair and yawned, reaching toward the ceiling in an overly stressed stretch that was obviously meant to tease his and everyone else around's senses. If there ever came a time she wasn't flirting, that would be the time to be concerned about her.

"Hold it right there, baby," the class clown, Gavin Myles, called out as he held up a camera and snapped a picture.

"Gavin," Charlie said. "Come on. Put the camera away."

"It's our last week, Teach, I'm trying to document everything!" Gavin replied, his goofy grin on full display.

"You mean play Peeping Tom on Valerie," Charlie argued.

"Oh, but you were watching too," the kid joked, and Charlie felt his face redden.

He turned away, shaking his head.

"Mr. Charlie, you goin' to the Grad Night party?" Valerie asked.

She had one finger in her mouth, putting on her best seductress routine. It would work on *everyone* else, but not on him.

"Val," Josie suddenly shot back, tilting her head to the side and bugging out her eyes.

Charlie hadn't heard about any party. Not that he would go anyway. It would be unprofessional.

They're graduating. Hell, it's probably after they graduate. It's not like they'll be students here.

No amount of mental arguing would make him okay with hanging out with students outside of school. That was the kind of stuff that got teachers fired.

"What?" Valerie asked Josie.

It seemed the two girls were engaged in some kind of silent fuss that involved exaggerated facial expressions accompanied by plenty of lip smacking and eye rolling.

"I hadn't heard about any party," Charlie replied. "Guess my invitation got lost in the mail."

By now, the rest of the class had entered. The two goth kids, as he thought of them, Rita and Bogdan, took their seats at the center of the room where they would be smooshed in among all the other personalities and therefore mostly ignored. They both dressed in black, wore black eyeliner and lipstick, and kept to themselves unless a social matter was brought up that challenged their freedom to be themselves.

Themselves. It's always about themselves. All of these kids. In their effort to be unique, they've become all alike. Even the goth kids. They're no different from all the other goth kids.

To be truly unique, kids needed to read the books they liked, not because someone else told them they should, but because they'd stumbled upon an author whose work they couldn't help but devour. Same with music. They should laugh at what they truly thought was funny, cringe at what bothered them, and fight back against matters that challenged their personal beliefs, not the beliefs of the "group" they belonged to.

They'll never understand what it is to be unique if they keep trying to be unique.

The two boys from the bathroom stumbled in only a minute after the bell. Some teachers would ask them to leave if they didn't arrive on time. That wasn't a battle he felt like fighting today. It wasn't worth it. Not during skate week.

Charlie returned to his desk, took his seat, and prepared a movie on his laptop. The girls were still bickering about the party when Drew got involved. His response was louder than the hushed whispers of his female counterparts.

"What invite?" Drew asked as he took his seat at the far back of the class.

Roth sat next to him.

"Roth," Mr. Charlie said.

He rolled his eyes, got up, and moved to the front of the class. Those boys knew damn well they couldn't sit anywhere near each other.

"An invite to the Grad Night party," Valerie whispered. "It just slipped. Sorry."

A few people shot her dirty looks, but nobody explained what was going on. The goth kids looked at each other, neither of them saying a word. It seemed nobody wanted him included in this shindig. That was okay. He didn't want an invitation anyway.

They better not have invited other teachers and not invited me though.

A wave of jealousy washed over him as he thought about some of the other teachers who might get an invite.

Ms. Peony, Lauren, was the computer teacher. Charlie was in love with her. He had been since the staff Christmas party last year. They'd left early to go have a drink together someplace quiet. It was a great night. They'd flirted nonstop and even held hands as they walked out to his car, but when he tried to kiss her at her front door, she pushed him away.

Since then, they'd gone out two other times and he'd been afraid to make his move. That sting of rejection had started to fade, and he didn't want to feel it all over again. Lauren was a couple of years older than he was, and she was what most people would call curvy, but she had the cutest damn dimples he'd ever seen and big honey brown eyes. She was gorgeous. The high school boys flirted with her nonstop. Several even asked her to prom. Of course, it had been played off as a joke in the end, but he knew the truth. She was a desired woman, and he thought about her often.

Then there was Mr. Cole. He was ex-military and as mean as could be. But he'd been here so many years most of the kids seemed to have respect for him even when they appreciated so few others. It was like he was a second father to many of them. He was a constant in a world where many of these kids had a revolving door of adult figures.

Charlie's buddy, Joel Mendez, was a music teacher, sang in a *bachata* band at Latin clubs part time, and many of the female students had a crush on him.

The list of invited teachers could be long. The only thing he knew right now was he was not on it. Maybe he'd been wrong about the kids liking him. The thought bothered him more than it should have. It kind of hurt. Like a bullwhip's lash to the soul. He'd get over it, but for the moment, it truly nagged at him.

"Enough about parties," he announced as he turned on the projector.

The class didn't quiet down at all. They were too caught up in their own teenage drama.

"Class," he said.

They seemed to grow even louder.

"Guys!" Bogdan, the goth kid, shouted. "Give the teacher some respect! It's not like we have much time left with him."

"It's not like we have much time left with him," Roth mimicked the boy in a high-pitched tone, followed by, "Shut up, girly boy. Doesn't surprise me that you want more time with him."

"Roth!" Charlie boomed loud enough to shut everyone up all at once.

Roth threw his hands up as if to say he was innocent. Charlie knew he wasn't, but again, this was the end of the school year, and inciting an incident right now would do nothing but put a negative vibe on the mood. It wasn't like he was going to change anything this late in their twelfth-grade year. He was lucky they continued showing up to class at all.

Sensing he finally had their full attention, he said, "It's funny you're all arguing about a party since I decided I was going to show you a movie that has quite a bit of partying in it. In fact, one of the characters says in it that she likes large parties. They're so intimate. Do you know what she means by that?"

Blank stares.

Of course, it was Josie who raised her hand, "I'm guessing it means that in small parties everybody's involved in everyone else's business. There aren't any secrets. No downtime."

"Oh," Valerie caught on and added, "and at large parties you can lose yourself in the crowd."

Several of the students nodded their heads and Charlie wondered how many of them wished they could get lost in a crowd.

"Nice," Charlie said. "Let's see if you still agree with those state-ments after watching the movie. It's based off of one of my favorite books of all time. I tried to get some of you to read it a couple of years back."

"Oh, not *Of Mice and Men*," Gavin complained.

"No," Charlie replied.

"*Pride and Prejudice?*" Valerie asked.

Both of the books mentioned had been huge flops. The kids went online to get the summarized chapter notes instead of actually reading.

"Nope."

He pressed play and waited.

It was all boos and complaints when the kids realized they were about to see the most modern version of F. Scott Fitzgerald's *The Great Gatsby*, until the opening credits began to roll, and Leonardo DiCaprio's name flashed on the screen. Then, the girls seemed to be fine with the selection. Eventually, the boys decided to give it a chance too.

4

LAUREN

Lauren walked into her living room and dropped her heavy bag full of papers onto the floor. She sighed and rolled her shoulders, finding the relief of weight to be damn near orgasmic.

"Oh, my God!" she yelled with a grunt into the empty space, expelling the workplace pressure, rage, and any other negativity pent up inside her.

This was her usual routine, so her only companion, her cat named Clyde, didn't even flinch. Instead, he made his way over to her and slid between her legs the way felines did, making sure she felt his touch and knew he was there for her.

"You understand me, don't you baby?"

She reached down, picked him up, and carried him into the kitchen where she set him down on a barstool at the center island and prepared his food. The cat ate better than she did sometimes. She actually had his meals budgeted alongside her car payment and utility bills. Anything left over and not spent on credit cards was thrown toward the cost of her own food. The thought made her laugh.

You're such a fucking loser.

She needed a shower, not only because she was dirty after a long day at work, but also because she needed to rinse free all the frustration, disappointment, and flirtatious comments from her male students. One boy in particular, Robbie Kline, never backed off. He was *that* kid. The one young female teachers got into trouble with all the time. She'd seen the news stories and read the articles: *From Teacher to Tutor to Baby Mama.* That was the last one she'd read.

Some of these young teachers simply couldn't resist the charms of their students, but Lauren could. She wasn't even tempted. At first, she'd found her students' comments flattering, endearing even, but after years of it, she'd grown tired. It was all a game to these kids. It wasn't like she was drop-dead gorgeous. Not even close. She had plenty of flaws, but to these boys, she was a challenge. One they'd never win, but also one for which they'd never stop striving.

I wonder if male teachers go through the same thing.

Lauren poured herself a glass of wine and took a long sip. Then she took another. She would shower, to rinse off all the bullshit, but first, she needed to bathe her insides with something that might give her a slight buzz and take the edge off. Wine wasn't strong enough. She eyed the bottle of tequila on the counter and laughed. She had to work tomorrow, so she couldn't overdo it, but a shot would be nice.

She didn't even search the refrigerator for a lime. She grabbed a shot glass from the cabinet, filled it up, and then downed it.

"Oh," she said with a wince. "Oh, wow."

Then she did it again.

With two shots of tequila warming her up on the inside, she took a hot shower to finish decontaminating. When she was finished, she dried off and then stood in front of the mirror and thought about Charlie. He seemed to genuinely like her, but he'd also quit trying, and she knew that was her fault.

They should have had a relationship by now, but as Lauren caught a glimpse of the hole in the bathroom wall, she was reminded of why it would never work with him. It might not ever work with any man. Of course, this hole had been caused by *her* when she'd accidentally flung the door open so hard the knob drove through the drywall, but it was so much like the holes that used to riddle the walls where she lived before this place. The holes *he* made.

How easily men punch through things.

She doubted Charlie was anything like that, but none of them started out that way. All men were the perfect boyfriend at first, then it always moved on to some rough lovemaking, then to some strong wrist grabbing in public, and eventually turned into full-blown violent arguments and forced sex.

Lauren stared at herself in the mirror and wondered if she were pretty enough to find a real man, a good man. Was she deserving of one? If so, why did she seem to attract the assholes?

Charlie had tried. They'd gone out on a few dates and he'd tried to kiss her that first night. It was too soon. He was smart to not try the second date, but on the third date, she thought she might give in to him. He took her home that night without so much as a kiss on the cheek. They'd missed their opportunity, and as much as she liked the handsome teacher, she figured their time had passed.

But she did think about him all the time. When she pleasured herself, it was usually him on her mind as she did it. With her in complete control, Charlie was an excellent imaginary lover. He did everything right, he was quiet, and he never pushed her beyond her limits.

Showered and in a pair of shorts and a T-shirt, probably the most unsexy outfit she owned – not that anyone was around to see her – she climbed into bed, picked up the TV remote, and put on the show she'd been binge watching for the past month.

Her sleep timer was set for two hours, which was almost the exact amount of time it took her to fall asleep every night. Her eyes were getting heavy and she'd missed part of the episode she was watching when the TV blinked out. It was time for bed.

In the darkness of her room and in the sudden silence, exhaustion forced her to ignore the sound that seemed to be emanating from the hallway. A low, odd growl shook the air. She imagined her air conditioner was acting up again. It often made weird noises when it did.

Then she heard footsteps. The neighbors overhead could have been walking. It could have been the guy next door. In a building like hers, strange sounds were common.

She shot upright in bed when she heard the creak of the living room floorboards. Clyde wasn't big enough to make it squeak like that. Besides, he was right here in bed with her. She reached out and pet his fur to make sure.

This time, the steps weren't only one or two, they were four, five, and six in rapid succession. The floor creaked with each one.

Lauren pressed both palms against her mattress, as if applying pressure there might help her launch up and out of the bed if the need arose.

She strained her ears and scanned her bedroom, seeing nothing except the empty blackness of night... and the open bedroom door leading out to the hallway.

Why did you leave the bedroom door open?

Had she left it open?

She was certain she'd closed it. She'd always hated sleeping with doors open. Even as a kid she'd insisted the closet and her main bedroom door be closed tight. If she was afraid, she would ask for her nightlight to be turned on, never the bathroom door left slightly ajar to allow a sliver of light to shine into her room.

But, her bedroom door was wide open right now.

You left it open. You had to have.

But, she hadn't. She remembered when she'd started to fall asleep and someone on the show she was watching knocked on a door. The banging was so loud she actually looked toward her bedroom door and for a second, wondered if someone had knocked on it.

It had been closed.

And now it was open.

Not that a cat could rescue her at a time like this, but she wanted something else living to be by her side. She needed to know she wasn't alone. She pulled the cat closer to her and stroked its fur, but Clyde fought to free himself from her grasp. He stood up and stared at the open bedroom door.

"Clyde," she whispered. "What is it?"

She'd heard the rumors that animals could see ghosts. She didn't know if there was any truth to it, but Clyde seemed to be tuned in to something. But what? Following her pet's gaze, she peered at the door.

Total silence, except for that thrum of her air conditioner. It never made this noise, and Lauren thought it reminded her of something she couldn't quite put her finger on. Suddenly, it came to her.

When she was a kid, she'd sit in front of an oscillating fan and speak into it, saying "Wow… wow… wow…. wow…" over and over again, finding the bladed chopping of her vocals oddly satisfying. She liked the way each wow became wa…ah…ow. It was similar to the sound she heard now, like someone's voice was being put through an oscillating fan, but it was a growl going in and something much more sinister sounding coming out the other end.

And with it… pitch black darkness.

Another footstep. Then one more. A third.

A scream built up in her core, deep down in her stomach, and was like a teakettle left on high. Any second now, the steam would rise to the top and she would roar. She would cry out in terror. She opened her mouth in anticipation, giving her voice the push she thought it needed, but no sound emitted.

Another footstep followed by the creaking of a board in her living room.

My phone. Where's my phone? It's charging. There.

Her cord wasn't long enough, and she always had to put it on the floor when it was plugged in to charge. She gritted her teeth and carefully pulled back her blanket, trying her best not to alert the intruder that she was awake. Maybe they'd think she was asleep and take whatever they'd come for and leave peacefully.

She had nothing of great value. Her TV wasn't brand new. Her stereo system wasn't either. Her purse. She'd left it on the kitchen island.

Fuck. Okay, no, this is good. They can take your money and credit cards and go.

But the footsteps weren't headed toward the kitchen. They seemed to be moving slowly in the direction of her room. They were coming toward her.

Of course, they wouldn't think she was asleep. She had the TV on until the timer turned it off. And they were already in the house when that happened. Whoever was in her apartment knew she was in the bedroom, they knew she was wide awake, and they were steadily making their way toward her.

Gathering all the courage she could, Lauren ripped the blanket the rest of the way off and slid out of bed. She crouched down on the floor, grabbed her phone, and pulled it free of the charging cable.

Then she heard the footsteps break into a run. Feet thumped down her hallway, racing toward her.

She panicked and leapt at her bedroom door, slammed it shut, and locked it.

Bang.

Something crashed against the door.

Someone.

Not so hard that it was trying to break it down, but hard enough to let her know someone was on the other side.

"Who are you?" she yelled. "What do you want from me?"

As she screamed, she dialed 911 into her phone and pressed the send button.

"Get out of my house," she threatened the unseen intruder. "Take what you came for and go."

The giggle that followed seemed inhuman. She backed away from the door and froze in terror as she was forced to hear the sound of someone in her hallway, stifling his or her own laughter. She imagined a cupped hand over a mouth and the laughter seeping through the gaps between the fingers.

And that strange thrum continued over it all.

"911, what is the nature of your emergency?" the tinny voice asked from her phone.

It took her a second to realize someone answered her call.

The laughter stopped.

The floor creaked back and forth, slow and steady, like someone was rocking back on their heels.

"Hello?" Lauren said into her phone.

"911," the voice replied.

"Someone's in my house!" she yelled. "They're right outside my room!"

"Ma'am, remain calm, and tell me where you live."

She heard the footsteps walk away from her bedroom door as she rattled off her address and explained what exactly was happening.

Fifteen minutes went by in silence. The operator remained on the line with her. The laughter on the other side of her door had stopped, but she was too afraid to step out of her room.

When the cops arrived at her apartment door, she was still hiding in her bedroom, and she only went out to answer when the voice on the phone assured her it was the police outside.

The intruder was gone.

Nothing had been stolen.

The only evidence of anyone having been in her house at all was the open terrace window and the envelope resting against her coffee table vase. It read: To Ms. Peony. From: Your Favorite Students.

She couldn't stop herself from trembling until she opened the envelope and saw it was an invitation to the Grad Night party.

"Is everything okay, ma'am?" one of the cops asked her.

She laughed under her breath and took a deep sigh, feeling utterly stupid.

"It was a senior prank," she replied. "Look…"

She showed the officer the invitation and he rolled his eyes before showing it to his partner who did the same.

"Kids these days," the second cop said, tapping her fingers against the pistol grip of her gun.

"They can be evil little shits if you don't mind me saying so," the first cop said.

"Absolutely horrid," Lauren replied. "Evil incarnate."

"Remind them tomorrow that they could get shot climbing through people's windows like that," the first cop said. "We live in a violent and paranoid world. Parents are accidentally shooting their own children who've snuck out to go to a party and then returned through a window. Just last week, a husband killed his wife because he was high on some kind of sleeping pill and woke up when his wife was returning home from her graveyard shift job. He thought she was a local gang-banger who'd threatened him earlier that day. Shot her right here."

He touched his index finger against the center of his forehead.

"I'm sure you see some brutal stuff," Lauren said.

"Ma'am, you have no idea," the second cop replied. "You take care of yourself and lock your apartment up tight. Let us know if you ever need us again."

The cops wished her a wonderful evening and left.

Before returning to bed, Lauren checked all her windows, locked her bedroom door, and then turned on the TV and deactivated the sleep timer. She doubted she would get any sleep the rest of the night, and she couldn't handle silence of any kind right now.

"Evil little fuckers," she said to herself, remembering the sinister giggle outside her bedroom door.

Putting herself through a mental police lineup, she pictured each of her students and tried to imagine them laughing on the other side of her door.

Who would do something so fucked up? Who has the balls for something like this?

Suddenly she found the whole ridiculous situation funny. Not light-hearted, romantic comedy kind of funny, but unbelievably wicked, a comical absurdity. Someone had scared the shit out of her only to do something sweet like invite her to an exclusive party. In addition to the party address, the words on the invitation instructed her not to tell anyone since only the graduating class's favorite teachers were invited.

She grabbed her big, body-length pillow and stuffed it between her legs, spooning it, and thought of Charlie lying next to her in bed. If he were here with her tonight, she would have felt a lot safer. He had such a calming way about him. His ability to see the good in people was inspiring and helped her remember why she'd started teaching in the first place.

These kids might be little shits, but they were *her* little shits.

Maybe there was still a chance for her and Charlie. He was sweet. In her mind, she revisited that first kiss he'd tried to press against her lips. What if she'd let him in that night? What if she'd allowed herself to be vulnerable? If she had, he might be here with her right now. That thought made her smile.

Tomorrow, she might talk to him and see how he was doing. Maybe he'd ask her out again. If he did, maybe she'd say yes.

She would also find out who broke into her house. Then, she might strangle him or her before giving them a goodbye hug.

And will you go to the party?

After they went through all this trouble? She would have to think about it.

You know you'll go. As much as they drive you crazy, you hate to let them down.

5

CHARLIE

"They could have been fucking shot," Mr. Cole yelled as he slammed a heavy book down on the teacher's lounge table.

Charlie's empty paper coffee cup rattled and nearly fell over. He silently thanked God he'd finished it in time. Coffee stains were a teacher's worst nightmare. He'd learned the hard way one morning on the way to school when he squeezed his Styrofoam cup too hard, his fingers went straight through and into the scorching hot liquid, and then it ran all over his pale-yellow shirt and the stack of graded tests he needed to hand back to students.

He was lucky this time around and took his final sip while talking to Mrs. Lowell, the history teacher, only seconds before Mr. Cole barged in and threw his temper tantrum. These two were both in their mid-sixties and rumored to have had an affair off and on again throughout the years. Neither would freely admit it and nobody would dare ask them about it.

Through all the yelling and barking, it took Charlie a full minute to understand what had the ex-military man so worked up. From what he pieced together, it seemed someone had broken into the old man's house only to leave a party invitation on his dining room table.

Mr. Cole was right. It was foolish and someone could have gotten shot. Charlie didn't doubt the man kept a gun somewhere near his bed. He probably slept with it under his pillow.

"Well, thank the Lord nobody was hurt," Mrs. Lowell said, patting Mr. Cole's knuckles.

It was a sensitive gesture that seemed to have a soothing effect on the old man. It led to a sudden silence that made Charlie feel uncomfortable, like he was an invisible soul witnessing the two share an intimate moment. But then the grumpy physics teacher huffed, shook his loose jowls, and everything was back to normal.

"Someone was in my house, Dawn," he said.

"I understand, but getting all riled up about it isn't going to change that. It was a senior prank. That's all. It's done and over with. It's not like you're going to that silly get-together anyway. Now, calm down before you end up giving yourself angina."

Mr. Cole stood and shooed her away. "Angina. Hubbub."

Mrs. Lowell turned her attention back to Charlie and said, "Someone was in my house too, but apparently my husband and I slept right through it. I tell you, when he's snoring, ain't nothing in the world that can disturb us. Not car alarms, not the bells of the church next door, and apparently not even a high school senior breaking and entering."

"You got one too?" Charlie asked.

He couldn't believe it. These two got invitations and he didn't? Mr. Cole he could understand. That grouchy son of a bitch had earned the students' respect, but Mrs. Lowell? She was high on back-pain medication half the time. He'd heard the students complain about her classes. She showed up late to most of them, needed substitutes to cover the other half, and even when she was there, she basically pointed at the whiteboard where she had the day's textbook assignment scribbled, and then she dozed off in her chair.

But nearly every student, even the worst of them, is passing her class? How can she possibly maintain grades the way she does? She has to be putting in fake numbers.

"Yes, I found it on the floor, propped up against my work shoes," Mrs. Lowell said. "Where did you find yours?"

44

He suddenly felt like the other Charlie, the one from *Charlie and the Chocolate Factory*, when the other kids were talking about how many Wonka bars they'd eaten in search of that golden ticket, and Charlie had to admit he'd eaten only two. But in this case, Charlie had *no* invitation.

Don't be so dramatic. Who cares about a teenage party? You can go to an adult fucking bar and have an adult fucking drink.

He could pretend it didn't matter, he could make a mental note of all the things he could do instead of joining the others, but it wasn't going to change the fact that two teachers he knew received invitations to the Grad Night party and Charlie didn't. He wasn't sure how to answer the old lady's question. She'd asked him where he'd found his invitation. He was embarrassed to tell the truth, but what other answer was there to give?

I found it right next to my broken heart.

He almost laughed out loud at himself and his pathetic joke. One of his students' sarcastic responses came back to him and he could practically hear it, the worlds tiniest violin playing a sad song solely for him.

"I didn't receive an invitation," he said, sucking it up and telling the truth.

Both of the other teachers in the room looked at each other. Mr. Cole pressed his lips together and shrugged his shoulders.

"Oh, Lordy," Mrs. Lowell said. "I'm so sorry. The invitation said we weren't supposed to tell anybody because not all teachers were invited. I don't know why I assumed—"

"—It's okay," Charlie assured her.

He meant to say more, but his eyes focused on the back of the book Mr. Cole slammed down against the table. He recognized it. Charlie turned the book over and saw the same dark cover he'd seen in his classroom the day before.

"*The Maddening* by T.K. Tantrum," Charlie read aloud.

"Huh?" Mrs. Lowell asked.

"The book," he replied. "Saw one of the students with it yesterday."

"I took that one off Becky Hayes," Mr. Cole said. "There I was spouting out my lesson, investing my time and energy in her education, and I see her snicker to herself. When I asked her what was so funny, she quickly closed that book. So, of course, I felt obliged to see what had stolen her attention away from physics. Garbage, that's what. Some kind of horror trash. Graphic too. Holy hell. Smut, that's what it is."

"Well then..." Mrs. Lowell said as she reached for the book and lifted it to her gaze. "Huh. Smut, you say?"

Mr. Cole laughed and walked to the coffee machine. Mrs. Lowell took her time reading the back of the book and then flipped it open and skimmed through a few pages.

"Do you mind if I borrow that?" I asked.

"I don't care what you do with it," Mr. Cole replied. "I've seen some of the language in that book and I can't imagine her parents would want her reading that rubbish."

Each time Mr. Cole disrespected the book by calling it garbage, trash, or smut, it felt like an invisible punch to Charlie's midsection. An author had poured his blood and guts into this novel. Like it or hate it, it took time to write, and it bothered Charlie whenever someone badmouthed any book or its author. He'd tried writing a book himself, but he wasn't disciplined enough to see it through to completion.

"I'll take care of it," he promised, "just in case."

Mrs. Lowell seemed reluctant to give up the book. Whatever she'd read in its pages had her fixated on the paperback. It wasn't until the bell rang signaling the end of the current class that she finally let go of it. She handed it to him, and he tucked it under his arm before heading to his class.

His next two classes weren't with the seniors, and he wondered if and when one of them might poke his or her head into his classroom and extend an invitation to the Grad Night party.

You don't want an invitation. The party will be lame. Plus, you shouldn't hang out with these kids.

He knew it was the truth, but he couldn't help feeling shitty that he hadn't even been considered for an invitation.

Do you really want someone breaking into your apartment and leaving one?

Thinking back to the fit Mr. Cole had thrown in the teacher's lounge, Charlie feared for the teenagers' safety. He decided he'd have a talk with them later on, because the old man had been absolutely right. These kids were lucky one of them hadn't gotten shot.

Or what if they'd given someone a heart attack?

He couldn't imagine catching someone breaking into his apartment. How did they do it? He could picture them wearing those Guy Fawkes masks from *V for Vendetta*. They could have frightened Mrs. Lowell half to death if she'd come out to her kitchen to get a glass of water last night when one of them was in her house.

Yes, he would definitely have a talk with them today. First, he wanted to peek inside this book and see what all the hoopla was about.

It didn't take long for him to get it. He read quietly to himself:

The smell of warm vanilla incense should have keyed me in. My last three attempts at making love to my wife had resulted in zilch. She had become a cold fish, my fish, in the only sea I was accustomed to. If there were any others, they'd already found the river's mouth and had begun swimming upstream to a higher elevation, where men had more money than I did and probably had bigger cocks. Maybe that was what she had in mind all along, to leave me for an upriver fish.

No, that wasn't it at all. It was the fucking game of it. A game I knew nothing about until it was too late. In the end, I was a champion of it, one of the few people who had lived long enough to figure it all out. But that night, the night of the warm vanilla incense, I was incredibly naïve, and I truly believed my wife wanted to make up for lost time. She'd called me earlier that night and asked me to pick up a bottle of her favorite sangria. As I set it down on the table, she stepped out of our room, completely naked, and holding a joint between two fingers.

She put it to her lips and pulled, lighting the tip up in red before seductively blowing out a ribbon of smoke. Neither of us had smoked since our college days, and I could only assume this was her way of saying it was time to let loose a little.

"Two glasses of wine and bring them to the bed naked," she said as she turned from me and made her way into our bedroom.

I was naked before I ever touched the wine bottle. As I poured the glasses, my cock stood at full attention, desperately needing something other than my hand to get off. She was in the other room, high and waiting for me. This was going to be the best night ever.

Charlie set down the book. "Whew. No wonder they're all reading this."

He chewed at the inside of his cheek and fought the urge to open the book and continue reading. Why did he feel so compelled to keep going? Did the students feel this way? Not only did he desire the words on the page, but he also remembered the teacher he'd had his sights set on for so long. Lauren Peony. He suddenly needed to talk to her. He laughed at the thought and put the book into his top desk drawer.

Are you hoping she'll tell you to grab two glasses of wine and come to bed naked? Damn right, I am.

"Hurry the fuck up so I can get my shit!"

As was often the case between classes, Charlie heard a ruckus kicking up outside his door. Most of the senior lockers were located in this hallway so he got to overhear a lot of gossip, plenty of complaints, and way more arguments than he cared to. The source of the voice now interrupting thoughts of the perfect date night with Lauren was obvious. It was the one kid at DS High who knew how to grate on his nerves.

Charlie threw open his door and caught Roth standing in front of Bogdan, their faces mere inches apart.

"What's going on out here?" he asked.

He knew damn well what was happening, but he wanted to hear it from the boy himself. Charlie couldn't stand bullies. He'd dealt with so many in his past that he wouldn't stand by and watch one of the good kids being pushed around.

"I need to get to my locker," Roth said, "and this little faggot is in my way."

"That's about enough of that," Charlie warned him. "I won't tolerate that kind of talk."

"What?" Roth asked, "Look at him? He wears mascara for cryin' out loud."

Bogdan's face reddened and his cheeks shook he was so mad, but he didn't say a word to stick up for himself. Violence was never the answer, but Charlie secretly wished the goth kid would flip out, turn green, and *Hulk* smash the shit out of the asshole of DS High.

"He's free to wear what he wants," Charlie said. "If you need to get to your locker, you can wait patiently for him to finish. If you're in a rush, you can speak to him respectfully and ask him nicely to let you get to your locker."

Roth scoffed. "You see, that doesn't work for me, Chuck."

Charlie couldn't believe his ears. "What did you call me?"

Roth shrugged, his smug grin returning to his face. "It's short for Charlie, right? What, Chuck doesn't work for you?"

"To the principal's office, now," Charlie ordered with a jab of his finger in the direction of the school's administration office.

Grabbing hold of the boy and escorting him there would be against school policy. It could be seen as roughing him up, overstepping his boundaries, and an all-around poor sense of judgement.

"I'll let them know you're coming," Charlie added.

Roth walked away, laughing, and called out over his shoulder, "You're lucky it's the end of the year, man. Both of y'all motherfuckers."

"I'll make sure I add that to your list of wrongdoings," Charlie replied.

"Whatever."

When Roth rounded the corner, Charlie returned his attention to Bogdan who'd gone back to silently pulling the books he needed for the last few hours of classes out of his locker and stuffing them into his backpack.

"You can be mad," Charlie told him.

Bogdan crouched down to zip up his backpack, refusing to look at his teacher. "What's the use?"

"Sometimes you have to stand up for yourself, Bog."

The boy stood and slung the strap of his bag over his shoulder.

Black tears were painted under his eyes, taking the place of any semblance of real sadness. Finally, he glanced up at Charlie who stood a few inches taller. "Confrontation with a kid like that would get me nowhere. I won't get into a pissing contest with a boy who pretends to be poor only because he thinks it ups his street cred."

Bogdan was way more observant than Charlie thought, and he wondered how many other kids knew the truth about the wannabe gangster.

"You're right," Charlie said. "He's not worth it, but listen to me now, Bog. There are three things in this world you always have to stand up for. Your family, yourself... and your beliefs. You lose any of those and you're an empty shell. There's nothing worse than that."

The boy stood there for a second, chewing on the words. Charlie only hoped he'd digest them rather than spitting them out and going on about his merry way. Bogdan nodded and walked away. "I'll see you in class, Mr. Charlie."

6

LAUREN

Every single one of her senior students could be the person who was in her apartment. That didn't sit well with Lauren as she looked out from her raised platform desk onto a sea of twelfth graders punching out the last words to their final essays. Instead of giving them an exam like most teachers were doing, she felt it made more sense to collect a written work from each of them explaining the strengths they'd developed in high school.

Some would take it seriously and mention things like responsibility, tenacity, or maybe even adaptability. Others would turn in lackluster work that described their strengths on the football field, their super-heightened ability to hook-up with the opposite sex, and quite possibly their capability of staying up over twenty-four hours to play video games and recharge with naps during their classes.

Yet, some of the know-it-alls would write something along the lines of: *Nothing. I learned nothing during my time in high school, because the teachers don't teach. It was a total waste of time, and I'd like those four years of my life back.*

It was always the teacher's fault.

Lauren wondered if any of them would create a five-paragraph essay explaining their new-found knowledge of picking locks, gracefully sliding through windows, and scaring their teacher half to death.

Finally, she could take no more, and she stood up with her hands on her hips, faced the classroom, and cleared her throat. "Something happened last night. I will not go into detail, but someone, more than likely someone in this room, knows exactly what I'm talking about. If that someone remains after class to talk to me about it, I would be rather grateful. If nobody does, I'll be taking major points off everyone's essay."

The class as a whole groaned. She was glad she couldn't read their minds.

Bitch. You can't do that, you dumb whore. Man, fuck you.

She'd hear more, much of it even worse than her own mind could conjure. Over the years, she'd been rocked by some of the things she'd heard in the hallway and even in her own classroom. These kids had no shame. Back in her day, she wouldn't have dared mutter even the word *crap*. Nowadays, that was a wimpy word. The school valedictorian recently used it in a speech addressed to the entire campus.

"We *will* succeed," he'd said. "We will take all the crap that's been handed to us and turn it into gold!"

Everyone cheered. No one flinched at the word.

Even *he* blamed the teachers. That *crap* was the education they'd received. He hadn't said it in such simple terms, but the overall idea was conveyed perfectly. He too couldn't wait to escape the prison of DS High.

These kids have no idea how rough life can get. High school is easy. Wait until they see what kind of crap the real world throws at them.

The way they'd all stood and cheered at that valedictorian's speech. Like he'd motivated them to charge forth into the world right this instant. He was that father patting them on the back and saying, "Go get 'em, tiger!" Lauren couldn't believe this was the end of it. These kids really were about to step out into the job market or onto college campuses.

She could almost hear Charlie saying, "They'll do great things. You wait and see." She would wait and see, because she had no other option. She only hoped she never ended up on an emergency room table with any of these kids wielding the scalpel.

Lord help us. This is our youth. This is our future. These are our business owners, politicians, and scientists.

She wished she could be even half as optimistic as Charlie. They'd discussed this over dinner one night. The way he spoke about the students with so much belief in their abilities to be all-around good people and with so much hope they'd actually succeed in life was quite inspiring.

Unfortunately, she didn't buy it. With these students at the helm, the world would never find a cure for cancer, discover life on other planets, or even create a bag of microwave popcorn that fully popped without burning. How could they when they were more concerned about taking the perfect selfie?

She considered pulling out her phone right now and snapping a picture of all their disgruntled faces. They didn't like her threat any more than she liked having someone sneaking around her apartment at night.

"It's simple," Lauren said after the groaning and complaining died down. "Someone only needs to stay and explain to me why it happened and why they, or if they know who did, then why that person, felt this was a smart thing to do. Finish your essays. I expect to see someone remain here after class."

Whispered conversations flew around the room, all too low for her to hear, but all carrying the resentful tone she expected. She only hoped it was someone here in this class, and not the boy she avoided in the hallways.

James Bender.

She knew so little about the teenager, but it didn't matter, he made her feel uneasy. It was more than that. Fear seemed like the wrong way to explain it, but whenever she saw him walking down the high school's corridors with his band of followers all around him, she found reasons to divert her course and take the more scenic route.

She'd never even seen the boy up close. He wasn't in any of her classes. She wondered if Charlie taught him. One thing was clear. When he was around, the air felt heavier, and she could swear the lights dimmed like it was their duty to keep him in the shadows.

One of her students raised her voice, angrily accusing one of the others. They were rooting one of them out. Somebody would approach her after class. The rest of the students would see to it.

She didn't expect it to be Elizabeth Cupo. Liz to her friends. Wicked Bitch of the East to the teachers. For anyone not involved in the educational system, they might think referring to a student in that way was harsh or uncalled for or even unprofessional. Even to those working in the field, it might seem wrong.

But this bitch... oh, this bitch deserves it.

She was eighteen years old, an adult as far as the rest of the world was concerned, and she was less than a week from never stepping foot on this campus again. She was beautiful, with long, straight, black hair and her family's tanned complexion. Other girls had to visit tanning beds, but not Liz. As with everything else in life, her beauty was handed to her.

Plus, the girl was well on her way to an easy future. She would either inherit one of her father's money-laundering businesses or would have a full, paid ride to her college of choice where she would drink, smoke, and probably fuck herself crazy while getting her degree solely because her father would shoot whomever had the balls to fail her.

She was evil. Lauren imagined her popping out of her mother's womb, snatching up the scissors, and snipping her own umbilical cord.

Lauren could spout out a dozen reasons she disliked the girl, but the worst was the time she told everyone a substitute teacher attempted to proposition her for sex. Her story went something like this:

"Mr. Matthews kept eyeing me in class. He insisted I sit up front, and twice he dropped his pen so he could look up my skirt. When I crossed my legs, he seemed disappointed. Then, when the bell rang, he called me to his desk. I was the only one in the room when he put his hand on top of mine and told me if I... if I... oh, God, if I sucked his cock, he would change half the grades in Mr. Goddard's gradebook for me. He said it would be easy to do because the teacher's book was in

the desk drawer and he wrote all his grades in pencil. I told him I would never do that, and he said… he said… oh, it still gives me nightmares. He said I was going to suck cock for a living anyways so I might as well get started with his. And then I ran from his classroom, crying. It took me two days to get up the nerve to tell anyone. I was just so embarrassed. Like it was my fault."

Mr. Matthews was gay, was married to a guy named Turner, and they had twin daughters. From his hospital bed, where he lay after Liz's father's goons got hold of him, he could barely return Lauren's gaze through eyelids so swollen he looked deformed. She'd gone to visit him because he was a family friend of hers. In fact, she was the one who'd helped him secure the substituting position at the school. So, she felt responsible when he whispered through lips too misshapen to open properly, "Why… why did she do this to me?"

The next day, when she'd asked Liz to stay after class, she put her job at risk by asking the young girl, "Did any of what you said really happen?"

If she'd thought the girl would be honest, she would have recorded the conversation, but none of it was planned. So, she was shocked when the bitch looked back at her, smiled, and said, "Of course, not. He's as gay as they come."

"Why then?"

"Because he threatened to leave a note for Mr. Goddard if I didn't work on my assignment in class."

"And?"

"And that's it. Nobody talks to me like that. I work when I want to work, and I don't when I don't want to. You know that."

After that, Lauren had spoken with the school principal and told him about the discussion. He'd only shrugged his shoulders and said, "Nobody believed her, Lauren. If what she'd said were true, we all know she would have punched him in the face. Mr. Matthews wasn't big enough or strong enough to be a threat to that girl."

"So, why fire Matthews then?"

"For his safety. Do you really think he'd return to this school anyway? This will never make it into his background files. Don't worry about that. Even the police know the truth. But who's going to go after Mr. Cupo?"

Nobody would. Her father was a protected man in this city. Protected from everyone, even the law. Mr. Matthews was lucky to be alive.

After that, Lauren had *never* had a one-on-one conversation with Liz. That was over a year ago. Since then, she'd only addressed the girl when in presence of the entire class. So, when Liz Cupo approached her desk as all the others walked out, Lauren felt a chill run down her spine.

She was afraid of the teenager. Not because of her father, but because the girl got what she wanted. If she decided to twist the words of this conversation to use to her advantage, Lauren was already done for. She couldn't say or do a thing about it.

"Elizabeth," Lauren said.

"Ms. Peony, it's Liz, please."

The girl giggled, as if she were the sweetest child on the planet. The game had begun. Lauren only needed to decide which move she'd make now.

She decided to smile. Two could play the *sweetheart* game. "Liz, I'm sorry. How have you been, sweetie?"

"Oh, you know." The girl put a hand to her head, the back of it, dramatically feigning exhaustion, like she might collapse from all the heat of the menacing sun's rays. The sun being the dull fluorescent bulb overhead. "A bit stressed."

"I'm sure," Lauren said, followed by another smile. "So..."

The girl had remained behind for a reason. Lauren wasn't going to lead her. Liz needed to do the talking.

"Right," Liz said. "So, about last night. I did it."

Lauren thought back to the girl's giggle when she'd corrected her on her name. It was not the same sound she'd heard in her apartment.

"You mean you sent someone," she goaded.

"Right, I mean come on. Please, I'm not going through all that trouble for a teacher."

Bite your tongue, Lauren. Bite it.

"I didn't even want you invited, to be honest," the girl continued. "It's for favorites, you know. Seems you're someone's."

Lauren chuckled. She remained silent for a second and looked over at the closed classroom door and the thin rectangular window at its center. She wondered if she were to grab Liz by her hair and drag her to the door, would the window break if she smacked the girl's head against it a few times?

No, it's too skinny. Too narrow. Even fucking better!

Liz smacked her lips together as if she'd just put on a fresh coat of lipstick and then turned toward the door. "Guess you got your answer."

"Wait a minute," Lauren said.

"I'm busy."

"Your essay?"

"Please."

That one word said so much. It asked, "Do you know who I am?" It said, "You can't make me." And, as she'd told Lauren when she'd asked about Mr. Matthews, it informed her, "I work when I want to work, and I don't when I don't want to. You know that."

"Excuse me?" Lauren found herself saying with a raised voice.

The girl had already turned her back to her and was headed for the door. She stopped and called out over her shoulder, "Give me the 'C.' Anything more than that and nobody will believe I did the work. Anything less and I'll make sure you don't work here next year."

"Elizabeth…" she started to reply.

"Don't," Liz warned her. "It's not worth it. Give me the 'C' and keep your mouth shut. Thank you."

Liz had her hand on the doorknob when Lauren said, "You know, he was right."

The girl turned and looked at her, her model-like beauty giving her an even more sinister appearance. "Who was right?"

Don't say it. Control yourself. Don't stoop to her level.

It seemed Liz only knew one level.

"Mr. Matthews. He was right about your future," Lauren said. "Might as well start now."

It took Liz nearly a full minute to remember her own lie, and when she did, she breathed deeply through flared nostrils. Lauren waited for the backlash. But then the girl coolly said, "Right. See you at the party, Ms. Peony."

She turned and walked out of the room.

Only then did Lauren realize she was clenching her fists so tight her nails dug into her hand. Alone in her classroom, Lauren wished she'd chosen to leave bite marks on her tongue rather than claw marks on her palm. At least she'd never have to face the bitch in the classroom again.

Reaching for her grade book, she wrote a big fat 'F' next to Elizabeth Cupo: final essay.

7

CHARLIE

This was his free period, and it was the only time he had left to do it. Charlie couldn't stop thinking about Lauren. He wanted to see her right now, and he wanted to take her out tonight. He thought he might understand why she was so hesitant to get close to him. She liked him too. At least, he thought she did, but he'd noticed during their last date that she flinched easily whenever someone raised his or her voice around her.

It was a horrible comparison, but she reminded him of a collie he once picked up from the pound. It behaved the same way, shrinking whenever there was loud noise or heated disputes. Thunder made it piss on the floor and action movies sent it cowering behind the couch. A vet told him it was because the dog had been abused.

Keeping that in mind, he decided he could move slowly. He only needed to show Lauren that he wasn't like anybody she'd dated in the past. He was one of the good guys. His wiring was different. While most guys he knew would probably think about getting into her pants, he hoped for simpler things like cuddling up with her and watching TV or spooning her in bed, fully clothed, and listening to a good audio book.

I am such a fucking dork. Who wants to lie in bed and listen to audio books? I do, that's who.

They'd spoken about exes only once. She'd listened to his story, but when it came time to tell hers, she'd only rubbed at her arms as if suddenly cold, and mumbled, "He was an asshole." For the life of him, he couldn't understand how anyone could be an asshole to her. She was wonderful, and he could wait for her if that was necessary.

Charlie knew he wasn't a bad looking guy. He'd had one-night-stands. He could go out to most bars and pick up a woman if he wanted to, but there was something about Lauren that always seemed out of reach. They worked in different wings of the school, so he really had to go out of his way to bump into her. Whenever he did, it made him feel like a stalker. Today, he didn't care. He wanted to ask her out, and this was the only way to get it done.

She was exiting her classroom when he approached.

"Charlie," she said with a smile that lit up the entire hallway.

She could illuminate any room. She was stunning. Charlie loved the way her brown hair was always up in a bun, but seemed to be haphazardly done, like she couldn't really be bothered with maintaining it. Yet, it dared not collapse completely. It owed her that much. Or, it was happy to be in her presence too, and therefore did its best to keep up with her. He liked that version better.

My God. I am a stalker.

"Ms. Peo... Lauren. Sorry," he said. "You headed out?"

"No, I still have two classes today," she replied. "I really need coffee though."

"So, let's go get some," he suggested.

She beamed. "Okay. I'd like that."

"I'll drive."

"Oh," she said, seeming surprised. "I uh... I meant in the teacher's lounge."

"The mud stuff?"

"The mud stuff. I mean, I'd love to go get a cup of coffee with you, but I wouldn't get back in time for my next class so... the mud stuff it is."

"How about I go out and get you some?" he offered.

Because your lips weren't made for cheap Styrofoam cups and your tongue should only taste the finest flavors.

She looked him in the eyes, and he saw hers sparkle. He loved being under her gaze. When she smiled again, it melted his heart.

Okay, Shakespeare. You're getting cheesy now. Ask her out.

"That's so sweet, really, Charlie. You don't have to do that though."

"It would be my pleasure."

"No," she said, shaking her head and blushing, "but if you want to go with me to the teacher's lounge, I won't cringe at the thought or anything."

Is she flirting with you?

"Absolutely," he said.

Oh, you didn't say the word 'absolutely.' That's the, "Will you accept this rose?" response on The Bachelor. "Absolutely. I'd love to accept this rose."

Charlie watched a lot of reality TV. They were his guilty pleasure. He liked all of them. The cooking ones, the dancing ones, and the dating ones. He wondered if Lauren watched them too. It seemed to be a single person's *thing*. Married people probably watched married-people shows. Programs that dealt with wives stealing the blankets, husbands working too late, kids failing school, and families getting over hardships together.

Those weren't his kinds of shows. He liked the trashy stuff. He wanted to see the drama, the cat fights, the cheating, the competition, and the tears that always accompanied them. If he had to pick a show to be on, it would be one that combined all of them. Like *Survivor* or *The Amazing Race.*

Yes, you are a dork, Mr. Charlie.

Side-by-side they walked to the teacher's lounge. They were half-way there when Charlie looked at his watch and realized they only had fifteen minutes before the bell rang for the next class. Lauren would get her coffee and then hurry back to beat the students there. Now was his only chance.

"Um," he started, "Lauren. Would you like to go out for dinner tonight?"

She stopped walking and stared straight ahead instead of turning to glance over at him. He wasn't sure how to read this. It almost seemed like he'd freaked her out.

"Or not," he said.

"I would love to, Charlie," she started.

Wait, what? Did she say yes?

"But..." she continued.

No, no buts. Come on!

"Tonight is the Grad Night party," she continued, "and I wasn't planning to go to that, but as ridiculous as this will probably sound, I kind of feel like I owe it to whichever student wanted me there. And I mean, to go through all that trouble breaking into my apartment to drop off that invitation. Talk about commitment."

"Broke into your place too, huh?" he asked.

"Oh, did they hit your house too?"

"No, I haven't gotten an invite. But Mr. Cole and Mrs. Lowell both had the same kind of story, so I wouldn't take it personally. Sounds like they daringly intruded on everyone's property."

"They're lucky they didn't get shot," she said.

He laughed. "Mr. Cole's words exactly."

"I'm sure you'll get one too," she said with a gentle hand on his shoulder.

He looked down at her fingertips and wished they'd remain there forever. He wondered what it would feel like to have those hands all over him. Or his on her.

What's wrong with you? Calm down.

"We could meet at the party," Lauren said. "The kids love you. I've heard plenty of them talk about you before. You'll get an invite."

"The party's tonight," he said. "Doesn't seem that way. But if I do, sure, we can meet there. If not... maybe another time?"

"If they don't give you one, come anyway," Lauren whispered and passed him a wink. "I can think of one person who'd like to see you there. I can give you the details. I'd rather hang out with you than wander around awkwardly at a party full of teenagers."

"We can make fun of them together," Charlie suggested.

"Absolutely," she replied, and he felt certain she too watched shitty reality TV.

If he didn't get an invitation himself, he thought he'd take her up on the offer and meet her there anyway.

Charlie returned to his class a few minutes before the bell rang. When he opened the door, he found the two goth kids sitting at their desks in the dark, holding hands across the aisle.

"Well, hello," he said.

"Hi, Mr. Charlie," Rita replied.

"Hope you don't mind us being in here," Bogdan added. "We'd rather deal with the silence in here than be out there roaming among all those animals."

Animals. Interesting observation. The school has become a lot like a zoo.

"Can't say I blame you," Charlie replied as he made his way to his desk.

He sat down, slid open his desk drawer, and pulled out the novel he'd gotten from Mr. Cole earlier that morning. He placed it on his desk only long enough to pull out his attendance book when Rita's voice yanked his attention up to where she was now standing next to him.

"Tell me you're not reading that too," she said.

He looked down at the book and said, "No. Well, the first page or two but that's it. Have you read it?"

"Please," she replied with a roll of her eyes, "wouldn't be caught dead."

"No conformity. Got it."

"What book?" Bogdan asked from his seat.

"That Maddening shit everyone's reading," Rita replied. She quickly turned back to Charlie and said, "Crap. Sorry, Mr. Charlie."

"It's your last day," he reminded her. "I suppose you've earned the right to say *shit*."

She laughed. Bogdan did too.

"It's shit," Bogdan agreed. "Don't bother. If all the other kids are into it, you know it's going to be dumb."

"It's no Vonnegut," Rita added.

This made Charlie smile. Did she enjoy Kurt Vonnegut?

"I'm sure you're right," he told her. "And, no, this isn't my book. I didn't buy it. But I am curious what has all the kids liking it so much."

"Don't bother reading it," Rita replied. "I can spoil it for you. It's full of graphic sex and violence."

That would be why Mr. Cole considers it smut. And quite possibly what Mrs. Lowell read that had her clinging to the book in that death grip of hers.

Charlie laughed and nodded his head. "Certainly seems that way at the start."

Then, as the other kids began filing into the room, Rita leaned closer to him and whispered, "Mr. Charlie, every student has an invitation to give to a teacher of their choice... you know... for the Grad Night party," she said, "and Bog and I... well, we both wanted to give ours to you. You're the only cool teacher at DS High, and we wanted to invite you to our senior party."

Charlie wanted to stand and hug the girl tightly. He looked over at Bogdan, who was nodding his head vigorously. He held a thumbs-up.

Not only had these two confirmed that at least someone in this school gave a shit about him, but they'd also given him the chance to see Lauren tonight. These two hadn't broken into his house to invite him in some dramatic fashion, but he'd finally gotten his invitation, and Charlie felt great. Rita handed him an envelope.

"You don't have to answer right away," she said. "We know some teachers don't feel comfortable with these kinds of parties, but the information is all inside the card. No pressure. If you come, we'll see you there."

She was about to walk away when she turned and leaned down once more, "And don't tell anyone, okay? Not all teachers are getting an invite so... you know..."

"Thank you," Charlie said, "to you both. You made my day."

Rita blushed and then turned and walked away. She shuffle-stepped back to Bogdan with her shoulders raised in a shrug that lasted most of the way to her desk. From the looks of it, her male counterpart was whispering something to her. Charlie imagined it was the question of whether or not he would show up, to which her shrug answered, "I don't know, but I tried."

I have to show up. If for no other reason, to say thank you to these two.

What would he wear to the party? Teacher attire? The typical dress shirt and slacks would make him stick out as an authority figure. Tonight, he wanted to be a guy who was invited to a new-adult party. Really, he wanted to look good for *his* girl.

He was nervous, he realized. That was odd. Why was he nervous?

Then, it hit him. He hadn't been to an actual party since college.

Holding it below his desk so none of the students could see as they entered, he read the information on the card.

Tonight.
8735 Wilshire House.
10 p.m. – Whenever we want
-B-

"B," he said a little above a whisper. "Bogdan?"

That had to be it. He'd gotten the boy's invitation. Each student must have written his or her name on it. Of course, Bogdan wouldn't be like everyone else. To do so would be an insult. He would sign with only an initial, and only for his first name.

The goth kids are fucking awesome.

When the bell rang, Joel stuck his head in the door and said, "Got a minute?"

65

"Got five," Charlie said, deciding he'd give up the chance to take a piss to talk to his friend.

That was one of the struggles of being a teacher in an overcrowded school. His schedule was packed with classes which meant the trivial things like taking a shit were always on the back burner.

You've never experienced real discomfort until you're standing in front of a group of teenagers, trying to show some enthusiasm for Walt Whitman, while squeezing your asshole shut. The only thing worse than coffee stains is diarrhea. That shit is a real pain.

When the class finally cleared out, Joel made his way over to Charlie's desk and sat down on the corner.

"Yo, you going to the party tonight?" Charlie's friend asked.

Charlie found it interesting how teachers were talking about this thing like it was a party meant for them. This was for the graduating students, many of which the teachers couldn't stand. He supposed, in some sick way, it was like the teachers were going only so they could confirm that these sinister ne'er-do-wells were really leaving. The Grad Night party was kind of like the students stepping onto a ship setting sail for a faraway continent, and the teachers were allowed to stand on the dock and wave goodbye.

Goodbye and good riddance.

"I got an invitation," Charlie said as he held his up for Joel to see.

"Sweet," he replied. "Let's go then."

"You really think it's a good idea?"

"Bro, it's free booze, and we're not responsible for these kids anymore. They've put us through the motherfuckin' wringer the entire year. I teach music, man. Do you have any idea how hard it is to get these kids to sing? They're twelfth graders and at least half of them don't even know the words to the school song. Their graduation is this evening and they *have* to sing it. So… it's gonna be a real shit show."

"What time's the graduation?"

"Five. So come watch them make asses of themselves for not working with me on this, then let's go get shitfaced and enjoy our weekend. We'll go, have some drinks, and then leave the party and go hang out at a bar or something. I bet Lauren will be there."

Charlie lowered his face and laughed.

"Yeah," Joel continued. "I'm sure she'll be there. We'll drag her out to a karaoke bar."

"Nah, no karaoke."

"Women like men who can make them laugh."

"My singing will definitely do that."

"Exactly! You need to unwind a little. I'll see you there."

Charlie took a deep breath and sighed. "Sure."

8

LAUREN

"Okay, what do you think?"

Lauren turned away from her floor-to-ceiling mirrored closet and looked down at Clyde who was busy giving himself a bath.

"You're not even fucking looking at me, Clyde. It's just like you to only focus on your needs. Now, give me an honest opinion."

The cat understood her. She was sure of it. He looked up at her, his eyes darting left and right, probably thinking about how odd it was that the room looked exactly the same behind her as it did behind him. All except her fat ass blocking this particular portion of the mirror.

No, not fat, honey. Phat. P... h... a... t... phat.

Did people even use that expression anymore? At one time, that was *the* saying. Now... not so much.

"Meer," Clyde said.

He'd never been good at doing the traditional *meow*. He sounded snootier than other cats. Clyde definitely had an attitude tonight. He didn't seem happy she was going out.

"I'm going to feed you first," she promised. "Then, Animal Planet. You'll love it. You can binge watch your favorite shows."

With his nose pointed at the floor, he lifted his gaze as if to say, "What else you got for me?"

She wasn't fully convinced she looked good in her black dress, but she was unwilling to wear anything with color tonight since she was unaware of the party's theme. She wasn't even sure about the location. It could be at a house, a country club, a restaurant... all she had was the street address, and that didn't ring a bell.

Clyde's bowl was full, his show was on, and he sat on the couch with his eyes glued on the TV when she finally headed out. She knew she'd deal with his attitude again later when she returned home, but if he was too rude, she'd kick his mean ass off her bed.

Maybe she'd bring Charlie home with her and really piss the cat off. She laughed, realizing how dumb it was that she was considering her cat's feelings when it came to bringing a man home. If and when it came down to that, she was sure she wasn't going to give a shit about Clyde's jealousy. It had been a long time since she'd been with a man. The thought of it excited her, and it gave her a jolt of exhilaration as she headed out for the evening.

Charlie will be there. It'll be great. Open up to him this time. Give the guy a chance. He definitely deserves it. You haven't made it easy on him.

She knew he'd get an invitation of his own. The students loved him, and he loved them right back.

That says a lot about him, Lauren. He's one of the good ones.

Maybe she really would invite him back to her place tonight and see where things went.

No. Bad idea. Teacher couples NEVER work out.

She'd seen colleagues of hers fail in the relationship department. She wasn't exactly sure what led to the splits, but she figured it had something to do with the constant stress and frustrations of dealing with children these days. Teachers knew better than to take that aggravation home, but they were human. It's what humans did.

Could make for some amazing angry sex though.

She laughed at herself as she got into her car and started it up. She should have never become a teacher. What would she do otherwise?

I'd be a stripper. Dance all night and get paid a lot more than I do now.

She giggled at the thought. She wouldn't have the guts to dance naked in front of people, but she liked the freedom she felt as she considered it.

Her ex would have beaten the shit out of her if she'd ever suggested such a thing. Back then, she wasn't even allowed to teach. She'd taken a break from her career after meeting him. *He* had suggested it at first, flaunting his money and claiming he could take care of her and give her the life of her dreams. She thought she'd take a temporary leave and rest up for later.

She should have known better. She should have seen the signs right away. That temporary leave turned into five long years of getting her ass kicked every night. He took care of her monetarily. In every other department, he was a selfish, mean son of a bitch.

Don't think about him. Do not let him ruin your mood.

She wouldn't.

Charlie.

Saying his name gave her an excited flurry in her gut. He was the cutest damn thing. They *would* make a good couple, if she decided to let it go there. If he really wanted it to go there.

Maybe we'll find out tonight.

She started her car and backed out of the parking lot. "Maybe teaching wouldn't be so bad if I had somebody to come home to." She'd said the words aloud, with nobody around to hear. She was wasting her time with such thoughts. She knew that. Ever since the ex, she hadn't been able to think about dating. She was terrified she'd fall into a similar situation. But she was tougher now. She was stronger. She'd never let a man treat her like that again. Never.

The convention center parking lot was full when she pulled in. She'd purposely arrived late to the graduation. She'd been to enough to know they always started late, and that always resulted in too much time spent awkwardly chitchatting with parents. She'd be forced to tell them how proud of the kids she was and how they were going to excel out there in the real world.

Some of them would. She had her favorites, of course. She liked plenty of students, but unfortunately, the majority of them graduating tonight were worthless. She couldn't lie to the parents this time. It wasn't in her. If she tried, the truth would be written all over her face. Liz's mother, Mrs. Donna Cupo, the mobster's wife, was the worst of them. The woman always dressed to kill, had gigantic fake tits, and had lips nearly as big. Botox hadn't been kind to her. She was the mom all the other moms flocked to.

And I wondered where her daughter gets it from.

By the time she found a parking spot and made her way into the building, the ceremony was well underway. Half the students had already walked the aisle, received their diplomas, and were seated side-by-side in front of the stage.

Mr. Joel Mendez was up there too, seated off to the side, waiting on his chance to lead the seniors in singing the school song. It was tradition. She couldn't wait to hear it this year.

The school's principal, Dean Mayer, was at the podium calling out his list of names.

Lauren stood at the back of the room, scanning the crowd for an empty seat. Her best bet was to stay standing. That way she could evacuate quickly when this thing was over. Teachers' attendance at the graduation ceremony wasn't mandatory, but it might as well have been. The principal was definitely making a mental checklist of everyone in attendance. Those who weren't here would hear about it later.

She'd decided to keep her spot leaning against the back wall, when she noticed someone standing in the dark corner on the opposite side of the room. While all the parents and other guests were glued to what was taking place on stage, a teenage boy wasn't interested in it at all. He was dressed too casually for an event like this. He wore stained white shoes, blue jeans, and a black zipped up sweater with the hood pulled down low and casting a shadow over his face.

James Bender. Why isn't he with all the other seniors? Surely, he's a twelfth grader and should be graduating tonight.

Now that she thought about it, she didn't know what grade he was in. She didn't know anything about any of the classes he took, but surely he was a senior. The rest of these kids wouldn't follow him around like they do if he were an underclassman.

She thought back to all her recent conversations in the teacher's lounge, and she couldn't remember a single teacher ever mentioning his classroom behavior. It was like he existed but didn't at the same time.

James Bender.

She didn't say the name out loud, but she might as well have. The second his name floated through her mind, the kid's head raised slightly. It was still pointed at the floor, but she could tell he was watching her. He pulled one hand out of his pocket, and she thought her mind must be playing tricks on her.

It was pitch black, balled up into a fist the color of tar. His wrist and the rest of what she could see of his arm before it disappeared into his sweater sleeve was the same color, or lack of color. He raised a finger to the dark void that was his face and held it there where his lips should be. He was shushing her, telling her to be quiet. She opened her mouth to speak, but only, "Wha..." came out. The word shriveled back into her throat as one of his long fingers unraveled from his closed fist and pointed at her.

A vision slammed into her like a freight train, throwing her mind into a nightmare-state where she no longer stood in this room. Electricity ran through her limbs and then she found herself in a different place, all alone. The parents, staff, and students all disappeared.

She lay naked with her wrists pulled apart and cuffed to a bed's headboard. Not her bed. It was huge, with a crimson colored comforter. Her legs were open too, and her feet were strapped to the footboard. A cool draft sifted up between her legs and threatened to enter her. She tried desperately to block it with her knees, terrified of what that frigid wind might put inside her.

"I'm coming, baby," a deep, hoarse voice said.

Her legs fell open and her heart plummeted. The cold draft no longer mattered. He was back. The sound of his voice had her pulling at her constraints, but it was of no use. She was trapped.

His feet slid down the hallway, the soles of his shoes pressing against the hardwood floor and dragging toward her. He used to walk like that sometimes, as if his drunken form couldn't be bothered to lift his feet up fully.

"You said you did the dishes, right?" the voice asked.

She couldn't remember doing any dishes, and she knew what would happen if she didn't. He hated coming home to a dirty kitchen.

"I did," she barely squeaked out. "I washed everything."

It was a lie. At least, she thought it was. She tried so hard to remember, but nothing prior to waking up strapped to this bed came to mind.

"All these knives too?"

What knives? Lie, Lauren. Lie to him. You have to.

"All the knives too," she said in a shaky, unconvincing voice.

His feet continued to drag against the floor, their scraping so loud it caused her to wince and grit her teeth.

Scrape... thud. Scrape... thud. Scrape... thud.

He was close. He was so close.

"You wouldn't lie to me, would you?" the man asked, coming closer. He was somewhere out in the hall now. He'd be here any second.

"I would never," she swore weakly.

"Then what is this?!" the voice yelled, as the scraping turned into a full-speed run.

Thud... thud... thud... thud.

"Oh, God!" she cried as she pulled on her wrist straps, feeling the leather dig into her skin, rubbing her raw. She yanked with her legs and barely budged. She could go nowhere.

His face came into view. His long, black hair, pinched nose, and gapped teeth. That bad boy look she craved the first time she saw him at the bar. The look that now made her stomach turn.

His nostrils flared as he yelled, "What is this shit?"

That voice. It wasn't his. It was more like a painful wail, a high-

pitched shriek that brought forth echo after echo after echo. His question repeated over and over.

"Leave me alone!" she screamed. "Go away!"

"What is this shit, Lauren?" the voice replied.

She'd had her eyes squeezed shut, too afraid to open them and see the man standing at the foot of the bed. He would jump on her like he used to. He would dig his nails into her arms and hold her thighs down with his knees. He would inflict great pain on her.

"Please," she begged.

"What is this shit?" he asked again. "If you cleaned them, then why are they like this?"

She opened her eyes, only because she wanted to make sense of his question.

He stood at the foot of the bed holding a large orange bucket. It was the dirty, faded one he took fishing with him on the weekends. He held it at waist level and tilted it forward so she could see what was in it.

The stench of it hit her first, causing her to dry heave. It was every foul odor she'd ever smelled. It was the stench of rotten eggs, fish guts, dog shit, and roadkill. She gagged and fought the urge to vomit.

Then she saw what was inside the bucket. A hundred dirty knives. Filthy, some with fish guts strung around the tips. Others with mold and chunky bits of rotting flesh.

"What is this shit?" he asked again.

"What do you want from me?" she asked, tears running from the corners of her eyes and into her ears where they pooled there with their wet stickiness.

He rocked the bucket back and forth, threatening to spill its contents on her in three...

She screamed.

Two...

"No, please!"

One...

Gripping the bucket tight, he launched its contents toward the ceiling and those hundred filthy blades flew high into the air and hovered for a second. She watched as they somersaulted toward the ceiling in slow motion. She could almost count them they rose so slowly. One blade in particular twisted, flipped, and pointed toward her. Wrapped around its tip was a fish eye and whatever tendrils of gooey matter that would usually keep it connected to its host.

As that one blade made its full rotation and was now pointed downward, the rest of the knives suddenly let go, like whatever had held them in pause was released.

The blades rained down on her.

She screamed.

A butcher's knife flipped toward her chest and hit her with a thwack. The blade buried itself into her, the pain shooting her eyelids wide open. Agony grabbed hold of her voice and pulled it back into her throat where pain wrapped her cry around its fist and wouldn't let go. She choked on her scream, coughing out phlegm and blood. That butcher's blade was like a hundred razor sharp claws flaying the flesh from her bones.

A steak knife plunged into her kneecap.

A paring knife sliced open her thigh.

So many sharp blades, most with names she couldn't identify, impaled her naked body. The giant chef's knife she kept in her kitchen fell across her abdomen and sliced her open.

Pain hit her in every part of her body.

The blades kept coming, puncturing the soft spot in the crook of her arm, driving into her pelvic area, cutting open her left breast and then her right.

Searing hot pain at every inch of her.

And his laughter. That cackle she'd heard so many times as he watched funny movies while she'd been lost in her own mind, trying to get as far away from him as possible without ever physically fleeing because of her fear of the unknown.

He laughed and laughed, even as the boning knife fell from high above her face. A hellacious howl ripped from her throat and then exploded in a gurgle as the blade pierced her throat, leaving her lying on her back, helpless, and drowning in her own blood.

That's when he stripped his clothes off and climbed on top of her.

Lauren returned to the convention center. Both hands clutched her throat and her fingernails pulled at it as if trying to break open an escape hatch for the breath that was caught inside her. The man standing next to her realized something was wrong and grabbed hold of her shoulder.

"Are you okay, ma'am?"

She swatted at his arm, fighting for breath, and feeling the way she had the last time her ex had kicked her in the solar plexus. James Bender had knocked the wind out of her, and no matter how hard she tried to breathe, she could only exhale.

Exhale...

Exhale...

Until finally her body gave in.

At the point of practically passing out, a loud gasp filled her with air in a reverse scream of high-pitched inhalation.

Clutching the man's arm, she rested her forehead against his shoulder and breathed.

"Just breathe... just breathe..." the guy said calmly.

"What's wrong with her?" a woman asked.

"I think it's an anxiety attack."

It's not a fucking anxiety attack. It's...

She looked past the man's arm and over at where the teenager had been standing before. James Bender was gone. Regaining her composure, she pushed past the man and walked halfway over to where the evil teenager had been only a few minutes before. The spot was filled by other people now.

He was there. He was right there.

But he was gone.

9

LAUREN

She'd seen him. She couldn't have imagined it. James Bender was standing right over there.

But had he been? Was it possible she'd imagined it?

"Maybe we should find you a seat," the man who'd helped her said.

She closed her eyes for a moment and tried to breathe normally. Her strength returned and she stood upright and strong. "I'm uh… I'm fine, really. It's nothing."

"Are you sure?"

Lauren closed her eyes and took a deep breath, nodding her head. "Really. I'm fine. This happens sometimes."

It was a lie. Like the lie that she'd cleaned the knives. The vision had been so real. She hadn't had a panic attack since being with *him*. Since the night she left him. Left him with a baseball sized knot on his forehead. Courtesy of the chicken frying skillet that had been in her family for four generations.

The man, and the woman Lauren assumed was his wife, finally let her be, but both looked back at her several times to ensure she was okay. It was a sweet gesture from two people she'd never met in her life. They were strangers willing to help. Good Samaritans who probably had children graduating tonight, teenagers who'd never lift a finger to help another soul.

Good deeds will die with my generation.

Lauren looked once more at where James Bender had been standing and tried to make sense of what she'd seen.

Was it the lights? Or the lack of light? That couldn't have been real.

She couldn't have imagined it, but now that the moment had fled, she felt stupid, like she'd let her mind get carried away. She'd seen that boy many times in the hallway, and she'd always felt there was something wrong with him, but this was silly. Of course, he didn't have tar-black hands.

"He was wearing gloves," she said under her breath, followed by a laugh. "You're so stupid. He was wearing gloves."

Lauren relaxed.

And the other part? The part where you were tortured by your ex?

She couldn't explain that, but any doctor would tell her she'd had an anxiety attack of some sort. It had been spurred on by that boy though. He was definitely an odd one, but he wasn't some kind of supernatural entity. Sure, he'd sit in front of the cafeteria, on top of one of the wooden picnic tables, and it was like the other students were drawn to him. He was a natural leader. That's all.

Thank God these kids are graduating.

The eleventh graders, who'd be seniors next year, had issues too. All kids did these days, it seemed. But they were nowhere near as bad as the kids grouped together at the front of the convention center.

Lauren carefully drew breath, too afraid to breathe normally. Her limbs still felt weak and her arms trembled. She looked through the crowd, hoping to see Charlie somewhere. More than anything, she needed a familiar face right now. Someone who might help her feel grounded, who might help her remember she was in the real world and not in some nightmare where demon boys shushed her, and ex-boyfriends pummeled her with knives.

Most of the teachers would be seated up front. That was the area designated for all the educators, but she knew it would be full by now.

She would have to wait until after the ceremony to find him, or she could see him at the party.

Are you still going to that party, Lauren? What if James Bender is there?

She hadn't considered skipping it until now. Her messed up mental state was ruining her plans. But this was a one-time thing. She'd never dozed off like that. She'd never gone into a full daydream so lucid as the one she'd experienced a moment ago. She had to go to the party. If not, she would be giving in to what her therapist used to call: *That monster from her past.*

"Some monsters are real, Lauren," she'd told her, "and you survived one. You are a survivor. It's time you live like one."

Her therapist had given her permission to get on with life, and she'd done such a good job at that. Other than opening herself up to the possibility of love, she'd gone out into the world and slayed it. She had her own place, her own car, and an overall decent life.

And you're ready to take it a step further. Fuck that little episode you had. Don't you dare give into that monster.

Joel Mendez had given her a heads up that Charlie would be there. He'd said it with a quick elbow nudge that seemed to say, "Now's your chance, girl. Go get him." That's exactly what she intended to do. Charlie had made his pass at her once before and she'd shut him down. She owed it to him to take the first step this time.

Or will that make him feel like less of a man? No, you need to do it. Or, should I let him?

She bickered with herself way too much. Even that had started with her ex, when she had nobody else to talk to about her problems, so she'd talk to herself. She'd have inner-arguments over everything from what she'd make as a chili dog side dish – frozen fries or tater tots – to what TV streaming series she could watch that would keep her ex far away from her. He'd hated chick flicks and avoided anything even slightly romantic like the plague. Her playlist always included titles with the words *love* or *lust*.

Lauren was in a half-dazed state through the rest of the graduation ceremony. Most of that time she stood questioning what drew her to her ex in the first place. She'd had this talk with her therapist time and again, but she'd always lied through it. She'd gone with the "daddy never loved me" excuse. There might have been some truth to it. But in reality, he'd reminded her of the frontman from Metallica. She'd had a major crush on James Hetfield growing up. It was that and the vicious way he'd take her sexually. It was rough, but it was a turn on. Until it wasn't anymore. It gradually became more aggressive until she began to feel that her life was in danger every time he touched her.

"Ms. Peony, you're here!" a young girl named Allison Warner sang as she excitedly waved at the teacher.

Lauren waved back and tried to mimic the girl's expression. She was sure she'd failed miserably, but it must have been good enough because the girl kept grinning until she was out of sight.

See? Some of your students love you.

She did her best to take her mind off her worries, so she thought of other mundane stuff as she mechanically waved at the students walking by and moved her mouth to express words like, "Congratulations," and "You did it!"

Her body was there, so they could see she cared, but her mind was elsewhere, floating around.

I wonder what Clyde's doing right now. I bet he changes the TV channel to porn when I'm gone.

What did my grandmother put in her sausage gravy that gave it that kick?

How did Facebook know I was searching Amazon for toe socks?

Which of these students will try to friend or follow me on social media?

Which will I block?

"Thank you very much," boomed a voice Lauren hated with all her heart.

During her momentary flight from reality, Liz Cupo had been called to the podium. Now, she stood in front of the microphone, her big fake smile plastered on the giant teleprompter screens situated on both sides of the stage.

She really is a pretty girl. If she remains exactly like this and never says another word or does anything evil, she'll be lovely.

But then she opened her mouth, and of course, total bullshit flowed forth.

"Good evening fellow graduates, parents, teachers, staff, and distinguished guests. I am so proud to stand before you as the president of our class, and on behalf of my peers, I'd like to thank you all for the time, effort, and invaluable guidance you've given us throughout our years at DS High. You've watched us grow, you've seen us struggle and overcome, and now we'd like you to see things through our eyes. Please watch the screen as I present to you our final year at DS High."

Lauren's heart skipped a beat as Liz lifted her arms, palms up – like the Antichrist raising the dead – and gestured at both screens. This was going to be bad. She knew it, and she was sure all the other teachers in attendance were also dreading what was to come.

It started out as pleasant as could be. From behind, the camera followed Liz as she walked from the parking lot into the school. There was a close up on the trees in the courtyard. On some flowers. On smiling kids' faces. But then the screen flickered, went dark, and music kicked on.

Violins raced back and forth hectically, symbols crashed, and drums beat to an invisible march. It was the soundtrack to a horror movie, and nobody seated at the graduation ceremony was going to be able to stop what was happening.

But then again, it wasn't so bad. The film focused on the students.

Drool dripped from a boy's mouth as he slept with his face down on his desk.

On screen, a girl leaned over to the student next to her and cheated on a test.

Punches flew back and forth as two boys engaged in a fistfight in the cafeteria.

The bell rang and a crowd of kids dispersed as they all realized they were late to class.

Smoke wafted out of one of the bathroom vents.

A kid pointed at words scribbled on a desk in black marker. The words read: Your mom gave me clamidia.

Of course, they spelled chlamydia wrong.

The very first few images were funny, but then they grew increasingly distasteful, and some were quite disturbing like that of a boy picking the wings off a fly.

Again, Lauren scanned the crowd, trying to gauge the audience's reaction. What were the parents thinking of this? It really didn't matter, she supposed. These students had graduated and were all eighteen-years-old or very close to that age. They were young adults. It wasn't like the parents would ground the kids when they got home. It was too late for that.

At least the parents get to see what we put up with. And they'll undoubtedly blame the school for this… which will trickle down to the teachers.

The camera focused on James Bender, with his head tilted down, his sweater hood pulled over his head the way it always was, his face never visible, but he was obviously looking down at the book resting on the desk in front of him. *The Maddening* by T.K. Tantrum. She'd seen that book. He was staring at it on screen, and then he handed it to whomever had recorded the video.

The screen went black with the words *We all go mad* flashing in white.

Suddenly Lauren herself was on the screen. She sat at her desk, chatting on her cell phone.

I never use my phone in class. Oh, my God. I never do.

She couldn't remember the last time she'd used her phone in class. They must have waited so patiently to get that shot. The only time she could remember pulling her phone out in class was… maybe when her mom was sick and was in the hospital.

It didn't matter. She was there on screen typing away. The camera zoomed in on her face and then did its best to see what was on her phone screen, but it was too blurry.

It cleared up and then showed a phone screen that wasn't hers, but nobody else would know that. On it was a chat message. It read: *Don't text me like that when I'm in class. You're making me wet.*

Lauren felt her jaw drop.

The couple who'd checked on her when she'd nearly fainted looked over at her. The woman was disgusted and shook her head slowly. The man laughed under his breath. Lauren could only imagine the dirty thoughts running through his mind.

I don't even have anyone to write something like that to!

The screen blurred and then cleared up on the screen of a different phone. On it read: *Don't act like you don't like it.*

Suddenly there he was, the sweetest teacher in the school. Charlie sat at his desk texting on his phone.

The audience gasped.

Through tricks with editing, these kids were making them both look like hornball scumbags.

Next up was Mr. Cole. He was on the screen screaming at his class. "Listen here you little shits! I've been teaching you since the beginning and there is no possible way you could be this damn dumb. It's idiocy at its finest!"

The graduate students in the front row laughed, clapped, and cheered. One of them yelled out, "We love you too, Mr. Cole!"

The parents in the crowd murmured to each other, obviously pissed off. But the video kept going, not giving anyone the chance to argue or voice their concerns.

Mr. Mendez was the next victim. On screen, he taught his music class. But the camera zoomed in on his hips. The music had clearly been altered and played *Closer* by Nine Inch Nails while he humped the air seductively, rolling his hips.

"I wanna *bleep* you like an animal," flowed through the speakers.

At least they'd had the decency to edit the song. Lauren knew the truth right away. He had Latin roots. He was probably playing a salsa song and many of those songs required a certain shaking and rotating of the hips. It looked like maybe the students had slowed down the action to make it look vulgar.

Again, the parents gasped. Joel got up from his seat and hurried toward a side exit.

The giant screens showed Mrs. Lowell smiling intently at her desk. Text began to appear letter by letter across the bottom of the screen until the sinister subtitles revealed: *She just returned from a lunch break and she's positively glowing. I wonder why.*

Then, the video changed in quality and looked like it was a recording from a shitty phone. But it revealed Mrs. Lowell driving into the teacher's parking lot. A couple of minutes later, Mr. Cole pulled in too. She was well ahead of him as she walked into the school, but she looked back at him and smiled. The camera zoomed in on her face, and the subtitles ran across the screen again: *Mr. Cole must be great in the sack.*

A cacophony of sounds lifted from the audience as everyone seemed to have something to say about that one, but the chuckling and giggling of the graduates was louder than it all. Some of them cheered again. "Mr. Cole handles it like a man!" someone yelled.

"That's enough!" Mr. Cole shouted as he stood up at his seat.

"You should be ashamed of yourself!" one of the mothers replied. "You are a sick soul, Mr. Cole."

"Do not speak to him that way!" Mrs. Lowell yelled, defending him, so naïve in her efforts.

The kids completely lost it, laughing hysterically.

"We all go mad," Liz said into the microphone.

A few of the graduates repeated the phrase. Others were still laughing. Random parents shouted objections that Lauren thought sounded like made up movie script phrases like, "This is an outrage!" And, "This behavior must stop!"

"Turn that off this instant!" Dean Mayer demanded.

Liz giggled once more and then said into the mic, "It was only a joke. None of that was true. It was a bad joke. Sorry."

Lauren couldn't watch any longer. She rushed out of the room shaking her head with disgust as she headed out of the building. She didn't give a shit about these kids singing their final goodbye song. They could all go fuck themselves.

It dawned on her that the video was probably made by a handful of them. Surely, they couldn't have all been okay with this. They may have ruined careers and quite possibly a marriage. Mrs. Lowell's husband probably wasn't in the audience. Teachers' spouses tired of all the school activities within the first few years of the job, but still, there was a good chance he'd hear about it.

Lauren expected to find Joel in the outer hallway, but it was empty. Nobody was there. Why would anyone be out here? They were all inside sitting in awe as they watched the entire staff at Darrius Sawyer High get picked apart by the senior students.

Fuckers.

She'd seen enough, had enough, and she had no desire to hang out with any of these assholes.

"Okay, it was just a joke," she heard Liz's voice echo through the hall. "We just happened to catch teachers at random moments, and we may have altered a few things to get a rise out of you."

Good catch, you fucking bitch.

It could have been worse, she supposed. She'd only been shown using her cell phone. The message on it was clearly edited. Sure, it was a violation of school rules. Teachers were never allowed to use their phones in front of their students. In fact, it was recommended teachers leave their phones in their lockers, but Lauren refused to do that. These kids were way too crafty. They could pick a lock in a matter of seconds.

They easily broke into your fucking apartment!

She'd be reprimanded later, she was sure of it, but again, it could have been worse. Joel looked like a pervert, and Charlie…

Have the students noticed something between us? It's not like we hold hands in the hallway.

They'd only been on a couple of dates. How would they have even known there was anything going on between them? It wasn't like they were sneaking off at lunchtime together. They weren't the youthful version of Mr. Cole and Mrs. Lowell. Suddenly, she laughed.

These kids are such assholes, but damn, they're good.

She'd never even noticed the elderly duo returning to school the way they'd been caught on camera.

Lauren walked out into the parking lot and found her car. She sat inside and turned on the ignition, thinking about the video once more. She laughed aloud as she thought about the lyrics to the song they'd put to show off Joel's dance moves. The guy was a looker, that was for sure. She knew most of the female students had at least a tiny crush on him.

Joel was too suave though, too much of a player. Charlie was more Lauren's type.

Charlie.

As she thought about him again, she began to change her mind about the party. A few minutes ago, at the height of her anger, she wanted nothing to do with their get-together, but now she remembered Joel and Charlie would be there. If they still went.

She pulled out her phone and found Joel's number in it. She could have messaged Charlie, but she felt like that would be too forward. Joel and she had exchanged numbers during a school project they'd worked on together. She punched a text message into her phone.

Lauren: Hey, you all right? That was pretty brutal.

After a brief pause, he wrote back.

Joel: Yes. I guess. They made me look really bad, Lauren. I might get fired.

Lauren: No, I'll help you explain it.

Joel: That was me dancing to Marc Anthony to show them how I wanted them to put effort into their performance. You've seen them. They are lazy. They fucked me, man.

Lauren: So... no party?

Joel: No, I'm going to that fucking party.

Lauren: Yeah? And Charlie?

Joel: Hold on.

Lauren waited.

Joel: He doesn't want to go.

Lauren sighed and thought about her response. If Charlie wasn't going to be there, she didn't want to go.

Joel: Never mind. I talked him into it. Free booze. These kids fucked us. The least we can do is drink all their booze, eat their snacks, and maybe give them a real farewell speech of our own. Fuck them. Charlie said he'll meet us there.

Lauren: Perfect. See you there.

She couldn't believe she was still going to the party after the stunt they'd pulled, but then again, had she really expected anything less?

Joel: See you at the party. Unfortunately, I have to go back in and watch them fuck up the school song.

Lauren laughed, and she hoped she'd laugh a little more before the night was through. With a little over an hour before the party started, she decided to get warmed up. If she showed up at the party the way she felt right now, she'd be a total downer all evening, and if she faced her students sober, she might say something she shouldn't.

She left her car at the convention center and walked to a nearby bar she was familiar with, where she ordered two shots of tequila. This would relax her a bit. She had a feeling she'd need it when she walked into that party.

10

CHARLIE

It was lower than he thought they'd ever sink. He'd expected so much more from them. Charlie felt so conflicted. How could he defend them like he did? How could he argue with Lauren about their worth and the great things he knew they'd accomplish in the future?

It was like someone had shoved a dagger through his heart. In all his years of teaching, he'd never seen a graduating class do something so messed up. And they'd targeted him. Not that it would have been okay if he'd been left out of it, but he couldn't possibly refrain from taking it personally when his face was on that screen and his hands were seen gripped with excitement, typing out a message he never wrote.

Then again, he was talking about a student body that consisted of violent offenders and sexual deviants. That was the truth of it, right? He tried not to see them that way. Every generation had its problems with raging hormones and testosterone-fueled brawls. So many movies had been devoted to these subjects. The 70s had *Carrie* and *Dazed and Confused* – okay the latter was made much later, but it did represent the decade. The 80s had *Fast Times at Ridgemont High*, the 90s had a whole slew of films dedicated to these issues... in all different genres.

A guy fucked an apple pie in one of them for God's sake.

But Charlie's students were different. He'd been nothing more than a naïve idiot placing his faith in kids who didn't deserve it.

When conducting normal classes, it was sometimes easy to forget about the old man murdered in the school parking lot, the teacher who'd gotten stabbed in her hand, and the porn that had taken place at the back of a classroom.

Little by little, the school principal had done his best to get rid of the students committing these horrendous acts, but Charlie knew the truth. Those were the ones who'd gotten caught. Mr. Rowen, the old man who'd been hacked to pieces in the parking lot... they'd never found his murderers.

It wasn't gang related. He knew that. It was *them*. Not all of them, but more than one of them. And they'd looked so happy up there with their caps and gowns and diplomas... all while waiting for that malicious video to play.

He seethed with anger.

Mr. Rowan had gotten murdered, and more than likely the killer was mixed in among the rest of the student body. He, she, or they were probably beaming with pride right now, clutching that certificate that told the world they'd completed their childhood commitment.

When it came to the murder, the worst part was, he doubted it was a total secret. He bet at least a few of these kids knew who'd done it. They loved to talk. They loved to gossip. It was quite possibly every single person graduating today was fully aware. Nobody liked Mr. Rowan.

How many of you know who did it?

He scanned the graduates, all sitting side-by-side. That asshole-indie film of theirs was finished, and Joel had returned to the stage. The poor guy. Charlie's part of the video wasn't *that* bad. Like Lauren, he'd gotten caught on his phone. The messages were obviously fabricated. That much was clear. It didn't take a genius to realize it.

Whatever. I'll get a scolding, not for the message, but for using the damn phone in the first place.

More than likely he, Lauren, and the others caught texting would hear about it with the rest of the teachers at a staff meeting. They'd definitely be having one to discuss all of the clips in the film. Yes, the students had definitely fucked them on this one. They'd hit Mr. Cole and Mrs. Lowell the hardest. They'd been having an affair, Charlie was sure of it, but he didn't know the students had figured it out.

At first, Charlie had wanted nothing more than to walk out in the middle of Liz's speech, go home, and watch TV. He figured none of the teachers would be attending the Grad Night party. That was until Mr. Lafferty leaned over and said, "They want to fuck us? Okay, cool. I'm going to drink all their liquor, and then when they come to me asking for a college recommendation letter... ha... they can go fuck themselves. Every last one of them."

Then Charlie had gotten the text message from Joel asking if he still wanted to meet them, Joel and Lauren, at the party. He'd said no at first, but then Joel convinced him. This *was* the perfect opportunity to spend more time with Lauren.

It was set. He'd watch the kids destroy the school anthem. Then, he'd meet them at this party and do his best to have a good time.

And destroy it they did. It was practically a different song altogether.

Oh, for the love of God, somebody make them stop.

At varying levels of volume and pitch – whiny sopranos, nasally baritones, and horrid groaning attempts at bass – the senior class fought its way through the lyrics to their school anthem. If the sound could be put into visual form, Charlie imagined it to look a lot like those old *Heathcliff* cartoons where two cats would get into a scuffle and a giant dust ball would kick up with arms and feet shooting out in all directions. The graduates' sound was a lot like the hissing, screeching, and squealing that always accompanied that animated feline battle.

It was bad.

When it was over, and after Dean Mayer said his final words of encouragement, the kids threw their caps into the air and joined their families for pictures. That was Charlie's chance to duck out and get some fresh air. He would be willing to bet not a single teacher would show up in a photo this year. They'd been attacked, and like Charlie, none of the others would want to be remembered on this day.

He wondered what Lauren was up to right now. Unfortunately, there was still an hour before the party would begin. Kids were already filing out of the building and heading to their cars. Surely, parents were inside the building, disappointed they couldn't snap one more picture of their baby boy or girl on his or her final night of high school. Sadly, instead of joining their parents for celebratory dinners, they were all headed to their drunken night of debauchery, and here Charlie was, wondering how long he should wait to join them.

Not wanting to go home, and having no other place to waste an hour, he decided to sit in his car and take a nap until it was time to drive to the party. He couldn't show up too early. He'd look like an idiot. Like he couldn't wait to go to their big party. Like he had no other option in life but to join them.

Charlie dozed off in his car, and when he finally came to, it was twenty minutes after the party was due to start. In his post-nap haze, he considered calling it off and heading home, but he thought once more of Lauren and decided he'd waited for his damn invite long enough. It was time to go to this party.

This was the place. The address matched and there were several cars parked outside. Yet, it didn't seem as packed as Charlie had expected it to be. He didn't see any familiar vehicles. Lauren's wasn't here, nor was Joel's. With his windows rolled up and the radio turned off, it was oddly silent inside his car. He listened to the gentle purring of his engine and wondered if he should back out and go home.

A leaf blew through the air and landed on his windshield where it skittered across the glass in jerky movements, like it was gripping the surface every few inches, refusing to take flight. He felt like that leaf right now, awkwardly moving along, unsure of whether he should hold on tight or let go and enjoy the breeze.

Outside, the wind blew violently through the trees, causing them to dance around the large two-story house that would be the party's host for the night. Through his rearview mirror, he saw the heavy pines behind him doing the same sway. It wouldn't rain tonight, but it would be great barbecue weather. Instead of karaoke, he thought about inviting Lauren and Joel over to his place so they could sit out on his balcony and sip wine. He imagined he'd have to get Lauren one of his heavy sweatshirts to drape over her shoulders and chest.

When Charlie glanced back through his front windshield, the leaf was gone. It had decided to go with the flow. "If you can do it, I can do it," he said under his breath, cringing at himself once again. He really was a loser, but he was happy this way. If he were going to follow the leaf's lead and join the party, he'd have to enter the enormous house in front of him.

Its upstairs lights glowed through the windows, well-kept flowerbeds sat on each side of the front door, and the lawn stretched out before him for at least fifty yards. It was gigantic, and he wondered which of his students was the proud owner of such a massive mini-mansion. He realized the house intimidated him. It was too big, too fancy, and too imposing. It almost seemed to say, "Don't bother coming in if you don't have something to offer those inside."

This was the kind of house that would proudly display Jean Valjean's silver candlesticks. The place definitely symbolized a good life.

Is that a good life though? Is that how you measure such a thing, with a large home?

Charlie wouldn't know, but he imagined Liz Cupo living in such a home and thought of her crime-lord father.

No, I guess not.

He contemplated staying in his car until one of his friends arrived. It would be much easier to strut through the door with Lauren and Joel by his side. He was about to lean his seat back and wait when a loud *tap* against his window scared the shit out of him.

Charlie jumped in his seat and turned to see Bogdan grinning at him on the other side of the glass. The boy's guyliner was on thick, and he even wore black lipstick that stretched beyond his mouth on both sides, giving him a Joker-like painted on smile.

"Jesus, Bog!" he yelled.

The boy raised his eyebrows, unsure of why he was on the receiving end of his former teacher's anger. Charlie rolled down the window and added, "Bog, seriously?"

Suddenly the boy got it and laughed. "Scare you, Mr. Charlie?"

Charlie took a deep breath to calm his nerves and looked at the paper bag the boy held. It was stuffed with what Charlie assumed was bottles of liquor. Bogdan seemed to be struggling a bit as he held onto it.

"Got enough booze there?" Charlie asked.

"For these lushes inside? Not even close."

"I'm not going to ask who bought it for you."

"Yeah, it's probably better if you don't."

Charlie hadn't thought about bringing something along to the party. If this were a dinner or a housewarming, sure, but this was a group of kids. Young adults was a better way of putting it. Still, what would he have brought? Chips seemed childish, and he wasn't about to become the adult responsible for providing alcohol.

Alcohol.

For the first time, Charlie realized he was about to walk into a party full of drunken kids, and he was an adult figure. Not only that, but he was a teacher. If the cops arrived and he was here, or God forbid if one of the kids got behind the wheel of a car and drove after this, he could be the one found liable for any harm done.

"So, you coming inside?" Bogdan asked.

"Bog, this might be a bad idea," Charlie replied. "I'm an adult, and if you're in there getting crazy, it might come back to —"

"—Mr. Charlie, this isn't *that* kind of party. At least not right now. The asshole kids won't show up 'til much later. When they do, I'd leave if I were you. You're right. You don't want to be responsible for any bullshit problems they cause. I might even leave after that. I wouldn't be here at all if Rita didn't want to come."

"Are you two *together* together?" Charlie asked.

The boy's painted on smile began to flatten out and it was clear his relationship with Rita hadn't evolved the way he'd hoped.

"Friend-zoned?" Charlie asked.

"Friend-zoned," Bog admitted. "But you never know."

"You never know."

"So, you comin' in with me or what?"

Charlie hesitated for a moment and then rolled up his window, locked his car door, and followed the boy inside.

When he stepped inside the house, it wasn't at all what he expected. There was no heavy veil of smoke fogging up the air. The faint scent of cigarettes was there, but the smokers must have been asked to do it in the backyard. The music wasn't blasting. It played at a reasonable volume, loud enough to enjoy and low enough that two people could have a conversation.

In the living room, Charlie saw many kids he recognized and some he didn't. What surprised him was the lack of teachers. A few lingered here and there. Mr. Toben, the art teacher, sipped from a red cup while leaning against the fireplace mantle. He raised his drink at Charlie and continued chatting with the young man standing in front of him.

Miss Arvis, the geography teacher, sat on a sofa with her hands folded on her lap. Charlie had always thought she was attractive in a teacherly kind of way. She was young, but very professional, like she'd finally stepped into the role she'd been preparing for all her life. She wore flowered dresses most days and kept her short blonde hair clipped back most of the time, but he didn't doubt she let it loose every once in a while. Right now, it was clipped back. She looked extremely uncomfortable in the environment. If someone didn't hurry and get a few drinks into her, she'd flee the scene within the hour.

"See?" Bogdan said as he handed the paper bag off to a boy Charlie didn't know. "It's pretty chill. Tyson owns this house. Or his grandfather does, I should say. He's a pretty cool dude. Came down earlier to have a smoke and took a small bottle of whiskey up to his room with him. He's pretty much stayed out of our way so far. He even said we could crank the music up. Said his hearing isn't good anyway."

The boy laughed and Charlie did too. He was a good kid.

"Thanks again for inviting me," Charlie said.

The boy nodded and then scrunched up a corner of his mouth, looking like he had something to say but was carefully considering his words first. Finally, he shoved his hands into his pockets, rocked back on his heels and said, "I'm sorry about the video."

"Yeah, the video," Charlie replied, wincing and sucking air through clenched teeth.

He wanted the boy to know the video wasn't cool. In fact, it stung.

"Just know, not all of us were in on that," Bogdan informed him.

"I didn't think you were, Bog, but damn. That was really uncalled for."

Bogdan nodded. "I know, and I know I've been quiet in class. It's a school thing, not a Mr. Charlie's class thing. I don't really have a lot of friends, you know? Just Rita and a couple of others."

"The goth kids."

Bogdan laughed and nodded. "That's what they call us."

"Sorry. I didn't mean to—"

"—No, don't be," Bogdan cut him off. "I mean it's what we are, I suppose."

"You're more than that, Bog. I shouldn't stereotype you like that."

Bogdan used his thumb and index finger to display the painted on smile he wore. "Dude, I've got black lipstick on. I get it. I'm fine with it. It's a phase. I know that. I'm not dumb enough to think I'll be wearing this shit at thirty, but for right now, it keeps me away from all the other scumbags at school. It makes me different."

"I get it."

The boy simply didn't want to fade into the background and join the army of selfie-taking, spray-on-tan, fake-friendly zombies. He would stand out, no matter the cost. The rest of the kids probably didn't like him and his group, but that was okay. They preferred it that way.

"So, why even come to this party?" Charlie asked. "Why not go... I don't know..."

"Hang out in a cemetery?"

It wasn't what he was going to say, but he shrugged his shoulders and laughed. "Why not?"

"We talked about it."

The boy who'd taken the brown paper bag came back with a beer for each of them. He handed one to Bogdan and the other to Charlie, who hesitated.

This is that moment. You take this beer and you're deciding to go that route. Are you the windshield, or are you that leaf?

"Mr. Charlie, come on," Bogdan prodded, banging his elbow against the teacher's arm.

Charlie reached for the beer bottle. "Fuck it."

Bogdan laughed. "That's the spirit."

"And call me Charlie now. You're not a student anymore. Congratulations by the way."

Charlie lifted his beer and Bogdan touched his to it. The bottles clinked together.

"Thank you," Bogdan replied. "Congratulations to you too, man. You did it. You survived my fucked-up classmates."

Charlie went in for his first sip of beer and said, "So did you."

"Yeah, so we talked about going someplace else and having a party of our own," Bogdan continued what he was saying earlier, "but in the end we decided it was *our* Grad Night party too, so we should be here."

"Hey, Mr. Charlie," Rita said as she walked into the room, stumbling a little.

"Charlie," Bogdan corrected her.

She stopped and cocked her head to the side before sticking out her tongue and blowing a half-drunken raspberry. "Okay, Charlie." She walked away mumbling something about the bathroom.

"So..." Bogdan said, acknowledging the awkward silence that arrived with her. "I'm gonna go hang out for a bit. Make yourself at home. Beer's in the kitchen. I think a keg is coming later. For now, the fridge is stocked with it. If you want a mixed drink, all that shit is on the counter."

"Got it," Charlie said, "have some fun. You deserve it."

So far, this party wasn't much different to any he'd partaken in back in his day.

Back in my day. I'm not an old fucking man. I'm not even old enough to be these kids' dad. Am I?

Again, Charlie glanced over at Miss Arvis, sitting alone. He decided to join her and sat in the armchair kitty-corner to the sofa. She lightened up when she saw him.

Miss Arvis, Rebecca, was single and was heavily involved with her church according to teacher gossip. It made sense she would be uncomfortable in this situation.

She looks like a wife. Like she was born to be a wife, yet she's not one. How odd.

"Hi," he said, trying to be cordial.

They'd only spoken a few times before when they were forced to during workshops or meetings. She was never rude or unpleasant, she simply wasn't *much* at all. It was almost like she didn't exist beyond her classroom. If Charlie had ever been asked to run down a list of all the teachers he worked with, he wasn't even sure her name would pop into his mind. That's how distant she seemed from everyone and everything.

"Jumping right in with them I see," she said, staring at his beer bottle.

"Figured if you can't beat 'em, join 'em," he said. "You should have a drink."

"I'm sorry. I'm not comfortable with that."

"Trying to quit?"

She didn't get his joke.

And the award for most awkward moment goes to...

"Okay..." he let linger as he tapped his finger against the neck of his bottle.

He desperately needed support. He was already drowning at this party, and he felt ridiculously out of place. Joel needed to hurry up and get here. Pulling his phone from his pocket, he texted his friend.

Charlie: You almost here? This is brutal.

He waited and then waited some more. The message wasn't going through yet. Then, it did, but it didn't seem as if his friend was online at the moment. The phone in his hand was the only respite from the woman sitting to his left, who he could see out of the corner of his eye was watching him the whole time.

I'll give it an hour, tops. If Lauren and Joel aren't here by then, I'm out of here.

Finally, he turned his attention back to Miss Arvis and smiled. "Rebecca right?"

"Yeah," she said, "and… maybe you're right. Sorry if I came across as a…" she leaned closer as if she needed to whisper over the music, "… a bitch. I think I'll have one of those beers now."

Maybe it wouldn't be so bad after all.

11

LAUREN

She'd managed to take two shots of tequila and down one beer before she gained the courage to head to the party. It was now twenty minutes to eight and her invitation stressed the importance of being on time. In fact, it read: ANYONE ARRIVING LATE WILL NOT BE PERMITTED. ABSOLUTELY NO LATE ARRIVALS. DON'T EVEN BOTHER.

Strict rules coming from a student body that couldn't follow a single one.

The thought made her giggle as she waited for the car she'd ordered. She'd leave hers in the convention center parking lot because she was already buzzing, and she was planning to throw back a few more.

Throw back a few.

Even thinking that term made her feel unladylike. It seemed reserved for dudes guzzling beers while watching the NFL or NASCAR.

Come on over, Joe. We'll order some hot wings and throw back a few.

Was it the thought that made her laugh or was it the alcohol racing through her? She decided it was a little bit of both. She wasn't a heavy drinker. In fact, she rarely had more than a glass of wine a night. That was her habit. Shower, wine, and TV. Tequila and beer most definitely were not part of the daily routine.

Nightly routine.

Even that made her laugh.

This is going to be a great night.

She wondered where Charlie was right now. Was he already at the party? She couldn't wait to see him.

A dark sedan pulled up at the curb and the passenger side window lowered.

"Arnold," the driver said. He was an older man, balding and happy-looking. He smiled and Lauren liked his dimples.

"No, Lauren," she replied.

He laughed.

"I'm Arnold," he said.

"Oh... oh. Okay." She finally understood that he was her driver. He was here to whisk her off to the party. "I'm sorry. I thought you were calling me... oh, never mind."

"You don't look like much of an Arnold," the driver said to her as she climbed into the backseat.

She chuckled and handed the party invitation to him, feeling suddenly important, like she had her own personal driver. Or was she simply discourteous for immediately choosing the backseat? She never knew if it was considered impolite to forgo the front passenger seat. In a taxi, she'd always climb into the rear, but these car services felt more personal, like it was a buddy picking her up and dropping her off at the party.

"You entered the address into the app," the driver said. "Remember?"

"Oh, yeah," she replied, laughing again.

It felt great being so silly.

The drive didn't take long. During it, she realized she recognized the area. She lived near here as a kid. But the car didn't stop outside a house, and when it slowed and pulled over outside the Harrison Park gates, she hesitated getting out. "You sure this is it?"

The driver lifted his phone and showed her the map. "This is the address."

"Huh," she said. "Odd place to have a party isn't it, Arnold?"

"Nothing surprises me anymore, ma'am. I once saw a nighttime party at a zoo."

The zoo's got nothing on these animals.

"Can you wait a second?" she asked. "Just until I'm sure there wasn't some kind of mistake?"

"Of course."

She climbed out of the car and shut the door behind her. The parking lot was quite dark with only one lamppost lit. Two boys stood at the entrance gate. She recognized them both from her classes. Brandon Pence and Jerome Knowles. These two hung out together a lot and liked to sit at the lunch table nearest the door so they could hiss and catcall at every girl who entered or exited the cafeteria, but they weren't particularly bad kids. Typical teenage hornballs was more like it.

Arnold rolled down his window. "This is it, right?"

She didn't really want him to leave, but she understood time was money. He had other people to pick up.

"Yeah, this is it," she replied, her buzz beginning to wear off.

"Have fun at your party," he said before rolling up the window and driving away.

"Oh, I'm sure I will," she said under her breath. Arnold was nowhere near close enough to hear her.

The chain-link fence in front of her surrounded the parking lot. Behind her, on the other side of the street, was nothing but trees. She'd played in this park as a kid, but it had always taken a bit of a hike or bicycle ride to get here. The nearby neighborhoods were at least a couple of miles away. It had always taken her a good thirty minutes or so to walk here. Wind shook the trees behind her. The boys inside the gate didn't say a word. They only watched her.

Lauren stuck a few fingers through one of the holes in the fence and steadied herself. On the other side of it, all the way at the back of the lot, she saw the path that led into the park. She'd walked it before.

This had always been one of her favorite places to visit as a kid. She'd chased boys along the wooden boardwalk trail that branched off into so many different pathways and had become an expert at hide and seek here. This park was where she'd experienced her first kiss. At night, the path was always illuminated by white Christmas-style bulbs that ran along the railings on both sides. She thought she caught a faint glimpse of them now back there within the trees.

There was something magical about the place. One could easily get lost if they ventured off the main path. Signs were posted to get people back on track, but it really was a labyrinth inside. Choosing to have a Grad Night party here was a strange decision; one that she couldn't believe would have been Liz's. No, that bitch was too prissy for this. She would want to hold the festivities in a grand palace, not outdoors.

But James Bender would like it here.

Where did that come from? She knew nothing about him, but she sensed evil in that boy, and thought he might like being under the moon, among the other animals in the wildlife, and in a place where he could be free to wreak havoc.

James Bender.

If she'd driven here, the mere thought of him might have been enough to cause her to turn around and go home. As his name echoed through her mind, the wind kicked up a notch. The trees behind her seemed to shush her. And she obeyed them, forcing herself to think of anything but the strange boy she dreaded. She hoped he wouldn't be here tonight. Even thinking about that kid gave her the heebie-jeebies. Wind blew dirt against her dress, so Lauren brushed it off and waited a moment before heading toward the entrance.

She nearly jumped out of her shoes when a car raced past and splashed through a puddle. She turned to look at it and didn't see one of the boys approaching.

"Ms. Peony," Jerome called out, causing her to jump a second time tonight.

She wheeled around and saw the boy on the other side of the fence.

"Told you she'd come," his buddy Brandon added.

"I agreed with you, jackass."

"No, you didn't."

"Boys," she interrupted. "I'm here. I wouldn't miss your Grad Night party."

As if she'd flipped a switch that turned their world to shit, both boys seemed to grow suddenly solemn. Jerome looked at his feet. Brandon took a deep breath and blew it out while staring up at the night sky. The change was strange, but it wasn't alarming, and she chalked it up to the boys being somewhat sad about leaving the only world they'd known for four years behind.

Graduating students were often like that. They all seemed to fall into one of two categories. They were either so thrilled to get out of high school that they completely lost their minds, or they pouted and cried, realizing life was about to transform drastically. Lauren supposed Jerome and Brandon fit into the latter. They'd probably spent all day feigning excitement to join their friends in celebration, but now that they were in a dark, silent parking lot facing their computer teacher, it might've finally sunken in that they were high school students no more.

"So..." she said, "you fellas want to escort a lady in?"

"Of course," Brandon said as he came out to meet her, took her gently by the hand, and led her through the giant gate. "You made it just in time. It's seven fifty-eight."

She glanced at her cell phone screen and saw he was right. "You were serious about not letting anyone in after eight I guess."

"Liz's strict orders," he said.

"Liz's orders," Lauren said, hating the taste of the girl's name in her mouth.

She couldn't wait to get home, gargle, and spit it out so she could never mention that name again. For now, she'd have to play nice. She silently thanked God the girl didn't have any younger siblings.

The Cupo curse ends with her.

"She doesn't want the party to be interrupted by late arrivals," Jerome added. "She said if the teachers really want to celebrate with us, they'll show up on time."

Something was odd about his voice. It was like he was reciting words without any meaning behind them. Like he'd been handed a script and was told to read it when someone arrived. When *she* arrived.

"Like you expected us to be punctual for class," Brandon said with the same coldness to his voice. "Her words, not mine."

"Got it," Lauren replied. "Well, I guess I fit the bill then, huh? I do respect you enough to arrive on time, even if I barely made it."

"You made it," Jerome said. "That's what counts."

Yes, they were good kids. At least these two were.

"Are any of the other teachers here?" she asked as she was led through the parking lot.

"Yes," Brandon replied. "You're the last."

The last. Why does he speak with that strange tone?

Lauren stopped and tried to get a clear look at his face. She wanted to read what was behind that voice. It didn't scare her, but it bothered her. Were these two high? That could be it. It wouldn't be unlike her students to smoke a little weed before the party. She was sure they smoked it on the way to school. Especially these two.

The darkness of the trees covering the moon, and the parking lot lamp at his back, kept Brandon's face hidden in shadows.

The James Bender kind of shadows.

"Saved the best for last," she finally said, holding up her end of the conversation.

"Definitely," Brandon said. "You know, this party is probably going to be boring for you, Ms. Peony. Are you sure you want to be here?"

His face moved into the light and she saw he was chewing on his inner cheek. He seemed almost nervous. Was he testing her? Or was he hinting there'd be a senior prank tonight he didn't want her falling victim to? Either way, she knew she needed to attend the party. To run away now would mean she was a coward. Besides, how bad could a prank be?

Worse case, they drop pigs' blood over you Carrie style. Best case, they egg and toilet paper your car.

Knowing how limited their creativity was, she wasn't *that* worried. Glancing back at the cars in the parking lot, she felt bad for the teachers. She was sure that was probably what was going to happen. The teachers would stagger half-drunk out to the parking lot later to find their cars undriveable. They'd have to peel off tons of wet toilet paper. Maybe there would even be shit smeared on the windshields. Liz Cupo was more than capable of pulling off a stunt like that. But Lauren hadn't driven tonight. She'd taken a car here with hopes to get a ride home later. If she needed to, she'd hire a car to take her.

Both boys waited on her decision. Would she turn around and leave or was she going to commit and make her way into the park?

"This is your Grad Night party, guys," she answered. "I'm honored to be invited, and I will definitely be attending."

Brandon nodded and smiled. He looked at Jerome and then back down into her face. It was amazing how tall these kids could grow. In the four years she'd known both of them, they'd shot up at least a foot.

"Oh, the time," Jerome said as his watch chimed.

"The party's in the park," Brandon advised her. "You see the lights? Follow that path and it'll take you straight back into the main playground area. That's where everyone else is."

"I know the place well," she assured them.

When she turned away, she heard them break into a jog, running toward the gate. She stopped at the entrance to the boardwalk path and looked back to see them securing the chain-link door with a giant chain and padlock.

Why are they locking us in?

She didn't like this at all.

"Boys!" she yelled.

The boys talked quietly among themselves and then Brandon took a few steps closer to her while Jerome wrestled with the giant lock.

"Ms. Peony?" Brandon said.

"Why are you locking us in?"

"I don't know," he replied. "Something about an agreement with the park. They don't want loiterers I guess. Liz said they only agreed to let us use the park if we promised to make sure nobody else got in."

"Liz's orders," Jerome said as he finally snapped the lock into place and turned toward her.

"Liz's orders," Lauren repeated for the second time tonight.

"It's fine," Brandon assured her.

She didn't like it, but again, she knew this park well. Better than they did, she was sure of it. Her concern was what would happen in the case of an emergency. What if they couldn't get that lock open? She knew a back way out, if it even still existed after all these years, but it wouldn't be practical for evacuating the entire party.

"You're holding onto the key?" Lauren asked Jerome.

He nodded and held a thumbs-up in her direction. Despite the feeling that something was *off,* she walked on, allowing herself to relax a little as she stepped onto the glowing path. Her hands slid over the white lights accentuating the railings. She felt wonderfully at home among the trees.

This was her safe place. It was her deserted island. She'd read so many novels seated on the park's wooden benches. She'd almost lost her virginity here but had denied the guy – more out of respect for the park than out of respect for herself – as she'd finally given into him later that night in the backseat of his car.

Holding her hands out at her sides, touching a few of the leaves that seemed to reach out to her, she imagined the place was welcoming her home. "I've missed you tremendously," she whispered, and she imagined the wind through the trees was them whispering, "We've missed you too."

Well, good to know the tequila is still working its magic.

Music flowed from deep inside the park. Its loud bass boomed in electronic rhythm. That hectic sound didn't belong here in a place so peaceful and calm. This was always a place of great silence and power. Its calming effect had helped her through so many troubles. These kids had no idea. They respected nothing. Already, Lauren couldn't wait for this party to be over. For now, she'd have to join them, until the time came for her to sneak out. She *at least* needed to make an appearance.

12

CHARLIE

Looking down at his cell phone, Charlie wished he'd at least see the blue checkmarks indicating his friend was reading his messages. They'd been received but not read. He added more to his message.

Charlie: Did you get stuck at the convention center?

Joel didn't answer.

Charlie: I'll wait here for a little longer, but I'm leaving if you don't show up soon.

"Is it me or is it getting hot in here?" Rebecca asked.

After her first beer, the quiet, awkward teacher had loosened up a bit. After her second, she was laughing a little more. After her third, she was practically wasted. He knew shit was getting real when she unclipped her hair and let her blonde bob fall freely above her shoulders.

Charlie was on his third beer as well, but he wasn't a small guy, and it took a lot more than that to get him buzzing. He'd already decided this was his last beer though. Unless Joel and Lauren arrived.

Right now, he felt like Rebecca's chaperone. If she had too many drinks, one of the high school boys might try to take advantage of her. It wouldn't be the first time it happened. The news over the past few years had been wallpapered with teachers succumbing to the sexual whims of their hormonal students. Some male. Some female. The behavior had become common, and Charlie wondered if it had anything to do with so many of these relationships popping up on TV programs. Things so taboo would have never been on the television ten years ago.

Glancing behind him, Charlie saw that one of the boys in the room did in fact have his eye on Rebecca. It was a boy from another school, but as the kid's buddy droned on about something obviously unimportant, this boy kept his eyes on the teacher. He looked past Charlie, as if he didn't even exist, and stared longingly at her.

Rebecca was cute. Charlie would give her that. Now that she'd let her hair down, he might even call her sexy. But she wouldn't pass for a high school student, not unless she was a character in one of the popular 90s sitcoms where all teenagers seemed to be played by actors over the age of twenty-five. That meant this boy knew exactly what he was doing.

"My last relationship was so dull," Rebecca went on. Charlie realized his repeated nods had kept him a part of her rambling. "I mean the sex was so mediocre. Every night was a decision, like should I lie back and take it, or should I read? I actually weighed my sexual desire against a good book. Has that ever happened to you?"

It suddenly dawned on Charlie that he and the pretty teacher had been given beers by the kids at the party. He hadn't gotten up to get a single one. He felt fine, but she was... not herself. Someone had put something in her drink. He was sure of it. It was made clear by the way she stroked one arm with the fingers of her other hand as she spoke. Beer might loosen someone up a bit, but it didn't usually result in sexual banter so early on. Rebecca was high.

He looked back at Peeping Tom again and realized he wasn't staring longingly like Charlie first thought. He was waiting patiently. Watching. When the time came, he would pounce on her. His plans were already in motion. When it became obvious she could no longer control herself, he'd slide in, flirt a little, and then whisk her off to one of the upstairs bedrooms.

You're being paranoid. Come on. That's the kind of shit that happens in movies.

It was exactly the kind of thing his students would pull. He was sure of it. And he didn't even know this kid.

"Stop drinking that beer," Charlie said.

"But I like it," Rebecca replied.

"Then drink mine," he said, realizing getting her to give up her drink would be more difficult than he thought.

As soon as he switched beers with her, the kid who'd been watching her scoffed in complaint and stormed out of the room.

Sorry to ruin your plans, you fucking douchebag.

He wondered what kind of parents the kid had. Would it be a father who'd slap him in the face for doing something so despicable, or was he the kind of dad who'd pat him on the back for following his directions? Charlie had met all kinds of parents. Some truly cared. Others only wanted their kids to sail through school and get the fuck out of their lives so they could travel or do other shit they'd never been able to since getting stuck with a child.

"Why don't you come and sit next to me?" Rebecca asked, flirtatiously smiling at him while patting the sofa cushion at her side.

He did, but not because he appreciated her sudden attraction to him, but because he needed to convince her to leave. This was a bad scene for her. Someone would snap a picture of her on his or her phone and then send it around to other kids, many of whom would still be students at DS High. Then it would quickly continue spreading until it reached a parent's phone who would undoubtedly seize the opportunity to destroy her career by sending it to the school principal.

This reminded him why he didn't want to attend the party in the first place. This was a bad idea.

"We need to get out of here," he leaned over and whispered to her.

She turned her face quickly so her lips could brush his. He backed up and chuckled. Then, she leaned over and whispered into his ear, "Why don't you take me home then?" It was followed by a moist tongue nipping at his earlobe.

Charlie was a man, like any other. His cock reacted the way any others would too, but his mind was strong enough to staunch his sudden excited energy. Physically, he was getting aroused while mentally, he knew better. This was not the time, nor was it the place.

You can take her back to her place though. Fuck her, Charlie. It's been a looooong time since you've had a woman.

It had been. He'd been practically celibate. In fact, he'd had such a dry spell he might as well have strapped on a clerical collar, carried a Bible, and preached sermons to his classes. The thought made him laugh.

"You want me, don't you?" Rebecca whispered. "I want you too."

Don't be a fucking idiot. Take her home! Lauren denied you, man. She flat-out pushed you away.

"I do," he said, but only because he thought that might help get her out of the house.

Charlie was a good man. He would *never* sleep with a woman who'd been slipped any kind of drug or who'd consumed so much alcohol she'd lost her inhibitions. She'd been extremely nervous when Charlie first walked into the house. She *did not* want him. It was the drink talking, or whatever the kid had put into it.

Charlie thought about this kid headed to college. What kind of damage would he do there if he was already a date-rape architect building bullshit sexual blueprints for his buddies to follow? How many of the kid's friends were trying this strategy right now with other girls at the party? This was the kind of shit that would land them in jail.

When his phone buzzed at his hip, Charlie practically leapt off the couch with excitement, which was probably a good idea because Rebecca had been moving closer with that wet tongue of hers. Surprisingly, none of the few kids in the room seemed to notice. Most of the partygoers were outside in the backyard. There couldn't have been more than fifty teenagers at this party.

Pulling out his phone, Charlie held a hand up to stop Rebecca and read the screen. It was Joel. Finally.

Joel: What do you mean when will I be here? I'm at the party.
Joel: Hello.
Joel: Where are you?

Charlie was confused. He looked around at the others in the room. Nobody had come through the front door in a while. He wondered if there was an entrance at the side of the house, maybe one that led right to the backyard.

"Come on," he said as he stood and took Rebecca's hand, only to help her get up.

"Yes, let's go," she said with a lazy grin painted on her face.

She thought he was taking her home and stomped her feet in disappointment when she realized he was dragging her toward the backyard.

"I want to stay on the couch," she complained.

"I'm not leaving you alone," he said.

In the kitchen, he saw two teachers. He waved hello and continued through the dining room and out onto the back patio. Outside, kids smoked cigarettes, vape pens, and joints. Most of the party was out here, but there weren't so many people that he couldn't tell them easily apart. He saw Bogdan standing next to Rita, who was telling a story that had her so excited she was throwing her hands around as she spoke.

He saw other kids. All good kids. Normal kids. Nobody who stood out as a serious problem student.

A few teachers mingled with each other and with students too.

But no Joel. No Lauren.

Rebecca plopped into an empty lawn chair while Charlie typed into his phone.

Charlie: I'm at the party. Where are you?

The message was delivered but wasn't read.

He wished he had Lauren's phone number. He'd had it at one point but deleted it one night after he'd had a few drinks. In a moment of self-pity, he decided he was at risk of seeming like a stalker, and she didn't deserve that. So, out of respect for her, he'd decided to leave her alone. He regretted it the next day, but at that point, it was too late to ask for her number again. He wasn't even sure how he'd do that when the time came around. He could always blame it on buying a new phone.

Or you can fess up and then lick her ear the way Rebecca did yours.

As always, his mind reverted to internal jokes to lighten the mood, but he didn't want to laugh. He wanted to find his friends. It made no sense. How could Joel be at the party if *he* was at the party. He typed into his phone again.

Charlie: I'm in the backyard. I'm with Miss Arvis. I see Bogdan, Rita, Mr. Fallon, Mrs. Welch. But I don't see you.

Finally the messages were received and read.

Joel: Backyard? What backyard? I'm at the fucking party, bro. At the park.

At the park. What fucking park is he talking about?

Charlie: What park?

The message wasn't going through. He waited, but it wasn't being received.

"Hey, Bog," he called out over the music.

It was something from My Chemical Romance or maybe it was The Killers. These kids wouldn't listen to anything too new and they weren't hippie-ish enough to listen to the classics. So they stuck with the in-between. The grungy, angsty, often angry rock. He liked this kind of music sometimes, he enjoyed the songs, but he didn't follow any of the bands.

Bogdan broke away from Rita's story and made his way to Charlie, smiling with a slightly drunk grin. The kid was having a good time and he deserved to. He was finished with high school. Charlie was proud of him, but he needed information.

"Where's the park?" Charlie asked. "Is there a park around here?"

"A park?" Bogdan asked. "I don't know, man. I don't live around here. This is a rich-person house. I'm not rich."

Charlie scratched his head. Bogdan looked down at Rebecca who was staring up at the stars, but her head was slowly bobbing and not to the beat of the music.

"Whoa," Bogdan said with a laugh, "Miss Arvis is wasted."

"Yeah," Charlie said, "between us, I'm pretty sure someone put something in her drink."

Bogdan looked honestly upset to hear it. "Doesn't surprise me. Some of these kids are friends of Anna, the host of the party. From her old school, I guess. Assholes, if you ask me."

"I agree," Charlie said.

As Bogdan watched Rebecca with the amusement of a child staring at a Fourth of July sparkler, Charlie scanned the faces at the party again and came to a conclusion. Every person at this party was decent. The students were good kids. Or at least not evil. Even the teachers here were pretty cool. These were the teachers never involved with any of the school drama. They were never mentioned as holding grudges with kids. They didn't storm out of heated parent-teacher meetings mumbling curses under their breath. They didn't go out of their way to get kids in trouble. They simply showed up to work, did their part, and went home. Like Charlie.

Joel had been involved in a few altercations. Lauren too. And where were Mr. Cole and Mrs. Lowell? A lot of people were missing. People who'd gotten invites and had talked about coming to the party.

"Bog," Charlie said. "Is there another party tonight?"

Bogdan shrugged his shoulders, but he wasn't very convincing. He knew something.

"Bogdan, what's going on?"

He took a drag from a cigarette and blew smoke off to the side. He wouldn't bring his eyes to meet Charlie's, which was odd with this boy. They got along well. There should be no reason to feel weird in his presence. Yet, Charlie sensed something was wrong. The boy was keeping something from him.

Charlie glanced at his phone again. His message to Joel had gone through but hadn't been read.

"Bog, I'm serious," he said. "Is there a second party?"

"Nah," Bogdan said. "This is it."

Charlie looked down at Rebecca, who now had her eyes closed and was moving her head around, this time trying to follow the beat of the music. Charlie knew this song. It was *Dope Show* by Marilyn Manson. The chorus played and he wondered if he was a star in the dope show. Was this party a façade? A fake front? Supposedly the *bad* kids were going to show up later. Why? What were they up to *right now*?

Fearing for the lives of his colleagues seemed a bit extreme, but he was definitely concerned.

"Is there a senior prank, Bog?" he asked.

Bogdan kept his attention on Rebecca.

"Bog?"

He didn't look at him when he replied, "Just drop it, please, Mr. Charlie."

"Drop what?"

"I gave you this invitation to make sure you came here instead. Just stay here. Trust me."

"Where else would I go?"

"Back to my place," Rebecca said.

Bogdan laughed.

"Don't repeat that," Charlie told him.

He nodded. "I wouldn't. It's not her fault. Someone definitely slipped her something. This happened to Rita once." He leaned in close and whispered, "It was the only time I had a chance with her, but you know, I couldn't do something like that."

Because he's a good kid.

"Come on," Rebecca said, tugging on Charlie's pant leg.

Charlie ignored her.

"What about you?" she said lazily to Bogdan.

"Sorry," he replied, "I'm a taken man."

Taken by Rita. He wasn't, but he hoped to be. Charlie wished they'd end up together too, but none of that mattered right now. He needed to find his friends.

"Bogdan, what's the prank?"

"It's no big deal," he replied.

"If it's no big deal, you'll tell me what it is."

Bogdan didn't answer.

"I swear to God, Bogdan, if something happens to them—"

"—They're at Harrison," he said under his breath.

"Harrison? Harrison Park?"

"But don't go there, Mr. Charlie."

"What's going on there, man? Are we talking a harmless prank, or do I need to call the cops?"

"No!" Bogdan said loudly.

Charlie looked around to see if anyone else had noticed. The music had covered him.

"They'll kill me," he added.

"Kill you as in be angry or *kill* you as in murder you?"

Bogdan laughed. "Come on, Mr. Charlie."

It did seem absurd. Of course, they wouldn't actually *kill* him, but then again, someone *had* killed Mr. Rowan. He was probably being paranoid, but Charlie couldn't shake the feeling that whatever they had planned would be really mean at the least.

Charlie ran through a mental list of the names of students who might be at that party.

Liz Cupo would definitely be there.

Drew Dryer.

Milton Rothmeyer.

James Bender.

He pushed the *call* button on his phone and listened to the phone ring.

"Wait, who are you calling?" Bogdan asked, nervously reaching for the teacher's phone.

"Get your hand away from me," Charlie snapped. "I'm calling Joel Mendez."

"He's there?"

"He's there."

"Shit."

The phone continued to ring.

"Hello," Joel said.

"Joel, what's going on there…"

"You've reached my voice mail," Joel continued. "Sorry I couldn't answer but leave a message and I'll get back to you as soon as possible."

"Fuck," Charlie swore under his breath.

"Language, Mr. Charlie," Bogdan said.

Charlie shot him a look that said, "You've got some fucking nerve." When it was time to leave a message, Charlie said into his phone, "Joel, get Lauren and get out of that party. I don't know what it is, but the kids are up to something. Probably some kind of stupid prank, but you know what they're capable of. They're probably slashing everyone's tires as I leave this message..."

It beeped on the other end, signaling his message was over.

"I can't believe you," he said to Bogdan.

"I was trying to save you," Bogdan replied.

"Save me from what?"

Charlie pulled his invitation out of his pocket and read it over once again. He pointed at the letter "B" under the address. He'd assumed it stood for Bogdan, but now, with a sick feeling in his gut, he realized it wasn't that at all.

"Save me from what?" he repeated.

"Nothing. I don't even know, but I knew if you were here with us, then you wouldn't be there with them."

"Dammit, Bog. You're a good kid." Charlie patted him on his back. "But I need to get to that other party and warn them."

Bogdan protested, but Charlie didn't care. He grabbed Rebecca by the hand and led her whining, complaining, refusing body out of the party and toward his car. He'd have to help her get her car back tomorrow, but for right now, she needed to go home.

The gothic teen followed them all the way out to Charlie's car and stood outside the passenger window as Charlie pulled on Rebecca's seatbelt.

"Mr. Charlie," Bogdan said, "Seriously. Don't go."

"Thank you, Bog," he yelled through the closed window as he stepped on the gas and gunned it. He had no time to discuss things with the kid now. He needed to get to party "A."

13

LAUREN

Lauren took her time walking through the winding boardwalk. She'd already decided she'd come back to the park routinely after this. She loathed jogging but could almost imagine enjoying racing up and down the trail's pathways as she reached out to slap the leaves with each completed lap. The wind through her hair would remind her she was still alive. She needed that reassurance nowadays. An empty apartment tended to do the opposite, and even Clyde's snuggling and loveable licks didn't help with that incessant loneliness.

She knew Liz expected punctuality from the teachers, and that might have been precisely what caused her to slow down and really soak up the scent of the night air. She listened to the variety of sounds coming from the swampy water below her feet. The boardwalk kept her safe from all the creepy crawlies that sloshed through the muddy water. She could only imagine what lurked in the darkness below.

As a kid, she'd toss Goldfish crackers into the water and watch them quickly disappear, snatched up and dragged under by what she knew were fish but often convinced herself were creatures who protected her in the park. She fed them and they made sure she was always safe. She remembered telling her friend, Courtney, about it. The little girl didn't believe her and made fun of her for always telling make-believe stories.

A moment later, a giant frog croaked only a few feet from them. It had somehow gotten up onto the boardwalk. Courtney ran screaming and never returned to the park again. "Tried to tell you," Lauren had said to the girl's back as she raced away. It never occurred to Lauren to be afraid. In her mind, the park really was taking care of her, even from brats like Courtney.

When she finally reached the end of the boardwalk, she was greeted with a beautiful sight. These kids had really outdone them-selves. Most of the park was accentuated with bright yellowish Christmas lights. Wrapped around a pole right next to where she stood, Lauren followed the wire that dipped low and continued to her far left where it met a post connected to one of the bars helping hold up a metal stage. The floor and backdrop to the stage were wooden.

A stage.

The park had never had a stage before. At least none she could remember. Who knew if it did now, but then getting a better look at it, she realized the thing would never withstand the rain, so it must have been erected for this one night only.

Lauren's eyes continued following the wiring from the lights as it ran behind the stage and reappeared on its opposite side, where it dipped across the sky and directly over a crowd of teachers and students gathered together and mingling. The cable reached the top of a slide.

The playground. It was right in front of where she stood. She smiled remembering all the time she spent dangling from those monkey bars, swinging as high as she possibly could on those swings, and racing face forward down that metal slide. Tommy Badger even knocked out his front tooth doing that.

Oh good times.

The golden lights dipped down low over a pair of rusting seesaws and then rose over the old metal carousel parents once used to scare the shit out of their kids. Children would yell out something like, "Spin me faster, Daddy!" Until gravity took hold and threatened to peel the skin from their faces and yank their heads off their bodies. Lauren remembered flying off it once and almost biting off the tip of her tongue when she hit the ground.

Ah... kids these days have never experienced the fun we had at our own expense.

What a good time!

She couldn't wait to have kids of her own so she could subject them to the same tortures she endured as a child. The thought made her laugh.

The Christmas lights continued past the playground and over to the roof of the covered basketball court to her right. Lauren had caught a boy looking under her skirt from beneath those bleachers. And once, for her birthday, her parents brought her and her friends to the park and turned that smooth court floor into a roller-skating rink.

She wondered how she could get onto the committee responsible for this park, if there even was one. This place needed to keep going. Kids deserved a park like this. And it loved the children right back. She could feel it. It remembered her.

Like a stalker staring out over the entire party, she didn't budge but continued surveying everything. Beyond the crowd of trees, she saw the hills that rolled up until the grass lawn met the trees again. The entire park was like a valley cut away at the center of a giant forest.

In the darkness, she imagined in front of her was the face of the trees and it was reaching out with giant bushy arms, its vine-entwined fingers scooping up everything in the clearing, pulling it in tight to its stomach. They were in the forest's embrace, and it was warm here.

To the left, far off in the distance, a train horn blasted, and she remembered walking those tracks with her friends. They'd walk along until they found a hole in the park fence where they'd all slip in. Then they'd trudge through the shrubbery and trees until they came to the park's center, where the students and teachers were gathered now.

In that crowd she saw so many kids she loathed and very few she got along with. Even the teachers were mostly the asshole ones. She'd been at the school several years and there were those teachers she would speak to and those she tried her best to avoid. Teachers weren't much different from the students when it came to foul gossip and mean-spirited remarks.

Mr. Cole was an asshole. Like a construction-team foreman, he walked around barking orders at everyone, stood up in meetings to discipline them all in front of the principal, and only seemed to have a soft spot for one person on the entire staff – Mrs. Lowell. Just like the kids had blatantly accused them of in their graduation video, the two were rumored to be sleeping together and had been for years. At this point, they didn't even hide it. Even now, they stood in front of the stage sipping wine from wineglasses, talking to... *the bitch.*

The bitch. You can do this Lauren. Find Joel and Charlie. That's all you need to do.

She walked into the opening and was immediately greeted by one of the teachers she ate lunch with often.

"Lauren!" Ms. Keen called out to her from her seat on one of the wooden benches at the playground.

At first, she wished the woman wouldn't have called her by her first name in front of these kids, but then she remembered they were no longer students. There was a good chance they'd be calling her Lauren all night, mostly to spite her.

"Paula," Lauren replied, returning the favor.

She approached her friend. Colleague was probably a better word to describe her. Even associate would do. Friend assumed they hung out after work, met for ladies' nights out, and told each other their deepest, darkest secrets. Their relationship was fairly one-sided.

Oftentimes Lauren would eat lunch while Ms. Keen spent the entire time ranting and raving about students, parents, and other teachers. She was kind of the school gossip, which was one of the reasons they'd never moved fully into the friend category. You had to be able to trust a friend. Lauren might think a lot of nasty shit in her head, but she rarely spoke any of it out loud. She didn't trust anyone at the school enough to do that. Many of the teachers would run back to other staff members and pass on things that were said. She didn't doubt that Ms. Paula Keen would do exactly that.

Sitting next to Paula on the bench was an ex-student, an older kid who'd graduated a couple of years before. He had definitely grown into a strapping young stud. Now, with facial hair, he was barely recognizable.

"You remember Scott?" Paula asked.

"Of course," Lauren said, holding out her hand. "How have you been?"

The boy pushed her hand away and stood up to hug her. "Great. You know, if I hadn't learned to type so well in your class, I'd be the shittiest journalist on my college newspaper."

"College newspaper," Lauren repeated. "Wow! Congratulations. Sounds like you're doing really well."

Behind Scott, Paula sat on the bench beaming. She was smiling a little too brightly and Lauren suddenly wondered if she'd interrupted a moment.

A moment? No way.

The thought seemed absurd. Lauren would never consider flirting with an ex-student. It was unprofessional. She'd been asked out before by a former student and had immediately but politely turned down the invitation.

Is there a point at which it becomes acceptable to see an ex-student romantically?

She didn't think so. It was kind of part of the teacher code. Teachers were supposed to be authority figures. They were supposed to help students sort out life, make sense of it, and plan for the future.

Oh, she's planning for the future all right. That's clearly written on her face.

When he loosened up his squeeze on Lauren's shoulders, Paula pulled the young man back down to sit next to her on the bench.

"Did you know he hated me?" Paula asked.

Lauren scrunched up her mouth and shook her head softly. She had no idea, but it didn't surprise her.

"Yeah," Paula continued. "He says I ruined his chances of getting into the first school he wanted—"

"—Only the school I dreamed about attending my whole life," he interrupted with a chuckle.

"Yeah, that," Paula continued, "because I refused to write a recommendation letter for him."

He turned to flirtatiously glare at her with one eyebrow raised. "Ruined my life."

"What? You were a terrible student. You know that."

"I was bad," he admitted, "but not *that* bad."

"I'll make it up to you," she promised.

On that note, Lauren thought it best if she leave. "Have you seen Joel or Charlie?"

"I saw Joel earlier," Paula said. "I think he's over there by the stage somewhere. Haven't seen Charlie though."

"Thanks."

She glanced around the playground and saw a few more teachers and some students sitting around. The cherry ends of cigarettes glowed in the darkness. Clouds of smoke rose into the air, the thicker vape smoke. These people were turning the park into a damn disco.

No respect.

As she turned to leave the playground, she saw something that made her freeze in place. Someone was sitting on top of the jungle gym. How she'd not noticed him before was a mystery to her. She'd been standing only twenty feet away or so when talking to Paula and Scott.

The silhouette of a boy perched at the crown of the jungle gym, unmoving, watching her, was too hard to miss, yet she hadn't noticed it at all. Now, she couldn't take her eyes off it. The shadow had hunched over shoulders, a rounded head, and sat in complete stillness.

James Bender.

She knew it was him. The oval-shaped void where his face should be was looking right at her. The boy was watching her. He was too far away to see clearly, but for a second, it seemed as if something glowed from beneath his hood.

Remembering the knives, she backed up a few steps, her arms and legs aching with coldness. As much as she didn't want to turn her back on the boy, she was afraid to look at him any longer. If his penetrating gaze grabbed hold of her again, she wasn't sure what she'd see next time.

One vision hit her. It came and disappeared so quickly she wasn't sure if he'd caused it or if her imagination had done it.

Her big toe was on her mattress, an open bottle of nail polish sat next to her foot. Bubblegum pink.

The scene seemed pleasant enough, until a pair of needle-nosed pliers shot into view, wielded by an unseen assailant. The tool went straight to her big toe, where the bottom piece of the pliers slid underneath her toenail and then the top clamped down. Lauren's ass clenched, and her eyes rolled back. "Ah... ah God," she cried.

The metal instrument jammed into the meaty flesh beneath the nail, and Lauren screamed in agony. The pliers were ripped up and to the side with a snap, tearing her toenail clean off. A thick line of snot-like goo stretched from her bloody toe to the nail being pulled away from it.

Lauren gasped as the vision faded, and she was left standing in the park, looking back at the silhouette of the boy. The strange vibrating thrum she'd heard in her apartment the night of the break-in played softly in the distance.

Is it coming from him?

The kid gave her the creeps. Looking once more over at Paula and Scott, who were now kissing on the bench like they didn't give a shit who might see them, it seemed Lauren was the only person concerned about the kid sitting so still, watching them all.

14

LAUREN

Fuck you, James Bender.

Lauren was here to have a good time. She wasn't going to let that sick little son of a bitch ruin it for her. He could sit there and stare all night for all she cared. Then he could go home and do whatever it was he did in private. She imagined he did really sordid shit like beat off to toy catalogues or talk dirty to a doll he'd created himself. Crude playthings he'd sewn together from ripped up pieces of Barbies and stuffed animals. An arm from one, the head from another, eyeballs plucked from a third, until he had a makeshift female Frankenstein of his own creation. She'd be named Cassandra or some other beautiful name that contradicted the doll entirely.

You are fucking crazy tonight, Lauren. Where do you come up with this shit?

Horror movies, that's where. She loved them. Only, she was usually too afraid to watch them now that she was always in the apartment alone. Sometimes she'd allow herself to view one, and every time she did, she'd pull Clyde close to her as if the cat was going to protect her from monsters, demons, and sadistic serial killers if and when one ever attacked.

This was one more reason she wanted to get to know Charlie better.

She missed simple things like having someone to cook dinner with, watch movies with, and take pre-bedtime baths with. Now, if only she could find him.

The crowd centered around the stage was small but thick. Bodies were nearly shoulder to shoulder as everyone seemed to be enjoying each other's company. The ex-students were dressed to impress, but it was damn near like club-hopping outfits. The girls wore tight, revealing clothing and too much makeup. The guys matched with clothing that showed off their muscles and tattoos.

It was strange to see them looking so adult-like. At school, they were forced to obey a strict dress code. Now, all that was out the window. It seemed that only about fifteen or so of the students were graduates from this year. At least ten others were ex-students. They were the most scandalous ones. The students who'd caused the most trouble or had gotten caught doing things in school students should never do.

A guy who'd gotten busted selling crystal meth two years back was here.

So was the resident marijuana supplier, her hair festooned with roach clips as if it were a big joke that she'd been booted out of school prematurely.

This year's pregnant student, Amber, who left long enough to have her baby and then came back to join the rest of her class stood near the stage sipping a drink and dancing sensually to the music.

Lauren spotted the couple who'd gotten caught having sex in a bathroom stall a couple of years ago. They weren't together though. The girl was talking to Joel. Being a newer teacher at the school, he probably had no idea who she was. Lauren decided to save him.

"Hey, Joel," she said. "Fiona, right?"

Lauren smiled at the girl who smiled back, "That's right, Ms. Peony."

Something flashed in the girl's eyes and Lauren had to wonder if she'd come across as rude, but all she'd said was the girl's name. Had the young woman realized she'd approached to save Joel from hooking up with the school slut? The menacing grin she now wore said that was exactly what she was thinking. Lauren had cock blocked her.

"Aww," Fiona said as she reached out and put her fingertips against Lauren's stomach, "Oh my God. You're pregnant?"

Lauren gasped.

No, I'm not fucking pregnant, you little bitch!

She wanted to say the words, but she couldn't find it in her to be that mean, even if the ex-student had decided to go there.

Joel's mouth opened wide in shock and he quickly used his hand to cover it.

Lauren steadied her nerves and finally said, "Umm... no. I'm not. But aren't you a sweet one?"

Fiona cocked her head to the side and squinted as if calling Lauren out as a liar. "Come on. Are you sure?"

If this were anyone else, she could see it being a total mistake. Lauren would be the first to admit she needed to lose some weight. She wasn't obese, but sure, she was curvy. She could stand to shed a few pounds. But this wasn't anybody else, and Lauren knew what the girl was doing.

On school grounds, Lauren might have bit her tongue a little better. At work, she could be fired or could at least be called into a meeting where she would be reprimanded by the principal and quite possibly the parents, but this was not that scenario, and Lauren was getting fed up with this bitch's comments.

"Yeah, I'm pretty sure," Lauren said. "And how about you? Find out who the fathers are yet?"

This caught the girl off guard to the point she only gasped, laughed under her breath, and walked away. Straight to Liz Cupo, where she whispered something into the girl's ear before walking away.

"Wow," Joel said, "What was that all about?"

"I have no idea," Lauren replied.

"Good comeback though."

"Do you know who she is?"

"No," Joel said. "Not one of our students though. I thought maybe a sister or a cousin of one."

"No, she's an ex-student. And a whore. Got busted having sex in a bathroom stall once. She also got caught sneaking into a guy's room on a field trip."

"Kids will be kids."

"Well, the dumb bitch isn't a kid anymore," Lauren said.

"You were like *this* close to kicking her ass, weren't you?" Joel said, holding his thumb and index finger an inch apart.

She laughed. She'd never let it get to that. Violence wasn't really her thing.

"You two having a good time?" Mrs. Lowell asked as she approached with Mr. Cole right by her side.

Both seemed to be slightly inebriated already. It didn't surprise Lauren. She imagined they drank quite often together, probably to help forget they were betraying their spouses.

"Lovely time," Lauren replied.

"Interesting crowd, isn't it?" Mr. Cole barked.

"It definitely is."

Lauren glanced around again and saw Mr. Lafferty, the English teacher talking to a student, Drew Dryer. Nearby, Coach McCall, the PE teacher, laughed it up with Gavin Myles – the class clown. Practically every one of the senior superlatives were here, all those voted for their class yearbook to be the most popular, best looking, funniest, most athletic, etc.

Oddly enough, even the main school security guard, Mr. Barry Jackson was here. The list of students he'd busted over the years was nearly as long as his sideburns. Lauren always thought he looked like a black version of Elvis. He had the long, slicked back hair Bruno Mars had brought back into fashion. Right now, he was telling a funny story with his arm around Franny, the cafeteria lady.

Valerie Kemper, DS High's resident Barbie doll, glided into the middle of the circle created by Lauren, Joel, Mrs. Lowell, and Mr. Cole. She had a tray in her hand filled with champagne flutes.

"Thank you all for showing up for us," she said in her sweetest voice, one Lauren knew she turned on only when she wanted something from someone.

What does she want from us?

"Please, take one," the girl said. "Only one, and don't you dare sip from it. Not yet. We need to make a toast first. Then we can really get the party started."

"I like the way you think," Mrs. Lowell said as she took two and handed one to Mr. Cole.

"Oh, you know I can't stand champagne," he complained.

"Do it for the kids, you mean old bastard," she joked.

It was the first time Lauren had ever heard her speak to him like that. She couldn't help imagining that was language she usually reserved for the bedroom. Then she caught herself actually imagining their bedroom extravaganzas and instantly felt nauseous.

Oh, God.

She almost laughed out loud at the thought of Mr. Cole's saggy balls teabagging Mrs. Lowell.

"What?" Joel asked. He must have noticed her reddening cheeks.

"Nothing," she replied. "Where's Charlie?"

"I don't know," Joel said. "He messaged me earlier about being here, but I couldn't find him."

Joel pulled out his phone and checked it. "Yeah, he hasn't replied. Or, it could be the shitty service in this park."

Because you shouldn't have to resort to playing on your phone when you're in a place like this.

Parks were sacred places. She hadn't been to one in ages, but she could imagine what she'd see if she did. Kids would be on the equipment while parents sat playing games on their phone, watching videos, or chatting on social media. In reality, the kids would probably be on their phones too. She could practically see the sandbox right over there with four kids sitting in it, each with a phone in his or her hand.

Do kids even know how to play anymore? Real games. Like Hide and Seek or Freeze Tag.

"Do you think it's possible he's here?" Lauren asked, still concerned about Charlie.

Joel looked at her, accidentally let his eyes drift down to her cleavage, and said, "Trust me. He wouldn't miss it."

"I hope not," she said under her breath, brushing off the music teacher's sneak peek.

Joel heard it and smiled. Mr. Cole and Mrs. Lowell had turned around to look toward the stage where Liz Cupo was now climbing the short staircase, making her way up to address her audience.

Her audience. All these years of trying to get her to pay attention and now we're all supposed to be excited to hear what she has to say.

After the speech she'd given at the graduation ceremony, the one followed by that vile video, Lauren wasn't looking forward to what was coming. Who knew what she'd say in a place where she needn't use a filter. Not that she used one most of the time anyway. Liz wasn't one to hold her tongue.

It seemed most of the audience looked forward to her speech. Most of the ex-students cheered for her, a few people whistled, and a couple of them even cried out things like, "Let's go, Liz!"

"Is this thing on?" she asked as she held the microphone up to her lips.

It wasn't.

Good. Make an ass of yourself.

As usual, a part of Lauren was mentally scolding herself for thinking such negative thoughts about a child, or a young adult anyway, while the rest of her wished the girl would trip, fall off the stage, and end up in the hospital like the substitute teacher, Mr. Matthews.

Liz tapped a finger against the microphone silently until it kicked on and sounded like thunder. The speakers at the sides of the stage squealed so loud everyone in the audience cringed.

Serves her right.

"Is it on now?" she asked.

It was.

"Good," she continued. "As you all know, my name is Liz Cupo. I'm the graduating class president. I take great pride in firstly saying congratulations to the rest of my class. You are all warriors. We've gone through so much together. Good times and some so very bad. You are fucking legends in my eyes. We made it through this together!"

The audience members did their best to clap and yell out with enthusiasm while holding their champagne flutes.

"Fucking legends," she mumbled and seemed to be trying to remember where she was.

You were being full of shit, as usual, Liz.

"Yes," she said loudly. "I am proud of you. I would go to war with any of you. We've shed blood, sweat, and tears together. You have had my back throughout these four years and some of you even longer than that. It's been a tough one. We've had our ups and downs. You teachers here tonight know that."

Teachers in the audience chuckled. Even Joel laughed. Lauren didn't. She began to feel that something was wrong. Far away, she thought she heard that vibration in the air, that thrum. It was faint, but it was the same sound she'd heard in her apartment that night and a few minutes ago by the jungle gym.

Plus, Liz's speech so far seemed more like she was speaking to a group of soldiers who'd made it through a great battle. Was her high school experience really like Nam or Desert Storm? Were the dead-beats in attendance tonight really like the heroes who fought for their country? And if it was a war, who was the enemy? Lauren looked at Mrs. Lowell holding up her champagne flute and smiling brightly. Mr. Cole was next to her looking like a proud father. None of the teachers in attendance were *really* hearing Liz's words.

You are all warriors. I'd go to war with any of you. You're all fucking legends.

Everything felt wrong. Why was it bothering Lauren so much? She scanned the crowd again and thought about how these teachers had made it their mission to see the *right kids* graduate. None of these kids in attendance were those kids.

Where are all the good kids? Where is the rest of the graduating class? And where the hell is Charlie?

As Liz droned on with her hypocritical speech, Lauren looked behind her, back at the now empty playground. Of course, Paula and the ex-student, Scott, were here in the crowd somewhere now. Only one person remained in the playground.

James Bender had turned toward the stage but still sat perfectly motionless at the top of the jungle gym. There he was, hunched over, his arms resting on his knees as he watched the rest of them.

"Teachers with us tonight," Liz continued, "I salute you for your willingness to push us through to the end. You are all a part of who we are now. We are stronger, more tenacious, and unwilling to roll over... because of you."

In the right context, the things she was saying might be positive, but as Lauren watched James Bender and listened to Liz, she couldn't help thinking these words could also be threats. They were stronger because the teachers had pushed them too hard. They were more tenacious because they'd had to become more stubborn in inventing new tactics to break old rules. Why? Because the teachers kept catching them. They were unwilling to roll over and give up... no matter how hard the teachers tried to get them to fail.

Those were the words she meant.

Yet, the teachers around Lauren cheered on the young girl as if her words were meant to show appreciation. They weren't. She was scolding them in her own way.

Lauren was the only one who noticed all the ex-students in the audience. While the teachers looked toward Liz, hanging on every word and giving the girl the attention she didn't deserve, the ex-students stared at the teachers. They weren't cheering. They glared at the teachers with squinted eyes and smiles that had flattened out to strange sneers. They wore vicious grimaces.

Bile rose in her throat, and Lauren thought she might be sick. *This* was it. Whatever these kids had planned, it was going down right now, and the other teachers were oblivious.

"Joel," Lauren said as she nudged her friend, too afraid to take her eyes off the young woman watching her with a piercing gaze.

Lauren missed the final part of Liz's speech because she'd zoned out, imagining the worst.

"... to you, our teachers, for making us the people we are today and for shaping who we will be in our future!"

On stage, Liz raised her glass.

Everyone in the audience did the same. Everyone except Lauren.

"Cheers!" Liz said.

"No," Lauren squeaked out, but it was at too low a volume. The word was drowned out by the teachers' response to the girl on stage.

"Cheers!" Everyone in the audience repeated.

"Joel," Lauren said again, looking back at the playground once more. James Bender had climbed down from the jungle gym. He now stood, still completely silhouetted, in the grassy area halfway between where she stood and the playground behind him. She thought she saw two yellow orbs light up inside his hood. "Joel, don't drink the—"

She turned toward him, "Don't drink the champagne."

She was too late.

Joel held his empty glass up to the air and licked his lips. The other teachers had all finished their glasses too. Lauren tilted her glass and let its contents drip onto the ground.

"DJ!" Liz shouted into the microphone, "Let's get this party started."

Whoever was the DJ for the evening put on a strange techno song that sounded like it could have come from the 80s, but with a more modern beat. The teachers began to nod their heads. None of them seemed to notice the slight difference around them.

None of the students were moving.

And none of them had drunk their champagne.

"Come on, let's dance," Joel said.

"No," she said, shaking her head. "I think I want to get out of here."

"Let's have some fun," he insisted, grabbing both her hands. "I'm sure Charlie will... wow."

He shook his head and opened his eyes wide. He stumbled a bit.

Next to Lauren, Mrs. Lowell collapsed onto her knees and said, "I feel funny."

"Get up and..." Mr. Cole began but then he too wobbled and collapsed.

Joel fell forward and caught himself with his hands for a second, struggling to remain up on all fours.

"Joel!" Lauren yelled.

The other teachers began to topple over, and as they did, Lauren heard laughter over the music. She'd crouched down to help Joel, and from that lower position, she looked up to see all the students around them laughing hysterically.

Mr. Lafferty was on the ground, completely out.

The security guard, Mr. Jackson, tried to remain up but slipped and reached for Franny, the cafeteria lady, and tore her dress from her shoulder as he went down. It only took that slight amount of pressure to bring her crashing to the ground on top of him.

And the students laughed.

They laughed.

They fucking laughed and laughed some more.

Scott, the ex-student had his hand up the now unconscious Paula's dress while his buddies around him cheered him on. "You'll never fuck me over again!" he yelled. They cheered.

"Do not act like an animal," one student yelled as she stomped over to him and kicked his knee hard.

It was Josie Simmons, one of the nicest, brightest students Lauren had ever taught. Why would she be here? What could she possibly have in common with these other kids?

Scott howled in pain as he pulled his hand out from under Paula's dress and stuck two fingers in his mouth, sucking on them and sighing with a satisfied, "ahhh."

Behind her, James Bender had gotten closer and now leaned against a tree watching.

"Fucking pigs," a boy everyone called Roth said as he spit on Mr. Lafferty and then pulled out his cock and pissed on his face.

With teachers passed out everywhere, some of the students began to dance, holding hands and moving in a circle as if they were doing a sick techno version of *Ring Around the Rosie*.

"What did you do?" Lauren yelled at them, looking up to see Liz watching from the stage with a look of satisfaction on her face.

Nobody answered her. Nobody would. She knew that.

"What did you do!" she yelled.

"Looks like someone didn't drink the champagne," Liz said into the microphone.

"I got her," a male's voice said from behind her.

A sharp pain at the back of her head caused her to fall onto Joel's chest. Everything went blurry. Then the world went black.

15

CHARLIE

Getting Rebecca home wasn't easy. At first, she only wanted to feel up his thigh, reach for his zipper, and stick her tongue in his ear. In any other situation, it might have been a turn on. He might have taken her home, let her sleep off the alcohol – or the drug someone had slipped into her drink – and waited to see how she felt in the morning. This wasn't that situation though and she was beginning to grate on his nerves.

His initial attraction to her, obviously fueled by her willingness to make passes at him, quickly faded when he let reality sink in for a second. He wasn't dumb enough to believe it wasn't the substances driving her to make bad decisions. He doubted she'd still like him tomorrow. In fact, he wasn't sure he'd feel the same way either. It was Lauren he always had on his mind. She was the one he wanted seated next to him in his car.

It's always Lauren.

It was the adorable way she tried to fit in with the students when the school would lighten-up the atmosphere by announcing Crazy Sock Day or Pajama Day. Lauren would wear one sock with cartoon characters so long it disappeared beneath her dress. The other sock would be short and have something random on it like pineapples. On Pajama

Day she'd arrive with her hair in pigtails, each one tied tight with a red-ribbon bow. Her baggy pjs were sexy in a way only Lauren could pull off.

Charlie had never participated in the events until he saw her doing it. Now, he looked forward to them. The last one was Wild West Day. He wore a red scarf around his neck and a cowboy hat. That was the day he was accosted in the parking lot by a group of gang members who threatened to kill him if he ever wore a red bandana again. He would never repeat that mistake. They were nice enough to advise him not to wear a blue, purple, or yellow one either unless he wanted to piss off the other gangs in the area.

He figured from now on he would avoid all the ROYGBIV hues. Each color of the rainbow seemed to have a violent gang affiliated with it. Even pink probably wasn't safe anymore.

We're West Side Rosebud, muthafucka!

It was the gangs committing most of the crime in the area. At least that's what the cops believed. Things were so bad. Mr. Rowen, that poor old man. The savagery of the attack, the way his right arm had been hacked completely off and his face so shattered the doctors said he was almost unrecognizable, supposedly proved it was a gang. Students could never do something so brutal.

They'll never do anything like that to the teachers.

No, they made empty threats and even when they did strike back physically, it was always amateur in nature. Juvenile-like. It was things like stabbing a teacher in the hand with a pencil or slapping them in the face.

Charlie tried to convince himself of the students' inability to do anything truly harmful. It killed him knowing Lauren and Joel were with them right now, and whatever was planned was bad enough that Bogdan didn't want him to be there with them.

Students would never hack a teacher up into little pieces. That was the mark of a gang.

Because that old man was such a thug he must have dissed one of the local gangs.

It was absurd. Charlie tried to imagine what the old man could have done to wrong one of the gangs. He wouldn't wear the wrong colors. The guy only wore brown and black and white. He was old school by default. His mind wasn't capable of creativity. It was all numbers, letters, and historical facts in that liver-spotted head of his. So, why would a gang come after him?

That thought scared him more than any other. If the students were involved in that attack, there was a good chance the ones responsible were at the park right now. Joel and Lauren could be targets of a mean-spirited prank or they could be victims of something much more violent.

"Dammit, Bog," he cursed under his breath.

The kid's attempt at saving him had also duped him to the point he feared he might be too late. He'd spent several hours at the *other* Grad Night party. The wrong damn party.

Charlie finally reached Rebecca's apartment, which took much longer than it should have since she'd started out unwilling to tell him where she lived. She'd seemed to think if she held back the information, he would have no other choice but to take her to his place. He'd almost considered it, but if all this worrying of his proved to be absolutely nothing at all, then he'd have to explain to Lauren and Joel why he had the high school geography teacher in his bed. Even if he wasn't in it with her.

"I need to take care of something," he told her, "and then I'll come back to your place."

"Mmm," she moaned and then giggled. "Yeah, you want some of this."

What the fuck did they give this chick?

He swore to himself he would not tell her about it tomorrow, no matter how much he'd want to. This was the kind of embarrassment one could never live down. He didn't want to have issues passing her in the hallway. Remembering the shy, sweet woman who'd seemed so uncomfortable before he'd asked her if she wanted a drink, made him feel bad. He might not have slipped her the drug, but he'd offered the drink in the first place, so in some roundabout way, he was responsible for her condition.

Finally, after what seemed like the longest drive of his life, he reached her apartment and walked her to the door where she once again tried to convince him to stay.

"Later," he lied. "Take a nap for now."

"I'll need my rest then?" she asked.

Dude! Take her inside and fuck her brains out.

His inner-fourteen-year-old was a horny piece of shit. The rest of him was starting to think the kid made sense. Charlie had to close his eyes for a second, breathe deep, and fight the inner-voice trying to convince him that his friends would be okay and he should stay with Rebecca for the night.

Right. So you can be the date rapist. Smart thinking.

"I'll be back," he repeated his lie.

She whined and entered the apartment, closing the door behind her.

With a slightly altered walk – slacks sucked when it came to hiding a hard-on – Charlie returned to his car and made his way to the park.

The park wasn't far from Rebecca's building. Only a few miles down the highway. He'd never been there before. He was from the other side of the tracks, where kids didn't play in parks because you never knew when a stray bullet might make its way through the swings and over the slides. Gangbangers didn't discriminate. When they had someone in their sights, they pulled the trigger. Who or what was behind them didn't matter.

Parking his car at the curb, because the gate had a giant chain wrapped around it, Charlie stared into the dark parking lot. The light was out. All the lights were out but the lot wasn't empty. There were cars crammed in, at least ten to fifteen of them as far as he could tell.

Why would anyone lock their cars in the parking lot?

An uneasy feeling came over him and he remembered words spoken to him a long time ago.

"Not everything dark is bad. Sometimes you just don't understand it. You can feel the real evil kind of darkness. It does this to you..."

Charlie was twelve years old and didn't have many friends. He lived in the best apartment his single mom could afford. She was never home. She took two buses to get to work and back and usually clocked out long past her scheduled shift to help her pay for their humble home.

His first summer living there sucked. He didn't like going outside to play because the other kids weren't nice to him. A Mexican family lived a few doors down. The two daughters, both right around Charlie's age, would stick their tongues out at him and crack jokes about him in Spanish. He knew what pendejo meant. Rather, he'd heard it in many gang-related movies, so he knew it wasn't something nice.

If he'd only known then he would one day lose his virginity with the oldest of the girls, he might have responded to their horrible attempts at flirting differently. Back then, it just seemed like everyone hated him.

Charlie was the only white kid in the whole neighborhood. At least, it seemed that way. He wouldn't have cared if it didn't mean he was always being picked on. He was called cracker and white boy and white bread and mayonnaise and pretty much every other thing that was pale in color. He was even asked one time by one of the kids in the neighborhood, "Hey, you like coffee?"

He didn't. He was too young for it and thought it was bitter. "No."

"That's 'cause it's black. I bet you like it when you put some white milk in it," came the response, followed by a middle finger pointed in his direction and laughter.

The entire first summer would have been spent indoors if Charlie hadn't met Junior. His skin was as dark as the blackest night, and he liked to wander around the neighborhood barefoot. Sometimes he'd stop by the apartment complex with no shirt on. Kids were like that in Charlie's day. Nobody was afraid of the sun yet.

Behind Charlie's complex was a grassy area. The fence at its rear was the only thing separating the neighborhood from the shopping mall on the other side. So, it was normal for kids to walk through his complex to hop the fence. The mall was where all the pretty girls hung out and was also home to the best arcade around.

Junior was passing through the complex one day, wearing his many necklaces of twine adorned with beads, shells, and even a few teeth. It was the teeth that got them talking in the first place. Charlie was sitting out back, leaned against a wall, reading a horror novel where people were having an orgy in a vineyard. He'd never read anything so crazy in his life.

He was completely entrenched in the paperback when he heard bare feet padding across the lawn. The sudden intrusion caused him to jump.

"I didn't mean to frighten you," the boy said.

Charlie eyed the frail boy's necklaces and noticed what looked like a human molar dangling from one.

"What are you reading?" the boy asked.

Charlie couldn't answer. He was glued to that tooth. The boy leaned down and peered at the cover of the book.

"Dominion. Bentley Little," he read out. "Is it good?"

He didn't answer. The boy looked down and saw where Charlie's eyes loomed. "Oh, this? This is my uncle Pierre's. He was a very lucky man."

"He's dead?" Charlie finally found his voice and asked.

"Yes."

"Doesn't sound very lucky to me."

The boy laughed. "My name's Junior. You live here?"

"Yeah, I'm Charlie."

They shook hands, and Charlie thought the summer might not turn out so bad. He was right, but it took two more weeks to start looking up. Junior stayed away for that long. The next time the boy showed up, it was right before what would have turned out to be the worst beating of Charlie's life.

He'd been outside reading again when the same group of thugs who always called him names passed him on their way to the mall.

"There goes white milk," the biggest and meanest boy, a kid named AJ, said. His friends joined in with harassing chants.

Charlie tried to ignore them and kept reading his book.

"Hey, I'm talkin' to you," AJ said. The boy stomped all the way

over to within a couple of feet of Charlie. His four friends spread out behind him in a crescent shape. AJ stepped closer and kicked his foot.

Charlie put his finger in his book to save his page and looked up at the group of boys.

"Y'all know why they call his people crackas?" AJ looked left and right, over his shoulders at his friends before turning his attention back to Charlie. "Do you know?"

Charlie shook his head.

"Y'all muthafuckas used to hit my people with whips. You know what sound a whip makes?"

He definitely wasn't going to respond to this question. Any answer he gave was likely to be the wrong one and might result in a beating. AJ threw back his hand and then brought it forward before yanking it back as if he wielded an imaginary whip. "Crack!" he yelled.

Charlie flinched at the boy's outburst.

"Crack! Crack!" AJ continued as he pretended to whip Charlie a couple more times.

"Is that true?" Charlie asked. He thought it probably wasn't, but it seemed almost logical. He'd never stopped to consider it before and was now genuinely curious where the derogatory term came from.

He set his book down on the grass and stood to face his problems like a man. He figured it would be better to take a beating in the upright position than to get stomped while seated. Fists hurt less than feet. At least that was usually the case.

The worst part was Charlie had taken karate for several years before moving here, so he was able to defend himself, but fear caused him to hold back.

"Are you callin' me a liar?" AJ asked.

"I think he is," one of his boys said.

"Oh, shit. That boy just called you a fibber," one of the other boys prodded.

They all laughed, and Charlie knew he was about to get his ass kicked. Nobody would be around to stop them, so he prayed it would be over with quickly. If he fell down with the first punch and covered his head, he might live through it. But then a miracle happened. Junior rounded the corner.

"Charlie!" he called out as he came into sight, obviously having no idea what was going down. He took a look at the boys surrounding him and said, "Charlie, is everything okay?"

"Um, not really," he replied. "Kind of in a bind here, J."

He'd taken to calling him J right after they'd exchanged names. The boy seemed to like having a nickname. Now, Charlie watched as AJ and the rest of his asshole friends backed away. Each step Junior took forward, they took two in reverse. It was like his friend had some kind of virus they were all afraid to catch.

"AJ," Junior said. "It's good to see you."

"You stay away from us," AJ said.

Junior grabbed hold of the molar around his neck, and the boys took off in a sprint, hopping over the fence faster than Charlie had ever seen anyone climb.

When Junior turned around, he simply smiled, putting his uneven teeth on display.

"What was that all about?" Charlie asked.

"They are afraid of me," Junior replied. "I don't know why." He was quiet for a moment and then shrugged. "I guess I do know why. I am from Haiti. My family is known, I guess. Our religion is... it is different."

The boy looked down at his feet and Charlie got the sense he was sad.

"Your religion is your religion, J," he said. "I don't even have one."

At twelve years old, he should have known at least something about Christianity, but his mom had never taken him to church and his dad left a long time ago. All he knew was Jesus died for his sins, but even that he'd learned on TV.

Junior smiled. "Have you ever seen a chicken foot before?"

"I don't know, I guess so."

"I mean not on its body."

Junior showed him a chicken foot. It was one of many strange items his auntie kept in her shack a few feet away from his house. They became good friends that summer. Charlie even went barefoot sometimes.

He was waiting outside Junior's house one night when he had to pee really bad. Of course, he wasn't going to piss on his friend's front lawn, so he snuck around to the side of the house so he could pee in a bush, out of view of the street. He wouldn't have wandered any further if he hadn't heard the chanting. Curiosity got the best of him, and he peeked over the rickety fence that led into the backyard.

That's when he saw Junior's auntie pouring chicken blood straight from its body into a bowl. She was chanting in a language he'd never heard before and it looked like her eyes had rolled back. They were completely white.

Charlie had gotten so scared he ran straight home. He avoided Junior for three days. From that point on, he read his books in his bedroom, too wary to go outside and read in the sunlight. He didn't know who he was more afraid to run into, AJ or Junior.

Junior tapped on his window one night, and he opened it to find his friend standing outside in the darkness.

"You are afraid of me too," he said.

A wave of guilt crashed over Charlie. He didn't know what to say. Of course, he didn't want his friend to feel bad, but he was scared. His aunt had been doing some kind of voodoo.

"It's okay," Junior said. "I understand. My auntie told me you saw her."

"She knows?" Charlie asked, feeling his heart sink down to his feet.

How did she know? Was she psychic? Was she watching him? What if she came after him and spilled his blood into a bowl?

"Yes, of course," Junior said. "You knocked over a trash can when you ran away."

He did? He didn't even remember that. He'd been so consumed by terror that he'd run straight home, where he hid under his blanket the rest of the night.

"I tried to come see you, but you never read outside anymore."

"I... I didn't want AJ to pick on me anymore," Charlie told a half-truth. The other half involved Junior. Inside his room, he felt safe from both boys.

"You don't have to worry about him anymore," Junior said. "I asked my auntie to perform um... a safety ritual for you. That is what you saw that night. She made sure they won't bother you anymore. You're protected now."

"You mean the thing with the chicken blood? That was for me?"

Junior let his gaze fall down to the window frame. He was ashamed when he nodded.

"Thank you," Charlie said. "I didn't know. You're a good friend. Hold on."

Charlie climbed out his bedroom window and the boys lay down on the grass together. They stared up at the moon.

"What is your God like?" Junior asked.

"I don't know," Charlie answered truthfully. "I've never met him."

They both laughed.

When the laughter died down, Charlie thought about something, and he hoped he was wrong. He had to ask, or he'd never know. "AJ isn't dead, is he?"

A long silence.

"What?" Junior finally asked. "Why would you ask that?"

"Because you said your auntie was taking care of him."

More silence. But then Junior burst into hysterics. He laughed harder than Charlie had ever heard anyone laugh before. "No!" he cried. "She would never hurt anyone!" He continued to laugh. "It was a good thing, Charlie. She was only protecting you, not hurting some-body else."

Charlie joined him in laughter, and it took a long time for them to quiet down.

"J, I'm sorry I was afraid of you," Charlie said.

"It's okay," Junior replied. "I understand. It was dark and you didn't know what my auntie was doing."

He felt lousy for doubting his friend. He'd asked his auntie to save

Charlie from the mean kids, and this was how he repaid him, by running away from him.

"Charlie," Junior said, "Not everything dark is bad. Sometimes you just don't understand it. You can feel the real evil kind of darkness. It does this to you..."

He reached out and grabbed hold of Charlie's wrist, squeezing it tightly and digging his nails into his skin. It didn't hurt, but it was strong pressure, so strong it kept his attention focused on it.

"Real evil won't let you move," Junior added. "When you feel that. That is when you should be afraid."

Now, standing outside the park entry gate, Charlie peered in at the darkness, but he didn't feel that grip of terror Junior warned him about. That had to mean something. He grabbed hold of the gate and gave it a sturdy shake to make sure the lock was actually fastened. It wasn't going to be opening anytime soon.

Charlie had hopped lots of fences in his youth. Once, as a kid, he landed on a barbed wire covered one and got the barbs caught on his shorts, right where his balls were. He'd had to stay there until his stepdad came to his rescue. Since then, he was smarter about scaling fences. This one had no razor wire or barbs. It was tall though and flimsier than he would have liked.

Staring once more at the parking lot, trying to decide whether he should or should not risk going over the fence, he studied the cars as best as his moon-provided night vision would allow. He didn't know what the teachers drove. Not most of them anyway. He was familiar with Joel's car. They'd taken it a few times to go off campus for lunch. He was pretty sure that was Joel's car in the far corner, but it was hard to tell in the darkness. Lauren's car wasn't in the parking lot at all. He knew her car because, well, it was Lauren's.

And you're a creepy stalker. Admit it.

He wasn't a stalker. Admirer, sure, but stalker was taking it too far. There was a fine line between liking a woman so much you noticed all the little things about her and stealing her panties to sniff them at night. Charlie wasn't a panty sniffer.

Did Joel and Lauren come to the party together?

They were friends, but Charlie had never known them to be *that* close. It didn't matter. Joel's car was here, and he could only assume the others belonged to the other teachers. He pulled out his phone and considered dialing 911. Then he remembered the new Dustin Hertz law.

Dustin was a young man who'd gone to prison at the age of fourteen for the murder of his grandparents. He went from a juvenile detention center to full maximum-security prison when he turned eighteen. There he remained until he died of a heart attack at the age of fifty-five. It was said health complications were a result of the unnecessary stress put on him at such a young age and that he'd continued to endure the rest of his life. He'd been issued three life sentences. When most boys were busy jerking off, Dustin was starting his life behind bars.

The details were complicated but, in the end, the Dustin Hertz law was put into place. It stated that anyone under the age of eighteen could not be issued a life sentence. At most, they would be locked up in a juvenile detention center and then moved to a working rehabilitation center, or WRC, where they would continue to be reevaluated each year to see if their minds had adapted as they grew into adulthood. All it took was a favorable evaluation for them to be released.

Since this law was put into place only five years ago, juvenile crimes had escalated. The gangs had grown more violent, often using children or young teenagers to hand out the harshest punishments. That way, if they got caught, there was a good chance they'd make it back out onto the streets. Adult violent crimes were at an all-time low. But teenagers were becoming evil.

At least some of them stayed in school.

It was the Dustin Hertz law that made Charlie decide against calling the cops. What would he say to them? A group of teenagers was probably going to play a prank on his colleagues? That would sound ridiculous. The police were probably out there dealing with real crimes. They wouldn't give a shit if some teachers were in danger of being embarrassed by their students.

With his fingers reaching through the holes in the fence, Charlie pressed his forehead against the cool metal and stared at the dark path he saw leading into the park. It was a pitch-black void between the trees, so he knew that was the real park entrance. Teachers would probably come screaming from that path at some point. But why?

Would they be covered in feces from shit-filled balloons thrown at them?

Charlie could see the students doing something so disgusting.

Would they be doused in liquid and told it was gasoline?

He could imagine them doing that too. Something so horrific was quite possible. Would it be real gasoline? He doubted it.

Or would they be chased by a deranged maniac wielding a chainsaw?

Even that wasn't too farfetched. Yet, a part of him held onto the hope that *his* students would never do anything too rotten. After all, they were kids. There had to be a hearty dose of innocence still in there somewhere.

They're your students, Charlie. Believe in them. They won't let you down.

Then he remembered the video and felt cold all over. They were capable of things he didn't think possible.

He needed to get in there and find out what they were up to.

Charlie gripped the fence and climbed.

16

LAUREN

"You're worthless. You know that, right? I only stay with you because we've put in so much time together and now we're stuck with this fucking house... in your name."

His words stung. They always did. When he had enough beer in him, he resorted to these violent attacks. He was never like this before.

Before.

Sometimes she thought if they'd never tried for a baby, they might have remained in love. No, the truth was, he had violent tendencies even that far back. When she got pregnant and lost it... that's when things got worse.

"Listen to me, you filthy fucking sow," he said as he pulled her attention back to him with a quick jerk of her ponytail.

Tears welled in her eyes as she fought the urge to cry. She knew if she begged him enough, he would leave her alone. He'd stick his cock in her mouth, she'd give him a blowjob, and then he would fall asleep. Tomorrow morning, all would be fine. At least he would see it that way. If she ever brought up his drunken fits, he'd accuse her of being a grudge-holding attention whore.

But this time she refused to beg him. She'd already given in too many times.

"No man would ever want your saggy tits and flabby gut. You're fucking repulsive."

He was right. She couldn't look in the mirror without being disgusted with herself. Her face was too round, her chin too soft, her tits too heavy, her stomach too big, and her ass too fat. He was the best man she'd ever get.

She kept her palms flat against the kitchen table and stared at the flowered tablecloth, forcing her eyes to cross until she swore the flower was moving. She would get lost there and ignore his ranting. She only needed to nod her head from time to time to show agreement. That would appease him.

"The fucking nerve of you to ask if I paid the electric bill. You gave me the cash for it didn't you? What else would I have done with it?"

He would have blown it at the tittie bar. She knew that was where he spent the three to four hours between the end of his workday and when he returned home. He always showed up with his breath reeking of liquor and in one of his sexual moods. It didn't matter if she wasn't turned on. Foreplay wasn't his forte. When he was horny, he only wanted a hole to put it in. She'd learned long ago not to push him away. That never ended well for her. So, she usually lay with her cheek against the mattress while he took her from behind. At least in that position, he wouldn't see her tears.

If he asked if she liked it, she would always say, "Mmm hmm."

Now, at the small dinette table, she refused to go to war verbally with him. She simply waited for the beating to come.

She heard his zipper lower.

She felt the weight of his cock against her shoulder.

Out of the corner of her eye, she saw the raised fist and knew it was one or the other. It was either a cock in her mouth or a punch to it. She parted her lips, stuck out her tongue, and closed her eyes.

"I'm the only one who'll want you," he reminded her.

Lauren woke with a copper tang in her mouth.

Blood. But why?

She couldn't see very well. Her head ached and her eyes were blurry.

"My hands," she complained.

Someone laughed. "Got one waking up over here!"

"What happened?" she asked.

"Yep, she's alive and well!"

"Okay, kids, this joke has gone far enough," Mr. Cole barked, only the strength was gone from his words. It was the man's voice, minus the authority.

Lauren's vision began to clear, and she looked down at her lap.

She was in a chair.

A wheelchair.

Why am I in a fucking wheelchair?

Her dream came back to her. This time, as she'd thought about *him*, it was a memory. The situation had actually happened, unlike her last dream about him with the bucket of knives. The bloody tang in her mouth reminded her of the mouth full of cum she always had to contemplate swallowing or spitting out. *He* had always hated when she spit. So, she sucked up as much of the blood as she could and spit it onto the grass.

The grass. Slowly, the world seemed to come into focus, and everything made sense in the most nonsensical way. She remembered everyone drinking from champagne flutes and then collapsing. The back of her head ached.

"Someone hit me," she said softly.

"Should have drank the fucking champagne, Ms. Peony," a male's voice said. She glanced to her left and between her and the next wheelchair, occupied by Mr. Cole, stood Milton Rothmeyer. The kid had his baseball cap on backward and was sucking on a cigarette. He blew a cloud of smoke down at her and chuckled. "You went down hard," he continued, "but I had to hit you a second time. You're tougher than you look."

"You have no idea," she said.

If he knew how she finally got away from her ex, he would think twice about hitting her.

"I like that," he said as he reached down and adjusted his cock through his jeans.

Teenage boys always grabbed themselves too much. She wondered if he'd caught crabs from one of his slutty female classmates or if he only liked to fidget with it. He disgusted her, and she couldn't wait for this stupid prank to be over with.

"Let me go!" a female voice cried.

Lauren looked right and saw Paula also strapped to a wheelchair. Then, she remembered that asshole ex-student, Scott, violating her when she was passed out. He'd stuck his fingers up her dress.

Is this a prank? Did he not realize I saw him?

She looked left and right and realized she was in a long line of teachers, all strapped to wheelchairs. No, zip tied. She pulled at her wrists and they were raw already. She would not be able to rip free of these things. Cops used them to subdue people. Her ankles were also attached to the chair. Every teacher was tied this way.

How the fuck did they get this many wheelchairs?

She didn't have to think about it very long. Liz walked past her, her hands behind her back, like a prison guard doing a spot check on her inmates. Lauren imagined, with the girl's father's connections, she could get anything she needed. Wheelchairs and zip ties would be no problem. Her asshole father probably did this to people all the time.

And then he probably drops them into the ocean.

To her left she saw Mr. Cole and his lover Mrs. Lowell. Beyond them was a woman named Connie who was a regular substitute for the school. She'd been around as long as many of the teachers. After Connie was Mr. Timms, the economics teacher, and then Mrs. Laymon, the guidance counselor. The list went on and on. She could see a couple other teachers beyond them and to her right was even more, including Joel, Paula, Coach McCall, and Mr. Lafferty, the English teacher.

Paula continued to fight in her constraints.

"Scott!" she begged. "Let me out!"

"Sorry, Ms. Keen," the handsome asshole said as he blew a kiss at the psychology teacher. "We could have been good together, but you had to go and fuck up my life."

"You were a bad student!" she yelled. "You know that! You admitted it."

Her voice lowered as she seemed to finally realize she wasn't going to be able to talk her way out of this situation. None of them would. They would have to wait until this terrible prank was over. For now, Lauren decided she'd keep her mouth shut and see what was in store. She was not going to beg them. She'd done enough of that to last her an entire lifetime.

The long crescent-shaped row of wheelchairs sat at the top of the hill surrounding the inner-park. Behind them was the forest and in front was the steep descent into the playground area where they'd been earlier, before being drugged by way of champagne toast. The Christmas lights strung across the park were on brightly, giving this situation a surreal feeling, like maybe this was all part of a ridiculous nightmare.

Because it was… ludicrous.

Students tying their teachers to wheelchairs in a park at night? How were they expecting to get out of this situation?

Beyond the playground, it looked like the lights to the trail had been turned off, plunging the rest of the park into complete darkness. Nobody driving by the main gate would even look twice at it. No one would see what was really going on back here.

The students who'd brought them all here stood fanned out in front of them. There were exactly fifteen of them, one for every teacher seated. Of course, Liz Cupo had returned from her prison-guard stroll and now stood directly in front of her.

"Look," Barry the security guard started, "if you're planning to leave us tied up out here all night, you're putting our lives at risk. These woods might have animals in 'em."

The kids all began to laugh.

"You of all people," another one of the assholes of the school, Kent Bluth, said, "are going to be the one to cry like a little bitch? Seriously? Animals? You have no fucking clue—"

"—That's enough," Liz said calmly. "Don't tell them anything. They'll find out soon enough."

"Elizabeth," Lauren finally allowed herself to speak, not to beg, but to try and talk some sense into this girl before she did something that would get herself into serious trouble.

"Liz, please," Liz replied.

"Liz," Lauren continued, "it's not too late to back out of this. Whatever you have planned. You're going to get caught. You have half the staff at DS High here."

"Oh, we know," Liz replied coolly. "Don't we?"

The rest of the kids laughed and cheered.

"What do you hope to gain from this?" Lauren asked.

"Good question." Liz pondered it for a moment and then said, "Notoriety, I think. It's about time that teachers realize the consequences of their actions. By denying a recommendation letter to a college," her attention turned to Paula. Then she moved her eyes down the line until they settled on Coach McCall, "Or taking someone off the school team when recruiters are coming to watch the game." She looked back and forth along the line until her gaze fell on Franny, the cafeteria lady, "Or by turning a student in because she's always too nauseous to eat, resulting in the school staff and student body finding out about her pregnancy and making her an example for the entire region. These are only a few of the things some of you have done to ruin the lives of your students."

"Liz," Lauren said, "everything you just mentioned was directly the result of students' inability to behave in class, complete the required assignments, or it had something to do with a student's safety. Keeping a pregnant student in class would have resulted in much worse immature gossip, hurtful remarks, and even deeper depression for that student."

Lauren looked for Amber, the girl who'd gotten pregnant. Her head was down, staring at her feet.

"A young mother needs to be able to take care of herself and her child without the ridicule of her classmates," Lauren continued, "and once that child was born, Amber was allowed to return to class, wasn't she?"

"A year after her friends had already graduated, Ms. Peony. She should have been part of last year's graduating class. She wasn't."

Lauren wanted to scream, "So fucking what?!" But she couldn't. That would only escalate matters. The truth was the girl had sex. Like everyone else, young and old, a certain amount of protection needs to be considered when participating in adult pastimes. She got pregnant. She needed to face the consequences, which in this case weren't so bad. She only had to miss a year of school.

"What do those things have to do with the rest of us?" Mr. Cole asked.

Lauren couldn't believe he had the balls to ask such a question. He who had a military background was the first to go the route of, "Why don't you let the rest of us go?" Lauren glared at him and then shook her head in disgust.

Where's Charlie?

It hit her. Charlie wasn't here because Charlie was a good person. He was the kind of teacher who knew how to create relationships with his students that didn't go beyond professional and at the same time didn't make anyone feel alienated or unworthy of his lectures. He was a good teacher. That's why he wasn't here. Lauren glanced down the row again and thought of other teachers not sitting to her right or left.

"This is absurd!" Mr. Cole continued. "You let us go right this instant!"

The kids seemed to be getting a kick out of his behavior.

"Don't be a pussy, dude," the meth dealing ex-student, Tom something or other, said.

The other graduates laughed. Only three of the students in the lineup didn't seem thrilled about being here. Amber, whose eyes remained on her feet. Drew Dryer, the basketball star who Lauren had talked to on several occasions about how she could help him bring his grades up so he could get back onto the court and the girl Lauren was still shocked to see at this party: Josie Simmons. She was the high school sweetheart, the all-American girl; the one Lauren could see being accepted into any university she wanted to attend. At the moment, she stared straight ahead, looking half in a daze.

"Mr. Cole," Liz said, "you are not innocent here, sir. Your friendship with Gavin's dad, has resulted in some fairly nasty beatings."

Gavin, the class clown, nodded. Lauren couldn't believe what she was hearing. This kid couldn't shut up in class. He was always laughing and cracking jokes. How could he be on the receiving end of beatings? When it was happening to her, she could barely force a smile onto her face.

"He's a knucklehead!" Mr. Cole said.

"Show him, Gavin," Liz said.

Gavin lifted his shaggy mane, only on the right side of his head, which was shaved underneath. A long scar ran from the top of his head all the way around to the back and over to his ear.

"You had to meet my dad for beers, Mr. Cole," Gavin said, his voice cracking in what appeared to be a mixture of anger and sadness. "What do you think happened every time you told him about the things I said or did in class? I was only playing around. Trying to cheer up my friends, but you had to tell him, didn't you? The last time, I was in the hospital for three weeks. I had to tell the doctors it was a skateboarding accident because my dad was able to do the same kind of damage a street curb could do with only his metal belt buckle."

Mr. Cole went silent. He tried to speak but his lips trembled. Lauren's heart broke for Gavin. She'd had no idea. She'd asked him to quiet down a hundred times, asked him to leave her class at least a handful. How many times had the school called his house because of her?

"Each person standing up here has been hurt by one of you," Liz went on. "Some of you have hurt more than one of us."

"Who hurt you?" Lauren asked. "We know it wasn't Mr. Matthews. He was innocent and you had him almost killed. Maybe you should be in one of these chairs."

She hadn't thought about the words before saying them, but they blurted out anyway. She couldn't help herself. She'd kept the anger in for so long. It had simmered inside her until it blew off the top. Now, Lauren would have to see where it got her.

"Mr. Matthews was a joke," Liz said with a roll of her eyes.

She still didn't think of the substitute teacher as any significant part of her life, even though she'd ruined his. The poor guy couldn't get a job as a teacher and was scared to death to speak up for himself now. Most of his days were spent inside his apartment trying to find work-from-home jobs.

"He didn't hurt me," Liz added. "But someone here did. We'll see if they come forward about it."

"You made up that story about Mr. Matthews," Lauren said. "How do we know you're not fabricating this one too?" Lauren saw the furrow in the young girl's brow and the downward shift of her eyes. No, she wasn't making this one up. Someone had gotten to her. "Why wouldn't you say something then?" Lauren prodded. "You had your dad's goons beat the shit out of Mr. Matthews and he wasn't even guilty."

For the first time since she'd met Liz Cupo, the young girl was silent.

"Because the truth is what hurts, isn't it, Liz?" Lauren asked. "It's easy to make stuff up and tell all your friends to get a good laugh at the destruction you've caused, but when it comes back to bite you, and something *really* happens, you don't want to cry wolf anymore. You just want to cry. Letting everyone know you're vulnerable is too much to handle."

She'd gotten to her and, for a moment, Lauren thought it might put an end to the situation. Maybe calling her out would prove to her friends that she wasn't so tough after all. The bitch of DS High wasn't immune to pain. She had experienced it too.

The opposite of what Lauren expected happened. Liz shrugged her shoulders and grinned.

"We'll see," she replied. "We'll see if the teacher responsible will come forward. Doesn't really matter if they do. I am now officially announcing the start of the first 'maybe annual' Grad Night party games."

The students to her right and left cheered. Even the kids who'd seemed unsure about being here shouted, whistled, and shook angry fists in the air. The only one who remained perfectly still was the kid seated at the top of the jungle gym.

James Bender watched them from his perch.

"Can we get on with this?" a woman seated to her far right asked.

Lauren looked her way and saw the school librarian, Mrs. Grainger, sitting calmly in her chair. She stared straight ahead, not even glancing toward Liz as she waited. Lauren barely knew the woman. She hardly ever left the library. Lauren wished she could be as ice cold right now as Mrs. Grainger was. She wanted to ignore the situation, to make the students feel like they'd never get a rise out of her. Maybe, if all the teachers did that, the ex-students would grow tired of their twisted game.

"We sure can," Liz said. "James, are we ready?"

Lauren realized she'd never heard anyone address the boy before. She looked toward the jungle gym and watched as he nodded and spoke the first word she'd ever heard him say. "Yesssss."

The word carried on, coming out as more of a roar. Wind blew with it, bringing his putrid breath at them. The foul stench of raw sewage, dead bodies, and cow shit hit her full on. The thrum Lauren had heard earlier rumbled through his voice, giving him an unreal, mechanical growl. Behind her, the trees whooshed, and sleeping birds scattered. Something screeched from deep within the forest. It was an animal fearing for its life.

"My God," she said under her breath, realizing this wasn't a prank.

This was something much worse.

James Bender, the creature disguised as a human boy, looked down at the bottom of the jungle gym where a giant potato sack sat on the ground. Something wriggled inside the bag as whatever was inside it dreaded the sound of his voice as much as Lauren did.

Teachers complained about the smell, about the thing moving inside the bag, or it could have been about both.

"What is that?"

"Oh, God, that's disgusting."

"I'm gonna puke."

Liz inhaled deeply, enjoying the scent. She grinned and said, "I suppose we should get this started then."

17

LAUREN

"Take your places, please," Liz said.

The kids cheered as they ran up the hill and each took his or her place behind one of the wheelchairs. Lauren leaned her head back and saw Liz had chosen her chair to stand behind.

"Was it me?" Lauren asked. "Have I hurt you in some way?"

Liz stared down at her and then with a short, quick motion, shook her head no. It was almost unrecognizable, but Lauren did understand that it wasn't her. "Then whom have I upset?"

The girl grinned that evil bitch smile of hers and said, "Live long enough, and you'll find out."

"Live long enough? Liz, what are you doing?"

Don't beg. Don't you dare beg, Lauren. You don't fucking beg.

To her left, Mr. Cole grunted in his seat as he struggled to free himself.

Mrs. Lowell cried softly beside him and that seemed to spur him on. He fought so hard Lauren thought he might hurt himself.

"Jeez, man," Gavin said as he held onto the wheelchair handlebars. He let out his trademark guffaw and added, "You're gonna give yourself one of them old man hernias, bro. Chill the fuck out."

"Gavin," Mr. Cole begged. "You have to know I would never purposely get you in trouble like that. I thought your dad found the stories as funny as I did."

"You found me funny?" Gavin asked, genuinely touched by the confession. "I thought you hated my jokes."

"Gavin," Liz said. "Get your head back into the race."

"What race, Liz?" Lauren asked.

"Let me out of this fucking chair!" someone yelled.

"I haven't done anything to you!" another teacher screamed.

Male and female voices shot into the night in the form of high-pitched wails. Some dipped down low in the form of groans and muttered complaints. Each teacher seemed to be digesting the situation in his or her own way. The librarian still sat silently, unwilling to give the students the satisfaction of scaring her.

Lauren refused to allow herself to beg for mercy. This was going to be a big ridiculous stunt in the end. They'd all be untied to find out there'd been pictures taken of them. Those photos would be handed out at school, of course, and the student body at DS High would laugh their asses off. That's all this was.

But what about James Bender? And that bag? And his voice? And that smell?

A hundred arguments ran through her mind as she played both sides. She wanted to believe this was only a nasty prank, but she felt in her gut this was something far worse.

Lauren clenched her jaw and zipped her lips. She would not scream, she would not yell, and she would not cry.

"Ladies and gentlemen," Liz yelled out loud enough to rise above the hysterical cries of distraught educators. "Start your engines."

"Woo hoo!" one of the kids yelled.

"Vrooooooooooooom!" another called out.

"Y'all are goin' down," someone else declared. "I fuckin' got this!"

"Hold on tight," Liz whispered to Lauren. "Not that you've got a choice."

"Bitch," Lauren said aloud for the first time in her career.

"That's the spirit, Ms. Peony," Liz replied with a giggle. "I knew you had it in you."

Lauren stared at the steep decline in front of her and felt the nervous pains of a giant pendulum swinging back and forth in her gut. Fuck butterflies. This shit was too serious for fluttering. These kids were going to push them down this hill and they'd have no way to protect themselves. These chairs would not make it. They would be pitched forward or might even flip.

"Liz, this isn't funny," Lauren said.

"Good," the girl replied. "It's not supposed to be."

A gun blast sounded off from somewhere, and suddenly Lauren felt a hard push at the back of her chair. Then she was careening down the hill, racing forward at a speed never meant for a wheelchair. The giant wheels in the back and tiny ones in the front bounced over the uneven grass, down a lawn filled with rocks and clumps of broken earth.

She screamed unwittingly, unable to stop the stuttered shriek that escaped her. It pitched forth from her throat, split her lips, and launched into the darkness.

Others screamed too. Everyone did.

Somewhere to her left she heard the tinny sound of cheap metal crashing against the ground and what sounded like the tumbling of a chair.

In front of her and to the right, a chair sailed over an uneven clump of grass that propelled it into the air a few feet.

Lauren bit her tongue and the pain shot from her mouth down her body and all the way into her toes. Blood filled her mouth and she clamped her jaw shut in case she'd bitten it off. She didn't want to leave her tongue on the grassy lawn.

"Holy shit!" one of the kids yelled. "Did you see that?! That motherfucker flew!"

She was still going, rolling toward the bottom. Many of the other teachers had crashed. This downhill sprint should have taken no more than a few seconds, but it felt like it stretched on for eternity. She could feel every jostle of her chair and could hear every scream of her colleagues.

One of the small wheels at the front of her chair snapped and Lauren leaned back hard to keep it from dragging on the ground and pitching her forward, but it seemed she'd overcompensated, and the strength of her backward push caused her to fall the other way. A new scream emitted as her body toppled back and her head smacked against the grass. Her forward momentum was strong enough to keep her sliding a few feet more, and then a rock dug into her scalp, pulling a final yelp from her before she finally grinded to a halt.

"Thought you had this, Tommy Boy?" one of the male students called out.

"It was the fuckin' chair, man!" Tom complained.

Lauren turned her head left and winced through the pain as she watched the blonde Barbie, Valerie Kemper, kick the chair of the woman she'd pushed down the hill. It was Mrs. Lowell's.

Every chair had fallen at some point during the race.

"I think you're the clear loser there, Val," Gavin joked as he made his way to Mr. Cole's chair, which had traveled most of the way down the hill. The old man was spitting dirt out of his mouth and had a nasty gash on his forehead.

"Nah, I think I'm the loser," Roth yelled as he stood over his chair, the one that had gone sailing through the air. From where Lauren lay, it looked like Barry's chair. "Get a load of this shit! Broke his goddamn neck."

"No way," Liz said.

"I'm serious as a heart attack," Roth said. "This motherfucker's dead. It's fuckin' gross."

"Ohhh shit," Fiona, one half of the kids who'd gotten caught fucking in the school bathroom said. "Isn't he the security guard?"

"*Was* the security guard," Roth said with a snort.

Her better half, the guy who'd been fucking her at the time but seemed to be clearly split up from her now, Steven, jogged over and then flinched as soon as he saw it. "What the fuck? His neck is like…" he tried to use his arm to show the angle of Barry's broken neck.

"He's dead?" Josie Simmons asked, now looking even more out of place among her peers.

"Shit just got real!" Roth announced.

Lauren tried to read the faces of her students but could only see some of them. It seemed half were completely fine with the situation while the other half weren't so sure.

Oh my God. Barry's dead. Barry's fucking dead. This isn't a prank. Barry's dead. Barry's dead.

She fought to control her breathing, holding back the panic attack threatening to cause a total breakdown. She couldn't appear weak in front of these kids. She needed to be strong. She had to find a way out of this. She wouldn't if she melted down right here in this chair.

The school security guard was gone forever, and these kids were responsible. They showed no remorse. *This* was their plan all along. They were going to kill the teachers.

Others cried and yelled around her, but Lauren's head buzzed so loud she couldn't make out any of their words. Not that they would matter. Nothing they could say would change anything. Liz had seemed to grow a cult-like following with these kids. She wasn't only their class president. She was convincing them to kill.

"Hey!" Liz yelled, snapping her fingers. "Josie, snap out of it. Ain't no backing out now. We talked about this."

Lauren's head cleared. The snapping of the evil leader's fingers yanked her back to reality.

"I know," Josie said. "No backing out."

"Dead is dead," Liz said, "but even dead doesn't make you a loser. At least not in this game. Mrs. Lowell is clearly the loser."

All the kids made their way toward Mrs. Lowell's fallen chair. Lauren had to lean her head to the side and glance up at an angle to see her. The old lady lay on her side, her face against the grass. She didn't seem to be fully aware of what was going on. She could have hit her head hard or was only shaken up by the rough downhill plunge.

"You get away from her!" Mr. Cole ordered, sounding like little more than a cracked shell of his old self. He wasn't commanding anything tonight.

"James?" Liz asked.

Lauren peered toward her feet and in the direction of the jungle gym where she saw James Bender lift the large sack, which was obviously heavy, as if it were weightless. He kept his left hand tucked into his dirty jeans pocket and walked slowly up the hill, his head down, his face concealed. He was in no rush and nobody told him to hurry up. They wouldn't dare.

His power over the rest of the students was clear. As he approached, each of them bowed their head as if the presence of this demon-god demanded it. Even Liz, the one who seemed to believe in nothing but herself, lowered her face to the ground and said, "Thank you for all you do for us."

The boy didn't respond with any clear word but growled instead. The deep throaty sound reverberated through the air. It was that speaking through the oscillating fan sound Lauren was so familiar with, only this was deeper, darker, and rattled with gravel. She swore she heard James murmur, "Mmm hmm."

James walked by Lauren and held out the sack so it would hover only a couple of feet over her face as he passed. She couldn't help but stare at the filthy brown material. She winced when she saw the bag move. Something was definitely in there. Lauren whimpered as he passed, hating herself for thanking God she wasn't the one he was approaching.

"Josie," Lauren called softly to the young girl standing only a few feet from her.

For a second, she thought she'd been too loud. Nothing scared her more than getting the attention of James Bender. But the demon boy kept walking, making his way over to Mrs. Lowell.

Josie heard her though. Her head tilted slightly to the right, letting Lauren know she was listening, even if she didn't turn to look at her.

"Get help," Lauren said. "You're not this person."

Josie stayed glued in place as if contemplating the suggestion. Then she shook her head, squared her shoulders, and moved toward the other students gathered around Mrs. Lowell.

"Okay everyone," Liz said. "You might want to back up. This could get messy."

All the kids moved away from the old lady and Lauren could tell the woman was finally understanding the dire situation. She'd lost the race and the kids were singling her out for punishment.

"Liz!" Mrs. Lowell cried. "You've known me since I taught your brother!"

"I have," Liz replied, "and I hated you as much then as I do now."

"But why? What have I done?"

"It's not what you've done to me, Mrs. Lowell, but if I remember correctly, it was you who turned in Alan, wasn't it?"

"He stabbed my nephew!" Mrs. Lowell yelled. "He tried to kill him."

"That's what he told you," the wiry Alan said, stepping forward to challenge the accusation. Lauren had only taught the boy one semester but knew he was a liar and had cheated on tests. "But he didn't tell you that he approached me at the party and punched me first. He didn't tell you that he'd beaten me twice before. Broke my jaw one of those times. He was a bully."

"And Alan was scared," Liz said. "So, naturally, he defended himself."

"He stabbed him in the throat!" Mrs. Lowell cried. "And he still suffers every day because of it!"

"He wasn't a good person," Alan argued. "I was fucking terrified of him. So… yeah, I stabbed him."

"You got away with it," Mrs. Lowell sobbed.

"No," he argued. "It wasn't removed from my record like they said it would be. My dream was to be a fucking pilot in the Air Force, Mrs. Lowell, but guess what. They looked into it and decided they couldn't have a potential psychopath join their ranks, even if I didn't kill him, and even if it was never proven. It was a decision based on information provided in my criminal file."

"But I didn't…" she cried.

"Get away from her!" Mr. Cole yelled.

"You shut your mouth, you old, filthy fucker!" Alan yelled at the old man. "Just 'cause you stick your dick in her doesn't mean you love her, does it?"

Mr. Cole gasped. Lauren had never heard anyone speak to him like that. He wasn't used to having little shits like Alan challenge him.

"Enough of the talk," Liz said, sounding bored. "Let's get on with this. Mrs. Lowell, you are the loser of our first game, and you are hereby terminated from your position at DS High where you will never again destroy a young life."

"But I didn't—"

"James," Liz said.

Everyone backed up. James approached with his heavy bag and lifted it up high. He held the top of the bag with one hand and palmed the bottom with the other. Then he tilted the top forward, let go, and shook the bag.

Dozens of multicolored snakes poured from the bag. Slithering, winding, curling bodies rained down over the old lady. Some fell onto her chair and flipped onto the ground. Others flopped onto the grass around her. But more than a few landed directly on her.

Lauren was close enough that she knew she too was in danger. Just like Barry had died during this game, she was also vulnerable. These kids wouldn't stop the snakes from coming her way. She wanted to yell at the lady and remind her to remain perfectly still. She didn't know much about snakes, couldn't tell what kind were in the fray, but she knew that with most animals, it was best to keep quiet and stay still. Yet, if she yelled or made movement of her own, it might draw some of the reptiles her way.

"Stay quiet and still!" Mr. Cole yelled, saving Lauren from having to risk it.

It was too late. Like most people would, if they had venomous snakes raining down over them, she panicked, and she lost it. Mrs. Lowell screamed louder than her vocal cords should have been able to handle. It ripped through her throat uncontrollably and her body shook in the seat. Lying sideways how she was, aggravated the slithering menaces. They moved toward her instead of away.

Either out of curiosity or aggravation, the snakes all converged on her, some going straight for her open mouth and others leaping at her trembling legs, shaking hands, and jerking stomach. The first bite

Lauren saw was at her forehead. Mrs. Lowell's eyes rolled back, and she screamed again until another serpent sprung at her lips sideways and bit down, stapling her cheek with its tiny mouth, its head holding on through the blast of agonizing cries emitting from her.

A brownish red snake bit down on her knuckles.

A black one tore into her stomach.

Even some of the students screamed when Mrs. Lowell's body began to convulse, and frothy saliva burst from her lips and ran down her cheek and onto the ground.

Her body twitched, but no longer with panicked fear. Now, it was only reacting to the sheer amount of venom coursing through her.

"Whoa!" Drew said, backing further away as a couple of the snakes slithered toward him and then darted past him and into the forest.

A guttural moan escaped Mr. Cole, but he quickly silenced it. Now that Mrs. Lowell was no longer thrashing around, the snakes seemed to get bored and let go of her. They moved calmly past the kids. Some of them ran screaming toward the playground, but the snakes wanted nothing to do with them. They'd only bit Mrs. Lowell because they'd been forced into the situation. They'd been dropped onto a screaming woman and perceived her as a threat. The threat had been eliminated and now they would be on their way.

From where she lay, Lauren looked into the face of the old woman who'd never hurt a soul. She'd never even raised her voice. She was one of the most levelheaded teachers Lauren had ever met. Sure, she was having an affair, but who knew what her homelife was like? Maybe her husband was having one too. They might have been fully separated by now. Even if she was fucking around behind his back, she didn't deserve this.

Finally, everything seemed to hit Lauren at once. She'd been so sure this was all a prank at first and then, even after Barry's death, a part of her had considered that a very bad accident, but now she'd been a witness to murder, and she knew these kids had no intention of letting her walk out of here alive. Lauren's stomach began to lurch, and she gagged. Lifting her head the best she could, she leaned as far left as she was able to, and stared once more into Mrs. Lowell's swollen, face frozen in horror. She heaved once, twice, and vomited on the back of her seat and the grass beside it.

"Ohhhh we've got a puker!" Gavin called out.

The other students laughed.

Lauren threw up again.

18

CHARLIE

The crack of the gunshot nearly knocked him off the fence. Charlie was half over it, one leg inside the parking lot and one outside, when he heard it. At least that's what he thought it was. Some of the fireworks nowadays sounded a lot like firearms. It was possible the sound hadn't even come from within the park. With all the gangs on the streets and the cops chasing after them, it could have come from somewhere else entirely.

Yet, his gut told him it came from within the park. Charlie whipped his leg through the air and over the fence to join the rest of his body before quickly climbing down and dropping to the ground with a thud. His feet hit the ground harder than he would have liked. He hadn't seen anyone since his arrival, but for all he knew, there might have been someone on lookout inside the trees.

Crouching down just in case, he duck walked to the first car and squatted behind it. From there, he spent a good thirty seconds watching the dark space that marked the park entrance. Not only did he not sense any nearby presence, the total silence made him question the trip entirely. The park was completely quiet. No footsteps through grass or leaves. No laughing or cheerful conversation. No music blasting. It didn't seem like the location of a party.

He glanced down at his phone and saw he had no bars. Of course he wouldn't way out here. Why would he? It would be way too convenient to actually have cell phone service when he needed it. This was the reason he'd considered changing cell phone companies, but it seemed like every time he was about to actually take his lazy ass into one of his provider's stores, he received some kind of sweet deal that gave him a month or two of cheaper service. It was like the phone company read his mind. It knew when it was dangerously close to losing his business.

Fuckers.

This time, there would be no backing out. He would change providers tomorrow, as soon as he finished up with all this Grad Night hoopla.

If it wasn't for Joel's car in the parking lot, which he was sure of now that he'd gotten closer to it, he would have climbed back over the fence and left. But he was here now. He'd climbed the damned fence and now he needed to follow through with this.

Charlie didn't want to enter the park. He realized that now. The entrance was nothing more than a break in the trees. They'd been cut to form an archway, and mere steps into the darkness, he realized the path was wooden. It was a boardwalk of sorts. Handrails were on both sides. They should have provided him some comfort, but they did the opposite. A wooden walkway similar to a bridge meant he was standing above water.

Dark, black water. Water that could be filled with anything from venomous snakes to crocodiles. Or alligators. Or whatever else might be in the water beneath him. Charlie didn't like reptiles. He didn't like anything smaller than him with such deadly potential. In fact, he didn't like things larger than him that could kill him either. Nor did he like things his exact size. Charlie didn't like anything that could cause him death or bodily harm.

Tip-toeing into the darkness, Charlie imagined spiderwebs overhead and an army of black widows descending on their silken strings, hovering overhead where he couldn't see them.

A sting hit his neck and he slapped his palm against it, damn near yelling out in the process.

This is fucking crazy. Who would have a party out here? Nobody would. Go back. Climb that fucking fence, Charlie. Get in your car and go home. Fuck it. Go back to Rebecca's house like you promised. That's safer. Lauren and Joel can both survive a prank.

Closing his eyes for a second, he waited for his nerves to settle and then finally glanced toward the sky. Moonlight broke through the canopy above, but barely, and the slivers of light weren't enough to prove to him there weren't any deadly spiders coming down around him.

Nor were they bright enough to light his path.

Use your phone, dummy!

If not good for phone calls, at least it could serve as a light. He flicked his finger across the screen, found the button for his flashlight app, and pressed it. It shined through the darkness, illuminating the path ahead. No alligator waited for him to mosey past. He aimed the beam at the water to his right and saw a fish break the surface. To his left was nothing more than water and trees.

I wonder if there are fucking monkeys here.

He was pretty sure there weren't any, but he was a literature teacher, not a zoologist. He didn't know shit about creepy crawlies or strange beasts in the darkness. He wished he had some sort of weapon with him.

Like what? What would you carry that might make a difference if you ran into a fucking monster in these woods?

Paranoia was real, and he was suffering from it at the moment. Through his flashlight beam, he noticed he'd come to a fork in the trail. It was more like a pitchfork. This was when things could get hairy. He had a decision to make. Keep going straight? Or take the path that veered to the right? Or go left? Running the beam along the wooden handrails, he searched the darkness for a sign that might point him in the right direction. But what would be the right direction?

Bogdan had told him there would be a party at the park, but he didn't say where at the park. Charlie didn't know if this was one of those camping parks with multiple sections to it or if all these trails eventually ended up in the same location. For all he knew, there might be a cabin or some kind of park main building of sorts where kids could rent out party rooms.

His mental cowardice was causing him to bumble around in the darkness. When the music kicked on, shooting from invisible speakers Charlie figured must have been hidden among the trees, he became suddenly aware that he wasn't alone in the park. This was the site of the party. The tune flowing from the speakers wasn't techno or pop or rap. It wasn't party music at all. In fact, it was *Dies Irae* the song that played in Stephen King's *The Shining* movie. Nothing made him want to get out of the forest more quickly than that spooky-fucking song.

His feet moved fast over the wooden boards and his right hand clung to the bannister while his left hand held the phone's flashlight out in front of him.

"Fuck," he swore under his breath as his fingertips caught a raised piece of wood and a splinter slid deep into the tip of his middle finger. "Dammit."

With the flashlight beam pointed at his hand, he saw the trickle of blood and the tiny brown stump protruding from his flesh. The locked gate was his first sign that something wasn't right here, and then the music played. That eerie music that didn't belong in this situation. That hadn't held him back either, but now, with a splinter in his finger, Charlie realized there might be something trying to hold him back. He wasn't invited to this party for a reason. Maybe it would be best if he turned around and left.

He was contemplating that very course of action, picking at his finger, when he heard a scream. It wasn't Lauren. The voice was much higher pitched, and it sounded like the woman was screaming, "Help us! Please! Please, let us go!"

Charlie's feet found that oomph he'd been hoping for all along. His body moved on autopilot, no longer giving a shit about his fear or his concern. He needed to get to the main park area and find out what the hell was going on. This was why he'd entered the park in the first place. Not to be a pussy. To be a hero.

Lights began to shine through the trees as the straight-forward path brought him to the main playground area. Before stepping out of the trees, he clicked off the flashlight and crouched down to get a look at what was going on.

He saw the backs of students. Girls wore incredibly short dresses, tight tops, and showed off tattoos in places he had no idea they had them. The boys were dressed in fancy attire, but some of them had shed their shirts and were now topless, obviously trying to draw the attention of the ladies. But where were the teachers? Where were Lauren and Joel? Mr. Cole and Mrs. Lowell?

Far away, a boy pushed a woman in a wheelchair, bringing her right toward Charlie. The kid had his head down as he walked, like he was ashamed of what he was doing. As they came closer, Charlie saw Mrs. Lowell's bloated, pale, veiny face slumped over. Her dead stare was on one knee.

My God. What have they done? What have they fucking done?

"Hurry up and get over here!" Liz Cupo yelled. Charlie would know her toxic voice from anywhere. She was the one in charge of all this. "Game two is about to begin."

19

CHARLIE

"Scotty, turn off the music," Liz ordered. "That's just mean."

"What? It fits the situation, don't you think?" Charlie recognized the boy speaking. He'd taught him a few years ago.

"That song freaks me out," Liz replied.

They seemed jovial enough. Maybe Charlie was missing something. No, he couldn't be. He'd seen Mrs. Lowell.

He crept through the bushes, tiptoeing through the mud, and even dropping to all fours when he needed to. He couldn't allow himself to be seen until he figured out what was going on. Teenagers were pushing teachers in wheelchairs, and it seemed like the teachers were tied down. A few of them yanked back and forth but barely budged.

The ex-students were leading the teachers toward the playground at the center of the park.

What the fuck is going on here?

Charlie looked down at his phone and saw it still had no bars.

Was this only a prank of some sort? Was Mrs. Lowell only knocked out in that wheelchair? Maybe she'd seen something that made her pass out. But what about how swollen she looked? Charlie had no answer for any of that.

"What are you going to do to us?" one of the female teachers asked.

Charlie couldn't make out her face, but it sounded like the school psychologist, Ms. Keen.

Lauren's chair finally went past. She was sweaty and her face was dirty and scratched. Joel was in the line as well. So was the cafeteria manager and Mr. Cole. The train of educators went on and on until they'd formed a group of parked wheelchairs between the swing sets and the slide, right in front of four multi-colored seesaws.

Liz walked in front of everyone, pulling their attention toward her. She stood with her hands on her hips like she was a real estate agent proud with her unparalleled ability to sell overpriced homes. She smiled under the Christmas lights, their glow shimmering off her eyes.

"You're doing so well," she announced.

Some of the students laughed. The teachers didn't.

"I think you might be finally getting what this is all about," she continued. "You've tried your hardest to mold us into the image you wanted for us. Some of those images were pretty disgusting. You wanted me to be the bitch of DS High. The whore whose dad helped her get away with everything, right?"

None of the teachers responded.

"It's okay," she continued, "you don't have to say anything. Your silence says enough. You wanted Drew to be the failed basketball player who never got to go anywhere but here. His life, if it were left up to you, would consist of working at a gas station and playing street-ball with his buddies on the weekend."

"That's not true," Coach McCall said.

"Is it not?" she replied. "You seemed to try really hard to make sure he didn't get to play. Likewise, Mr. Lafferty, our resident grammar expert, loved to make fools out of all of us in every single one of his classes. A little humility would have gone a long way, but no, he had to make every class a fight for survival. Do you remember the games you had us play? The ones where we had to sit on top of our desks and when the ball came to us, we had to catch it and answer a grammar question out loud. If we got it wrong, you would lead the rest of the class in laughing at us."

"It… it… dear God, it was a learning tool, Liz," Mr. Lafferty cried out.

"Absolutely," she agreed, "and that's what we have for you now. We've put together a learning tool game based on the same concept you used, Mr. Lafferty."

At the top of the large, round jungle gym, a shadowy figure watched over them all.

James Bender.

He didn't need a reason to believe it was the boy keeping an eye on them. It had to be. It was his way. Liz might have been the voice of the graduating class, but James was the hidden leader. He was the one pulling the strings tonight. As if he'd stepped out of the pit of hell and slid right into the graduating class of DS High, James Bender seemingly appeared from out of nowhere.

Charlie had met with many students and their parents. He'd always taken great pride in getting to know his kids as well as possible. Every student graduating from the high school had to take his literature class at least two years. American Literature and British Literature were mandatory. Yet, he'd never seen the boy in any of his classes. He'd never met the parents. He'd never even heard any other teacher mention the kid other than pointing out the fact there was a strange boy in the hallways who gave them all the creeps.

From atop the jungle gym, the hooded figure looked back at him, and Charlie could feel his invisible eyes burning into him. He wasn't hidden from that boy. Junior's words from so long ago came back to him again.

"Charlie, not everything dark is bad. Sometimes you just don't understand it. You can feel the real evil kind of darkness. It does this to you…"

He could feel that right now. With James Bender staring back at him, he felt Junior's grip on his wrist, but this was stronger, and it seemed to grab hold of his stomach and squeeze with both hands. It reached into his soul and wrung it out.

"Real evil won't let you move," Junior told him. *"When you feel that. That is when you should be afraid."*

Charlie was frozen in place, and he was afraid. His heart rate picked up, slamming in his chest, and his breathing became heavy, like he was fighting through a chest cold. Junior was right. There was a different kind of darkness. This was pure evil.

James Bender tore his gaze from Charlie and looked at the set of seesaws.

There, squished in among all the others was Lauren. She squirmed in her seat, and Charlie wanted so badly to rush in there gallantly and save her. He might have done it if he didn't notice one of the boys, another former student named Tom, fidgeting with something tucked into the big pocket at the front of his sweater. He knew it could be a gun.

"What do you say?" Liz called out. "Any volunteers for round one?"

Don't volunteer, Lauren. Don't volunteer.

After a moment or two of silence, Mr. Cole's loud voice broke through with, "I'll volunteer."

Why would he volunteer to do anything with this group of kids?

Mrs. Lowell. He's in love with her and if... if she's dead... he might feel dead inside too.

But she couldn't really be dead. It had to be a prank of some kind. Whether it was a joke or not didn't matter, they'd already won the round. Charlie had never seen Mr. Cole looking so defeated. He had a wife and kids, older kids, but his newfound zest for life had been all about Mrs. Lowell.

"We have a volunteer," Liz announced. "Great. Wheel him over to the first seesaw."

Roth wheeled over the old man, parked him in front of one of the seesaws and then rushed over to grab the back of Mr. Lafferty's chair. He clearly wanted to make sure the grammar teacher was involved. Charlie remembered Roth's hatred of the man the other day when he'd caught him and Drew Dryer talking shit in the boy's bathroom. This was Roth's chance to get his revenge, so he pushed Mr. Lafferty toward the second seesaw, making sure his face was situated right above the metal seat.

"Guess that makes two," Liz said.

"I didn't volunteer," Mr. Lafferty complained.

"This game was created specifically for you," she informed him. "Volunteer or not, you *will* play this game."

Silence.

Charlie got a sick feeling in his stomach. He knew Lauren hated Liz, but he didn't know if Liz felt the same way about her computer teacher. He feared she might call on her.

Liz asked, "No more volunteers? I'm disappointed in you all. If I remember correctly, you teachers were always going on and on about self-confidence. When we were nervous or shy, you'd tell us things like, 'Go ahead and get it over with.' Or, 'If you go first, everyone has to measure up to the standard you set instead of the other way around.' Fucking hypocrites. So, I guess I'll go ahead and pick two more."

Charlie held his breath, praying she wouldn't choose Lauren. He saw Joel seated a few chairs behind her and quickly added him to the prayer.

"Somebody please wheel over Mrs. Moreau and Mrs. Connie," Liz said.

He breathed a sigh of relief and instantly felt bad for it. The French teacher and the substitute had been chosen. For now, Lauren and Joel were safe.

And Joel was looking right at him.

Does he see me?

His heart skipped a beat. If he looked at him for too long, one of the students might notice. But then Joel turned his defeated looking face back to the game going on in front of him.

"We've always been forced to keep up with our English work even when bombarded with vocabulary and grammar from a foreign language," Liz continued. "So, Mrs. Moreau, let's see how you do. Likewise, Connie, you get to come and go as you please at the school. You should have plenty of rest. Your mind should be fresh and ready for the game."

Charlie looked over the students gathered behind the teachers and couldn't believe some of the faces he saw. Gavin, the joker. Valerie

Kemper, the flirt. They weren't *bad* kids. They got into trouble like anyone else, but they weren't evil. Then he saw Josie Simmons and his heart ripped in two. Someone tore it in half, then into tiny pieces and tossed them into the wind. His faith in his students wilted right then, and he knew now nothing would restore it.

"Liz, please," Connie begged, but the leader of these kids didn't listen to her.

Mrs. Moreau looked left and right as someone grabbed the handle-bars behind her chair and pushed her forward. She struggled to get free from the zip ties keeping her wrists bound to the wheelchair. Yet, Charlie didn't think either woman seemed truly terrified. So, again, he wondered how bad the game could actually be.

"Kent, grab one of the chairs," Liz instructed. "You know the drill. You should be happy to play in this one."

Kent was one of the largest boys in the group. He'd been on the wrestling team and was a football offensive lineman until he'd been removed from both teams until he could go through psychological evaluation. None of the teachers knew the real reason why.

"Ok, I'm ready," Kent said as he dragged a metal folding chair over to the opposite end of the seesaw in front of Mr. Cole and then lifted his end as high as it would go, which in turn pushed the seat on the teacher's side down, so it was against the ground. Standing on his chair, Kent gripped the seat above his head and readied himself.

"Gavin," Liz said, giving the class clown the go-ahead to help prepare Mr. Cole for his round of the game.

Charlie watched from behind a thick bush as Gavin wheeled Mr. Cole closer to the seesaw, until his face was directly over the metallic seat on his end. The physics teacher struggled and leaned away from it, throwing his neck back to keep it far from the seesaw.

"Plywood," Liz ordered.

The kid Charlie recognized as Scott carried over a large piece of plywood and placed it behind Mr. Cole's back, where he then pushed on it hard, forcing the old man to lean forward in his seat. Gavin assisted and the two young boys were finally able to get the old bulldog of a man into position. With his wrists still zip tied to the chair's rails, Mr. Cole couldn't budge. He could only wiggle from side to side. The kids waited until he'd exhausted himself.

"Done now?" Liz asked.

"He's fuckin' exhausted," Drew Dryer said.

Charlie had always liked Drew. He was a good kid. Surely, this was all an elaborate prank.

"Mr. Cole, relax, please," came the sweet voice of Charlie's favorite student, Josie.

What was she even doing here? Charlie found himself scanning the area around them, searching for any kids who might be taking pictures of this. Maybe they only wanted to scare the teachers and were going to create another shitty video to spread around the campus.

Good one, kids. But now it's time to stop, don't you think?

"Now now," Liz said in the condescending voice a stepmother might use when about to tell her stepchild it was time to mop the floors. "Don't you think you're overreacting a little, Mr. Cole? Relax so we can get on with this."

"You're sick," Mr. Lafferty said.

"Glad you think so, you old asshole," Roth said from behind him. "Because you're next."

Mr. Cole leaned forward in his seat, his tongue lolling out. The boys had exhausted him, and he had no other choice but to remain in position with the seat of the seesaw on the ground below his chin.

"So, in the spirit of Mr. Lafferty and his grammar teachings, we've devised a game," Liz informed them. "One round for each of you. Get it right and you coast right through. Get it wrong, and, well, you don't. So… starting with Mr. Cole."

She paused for dramatic effect. No one made a sound.

"Mr. Cole," she continued, "in the following statement, Andrea stayed an actress, what is the predicate noun?"

Mr. Lafferty opened his mouth to say something and Liz pointed a finger at him, "Cheat and you die."

"I'm not an idiot," Mr. Cole replied. "Actress would be the predicate noun."

"Very good," Liz congratulated him. "Now onto Mr. Lafferty."

Kent moved the chair over to the next seesaw and positioned it the same way. Mr. Lafferty didn't fight or squirm, but Scott put the piece of plywood behind him in case he tried to at the last second.

"Mr. Lafferty, you are the grammar teacher, so we are expecting you to get this correct. Listen to me closely. Your question begins now. That was a *near* miss. What part of speech is *near*?"

Mr. Lafferty leaned his head forward and thought for a second before proudly declaring, "It is an adjective."

Applause went up from the students. A few of them groaned in complaint.

"Wait, was that right?" Roth asked.

Charlie shook his head. Of course, the boy wouldn't know.

"Seems you have a couple of fans," Liz said, ignoring Roth. "Good for you. Now, moving on, I'm curious to see how our French teacher will do. Mrs. Moreau, are you ready?"

The French teacher, a dainty, pretty woman thrashed around wildly in her seat. She pulled at her constraints until blood seeped from them. The kids all around her watched. Kent moved his chair over and made sure her seesaw was positioned the same as the others, high on his side and low to the ground on hers. Scott placed the plywood behind her back and pushed forward while Mrs. Moreau continued to fight.

"Why?" she yelled. "Kent! Kent please. You know why I turned you in!"

Charlie had never gotten the story. He'd never heard the issue between them.

"It was inappropriate!" she said. "It was so inappropriate. And it could have gotten me in big trouble. If anyone got ahold of my phone..."

"I loved you," Kent admitted. "I loved you so much."

His face was blank, as he was clearly reliving something in his mind.

"I know you did," she replied. "I believed you, but I couldn't be that person for you. I'm a teacher, Kent. I'm much older than you. I could lose my career over it."

"So, you showed them the pictures I sent you," he replied. "You took them to the principal and now look at me... I got kicked off the football team. And off the wrestling team. And I have to see a therapist now. I barely fucking graduated! For what? Because I was sexually attracted to the most beautiful teacher in the school?"

"Kent, don't make me say it," she begged.

"You ruined me," he replied.

"Kent."

"You turned me in, and everyone thinks I'm a freak."

"Kent, you sent me pictures of yourself masturbating. Pictures of your penis... every single day. I begged you to stop. I even blocked you, so you found me on Facebook and continued..."

"You asked me for those pictures," he cried, with tears actually streaming down his eyes.

"I never—"

"—No? You didn't? Look here, everyone."

Kent held up his cell phone like everyone would be able to see his tiny screen. He read from it, "Sure, go ahead and send it."

Mrs. Moreau was shocked. "I didn't... no... what was that in response to?"

"I told you I had something I needed to show you, and you told me to go ahead and send it."

"I thought it was homework related," she defended herself.

"And this, ladies and gentlemen, is why you shouldn't be text messaging your students," Liz announced. "I think that's enough explanation. We know how you teachers are. I'm sure you took that picture of his cock, masturbated while speaking your French ooh la las, and then played little Miss Innocent and turned him in to ruin his life."

"I would never—"

"—Enough," Liz cut her off. "Kent, we are ready now. Mrs. Moreau, your question is this..."

As Liz prepared to read the question, Scott pressed harder on the plywood, and Mrs. Moreau's face was forced to hover over the metallic seesaw seat. Kent pressed down ever so slightly to give himself some leverage. The French teacher's eyes poured tears.

All Charlie could do was watch and hope this was part of the big prank. They'd made a fool of her already. Now, they'd show her trembling in fear, maybe she'd piss herself, and then this would all be over.

Charlie considered running out into the playground and ordering them to stop, but if he jumped out there now, they could easily grab him and tie him to a chair like the others.

"Mrs. Moreau. Listen carefully," Liz continued. "This is nowhere *near* good enough. What part of speech is *near*?"

As the question was asked, Charlie saw James Bender's silhouette stand up on top of the jungle gym as if he needed to get a better look or wanted to oversee what was to come. Charlie would swear he saw a dull yellow glow from within the boy's hood. Again, that gripping sense of terror overcame him and he found himself glued to his position behind the bushes, unable to move.

Mrs. Moreau trembled and looked right at the substitute teacher next to her who seemed more lost than she was. She looked left, searching for help on that side, and just as Mr. Lafferty opened his mouth, Roth slammed a piece of plywood against the back of his head. A grunt left his mouth and then his head lolled forward and drool dripped from his lips.

"Your answer?" Liz asked.

"Umm... umm... can you repeat the question?" Mrs. Moreau asked.

Liz laughed and nodded. "I guess, given the circumstances, that's only fair. This is nowhere *near* good enough. What part of speech is *near*?"

Mrs. Moreau lowered her face and breathed deeply. Tears fell onto her lap.

"I don't know," she admitted.

"Is that your final answer?" Liz asked.

"No!" she shouted. "Umm... umm..."

"Adverb," Charlie whispered to himself too far away for her to hear.

"A preposition?" the French teacher asked.

It often was a preposition, and he hoped the students gave her credit for that. Surely they would.

"Ooooh," Liz said, sucking air through her teeth. "So close."

"I'm wrong?" Mrs. Moreau asked, seeming to accept her fate. "Please… please no snakes."

"No snakes," Liz promised. "But yes, you were wrong. The answer was adverb."

Some of the students cheered, some booed, Kent smiled.

"Now?" he asked.

"Now," Liz said.

"No," Mr. Cole said, "Take me."

"Your time will come, you old bastard," Gavin said from behind him.

"Thank you for your service," Liz told Mrs. Moreau while reaching down to give her shoulder a squeeze. "You're going to feel a little pressure."

Liz laughed and nodded at Kent.

A transformation came over the boy. He'd always been big, but what Charlie saw now frightened him. His eyes seemed to go blood-shot with rage. He gritted his teeth, leapt high out of his chair, gripped the seat on his side of the seesaw, and threw his body onto it.

"No!" Charlie yelled as he threw himself forward but found himself stuck to his position by some sort of supernatural force.

James Bender looked his way. Charlie fought and screamed, "No!"

It was too late.

All Kent's weight came down hard on the seesaw and as he plummeted toward the earth, the opposite end shot upward with the strength and speed of a Mack truck.

The metal seat rocketed upward, peeling the skin from the front of Mrs. Moreau's neck.

It struck her chin and there was an audible crack as it threw her head back so hard her neck snapped and fell to one side.

The second crunch came with the weight of her head hanging loosely by nothing but the skin encasing her neck.

Without it, her lifeless head would have bounced off the ground.

Charlie's feet became unstuck and he pitched forward into the bushes, rolling out of them and onto the grass where he faced the crowd of students and teachers.

Nobody had expected him, and he didn't wait for their reactions.

He ran to the dead French teacher, unable to fathom that she was actually gone.

Her wrists leaked blood where the impact had practically launched her entire body out of her seat. Only the zip ties kept her locked in place. Her throat was ripped open, the jagged shards of her shattered trachea had punched through the thin skin. Blood pooled in her lap and down to the ground beneath her chair.

Connie screamed so loud and shook so hard Charlie thought she might pass out. He grabbed her chair and pulled her away from the seesaw where she wouldn't be able to see what had happened to the French teacher.

"What are you doing here?" Liz yelled at him, but he couldn't pay her any attention. He was busy trying to calm Connie down.

The substitute teacher wouldn't close her mouth. It was stuck in the open position with wails emitting so loud he was afraid she'd damage her throat. Her eyeballs shook and her fingers curled up in claws, scratching at the rubber of the wheelchair.

"Connie," he said, "calm down."

He said the words, but inside, he was having almost the same reaction she was. Mrs. Moreau's head had been torn almost completely off. Charlie looked back at Kent who was laughing his ass off and pointing at the dead teacher.

"You fucking coward!" he yelled at Kent.

"What did you say?" the boy asked, spit flying from his lips. He was still in his crazed state, and it was clear he wanted nothing more than to end another life.

Charlie welcomed the piece of shit. "Come on!"

"Charlie!" Lauren yelled.

"Charlie!" Joel joined in. "Run! Get help!"

He wasn't thinking straight. Of course, he needed to go get help. His car was out by the road. He only needed to—

Something hit the back of his head and he was out cold.

20

LAUREN

Why would he do that? Why would he run out here like that? He could have saved us. He could have saved us all if he would have gone for help. What was he thinking? Oh, my God. I'm going to die. We're all going to die.

Lauren was going into a full-blown panic attack. Her chest heaved up and down, and her throat constricted the way it did the first time she had to speak in front of a crowd. Black spots pocked her vision. This hadn't happened since the last time her ex hit her and then threatened to leave. She'd been lying on the kitchen floor, doubled up in pain from a punch to the gut, and had been more worried about the man walking out the front door than she had about her own well-being.

Since getting rid of him, she'd sworn to never feel this way again. Yet, here she was, all the strength in her body reduced to short gasps. If she began to cry, she knew she'd sound like a child who'd been spanked at the grocery store and was throwing a fit in aisle two, complete with wracking sobs that would make her words come out one at a time between sniffles and gulps of air.

It was a slap across her face that brought her back to reality.

"Don't even think about losing your shit," Liz warned her. "You're in this for the long run. After all, you're my favorite teacher."

"What are you going to do with Charlie?" Lauren asked, ignoring the girl's bullshit declaration.

"Ouch," the teenager said. "So, I'm not your favorite student?"

Lauren glared at her and bit her bottom lip to stop herself from saying something that might get her hurt. The pain from her own chomp calmed her breathing down a bit. She closed her eyes and sucked air through puckered lips.

"He wasn't supposed to be here at all," Liz said. "Believe it or not, he was voted out of this mess. Some of the kids thought he should be included but a few were adamant that he should not be invited to this party. His dumb ass just couldn't stay away."

"Liz, please," Joel said. "You know us. We're not bad people. Sure, mistakes have been made, but come on. You've totally made mistakes of your own."

Liz ignored him and turned back to the others. "Put Mr. Charlie in Mrs. Lowell's chair. It's not like she needs it anymore."

A few of the students laughed.

"Where should we put all these bodies?" Scott asked.

She rolled her eyes. "Scotty, you know that control you always take in the bedroom? Take some of that and use it now. I can't make *all* the decisions."

Liz is fucking Scott. Noted. How can I use this information against them?

She scribbled the note into her mental journal and fought to memorize it through the cloudy haze that had become her thoughts. She only wanted to get out of this park. These kids had tainted the place that once held her fondest memories. If she lived through this, she would never come back here. This park was now a place of unspeakable evil. It was the site designated for the offing of the teachers.

Why kill us? What do they hope to gain from all this? They're finished with school. Why would they do this now? Why not last year or the year before? This is absurd.

"Let's move on," Liz announced to the rest of the kids. "Back to the stage so we can play our version of the spelling bee."

Lauren's stomach dropped. She was a horrible speller. She spent all her time around computers. Spell check was very real, very useful, and very necessary in her life. She'd never been good at spelling tests, spelling quizzes, and especially spelling bees.

Charlie wasn't far from her, so she tried to wake him up. "Charlie, psst."

"Shut up," Kent said as he struggled to move Charlie's chair through a patch of muddy soil.

Arguing with the boy or trying to plead with him would be useless. He'd lobbed off the head of the woman he was supposedly infatuated with.

What kind of human could do such a thing?

"Why?" Lauren asked as she leaned her head back and looked up into Liz's face. "Why are you doing this? What do you hope to gain from this?"

"Have you ever read the book *The Maddening* by T.K. Tantrum?" Liz asked, wrinkling up her face as she pushed Lauren's chair up the slope and toward the stage.

Lauren had never even heard of the book. Was this another of the reading fads going on? Most of her students didn't read until a book came along that was deemed "cool enough" to get their attention. First, it was the *Harry Potter* books. That kept the kids enthralled. Only the truly dedicated students made it past book one. Then, it was the *Hunger Games* series. Kids killing kids? How could that not get their attention? After that, there'd been a lull until the *Fifty Shades* books came out. The school had even held a meeting about keeping those books out of the classrooms. Some of the students switched the dust jackets with other books, as if any of the teachers would really believe they were suddenly interested in *War and Peace*.

Once the movies were released, the kids even lost interest in that story. Going to the theater cost half as much as the book and took a lot less time out of their hectic schedules.

Was the new "it book" this Maddening story Liz mentioned? If so, what could it possibly be about? What was the natural progression when going from a school of wizardry to murderous students to BDSM and other sexual acts? What could possibly come next?

Murdering your teachers – obviously.

"I'll take that as a no," Liz added.

Lauren hadn't even realized she'd failed to answer the girl. She hadn't meant to.

"I haven't," Lauren finally replied.

"You should." The girl laughed. "Well, I suppose it's a little too late for that now, but it's a good book. You see? It's a novel. Fiction, but its message is clear and is so appropriate for the day and age in which we live."

She spoke so formally about it, one might suspect she'd written it herself and was now sitting on the sofa at *Good Morning America* explaining its importance to the world.

"It's all about how the world is going mad and how the strong will survive," Liz continued, "and the only way to ensure that's the case is to be the maddest of the mad and be the first to lose yourself in The Maddening. With so much suffering, anger, hate, rage... with so much of that out there in the world already, why not embrace it rather than try to fight it? We were created with an animalistic side, a desire to kill rather than be killed. Only when we open ourselves up to our true nature, will we really be free. The world wasn't meant to be tamed, Ms. Peony. It's a mad world, and we're embracing it tonight."

"So, this is all because of a book?" Lauren asked.

These kids who seemed to learn nothing taught to them were following the instructions of a fucking book?

"You don't understand," Liz replied. "Not that I expected you to and not that I care if you do. It's too late for that."

There would be no swaying her.

"Maybe you should have put all this into your final essay," Lauren said, "and then I wouldn't have had to give you that 'F.'"

Liz ignored her. They'd reached the stage. Lauren glanced up into the spotlights shining down onto it and saw that someone had been busy while they'd been playing the other "games." A wooden post was erected at the middle of the stage, standing about ten feet tall. At its top was a circle of smaller posts, extending out from the center, like the spokes on an umbrella if the canvas covering had been torn free. Dangling from each of the wooden spokes was a thick rope tied into a noose.

It was a hangman's carousel. Lauren didn't need the rules explained to her. It was obvious what would happen. She could see the trap door in the stage at the front and center. They would be made to march in a circle, each taking his or her turn standing on that trap door.

"This is sick," she muttered.

"No, Ms. Peony," Liz argued. "It's brilliant."

Lauren wondered who would build such a thing and how would they have time to do it?

"It wasn't easy talking Mr. Marsh into making this, but you know, Daddy has lots of money and will do anything for his little girl, so... Mr. Marsh won't need to do janitorial work at the school anymore."

Harold Marsh. He was the high school's Mr. Fix-It who was constantly ridiculed and treated like shit by the students and staff alike. For a man with so little respect, it probably didn't take a lot of prodding to convince him this was worth it. A janitor's salary wouldn't provide much. This was his opportunity to escape the clutches of poverty and move onto a mediocre but comfortable life.

"Heading home," came a hoarse voice Lauren was all too familiar with. She knew before seeing him walk by with his shoulders slumped and his Detroit Lions baseball cap pulled down over his eyes that it was Mr. Harold Marsh himself. This was Dolphins territory, but the man remained loyal to his back-home team. Once, the teachers had pitched in to buy him a Miami hat for Christmas. He'd laughed at it and then stashed it away somewhere, or threw it away, never to be seen wearing it.

"You don't want to stay and watch the show?" Liz asked.

"No, thank you," he said.

"The gate's locked," Liz reminded him. "Scotty, can you take care of that?"

In front of everyone, without even a second of hesitation, Scott walked over to Harold, raised a gun to his head, and pulled the trigger.

Mr. Fix-It's brains exploded in a gust of red mist riddled with bone fragments. His body collapsed. Liz snickered. Lauren gasped.

"What?" Liz asked, now looking down at Lauren. "You didn't think I was going to actually pay him, did you? He's one of you. Do you have any idea how many times he's gotten students in trouble for smoking in the bathrooms? Who do you think turned in Janie Ross for giving Levi Levitz a blowjob behind the stadium bleachers? Mr. Marsh. Couldn't include him in the games because I needed his help creating them, but... you know... when it's your time to go, it's your time to go."

And when it's your time to go?

Lauren wished she held the skills of so many movie badasses. If she were only a *La Femme Nikita* type, she'd rip her arms free of this wheelchair and bury one of the metal bars into Liz's belly. Then, she'd snatch Scott's gun and shoot all the rest of these vile little bastards. But she wasn't like that at all. She was Lauren Peony, a high school computer and typing teacher. She might be able to bore them all to death with one of her lectures, but other than that, she had no skills in the deadly arts.

"Hey, wake up," Kent said as he slapped the back of Charlie's head.

Charlie wasn't a tough guy either, but Lauren was pretty sure he could kick Kent's ass if he wasn't zip tied. Joel could probably do some damage too. Mr. Cole definitely could. He was old, but he had military experience. That had to count for something. None of it would as long as they remained in their restraints.

Lauren looked left and then right. She counted thirteen teachers. There had been fifteen to begin with. Three were dead, if she included the school security guard in her numbers, but Charlie had been added at the last minute.

Unlucky thirteen.

Who was left? Herself, Charlie, and Joel. Mr. Lafferty, the grammar teacher sat sullen in his chair, unresponsive to the questions and complaints of the other teachers. Mr. Cole was barking orders to untie him again. Franny, the cafeteria manager, was doing the same.

Coach McCall sat as stiff as a board. Paula, the psychology teacher who'd thought this night was going to end with an ex-student in her bed, tried desperately to get her hands close enough to her face to catch her tears. Then there was the substitute, Connie, and the three teachers silently trying to work themselves free of the zip ties. Mr. Sterling's knowledge of government and politics wasn't going to get him out of this trap. Mrs. Laymon had done a *shit* job of counseling or providing any kind of guidance to these kids. She deserved to be here more than any of them. Mr. Timms could know all there was to know about economics, but that wouldn't set him free from that chair.

Then, there was the librarian, Mrs. Grainger, who didn't seem to have a care in the world. Her giant goggle-like glasses, with their thick lenses and oversized brown frames, rested at the bridge of her nose. She could have been an audience member at the symphony orchestra, the lady behind you in line at the grocery store with her cart full of casserole ingredients, or even the single mom at church every Sunday because her husband and kids refused to join her. Looking at her, you'd think she was anyplace but here.

"Mrs. Grainger," Lauren whispered to her.

They weren't friends. Lauren wasn't sure she had many. The librarian generally kept to herself. In fact, Lauren couldn't remember seeing her at any school function, staff meeting, or unscheduled complaint session inside the teacher's lounge. She had her own world inside her cathedral of hardcovers, paperbacks, outdated magazines, and that shelf of newspaper articles nobody ever touched.

Only kids like Josie Simmons visited her in there.

The Josie Simmons who doesn't belong here. Why would she get mixed up in this?

"Mrs. Grainger," Lauren tried once more to get the woman's attention.

Liz didn't hear. She'd left Lauren's chair and made her way onto the stage to oversee things up there. Mrs. Grainger turned to look nonchalantly over at Lauren. Her hair was its usual muss. Her tight leathery-brown swirls hugged her head and jutted out in haphazard tufts, like someone had grabbed hold of patches and pulled. Or like she'd rolled out of bed and realized she was late for this maniacal party, only grabbing her keys on her way out the door. Her sanity stayed home.

The older woman only stared at Lauren, looking so serene. Had she been drugged? Didn't she understand she was about to be forced to play a deadly spelling bee? Even saying the words in her own head sounded so insane. So absurd.

A fucking deadly spelling bee?

"Why are you here?" Lauren asked her.

She stared back, stone-faced. Lauren couldn't imagine what she might have done to upset even one of these kids. She didn't ram homework down their throats or grade term papers. She didn't even have to teach them that damn Dewey Decimal System. In fact, Lauren couldn't imagine any of these kids even stepping foot inside the library. Not with Google readily at their fingertips. They didn't need to look anything up anymore and most of them didn't read for pleasure.

"What are you doing here?" Mrs. Grainger replied with all the calmness of someone who might have bumped into her friend at the supermarket.

"I don't know yet," Lauren replied, "but you... you couldn't have done anything to upset them."

"We all have," she said.

With her words, it seemed the rest of the world went silent. Lauren's mind buzzed. The coolness of the librarian's words. No question. No doubt. She seemed to understand something Lauren hadn't yet wrapped her head around. Mrs. Grainger had made peace with the fact she was going to die.

The librarian turned back to the stage and sat quietly in her chair to await her turn.

"Wake him up," Liz ordered from the front of the stage.

She was talking about Charlie, who'd started to come out of it. His head hung down and his eyes were on his lap, but his head was moving slowly from side to side. He was the *Wizard of Oz*'s Tin Man and only needed some oil in his neck to bring him back to life.

Instead, he got a slap to the back of his head by the heavyset Kent.

The boy guffawed as he did it. He was having too much fun with this. Any of the hesitation or doubt he'd shown before the seesaw game had disappeared completely. Now, he was a coldblooded killer only waiting for orders to carry out his next deadly move.

"Wake up, fucker!" Kent yelled at Charlie, bringing his face close to the teacher.

Charlie reacted with a headbutt that nailed the teenager right in the nose. Lauren swore she heard the crack of the cartilage crushing beneath the teacher's forehead. Blood ran from the boy's nose, showering his T-shirt in crimson.

Lauren wanted to stand up and cheer. At the same time, she was worried about the repercussions. As much as she hated that Charlie had shown up, having someone here willing to fight back made her feel that all hope wasn't lost.

"Let me out of this fucking chair," Charlie spat.

"Ohhhh," Liz cheered him on. "That was awesome."

"Did you see that?" Scott yelled, throwing his hands up into the air in victory. "Holy shit, Mr. Charlie. I didn't know you had it in you."

"Come here," Charlie told the older boy. "Let me tell you a secret."

"Nah, man. Fuck that," Scott replied.

Charlie hadn't seen the boy shoot the janitor. He'd been out cold when it happened. If he had, he might not be playing so tough right now. She needed to warn him. If he went too far, they might lose patience with him and do something drastic.

"Charlie," Lauren said.

He turned toward her, and she slowly shook her head *no*. She would have loved to see him torture a few more of these monsters, but she didn't trust that they wouldn't grow tired of his attitude and put a bullet in his head.

"What are you doing here, Mr. Charlie?" Liz asked. "You weren't even invited."

"I felt left out," he said, still looking groggy.

"Aww, you thought we didn't like you?" Liz asked.

"Something like that."

"If you only knew we liked you more than the others…" she

seemed to be considering how to finish her statement. This part wasn't scripted. Charlie wasn't supposed to be here. He'd interrupted their plans. "... maybe you wouldn't have come..." Liz stopped talking for a second and looked at Lauren. Then she glanced at Charlie again. Back to Lauren. "Oh, hold on a second. You didn't come here because you felt left out. You came here because you have a thing for Ms. Peony."

"Oh, shit," Scott said.

"Fucker broke my nose," Kent complained. "Scott, shoot this prick."

"Go clean yourself up," Liz told the boy.

"But I'll miss—"

"—You won't miss anything. Hurry up."

Kent obeyed her and scurried away.

"So... Charlie and... and Lauren," Liz said. "Are you two fucking?"

"No," Lauren answered.

"Wow," Liz replied. "That was a fast answer. So you want to be fucking him?"

She was right. Lauren had been hoping tonight might lead her down that road, but she couldn't think of any benefit to admitting it.

"Well, let's do these two a favor." Liz put her hands on her hips, looking too cutesy given the situation. It was a stance she'd perfected over the years, bouncing around from the cheerleading squad to the dance team to even the step team. She'd done it all and seemed to be allowed to come and go from the teams as she pleased. Everyone, from the students to the team coaches, was afraid to tell the girl no.

"How about we only make one of you play this game?" she offered. "We'll let you decide which of you will participate. The other can watch and cheer on his or her lover."

"We're not lovers," Charlie reiterated.

"Whatever," Liz replied. "Call it what you want, but it's pretty clear you want to fuck Ms. Peony, so we'll just consider you lovers. I mean why else would you risk coming here?"

"The gate was locked, man," Drew Dryer, the basketball star said.

"Did you fucking climb over it?" Roth asked. "You did."

"He did," Drew said. "That's mad skill, teach."

"Yeah, they're fucking," Liz added. "No way he'd hop over the fence, go through the dark park, and jump into harm's way because he was interested in our party. So, which will it be? Who's participating?"

21

CHARLIE

His head hurt and his stomach threatened to empty itself all over his lap. He wanted Scott to come closer so he could shower him in vomit, but the boy wouldn't be stupid enough. Not now. Not after what he'd done to Kent. With his head swimming, he tried to focus on the young lady standing center stage. No, she wasn't a lady. This chick was batshit crazy.

"So, who will it be?" Liz asked.

She'd called him out. He and Lauren actually. The girl was right, but it was none of their damn business. Now, she was asking them to choose which of them would be sacrificed to this game and which would be forced to sit and watch it happen.

A game. What kind of sick shit is this?

He was having a hard time understanding it all. He'd come to the park convinced there'd be some sort of mean-spirited prank pulled on Lauren, Joel, and the rest of the teachers, but what he'd seen was incomprehensible. Kent had stood over a seesaw and with one wrong answer had thrown his weight down and practically ripped the head off Mrs. Moreau. The French teacher's throat had been torn open and her head had hung to the side like a fishing bobber kept afloat by little more than a string.

"You killed her," Charlie whispered.

"I'm sorry?" Liz said.

"You killed Mrs. Moreau."

The girl laughed. It was more like a cackle. Charlie's comment caught her by surprise. She would have spit out her drink had she been sipping on one. "That's kind of the point."

"Nobody is meant to survive these games, are they?" Lauren asked.

Her question helped Charlie understand better.

"Three of us down already," Lauren added, "and you won't let any of us walk out of here."

"Just shut up and play the game," Mrs. Grainger said so loud it seemed to carry with it the crack of a whip.

Everyone looked at the librarian.

"Seems Mrs. Grainger gets it," Liz said. "Better to get it over with than to dwell on it. Yes, Ms. Peony. I hope you don't mind if I call you Lauren from now on. Seems less formal, and let's be honest, I'm not a student anymore, and I never fucking liked you anyway, so Lauren it is. You're right. You're not meant to survive these games. But that doesn't mean you won't be playing them."

"Why would we play in games we know we're going to lose?" Joel asked.

It was the first time Charlie had heard him speak since his arrival. The teachers all seemed to have given up hope, but he hadn't. Charlie would get out of this somehow. While the others were preoccupied with questions about playing the games, he understood that surviving each moved him closer to the point of escape. He was a good speller. Years of reading, studying, and discussing literature had made him quite astute in vocabulary and spelling. He could beat this game. Then, when he was moved on to something easier to escape from, he'd make his move.

The bickering of the others drowned out as he focused on the students around him. Scott, who Charlie barely recognized as an ex-student of the school, wielded a pistol. Gavin, the class clown, carried a baseball bat. Roth, that piece of shit, had a lead pipe.

One of the girls, Charlie was pretty sure her name was Layla, looked like she had a gun tucked into the waistband of her pants. She was high half the time she'd been in school, and even now decorated her hair with roach clips and feathers. She reminded him of a member of the 1970s Manson family. He was tempted to tell her he liked her costume but thought better of it. He didn't need another strike to the back of his head. The last one made his brain feel like scrambled eggs.

"So, uh, can we get back to the program?" Liz asked. "Who's it gonna be? Charlie or Lauren?"

Lauren looked at him and took a deep breath.

"I'll—" she began but was cut off by Charlie.

"—Me. I'll go. Leave her alone."

Liz cupped her chin under both palms and batted her eyes like a lovestruck teenager instead of the twisted bitch she was. "Aww, that's so fucking sweet. I'm secretly shipping the two of you. That is, if you can make it through this game, Charlie."

Shipping. Charlie wasn't sure where the term had come from, but he understood its meaning. It meant she was secretly hoping he and Lauren would end up together.

She sure has a funny way of showing it.

"But, you know, sometimes you must kill all your darlings," Liz added. "See? I did pay attention in your class, Charlie. Fitzgerald said that, right?"

"Faulkner," he corrected her.

"Close enough," she said, throwing her head back. Charlie knew it was accompanied by an eye roll, even if he couldn't see her closely enough to be sure.

It wasn't close enough. It was like claiming Poe had written *Othello*.

"Get him up here then," Liz commanded.

Scott stepped toward him and Charlie wished he had the skills to knock that gun out of his hand. He was only a high school teacher though. He could handle himself well enough on the street. He'd been in a tryst or two, but even the fact he'd mentally used the word *tryst* instead of fight reminded him he better not go for that gun yet. With all the other teachers still stuck to their chairs, he would be alone. Charlie versus all the toughest graduates from DS High.

"Get him out of the chair," Scott ordered Drew and Roth as he kept his gun trained on the teacher.

"I'm not going to fight," Charlie said.

"I hope you fuckin' do," Roth replied.

"Please don't," Drew said.

Charlie couldn't stand Rothmeyer, but he'd always had a decent relationship with Drew. He thought back to the other day when he'd heard the boys discussing their problems with Mr. Lafferty in the boys' bathroom.

"I should have turned you in," Charlie said.

"Whatchu mean, punk?" Roth asked, trying to sound gangster as he usually did.

"When I found you in the bathroom with that vape pen," he said, "talking about how badly you wanted to beat the shit out of Mr. Lafferty."

"What?" Mr. Lafferty asked.

"I should have gone to the principal with that info," Charlie continued, "but I didn't. Because I wanted to make sure you both graduated. Now, I wish I would have turned you in."

"And I wish I would have invited you to this party in the first place," Roth said. "I tried to, but Drew here wouldn't allow it. Then fuckin' Josie had to get involved and they shut me down. But look at you now, motherfucker. Look at you now."

"Look at me," Charlie replied. "All zip tied and helpless. It takes a big man, a real *gangsta* to handle a man who can't fight back."

"Oh, you want to fight back?" Roth asked.

"Shut up, man," Drew told him. "Mr. Charlie would kick your ass."

"Stop letting him get to you," Scott said. "Get him out of the fuckin' chair and haul his ass up to the rope."

"You know he can't kick my ass," Roth mumbled his disagreement as he put a hand to Charlie's chest and pushed on him firmly. Drew used some wire cutters to snip the zip ties at his wrists. Before Roth could register what was happening, Charlie threw his right fist upward and smashed it against Roth's chin. The wannabe gangster flew backward, slipped on the moist grass, and went down hard on his ass.

Scott stepped forward; making sure Charlie saw the gun and calmed down.

Drew sighed and grabbed Charlie's shirt collar. "Fuck, Mr. Charlie. Come on, now."

All the other kids started laughing. The teachers struggled in their chairs as if they might stand by his side in his attempt to overthrow the students one at a time. Unfortunately, the punch was strong, but teenagers were good at taking a spill and bouncing right back up. Sports and routine fights at parties and late-night drunken gatherings had, if nothing else, taught them to take a hit.

Roth was back on his feet by the time Drew led him toward the steps to the stage.

"Try that again, motherfucker," Roth threatened.

"I will," Charlie promised.

He wasn't sure where this bravado had come from, but he was embracing it. He didn't know what would come of it, but at least he'd gained the respect of some of the teenagers and pissed Roth off to the point that he might try something stupid later. He was the kind of kid who couldn't stand being disrespected in front of his peers. Inside, he was probably too afraid to make a move on the brave teacher, but on the outside, he wanted all of his classmates to think he really was this hardened bad boy. He would have to make a move at some point, and when that time came, Charlie would be ready.

The crowd murmured like they were the residents of the town in Shirley Jackson's *The Lottery*. They all anxiously awaited what was to come. Seeing their teachers strung up by the neck was the highlight of the evening. Or the highlight so far. Charlie imagined each and every new game would be worse than the one before. These kids were fucked in the head.

"We have only eight ropes," Liz announced, "as I'm sure you've already counted."

Charlie hadn't had time to, but now that he was being led to the one in the front of the stage, he did count and she was right, there wouldn't be enough for all the teachers.

"So, to be fair, we won't involve the teachers who played in the last game. Plus, as I promised, Lauren will be exempt. So, I'll go ahead and call out the teachers who will be playing this game. Scott, if you would be so kind as to help them up."

"Of course," he replied.

His position at the front of the stage made him the first teacher in danger. Drew lowered the heavy rope down over Charlie's head and pulled it tight. Breathing wasn't difficult, but there'd be no escaping.

"Hands behind your back," Drew said.

Charlie knew he could try and fight, but Scott had his gun pointed directly at his face. If he even twitched, the nervous boy might pull the trigger. As it was, his knuckles were white with anticipation. He was squeezing that pistol grip with all his might, impatiently waiting for the chance to shoot.

When Charlie hesitated, Drew said, "Mr. Charlie, please. Scott already shot Marsh."

"The janitor?"

"Yeah."

Why would he shoot the janitor?

"Who else has died tonight?" Charlie asked.

"I shouldn't even be talking to you," Drew said as he pulled Charlie's hands back behind him and zip tied them together.

"Fuck, man," Charlie complained.

"Too tight?"

"Just a little bit. Damn."

"Sorry."

"Drew, you shouldn't be involved in this. You're a good kid, man."

"It's The Maddening, Mr. Charlie," Drew replied.

"What the fuck does that mean?"

He thought about it for a second. He'd seen that somewhere.

The book.

"Wait, like the novel?" he asked the boy.

"I've already said too much," Drew replied as he lowered himself and said, "I'm going to tie your ankles together with this rope. Don't kick me. Even if you do, someone else will come up here and wrestle your legs together."

"I'm not going to kick you," Charlie promised. "Just tell me why you're doing this."

"You're going to die tonight." Drew pulled the rope tight. "You're a sacrifice to the start of The Maddening. To prove we're not held back anymore. We're founders of The Maddening, key players in its initial round."

"Initial round?" Charlie turned that over in his head, dissecting it, and still it made no sense.

"Mrs. Grainger," Liz said. "You're next up."

"Drew, this is nuts, man," Charlie struggled in his constraints. "You could be going to a good college."

"Don't struggle," Drew warned him. "With your hands cinched and your legs tied, if you fall... you're dead."

"Come on," Scott said as he grabbed Drew's arm and pulled him toward the stairs.

The two boys walked into the group of wheelchairs, cut Mrs. Grainger free, and waltzed the librarian right up to her noose. She didn't say a word. She didn't fight. She didn't even struggle in the slightest. Charlie turned on his rope and saw her a few nooses away. She didn't even seem worried.

"Mrs. Grainger," he said. "Are you okay?"

"I'm dandy," she replied.

He'd spoken to her several times. Charlie didn't know her to have many friends, but he'd had many discussions with her about the books that surrounded her every day. He'd always thought being a librarian would be an amazing job. He'd much rather spend his days with hard-cover and paperback friends than speaking to a crowd of unwitting students who'd only go look up the books he assigned online and regurgitate the chapter summaries. Only a handful of students actually read what he assigned. They were all at the *other* Grad Night party.

All of them except Josie Simmons. Charlie turned toward the crowd and found her. She refused to look his way, and it was very obvious. She glanced left, right, up, and down. But she never looked toward the stage.

"Why is Josie Simmons here?" Charlie asked aloud.

"Why wouldn't she be?" Mrs. Grainger replied.

Charlie turned once more to see her looking straight ahead. There was no emotion on her face. Until suddenly he saw the faint hint of a grin forming. The corners of the woman's mouth crept up so slightly it was impossible to tell if it was done on purpose or was only her relaxed state of mind causing it.

What did she mean? Josie Simmons was his best student.

"Because she's a good kid," he replied.

"They're all good kids, in their own way," she said.

No fucking way. These were the bottom of the barrel kids.

He used to believe they could be something, that they were something, but not anymore. He'd lost his faith in his students. He'd lost his faith in society's youth as a whole.

"Maybe your belief that they're nothing is one of the reasons we're here," she added. "We blame them, but have we *really* tried to reach them? Have we given our all?"

"I have," he said, but his voice came out on autopilot while his mind retraced his steps, thinking back to so many classes he'd taught. Had he *really* worked as hard as he should have? Had he put all his effort into each student? Or had he focused on the *good* ones like Josie Simmons?

"Perhaps you have," she said. "And that's why you weren't invited here."

"But you don't even teach them," he said. "Why are you here?"

"Neither did the security guard and he's dead."

"Mr. Jackson?"

"Yes. Mrs. Lowell too. And Mrs. Moreau."

He'd only known about Mrs. Lowell and the French teacher.

Charlie hadn't heard the next teacher being called to the stage, but suddenly Franny was there. The cafeteria manager was strung up to his right. She begged for her life and the kids laughed along with each of her wails.

"Please! I tried to be nice to everyone!"

They were in hysterics. Charlie heard the sound of dripping water and looked down to see the puddle running toward his shoes. Franny had pissed herself and the kids thought it was the funniest damn thing they'd ever seen.

"Please!" she cried. "I'm begging you. I'm begging."

She began to sob, whispering a desperate plea only she and Charlie could hear. He wished he could tell her it would be okay, but it wouldn't. At least not yet.

Next up was the economics teacher, Mr. Timms, and then the guidance counselor, Brenda Laymon. The kids usually called her Brenda. She was okay with that. If she'd been more into actually counseling them instead of making them all take those stupid tests that tell them what job they'd be good at, then maybe none of them would be here right now. Charlie had complained about her a few times. The kids felt like she wasn't interested in helping them prepare for the SAT or ACT. Instead of assisting them with college entry essays, she would walk through the school reprimanding them for violating the dress code or for running in the halls.

Charlie had been silently stewing in his anger when the rest of the teachers were marched into position. Mr. Sterling, Joel, and the substitute teacher, Connie, joined him on the stage. Charlie moved his feet, stepping down hard, and was reminded that he stood over the trap door. It shook slightly and rattled beneath his feet. He was in the killing position. He would be the first up to bat. The first speller.

22

CHARLIE

Lauren watched him tearfully. He wanted to console her. Here he was, the one in harm's way, and his thoughts were on comforting the woman he loved. His life was in danger, so maybe that's what made him realize it. His infatuation with her had become so much more. He was *in love* with her.

She shook her head slowly from side to side and it was clear she couldn't come to terms with the fact he was willing to die for her. This whole game, this whole night really, seemed like a sacrifice.

To The Maddening? What the fuck is in that book? And why do these kids hate us so much? This is like some sordid sacrificial Olympics. But to what are we being sacrificed?

"I'm so glad it's you eight in those nooses because I'm really not a good speller," Liz joked.

She was so relaxed in this role. She had no fear of public speaking. She was the leader of her class and they all watched her, waiting for the class president to issue orders, ask a question, or start the game. They hung on her every word.

"This is so exciting, isn't it?" Liz asked.

The students cheered.

"I'm not a good speller," Joel said. "I'm so fucked."

"I'm okay," Connie said. "I won a few spelling bees as a kid, but I mean... that was years ago."

"Sound out the words," Charlie told them. "Don't spell too quickly and trust your instincts. Most of the time people are right the first time but convince themselves they're not."

He wasn't trying to be a know-it-all. He wanted them to survive. They were right. In their profession, especially now that so much technology was used in the classrooms, it was rare they needed to spell. Only the old-school teachers wrote everything down on the white board. Chalk boards were extinct at DS High. He imagined Mrs. Grainger might do well since she was well-read.

"You're up, Mr. Charlie," Liz announced. "By now, you've noticed the trap door at your feet. The rules are simple. I say a word. You spell it. No asking for the word to be repeated, no definition, and no using it in a sentence. You spell it and you live. You misspell and you die. It's that easy."

Easy. Only if you know words really well.

She was breaking every rule to every spelling bee ever performed. How could they be expected to do this perfectly without asking for a word to be repeated or to be used in a sentence? The answer was simple. She didn't expect them to do this perfectly. She wanted them to fail miserably and die.

Tears now fell freely down Lauren's cheeks. She mouthed his name over and over again. "Charlie... Charlie... Charlie..." Her brow furrowed and her head tilted to the side in defeat. He realized, she blamed herself for this and thought there was no way he'd make it out alive. She needed to have more faith.

"Lauren," he said, "cheer up. I'll be back in a second."

"Ohhhh," a few of the kids said with their hands cupped around their mouths.

"Damn, Mr. Charlie's not afraid at all!" Valerie Kemper said.

"Of course he's not," Drew said barely loud enough for Charlie to hear.

"Hang that punk bitch," Roth yelled.

"Only if he fails," Gavin replied.

"Fuck you!" Roth yelled at the class clown.

"Boys!" Liz interrupted. "None of that. It's *us* against *them*. Not *us* against *us*. No matter what."

It was naïve to think he could win them over, but Charlie did think he might be able to reach some of them if only he could live long enough. His reason for his confidence was easy. Franny was terrified. She'd pissed herself. That got her nowhere. So, what difference would it make if he talked shit to them and pretended to be the badass none of them expected? If he were going to die tonight, he didn't want to go out crying like a little bitch. He wanted to stand up tall, the same way he had every day in class.

Beyond her, far behind the rest of the crowd, a figure sat atop the jungle gym, his elbows on his knees as he spied the show like someone not given tickets to the good seats and was stuck in the stadium's nose-bleed section.

James Bender. What role does he play in all this? Why is he here but so far apart from the others?

"Are you ready?" Liz asked him.

"Guess it wouldn't matter if I wasn't," Charlie replied.

"That's the spirit. Ready or not, your word is: Prospicience."

Charlie breathed an internal sigh of relief as he sounded out the word in his mind and slowly spelled it aloud. "P... r... o..." he broke it down into familiar pieces and continued, "s... p... i..." and he knew the rest was like science minus the *s*, "... c... i... e... n... c... e. Prospicience."

"Well, I'll be damned," Liz said with a chuckle. "Correct. Crank it."

Someone followed orders behind the scene, and the wooden beam at center stage began to turn like a carousel, yanking on their nooses. The sudden jerk forward could have knocked any of the teachers off their feet and to their death, but sheer terror along with the will to live snapped them each into action and they all shuffled along with the turning of the axle. A few teachers complained, whined, and moaned, but in the end, they all moved into the next position. This placed Franny over the trap door.

The cafeteria manager freaked out. She thrashed around and came too close to falling. Stumbling, she got her footing again and quieted down, seeming to understand that she was about to cause her own death.

"Franny," Charlie said, "Calm down. It's only a word. You can do this."

"If you help her, you will get a bullet in the skull," Liz warned him.

Franny's feet tapped against the trap door as she danced in place. "Please don't do this. I serve your food. That's all."

"Oh, don't pretend to be innocent, you conniving cunt!" Amber yelled from the crowd at the front of the stage. "You're the reason everyone found out I was pregnant."

"It was for your own good!" Franny yelled. "You were keeping it a secret and you weren't eating right. You were smoking under the tree with all your friends."

The tree was the spot all the rebellious teenagers used as a smoke pit. They'd meet up there before school, at lunchtime, and after school to pass cigarettes and other illegal paraphernalia around.

"I knew what I was doing," Amber said. "Besides, I killed that baby anyway."

A murmur went up in the crowd as these ex-students and the teachers in the wheelchairs heard of this for the first time.

"Got an abortion," Amber added.

"You were too far along for that," Franny said.

"You're never too far along if you don't want it."

Franny didn't reply. There was no response. What could she say? But then she did say something. "I hope you rot in hell!"

Silence.

"I hope you all rot in hell!" Franny declared with a sudden strength she hadn't had previously.

"Franny," Charlie said, trying to calm her down.

"Burn in hell!" Franny yelled louder.

Liz giggled and said, "Your word is onomatopoeia."

"Burn in..." Franny continued but then transitioned into, "... onomato what?"

"Spell your word," Liz warned her.

"But I didn't hear it."

"Then I guess you shouldn't have been yelling at us."

Spell it, Franny. That's an easy one. You've got this.

Charlie spelled it in his own head. Franny was trembling. She had already given up having not heard the word.

"Just give it to her again," Charlie said.

"Charlie shh!" Lauren warned him.

"Liz, you have to be fair in this," Charlie said.

"I don't *have to* do anything," Liz replied. "Spell your word, Franny."

"Spell it, you lousy bitch!" Amber yelled.

So much hatred brewed inside Amber. If she hadn't been exposed, would she have gotten rid of the baby? Did she actually blame Franny for the loss of the child? Was she that jaded that she didn't understand who was really responsible?

Franny sobbed.

"Oh, kill her already!" Amber shouted.

"At least try," Joel said.

"Try," Connie added.

Liz stepped closer to them. "I'm warning you all to shut the fuck up."

"There should be a time limit," Amber announced. "I mean we can't let them stand there all damn day."

"New rule," Liz agreed. "You have ten seconds to begin spelling. One... two... three..."

"Try, Franny," Charlie urged.

"Shut up," Liz said, "four... five... six..."

"I can't," Franny said, "Okay, um... O... n... o... m..."

Doing good, Franny. Keep going. A... t... o... say it.

Charlie thought so hard on the letters he imagined they might sink into her skull and fall upon her tongue so she could relay the rest of the word in correct order.

"O... I mean... I mean a... no, O..."

Liz shook her head. "I'm sorry. No."

"But I..." Franny tried to explain herself when Liz pointed to the back of the stage. Someone, somewhere, must have pulled a lever.

The trap door opened.

Franny had no time to scream.

Connie did. She screamed so loud it drilled a hole into the back of Charlie's head.

Worse than the sound of the substitute's yell was the thump.

Franny fell through the trap door. The weight of her entire body pulled on the rope until it jerked tight.

Her neck snapped.

Her tongue lolled out.

Her eyes bulged.

Shit and piss ran down her leg.

Franny was dead, her neck snapped immediately.

There was none of that movie struggle. The kind where the person kicks his or her feet and struggles for a while. Maybe that would happen to one of the others, but for Franny, she was dead instantly. Roth and Drew hopped onto the stage and pulled her up out of the hole. The trap door closed, and Franny's body was left dangling there in front of the rest of them.

Connie kept screaming. It was her turn next.

The wheel turned, dragging Franny's body as they each moved over one space. A long smear of feces trailed behind her. It ran down the woman's shoe, drawing a thick line across the wooden platform. Charlie watched the cafeteria manager's lifeless face hang to the side, wondering if the pressure would pop her head off. In his mind, it came off at the neck and blood spurted everywhere, pooling at their feet. In reality, she kept sliding across the ground with each stutter of the wooden wheel overhead. It seemed to strain a little with her weight being pulled along.

Connie's turn came and she couldn't stop sobbing. She was gasping too hard to spell anything. She'd only recently calmed down after losing it over the French teacher's demise. Now, her hysterics had started all over again.

"Get yourself together," Liz warned.

She couldn't. She looked toward Charlie and then over at Joel. She begged Mr. Timms to help her and even turned her attention to the librarian, but Mrs. Grainger could offer her no assistance.

"How does it feel to be left hanging, Connie?" Valerie Kemper yelled as she stepped in front of the rest of the kids.

Connie didn't say a word. Snot ran from her nose as she stopped fighting the tears and allowed herself to zone out.

"You need to know why you're here," Valerie said, "You see, she thinks she can come and go as she pleases. She shows up, subs a class or two, treats us like shit, and then leaves."

"No," Connie said.

"Yes," Valerie argued. "We had a disagreement in class once. I had bad cramps and you wouldn't let me rest. I only wanted to put my head down on my desk, but you forced me to sit up straight and participate. Until I couldn't take it anymore and put my head down anyway."

It didn't seem like a good enough reason to kill her, not that any of the reasons were good enough.

"And then when I was in the bathroom after class, and I got stuck in the stall because I didn't have a tampon, you came in. I saw you through the crack in the door. I begged you to please get me one or find one of my friends who could. I saw you turn and look at the stall. And with that bitchy grin of yours, you left me. You left me hanging. Do you know how embarrassing it was to leave the bathroom like that? I had to go home because I bled straight through my skirt."

Liz sucked air through her clenched teeth with a hissing sound and said, "Damn, that was cold, Connie. You left the girl hanging."

Connie begged and almost slipped she fought so hard to get out of the rope.

"Let's see if we leave you hanging," Liz said, "Your word is cul-de-sac."

Charlie breathed a sigh of relief. She would get this one easily.

Liz counted and the students joined her, "One... two... three... four... five..."

Spell the word!

"Six... seven... eight..."

"C…" Connie started, "u… l… d… e… s… a… c."

Yes.

"Wrong," Liz said.

What? No.

"There are a couple of hyphens in there," Liz informed her. "Can't skip right over them, right, Mr. Lafferty?"

The old man started to speak but held his tongue. That was exactly what he would say if one of them left the hyphens out in an essay. Charlie had heard him joke about stuff like that in the teacher's lounge, about how close one of the kids was and how he'd had to pull the rug out from under him. He seemed to take great pride in making his students squirm.

Charlie heard the crack of the lever.

Connie dropped.

"No!" Lauren yelled.

The substitute did struggle for a few seconds, maybe five or six, snot shooting from her nose and joining the slobber at her lips. If her hands were free, she would grasp at the rope, trying to claw her way through it, but the kids had taken that small mercy away from her. She could do nothing but hang. So, she did until she stopped shaking, wiggling, and sputtering. An eerie silence settled over the stage as she finally died, and the boys lifted her out of the hole.

With no warning, the wheel above jerked again, pulling them on. This time it dragged both Franny and Connie.

Joel was next.

"No!" he yelled.

Lauren cried in the audience. "Please, please stop this, Liz! You can stop this."

"Josie!" Charlie yelled at the girl in front of the stage. His straight-A student, the one who still wouldn't look at him at all. She was mortified, but she did nothing to stop it.

"I'm not a good speller, man," Joel warned.

"Liz! That's enough. You've killed two already!" Charlie yelled.

"Can I shoot him please?" Scott asked, approaching Charlie.

"Not yet," Liz said. "I want him to see this. Joel…" she chuckled again, knowing she was picking a word Joel couldn't possibly know. "Your word is appoggiatura."

"What the fuck?!" Joel yelled, thrashing around. "I don't know that fuckin' word!"

He went so wild that he lost his footing and fell. The rope around his neck held him up, but it cut off his air and he dangled for a second, wheezing with his face beet red.

"Help him!" Charlie yelled. "Joel, fix your feet!"

"We can't help him," Liz said.

She didn't have to. Joel struggled but then found his footing, and in all the commotion, Charlie was able to give him a message. He quietly whispered, "It's a musical term. Double *p* double *g*."

Charlie couldn't remember the definition of the word, but he knew it had something to do with music, which was Joel's specialty. Maybe he'd heard the word. Hopefully he'd heard Charlie's message. Nobody else seemed to have.

"Despite the total waste of time we just experienced," Liz went on. "You will get your full ten seconds to begin spelling. Starting now."

"But what have I done to deserve this?" Joel asked in a weak voice, his circulation starting to come back to his face, but his cheeks were still redder than Charlie had ever seen them.

"Do you remember making Marcia Tucker sing on stage last year?" Liz asked.

"I didn't make her," Joel replied. "I selected her because she has an amazing voice."

"Did she not tell you no? Did she not tell you she was too embarrassed and had stage fright?"

"All kids have stage fright until they perform."

"Did you see the video of her singing, of her voice cracking, online?"

Charlie hadn't seen it. He'd never even heard of it. Then again, these kids kept damning information secret. They teased each other, ridiculed one another, but they rarely got the teachers involved because they would only squash it. They would take it to the principal and put an end to all the fun. Cyber bullying was all too real now.

"I was bullied online because of you, Mr. Mendez," Marcia Tucker said as she stepped forward in the audience. "I can't take the video down, and every time I report someone for putting it up, it gets removed but then pops up again later."

"Marcia, I'm sorry," Joel said. "I didn't know. I picked you to sing in the show because you're so talented."

"So beautiful you mean," Liz interrupted.

Marcia was a pretty girl. She had a style all her own. She seemed to have only a few friends, wore classic rock T-shirts, and drew digital art on her tablet whenever she arrived early to class. She kept to herself but often got in trouble in class for snapping at students who challenged her ideas. She was the curse-word champ. It was common for her to belt out, "Go fuck yourself," if someone disagreed with her point of view. She wasn't the debate-team type.

"I'm not following," Joel replied.

"Did you or did you not flirt with her when you worked after hours with her?" Liz asked.

"Of course not," Joel replied.

Charlie was sure he hadn't. He remembered the two of them discussing Marcia and how shy she was when they were working together. He rarely remained alone in a room with students. Every teacher on campus knew the danger of that. But being the music teacher, sometimes he had to coach students who were embarrassed to make mistakes in front of others.

"Did he, Marcia?" Liz asked.

Marcia nodded her head. She was shy even now. "Yes, I... I think so."

"You think so?" Charlie asked. "Liz, this is going too far. You're not getting justice. You're falsely accusing your captives."

"Mr. Charlie, if you interrupt me again, I will have no choice but to put you back on top of that trap door and pull the lever," Liz threatened.

He wouldn't win this battle. Neither would Joel.

"Enough of this nonsense," Liz announced. "You have ten seconds, starting now. One... two... three..."

"Oh shit," Joel said. "Uh…"

It wasn't an easy word to remember.

"Four… five… six…"

Joel looked at Charlie and began spelling, "A… p… p… o…"

Charlie nodded. He was doing it.

Dear God, please help him do this.

"G… g… i… a… t… u… r… a," Joel finished.

All was silent.

"I'm sorry," Liz said. "But that is incorrect."

It wasn't incorrect. He'd spelled it correctly.

"Check again!" Charlie demanded. "He was right."

"I'm sorry," Liz said, "but according to my list here it's—"

"—He was correct," Josie Simmons announced. "Your list is wrong."

"A… double p… o… double g… iatura," Joel repeated.

Liz checked her list again. "What to do?"

"There's only one thing to do," Charlie yelled. "You created the games. You have to be fair."

"Mr. Charlie's right," Josie said.

As pissed off as he was that she would even be involved in something like this, Charlie wanted to hug her for coming to his rescue. Without her, Liz would surely have that lever pulled and Joel would drop to his death like the other teachers.

"Okay," Liz agreed. "I guess fair is fair. Next."

The wheel overhead turned and yanked them by their nooses again until, struggling under the weight of the dead bodies, it pulled them into the next position.

"Mr. Timms," Liz said. "He who thought it was okay to staple applications for all the famous fast food chains to our final exams last year."

"It was to motivate you," the economics teacher declared, "and I only did that to the failing grades. It's not my fault you didn't study."

"Right," Liz said. "Your word is feuilleton."

She'd mispronounced it, but Mr. Timms began spelling anyway. He fucked up on the fifth letter.

The trap door opened, and he fell.

Snap.

Dead instantly.

The boys pulled him up, the wheel turned, and now it was Mrs. Grainger's turn. She calmly stood still. No arguing, no fighting, no thrashing around. She remained at ease even as Liz said, "Your word is ursprache."

Standing on the rickety trap door, the older woman leaned left and then right, causing the door to creak.

"U...r...e...s—" she began.

"—Wrong," Liz announced.

"Don't do it, Liz," Lauren begged. "Hasn't there been enough?"

"There hasn't been nearly enough," Liz replied. "I'm sorry, Mrs. Grainger, but you are wrong."

Mrs. Grainger closed her eyes and accepted her fate. She didn't even ask why she was here or whom she had wronged.

"I will go be with my husband then," the librarian said, and Charlie finally got it. She wasn't worried because she'd wanted to leave this world behind. This was an escape for her. After a moment of silence, she added, "Get on with it."

Liz nodded to the back of the stage and the trap door opened. Mrs. Grainger fell but instead of that quick, nasty jerk, her rope came loose and fell with her into the hole.

"Whoa," Scott yelled. "Did you see that?"

"Talk about divine intervention," Roth called out.

"That's not supposed to happen," Liz announced, anger written all over her face. "Go in there and finish her please."

Roth leapt onto the stage to volunteer. He'd traded his lead pipe for a machete. After touching the tip of the blade to his forehead in a threatening salute aimed at Charlie, he dropped into the hole and disappeared from sight. Seconds later, Mrs. Grainger screamed in agony. The sickening thwack of the blade biting into her muscle and bone caused Charlie to flinch.

"No," Joel said. It was only one word and had no real meaning behind it. But what else could someone say in this situation?

The only teachers on stage now were Charlie, Joel, Mrs. Laymon, and Mr. Sterling. The guidance counselor leaned forward as far as the rope would allow and threw up. Her vomit splashed against the stage and the history teacher did his best to avoid it, hopping out of the way.

"God, make her stop," Mrs. Laymon begged. "Make her stop."

"She will stop any second now," Liz promised.

A final thwack of the machete under the stage and the librarian was silent.

"Hasn't that been enough death?" Lauren asked. "My God! Liz, Josie, Drew... all of you... hasn't that been enough? You've made your point. We were wrong. We were all wrong."

"Keep going," came a deep groan that seemed inhuman. It shook the air and came from deep within the park, quite possibly from all the way back in the trees. The words slithered between the remaining teachers and nipped at Charlie's ear. "Kill them."

Those last two words vibrated through his ear and squeezed his brain. Charlie would have doubled up in pain if his body would have allowed it. It wasn't coming from the trees. It was the voice of James Bender.

Why don't you come over here and kill us then?

He wanted to yell the words, but he couldn't. As brave as he'd been, daring a demon like the one seated on the jungle gym took a different kind of strength. Charlie was afraid of the boy.

"Who is that?" Mrs. Laymon asked.

"What is it?" Joel replied.

Nobody was going to answer them. Roth pulled himself free of the hole in the ground, sliding his bloody machete across the stage. He stood, raised his hands above his head like the night's champion, and accepted the applause that followed. Then he looked back at Charlie and said, "You don't look so tough now."

Charlie wanted to reply, but he couldn't. The demon's voice had drained him for the moment. He could barely stand, let alone talk back to the kid.

Liz gestured for the wheel to turn. It did, squeaking overhead, dragging the bodies along... all except for Mrs. Grainger who remained beneath them, her blood surely soaking into the dirt below.

Charlie found himself wondering about the park. How many families would come here tomorrow, oblivious to the violence that occurred tonight? How many children would kick blood-stained dirt at each other or roll around in the shit-soiled grass? Hanging does something to the body. It lets loose everything.

The air wreaked of piss, shit, and vomit. There would be no washing that free tonight. Only a storm could rinse some of it away. The rest would remain deep in the soil.

Mrs. Laymon stood over the trap door. Liz laughed. "The guidance counselor who offered no guidance. You were more like a disciplinary officer, weren't you, Mrs. Laymon?"

"I only wanted you to succeed," the counselor swore.

Liz gave her a word that was too easy in Charlie's opinion. It dawned on him that he was betting against the counselor. He'd never cared much for her. In fact, she often seemed to oppose the teachers who tried to help the students. It was like she couldn't be bothered to do her actual job.

What kind of person are you to hope she gets a difficult word?

Mrs. Laymon spelled her word with ease and then let out a trail of nervous laughter. It was that "barely made it" release of energy that could only float on a brief chuckle.

She looked at Charlie, breathed deeply, and then laughed once more.

"That was good," Liz said, "but I think that might have been too easy for you."

Mrs. Laymon gasped and then her eyes went wide and she moved her focus from one person in the audience to the next, reading their faces. It was like her brain was trying to process what she'd heard by gauging the expressions of everyone in front of her. Had she actually heard what she thought she'd heard. "What? What do you mean? I spelled it correctly. It's not my fault if it was too easy."

"It's not my fault either," Liz replied. "It never was. But my mom sure seemed to treat me like it was. Like I was the reason she couldn't keep her man. Her *mom-bod* would always be a turn off. I suppose it's time to reveal my story."

Mrs. Laymon's face blanched. Charlie could tell she knew what was about to be revealed.

"You know," the guidance counselor said.

"I always have," Liz replied. "Just like I know how you got the job at the high school. Tell the truth, Mrs. Laymon. You have no college degree. You're not a counselor of any kind, are you?"

"I... I..." Mrs. Laymon stuttered.

"You what?"

"I..."

"You're the reason my mother's an alcoholic?"

"Liz..."

"Mrs. Laymon, being my father's whore was never going to make you a Mrs. Cupo."

"I never wanted to—"

"—I heard you! And I saw you!" Liz's raised voice quieted the counselor. "I was ten years old. It was the day after my birthday and my dad was taking me to buy ice skates. He'd promised. But he needed to stop by his office first. I was supposed to stay in the waiting room. He took too long, and when I peeked through his office door, I saw his assistant riding him at his desk."

Charlie couldn't believe it. He could... but he couldn't.

"And do you know what she was asking with each thrust of that nasty cunt of hers?" Liz asked everyone around her.

Nobody answered. Even the other students seemed to sense this wasn't the time to piss her off.

"When... are... you... going... to... leave... your... fuck... ing... wife?" Liz said word by word, gasping with each, as if she were in the throes of sex.

The students remained quiet.

"But he didn't, did he?" Liz asked.

Mrs. Laymon looked down at her feet and softly shook her head no.

"He would never," Liz said. "Don't you see that? She's his wife.

She's there for him through thick and thin, but she found out about you and his other women. That's why she drinks so much and does all those stupid fucking surgeries. She has to compete." She turned toward the audience and said, "And that, ladies and gentlemen, is how our esteemed guidance counselor got her job. My dad wouldn't marry her, but he'd shut her up with a high-paying position at the school. The only reason our principal isn't here tonight too is because my dad needs him in that position."

Charlie had always wondered about the girl's pull. Her dad had the school heads in his pocket. It made perfect sense.

"So, let's try this again, shall we?"

"Liz," the counselor said. "Please."

"Ohhhh please," Liz mocked her in a whiny voice while rubbing both fists at her eyes, making the *crybaby* gesture. "Is that how you begged for my daddy's cock?"

Everyone laughed. Everyone except the other staff members forced to watch, each surely wondering when it would be his or her time to have the rules flipped on them at the last second. The danger of the games became so much more real. Even winning wouldn't ensure their safety. There was no safety when it came to these kids. They wanted revenge.

Mrs. Laymon looked at Charlie as she heard the next word she was expected to spell. Charlie couldn't believe it. This was the kind of word reserved for the championship round of genius-level spelling bee competitions. It was clear from the look on her face that she was done for. She had no idea how to spell the word, and as the counselor tried, Charlie hit a snag in his brain and realized this would be the point when he, too, would be dead. He wouldn't survive it.

They would have beaten him, only it wasn't him standing on the trap door, and as Mrs. Laymon misspelled *scherenschnitte*, he closed his eyes and listened for the blast of the doors falling open and the snap of her neck breaking. It happened quickly with her. A fresh coat of shit was painted on the breeze. The counselor was gone with that sickening crack, and Charlie thought he heard her grunt one final explosion of breath from her gut. It was her final, "Fuck you."

Mr. Sterling wasn't even given a word. When his turn came to pass, Liz seemed to have grown impatient. She shrugged her shoulders and said, "You seemed to have great fun ridiculing us in class. Do you remember the time I confused the death of Marie Antoinette with that of Susan Newell?"

"I do," the teacher said.

"Do you remember how you laughed, and the students joined in? Everyone laughed at me."

"I do and I'm sorry."

"It's a little bit late for that, isn't it?" she asked. "You did this with all of us. You made fun of us for our lack of knowledge."

"Your lack of willingness to learn," he corrected her.

"Whatever."

"But I—"

"—Marie Antoinette was beheaded. How did Susan Newell die again?"

"She was the last person to be hanged in Scotland," Mr. Sterling said.

"To be what?" Liz asked.

Don't say it. Don't repeat it.

"To be hang—"

The history teacher didn't even get the full word out of his mouth when the trap door opened. He dropped hard but didn't die right away. Liz laughed and laughed. She raised her hands as if leading a satanic orchestra and suddenly all the kids in the audience laughed with her. Everyone cackled and pointed fingers at him. Some even applauded. It was the last thing Mr. Sterling saw before his face turned a shade of blue and he stopped fighting for breath.

Only Charlie and Joel remained on stage. The game was over.

23

LAUREN

She was in second grade. Her blonde pigtails were wrapped up in red ribbon, her heart thumped in her chest, and her eyes focused on the Bingo-like scorecard she held in front of her. It was filled with stars and she needed only one more. Mrs. Lawrence said the student to get the next question right would get a star added to their tally. This was Lauren's moment. It was all she wanted in the world.

Filling up the card completely meant a trip to the class store at the back of the room. Of course, it was nothing more than a storage closet with one shelf dedicated to prizes the kids could win if they behaved well enough and performed at a high enough level to collect a card full of stars.

She only needed one more.

"Your question is," Mrs. Lawrence began.

Lauren squeezed her legs together to stop herself from peeing. She was so excited she knew it might trickle down onto the floor, and that would be the worst nightmare imaginable. Alexander sat behind her, and he was a real jerk face. Every single day when she sat down at her desk, he would point a finger at her and start counting. "One... two... three..." and he would keep going until he'd pointed out each and every freckle on her cheeks.

Her mom had called him a little asshole, but Lauren would never repeat that. Her dad would take the belt to her if she did. She knew better. She preferred the belt to remain around his waist or hanging in the closet. When it struck her backside, it hurt horribly. He usually only beat her when he was drunk. Today was Friday and Daddy always drank to the start of the weekend.

If she had a card full of stars and a new prize to bring home, he wouldn't lay a hand on her. He would be too proud.

"Are you all ready?" Mrs. Lawrence teased, pausing her question to heighten the suspense. She always did that. Even at lunchtime she would have them stand by the door a full three minutes before the bell rang and would remind them how much time they had left practically every few seconds so that by the time they could leave, everyone ran like wild animals out the door.

But Lauren liked Mrs. Lawrence. She always asked about the bruises on her leg. Once, one of her friends, a pretty lady named Susanne stopped by the class to see the bruises. She wasn't so smart though. She believed Lauren when she said she hurt herself wrestling with her older brother. She didn't have an older brother.

"Okay, I won't tease you anymore," Mrs. Lawrence said. "Your question is, which U.S. presidents' faces are on Mount Rushmore?"

"Oooooooh!" Lauren groaned as she stretched toward the ceiling with one hand up so high she thought she might scrape the tiles above.

She could hear Alexander behind her, whining as he stretched his arm out too. Lauren wanted to turn around and slap his hand down. He only had five stars out of twenty so this wouldn't even help him much if he got it right. Lauren needed this one.

It's Friday. Please. I only need one more star. Ohhhhhh, please.

Mrs. Lawrence looked right at her and Lauren beamed with antici-pation. She was going to be picked. She smiled as wide as she could, being sure to show teeth the way Mama always told her to.

"Don't hide your pearly whites," Mama would tell her.

She didn't hide them today. She smiled so hard the corners of her lips hurt.

"Yes?" Mrs. Lawrence asked, and Lauren waited for her name. She

couldn't answer until she was called upon, but her response was so ready to spill from her lips.

Then it happened.

She felt the warmth spread across her underwear first and knew that her light tan pants would do nothing to hide the widening dark spot.

Alexander sniffed the air behind her, louder than was necessary.

"Yes, Alexander?" Mrs. Lawrence asked.

Right away, Lauren knew why. That one second it took for her to realize she'd peed her pants stole her attention and made her lower her arm enough to look like she was unsure of herself.

"Oh, Mrs. Lawrence," Lauren begged.

"Lauren," the teacher said. "You wait your turn. I called on Alexander."

"Umm," Alexander started.

And he didn't even get one of the presidents correct. His very first answer was, "John F. Kennedy."

"No, Alexander," Mrs. Lawrence said. "I'm sorry, but that is incorrect."

"Oh, I know!" Lauren cried out.

"Ronald Reagan!" Alexander tried again.

"No, I'm sorry. That is incorrect. Lauren?"

Now was her chance, but as usual, Alexander ruined it.

"Eww," he said, "Did you... did you pee your pants?"

A puddle had spread beneath her seat and she was sitting there in a wet, plastic chair. She couldn't move. Every kid in the class turned toward her. She froze. No answer came to mind.

"You did!" Alexander yelled as he backed away from her desk and pointed at her, leading the rest of the kids as everyone began to laugh.

"You stop it!" she yelled at him, and as she turned to face him, her elbow brushed her golden star-covered score card, knocking it off her desk where it floated lazily down to the floor and landed in her puddle of pee.

It was the end of life as Lauren knew it. She now had no chance to win a prize. She'd proven herself nineteen times this quarter. She'd behaved well enough and answered all of the difficult questions. She'd spelled words correctly and had begun learning her times tables. She'd eaten all her lunch and had sat quietly when all the other kids were being loud and rambunctious.

But her proof of all that was now soaking up her pee.

"Mrs. Peabody wants to answer the question, Mrs. Lawrence," Alexander said.

"Mrs. Peabody," someone else repeated.

"Make her count to one, two, pee," someone else said.

Her mind raced, her vision blurred, and her tiny second-grade hands curled up into tight fists.

"Stop it, everyone. That is not nice," Mrs. Lawrence said.

"But she peed all over the floor," Alexander replied.

"Don't make me do the Muffle Mouth punishment," Mrs. Lawrence threatened.

That should have been Lauren's cue to stop. The Muffle Mouth punishment was the most embarrassing thing a kid could go through, but right now, all she could see was Alexander's ugly face cupping a hand over his mouth and hissing through his fingers with laughter.

All of her pent up little-girl rage boiled inside her until it ripped from her throat in a shriek that could have rivaled scary movie scream queens. With all the strength Daddy used when he brought the belt down on her, she raised her fist and socked Alexander right in the eye. The kid fell to the floor, holding his face, and crying.

"Lauren!" Mrs. Lawrence cried. "My God!"

The teacher was much bigger and so much stronger than Lauren so when she grabbed her wrist and pulled, it practically yanked her off her feet. Lauren's shoes slid through her pee and then the teacher was lifting her up and over Alexander.

At the back of the classroom, there were two storage closets. One was the good one. It was the class store, filled with goodies. The second was the bad closet. Mrs. Lawrence reached into the closet, retrieved her giant roll of silvery grey duct tape, yanked off a large strip, ripped it off with her teeth, and then pulled it roughly across Lauren's mouth.

"I have never seen such bad behavior in all my life!" Mrs. Lawrence yelled. "You will never get another gold star from me young lady. First, you soil yourself and pour your disgusting urine all over the floor. Then you physically strike a classmate? You are a pitiful child, you little Muffle Mouth, you! You will stay here through lunch and remain here until your parents come to pick you up."

Mrs. Lawrence slammed the door shut, with the lights off, and left Lauren to sit in her pee-stained underwear and pants. She knew she needed to stop crying because tears only made her nose clog up and then she wouldn't be able to breathe very well. That's what happened to Peter Gibbs when he was a Muffle Mouth. Lauren didn't know Peter, but everyone heard the story. The kid almost died in this closet.

Lauren thought about removing the tape from her mouth, but she knew if Mrs. Lawrence came in to check on her she would be in even bigger trouble.

On the cold tile floor, Lauren lay down and rested her face against her folded arms. There, she cried herself to sleep, knowing her parents were going to be so angry with her.

Tonight was Friday and Daddy would put the belt on her for sure.

Lauren had to piss so bad. She'd been tied to this wheelchair for so long her ass and legs were going numb. As a kid, she had a problem with peeing herself whenever she got overly excited or nervous. Now, she refused to do it. Her father had put an end to her problem by beating it out of her one day when she'd gotten locked in the closet by her second-grade teacher.

Back then, teachers got away with unspeakable things. The principal himself would issue beatings with a giant ruler, and the parents had to sign a waiver allowing him to do it.

The music teacher used to grab students by their ear and lead them around the room if they weren't listening. She told them, "If you want to act like an animal, I'll put you on parade like one."

In high school, it was rumored the chemistry teacher was sleeping with one of his students. It was never proven, but he was asked to leave the school anyway. Less than a year later he married that student.

Things were fucked up back in the day.

Yet, not once had Lauren considered murdering any of her teachers. Thinking back on it now, she'd love to take a baseball bat to Mrs. Lawrence's head.

And be like these kids, Lauren? Do you have that inside you too?

The Maddening. These kids were following the message in some book, and it wasn't even a how-to manual or a self-help book. It was a novel. How did they get the message they should string up their teachers in a sadistic spelling bee?

Fuck, I really have to pee. Don't you do it, Lauren. Hold it.

She was tempted to bring it up, to tell Liz she needed to use the bathroom, but it felt wrong. She'd witnessed many of her colleagues hanged in front of her. Only two of the eight who'd gone up to the stage in the first place were still alive. Her need to piss didn't seem like a priority. She doubted Liz would allow her that small comfort anyway. Why would you let someone take a piss when you're planning to lob off their head anyway?

"Cut their ankle ropes," Liz ordered, "and the ties at their wrists. If any of them make a move, put a bullet in them."

Kent was back. He and some of the other boys cut the ropes off the ankles of Charlie and Joel.

"You know what? Cut them all free. They'll need their hands and feet for our next game. They'll need to be able to run," Liz said.

"Run, baby, run!" Kent hollered.

"We're clearing them out nicely," Scott said. "Right on time too."

"On time for what?" Lauren asked.

Liz shrugged her shoulders. "Wouldn't you like to know? Well, you'll find out soon enough, I suppose."

"How many teachers do we have left?" Scott asked.

Liz counted, saying the numbers so only she could hear as she turned to point at each remaining teacher. "Seven. Mr. Charlie's arrival has really fucked up our numbers, hasn't it. What to do? What to do?"

As she worked on a solution, the teachers were marched toward the basketball court. Their chairs were left behind. The ex-students strolled along both sides of them raising their weapons and blowing smoke into the air from vape pens and rolled joints.

Lauren couldn't help but be reminded of William Golding's *Lord of the Flies*. These kids were like the ones dancing around the fire with sharpened spikes, taking advantage of every second they didn't have to be under strict parental control or laws governed by their military school. Only instead of tribal-like weapons, these kids raised machetes, bats, pipes, guns, and knives.

"Are you okay?" she heard Charlie ask from behind her.

"I should be asking you that. I can't believe you volunteered—"

"—Shh. We don't have much time to waste. I don't suppose you have your phone on you."

She didn't. She was wearing a dress, so no pockets and her purse had been taken when she'd been knocked out after the toast.

"No," she said.

"Me neither," he replied. "They took it."

She knew. She'd seen them empty out his pockets. They'd taken his wallet and car keys too, all while he was knocked out.

The teenagers to their left and right chanted something in a foreign language. It sounded like Latin. Lauren imagined it was something they learned from playing a death metal record in reverse. Everything about this night screamed Satanic.

"Whatever this next game is," Charlie whispered, "this is when we have to make our move."

"What move?"

"I don't know yet, but at least we're not tied to those fucking chairs."

"They have guns."

"If we're going to be killed anyway then we have to at least try. We still have the strongest teachers. We might be able to overthrow them."

Lauren looked in front of her and saw Joel and Mr. Cole. Behind Charlie was Mr. Lafferty, Coach McCall and the psychology teacher, Ms. Paula Keen. There were only two female teachers left and Lauren was one of them. Charlie was right. The teachers who remained were the toughest in the bunch, but could they go up against the school's strongest students?

Slowing down so Charlie would be closer to her, Lauren said, "Maybe we should make a run for it now."

"No. They're on both sides of us. We wouldn't make it ten feet before we got stabbed or shot in the back."

He had a point. They were all riled up right now, chanting and jabbing sharp instruments into the air. They needed to be caught off guard if they were going to have any chance at getting away.

Over the green grass hills and through the playground they marched. One of the kids smacked a lead pipe against the monkey bars. Kent pushed the seesaw down and laughed, obviously remembering how he'd murdered his teacher crush. Lauren had never wished harm on any of her students, but tonight, she hoped that boy would die a horrible death for what he'd done. He didn't deserve to go home, kiss his mom on the cheek, and tell her about the great post-graduation party he'd enjoyed. Not with Mrs. Moreau's blood on his hands.

When they reached the basketball court, most of the ex-students made their way over to the metal bleachers and sat down. Only Liz, Scott, and Drew remained standing. The three formed a triangular shape around the teachers.

"Seven of you," Liz said. "Interesting. Well, since we know Mr. Charlie and Lauren here are fucking on the weekends, we might as well pair them up together. To help even the odds, we'll put Charlie on a team with our two ladies and weak-ass Mr. Lafferty. Lauren? Ms. Keen? Are you okay with that?"

Lauren refused to answer. Paula shrugged her shoulders.

"That puts you two young women with our youngest and oldest male teachers," Liz added. "So, you four against our two other old men and our suave Latin stud here."

The Latin stud she was talking about was Joel. The other two were Coach McCall and Mr. Cole. Their team consisted of a music teacher, who Charlie knew played soccer on the weekends, a physical education coach, and an ex-military physics teacher. Their four against these three still weren't great odds.

"We're going to play basketball?" Charlie asked.

"Right," Scott said. "That's all."

On the bleachers, a few of the ex-students laughed.

"Yep, that's all," someone called out.

So, that's not all.

Liz shook her head. "Hardly. You see, you can thank Coach McCall for this one. The school physical education teacher who wished so badly he was the basketball coach that he decided to punish the school and the *actual* team coach by making sure the star player was benched."

"I would never," Coach McCall argued.

"Fuck you, man," Drew shouted as he pounced forward and smashed his fist against the PE teacher's jaw.

Scott grabbed Drew's arm and pulled him back while the coach spit blood on the ground.

"It's kind of hard to get into a good college with a basketball scholarship," Liz said, "when you've rode the bench most of your twelfth-grade year."

"Ridden," Mr. Lafferty said.

Lauren couldn't believe her ears. Hadn't the grammar teacher learned anything by watching the spelling bee? Liz hanged the history teacher for correcting her in class. Now was not the time to teach past participles.

"Excuse me?" Liz asked.

"When you have ridden," Mr. Lafferty said, "not rode."

"Drew," Liz said.

Scott let the boy go and Drew once again launched himself forward, this time with a fist aimed directly at Mr. Lafferty's face. The older man was quicker than expected though and moved out of the way, sending Drew sliding across the floor.

"Whoa!" Roth stood up and yelled from the bleachers. "Holy shit! Mr. Lafferty's got skills. Can I kill him please?"

"Not yet," Liz said. "We have a game to play. Trust me; it'll be a lot funner if we watch him get his ass kicked in the game." She looked over at Mr. Lafferty, winked, and said, "Kidding. It's *more fun,* right?"

She'd stolen Mr. Lafferty's attention long enough for Drew to regain his footing and swing at the teacher once more. This time, he landed a powerful blow to the teacher's jaw, knocking it off kilter. His jaw went lopsided, dislocated, and Lauren almost threw up.

"Oh, my God," she said.

"Ugh," Mr. Lafferty moaned, unable to speak. He put a hand to his face and touched his jaw gingerly. Even the slightest touch made it move. Lauren thought of all the movies where someone only needed to pop a shoulder back into place. She wondered if that was the case with his jaw. From the look of it, it was beyond that. It was shattered.

"Well, this should make the game a lot more interesting," Liz said.

The kids seated on the bleachers laughed and pointed at the teacher. Mr. Lafferty turned toward Lauren with his mouth partially open. "Uh," he tried to speak again. The kids pointed at him and made fun of him. They chanted something in that foreign language again.

"How does it feel to be laughed at, motherfucker?" Roth yelled, antagonizing the teacher. "Remember how you used to call my attention in class? How you used to call on me when you knew I didn't know the fuckin' answer? How you'd call on somebody else to save me? To show how fuckin' dumb I was? Who's the dummy now, you piece of shit?"

So much rage. The other kids seemed to be energized by his outburst, motivated by it, like he was reminding them of why they were all here. They'd all been ridiculed in class.

"I was made fun of too!" Lauren yelled.

"Lauren, no," Charlie said.

"I was locked in a closet with duct tape over my mouth," she added.

The kids stopped chanting, laughing, and jeering. They actually seemed to be listening.

"I cried myself to sleep while my teacher continued on with the lesson on the other side of the door," she continued, "and then when I got home, my father beat the shit out of me as punishment for peeing my pants in class. But I didn't kill any of my teachers. This is wrong. You're becoming adults now. You're going to make mistakes. Like you have as children and teenagers. You'll make some as adults too. Like this. This is a big mistake. Nobody should be murdered for their wrongdoings."

They were silent. Liz had her head bowed. Drew stared at his feet. Scott looked over at the playground. She was getting to them. She was convincing them that they were wrong. This was their chance.

"I was a student too and a teacher did me so wrong. Our school principal used to beat us with a paddle, so I had no hope he'd save me. I cried myself to sleep, in a dark closet, with my mouth taped shut, soaked in my own piss. Only so I could go home and have my father beat me as punishment for being punished in class. Everyone was against me. So, I understand what you're going through. I feel your pain."

"Maybe she's right," Josie Simmons said, and that gave her hope. If she could reach one of them, she could reach them all.

"No," came a voice from behind her. It wasn't one she knew well, but one she'd heard before.

Lauren turned to see Mrs. Grainger, the little old librarian, walking through the playground and stepping through the darkness into the overhead lights of the basketball court. She didn't have a scratch on her. Her neck was fine. Her arms and legs were free of blood.

That's impossible. She got hacked up with a machete.

It made no sense.

"Surprised to see me?" Mrs. Grainger asked.

Applause went up from the bleachers. Students clapped, stomped their feet, and cheered her arrival.

24

CHARLIE

Like an angel of death stepping into the bright stadium lights, Mrs. Grainger moved toward them with those random patches of untamable hair jutting out like someone with serious bed head. Her lipstick was smudged and one of the lights cast an eerie glow around her that almost made her look demonic.

It didn't make sense. Seconds before, Lauren had seemed so close to reaching these kids, only to have that moment stolen away from one strange looking librarian who should have been dead. Charlie moved to Lauren's side. "What the fuck?"

Joel's mouth hung open in awe. "Impossible."

"I wasn't planning to make my grand re-appearance so soon," Mrs. Grainger said, "but I have to admit, your little speech was inspiring, and I couldn't have you swaying the minds of our tormented youth."

The old lady's eyes were locked on Lauren who said, "I don't understand."

"You're not supposed to, dear," Mrs. Grainger replied. "You see, we've been blessed with a visitor. A higher power, if you will. He watches over us all, keeps us safe from harm, and helps us find our way... but he can't do it all himself. There's that whole free will situation, and he can only provide the tools to help us see this through."

James Bender. She was talking about the demon boy. He was nowhere in sight, but Charlie knew he was out there in the darkness, watching their every move. His plan to escape suddenly seemed hopeless. *He* wouldn't let that happen.

"Liz has done a swell job of gathering like minds together," Mrs. Grainger continued, "but without a little bit of guidance, she would have been lost. I knew when I came across T.K. Tantrum's book that it wouldn't do much sitting on a dusty shelf. DS Publishing... DS High... the two seemed to be a match made in heaven... or hell. You choose. Do you know what the DS in DS Publishing stands for?"

Nobody answered.

"Why, Diablo Snuff Publishing, of course," she supplied the answer.

"Is that supposed to ring a bell or something?" Charlie asked.

"I highly doubt it," Mrs. Grainger replied.

"Of course," Lauren said. "Only the librarian could convince these kids to read."

"Is that an insult?" Liz asked.

"Ung," Mr. Lafferty moaned, and Charlie got the sense he was trying to warn her to shut up if she didn't want to end up like him.

"What do you plan to gain from this?" Charlie asked.

"The Maddening is coming," Mrs. Grainger said. "James Bender has shown us that. Humankind will once again be like it was in the beginning. Animals, beasts, completely uninhibited, totally untamed, and free to follow every impulse and instinct. It will be mad!"

Her voice rose with that last word and with it the applause of the crowd from the bleachers. Mrs. Grainger turned to her minions and put her hands on her hips, transmitting a power that seemed to flow from her onto them and then right back to her.

"The world won't understand what happened here tonight," she continued. "Not at first anyway, but they soon will. Liz and her friends will be heroes of horror, pioneers of pain, masters of mayhem—"

"—Knights of Nuisance," Charlie interrupted. "That's all you are. You're nothing more than misguided youth following the whims of a nutcase librarian."

"Drew," Liz said.

Drew looked at Charlie. It was clear he didn't want to punch his teacher. Charlie had been hit many times growing up. He was no stranger to a sucker punch, so he knew he could handle one that was expected.

"Drew," Liz repeated with raised eyebrows.

"Sorry, Mr. Charlie," Drew said.

Drew swung at the teacher's head, and Charlie tilted his face at the right moment, causing the kid's fist to collide with his forehead. He heard the hand crunch and knew he'd broken it. Drew howled in pain and Charlie winced through his. The boy could hit hard and probably would have broken his jaw if he'd remained upright.

"Clearly, you're letting this one get away with too much," Mrs. Grainger said.

"You can't strike people and expect them not to strike back," Joel said.

Scott pistol whipped him across the mouth. Joel grunted with the hit, and then spit up blood.

"Please, stop," Paula begged.

She was the psychology teacher, and Charlie wondered if there was anything in the textbooks that would help explain the things going on tonight. Was it mass hysteria? Liz, the librarian, or the demon boy having a God complex? He imagined this group ran the gamut. Everything in that damn book could be used to describe these insane bastards.

"Everyone just shut up," Mr. Cole ordered.

The old man had given up. Charlie had never seen him looking so weak. His shoulders were slumped, the crow's feet at his eyes seemed much larger than usual, and he breathed heavy sighs.

"Let's get this over with," he added. "I want to see Dawn again."

Mrs. Lowell. He really did love her, didn't he?

Mrs. Grainger smiled and walked toward the bleachers, calling out over her shoulder, "I think I'll take a seat. Liz, please go on with the game."

"Of course," Liz said, clapping her hands together and keeping them clasped as she eagerly retook hold of the reins. "What I was getting at before Lauren decided to try and brainwash us all with stories of pissing on herself and sleeping in closets, was this will be much more than a basketball game. We'll call this Dodge Basketball."

"Hell yeah!" Gavin yelled.

"This is gonna be a fuckin' riot!" Roth cheered.

"Dodge Basketball," Charlie repeated.

What the fuck are we going to be dodging?

"The object of the game," Drew took over, while clutching his now broken hand, "is to put the ball in the hoops."

Roth produced a ball and tossed it toward his friend. It bounced a few times as it made its way over and Drew had to stop it from rolling away with his foot. He bent over, picked it up, and dribbled it a couple of times with his good hand.

"Sounds easy enough, right, Coach McCall?" Drew asked.

When the coach didn't respond, Scott pointed his gun at him. "Don't be rude."

"Yeah," the coach said, "yeah, sounds easy enough."

"Ready for the fun part?" Scott asked. He turned his attention to the bleachers and asked again, "Are *you* ready for the fun part?"

Their answer came in a loud cheer. They yelled things like:

"Fuck yeah!"

"Do it!"

"This is gonna be lit!"

"Fucking do it!"

Charlie wanted to knock that smug grin off Scott's face. This was one of those kids who'd never suffered a difficult day in his life. If he could only get that gun away from him, he'd knock him down and pummel that goofy face of his.

"And the fun part is," Liz said. "Go ahead. Tell 'em Scotty."

"Coach McCall, you know how we always played shirts versus skins in class?" Scott asked.

The school had since banned that practice in favor of having some kids wear cheap jerseys instead of removing their shirts, but Charlie was well aware of what he was talking about.

"Of course," the coach answered.

"Well…" Scott said, leaving the end off so they could guess the rest.

"You're not serious," Paula said, figuring out where they were going with this.

"Yep," Liz said. "And for the pleasure of the crowd, your team gets to be skins."

"No," Lauren said.

"No?" Liz asked.

"Liz," Lauren replied.

"Those are the rules," Liz said. "Follow them and you may live through this. Don't and you die."

Charlie had seen what could happen mid-game. The rules were subject to change. Liz didn't like losing and if it looked like things weren't going the way she wanted, she had no problem with switching things up at the last second.

"Okay, Mr. Charlie, Ms. Peony, Ms. Keen, and Mr. Lafferty… strip," Scott instructed.

Mr. Lafferty didn't argue. He unbuttoned his dress shirt easily but then hollered in pain as he pulled the collar of his crew-neck undershirt over his broken jaw.

"Oh, that had to hurt," Scott antagonized him.

Charlie followed the older teacher's lead and did the same, removing his outer shirt and the tank top he wore beneath. He tossed them both off to the side. Lauren hesitated. So did Paula. It wouldn't be so easy for them. They both wore dresses.

"Paula, come on," Scott said, stepping closer to her and pressing his body against her.

Liz laughed. "That's right. You were trying to fuck my boyfriend earlier."

"I wasn't," Paula said.

"Your boyfriend?" Scott asked.

"Scotty, don't make me regret saying that," Liz replied.

"Yeah," Scott agreed, "she totally wanted my dick. A few more drinks and I think she might have blown me right there on that park bench."

"Go fuck yourself," Paula said.

"Take off your dress," Liz ordered.

Paula refused.

"Scotty," Liz said.

Scott pointed his gun at the counselor's feet and pulled the trigger. The shot echoed through the open-space arena and a ping of dust popped off the concrete basketball court next to her shoe.

"Okay!" Paula screamed, tears running down her face as she pulled off her dress, exposing the red lace bra and matching panties she had on underneath.

"Bra too," Liz said. "I said shirts versus skins. Not shirts versus bras."

Scott pointed his gun at her again. This time he didn't need to pull the trigger. She removed her bra and let it fall to her feet with her dress. She covered her small breasts with her arms and shivered in the night air.

Lauren must have decided she didn't want to leave the other woman standing there alone like that because she suddenly yanked her dress over her head and unclasped her bra. She bent over to pick up Paula's clothes and then stepped closer to the side of the court and tossed them near Charlie's shirt.

Charlie felt his breath catch in his chest. This wasn't the time to be admiring her beauty, and this wasn't how he expected to see her like this for the first time, but he found himself gawking at her the same way the kids were. She stepped toward the bleachers and spread her arms wide, her back to Charlie, but he could imagine the eyeful they were getting. Her big, beautiful breasts were on full display.

"Do you like what you see?" Lauren asked.

"Damn, baby," Roth yelled. "Lookin' fine, but the granny panties gotta go."

"I knew you had a rockin' fuckin' bod," Tom, the crystal meth dealer said. "You have any idea how many times I've jerked it to thoughts of you?"

The kids around him laughed.

"You too?" Gavin asked, even now the class clown.

"Laugh it up," Lauren said, "this might be the only time you get to see a real woman."

"Liz's are better," Scott said.

"Aww thanks, baby," the bitch replied.

"Don't act like pigs," Josie Simmons told the kids seated around her.

"Fuck off, nerd," Roth replied.

Josie kept her mouth shut. Lauren turned back to Charlie and for the first time, he got a really good look at her. Again, he found it hard to breathe. Finally, Paula let her arms fall too and hers were smaller, perkier. Charlie looked down at his own body and despised his man boobs. He wasn't overweight, but he didn't do enough pushups to keep himself in great shape. He was flabby in all the wrong places. Mr. Lafferty, even at his older age, had a nicer chest than he did.

"Lookin' good, Mr. Charlie!" Valerie Kemper teased. She was lying, of course. She was the hottest girl in school. He'd always found his way with girls in his youth, but never with one like her. She was only messing with him.

"Make them take off their pants too!" Amber yelled.

Charlie was so tempted to yell something mean back like, "Maybe if you stopped saying that, you wouldn't get knocked up."

Yet, even now, when he hated every single one of these kids, he couldn't bring himself to be the bully. He couldn't say anything so hateful, so spiteful. The girl had gotten pregnant because she'd fucked her boyfriend at the time. How many other teenagers did the same thing but didn't end up with a baby? It wasn't her fault. Well, not *only* her fault.

"Yeah, pants too!" the girl with the roach clips in her hair yelled.

"Hear that?" Liz asked. "Seems your fans want to see a bit more."

"We won't be able to play basketball—" Charlie began but was cut off.

"—Dodge Basketball," Scott reminded him.

"Dodge Basketball," he corrected himself. "We won't be able to play Dodge Basketball, whatever the fuck that is, if we don't have any pants on."

"Oh, I think you'll manage," Liz said. "Pants off, please. Underwear too."

"You're going too far!" Mr. Cole yelled and stepped toward Liz with his hands up.

Scott must have taken it as a sign of aggression because he pointed his gun at the teacher's thigh and pulled the trigger. The gun cracked through the air again and the bullet slammed into his leg. Blood sprayed out the back as the bullet continued through, hit the ground, and disappeared into the night.

Mr. Cole screamed in agony and fell to the ground, clutching his leg. Blood spread out beneath him and he began to shake, probably more from fear or shock than from anything else.

"Fuck, Scott!" Charlie yelled as he bent over and pressed his hand against the wound. "What the fuck is wrong with you?"

"Take your fucking pants off!" Liz yelled.

Charlie looked back at the bleachers and watched as Mrs. Grainger shrugged her shoulders, palms up, as if to say, "Better do what they tell you."

"You want my pants off?" Charlie asked. He dropped his pants, making sure his fingers hooked the waistband of his boxers, so they'd come off too. His cock hung freely. "There you go." He pulled his shoes off only long enough to remove his pants and underwear. Then he slid his feet back into them.

He felt like a lunatic standing stark naked in a pair of dress shoes.

The girls in the audience cheered. Valerie Kemper's mouth hung open. The girl with the roach clips in her hair clapped. Josie Simmons turned away. Liz whistled.

"Gotta be honest with you, Mr. Charlie," Valerie said, "I thought you'd be bigger."

That was the problem with TV and the pornos these kids probably watched. Everyone was huge. Charlie was average in size, and standing in the cool basketball court, with all these people gaping at him was definitely causing shrinkage.

"Guess he's a grower," Amber joked.

Laugh it up. Keep the jokes coming.

Lauren and Paula pulled their panties off. They'd share the ridicule now. Both women had worn shoes that wouldn't be very useful in this game, so they kicked them away, opting to go barefoot.

Charlie respectfully kept his attention away from them. He hadn't meant to gape at their breasts in the first place. Now that he had his wits about him, he could keep his eyes averted. When he looked back at Mr. Lafferty, he too had dropped his pants and underwear.

"Isn't it interesting how this was the way *your* God wanted you to be?" Mrs. Grainger asked. "Stark naked, playing hide and seek in a garden, innocent and naïve? When you think about it, we're only bringing you back to the basics."

"You should come join us," he said.

The librarian scoffed. "You wish."

"Someone might want to help Mr. Cole," Liz said. "A bullet in the leg is no excuse for breaking the rules."

Nobody moved.

"Scott, put another bullet in him," she ordered.

"No!" Charlie yelled as he scurried over to Mr. Cole's side.

"I'm okay," Mr. Cole assured him. "Just help me up. I can play."

Joel and Coach McCall helped him lift Mr. Cole back to his feet.

"Look at the two teams working together," Liz said. "How sweet. Oh, I almost forgot. The *dodge* part of the Dodge Basketball. Tom, is your brother ready?"

"Yep," Tom replied.

At the bleachers, Tom was helping a grown man make his way to the top row. The guy held a rifle in his hand. Where he'd come from, Charlie wasn't sure. He'd been too preoccupied with the bloody mess that was Mr. Cole.

"Have you met Blind Terry?" Liz asked.

Charlie hadn't and he doubted the other teachers had.

"Terry Boyle?" Coach McCall asked.

"Bingo," Scott said.

"Yes," Liz said. "Guess Mr. Timms was right about one thing.

Some of us would graduate and work in fast food. Not that there's anything wrong with that. That's what Terry did. Freak accident, slipped on the floor and fell face first into hot oil, blinded him. So, we call him Blind Terry. He's cool with it. Got a pretty big settlement so he lives like a king even if he can't see shit."

"He can listen though," Scott said. "Tom read *The Maddening* to him and needless to say, he liked what he heard. Society treats him like shit every day. This is his chance to fling a little bit of shit himself. He was all for helping us out tonight. Was kind of pissed Mr. Timms is dead already, but hey, maybe he'll get to kill one of you."

"Let us know when he's ready!" Liz called out.

"Oh, he's ready," Tom yelled.

"I'm ready," Blind Terry replied.

Ready for what?

Charlie looked once again at the rifle in the man's hand. They couldn't be planning what he thought they were.

"Don't shoot until Drew blows the whistle!" Liz instructed.

"Got it," Blind Terry said.

"We're dodging bullets?" Charlie asked.

"Fuckin' ridiculous, isn't it?" Scott replied.

"Oh my God," Paula cried.

"You can't be serious," Lauren said.

"I'm *dead* serious," Liz replied. "When Drew blows that whistle, the game begins. Shirts versus skins, with a blind man's bullets flying down range at you."

"This is insane," Charlie said.

"We'll all die," Joel added.

"Not if you're lucky," Liz said. "Come on, guys. You can do it. After all, he *is* blind."

She walked away from the court and sat down. Drew and Scott followed, sitting between her and Mrs. Grainger. Then Drew blew the whistle.

25

LAUREN

Drew blew the whistle, and with it came the first gunshot. Everyone yelled or screamed but nobody howled in pain, so Lauren knew the bullet had missed. They couldn't remain in the same position though.

"Forgot to give you the ball!" Drew yelled. He tossed it onto the court and Joel scooped it up.

"Are we seriously playing this?" Lauren asked.

"If you don't play," Scott warned, "those of us with eyes will start shooting too."

Joel moved down the court, dribbling the ball, picking the side of the court that would be his team's hoop for the game since none had been established beforehand.

"Over here!" Coach McCall yelled.

Joel passed it to him, and Charlie ran between the two men, swiping the ball out of thin air and turning toward his hoop. Lauren wasn't sure whether to cheer or not. To make it back to the side they needed to score on meant crossing that middle mark where she assumed Blind Terry would be more likely to hit his target.

Charlie seemed to have realized this too as he slowed down for a second.

This entire game was ludicrous. Charlie was completely naked, except for his shoes, dribbling a basketball with his dick hanging there for everyone to see. Behind her, on the bleachers, the kids cheered, and she knew it didn't matter to them which team won. She wasn't even sure what would happen to the losing team, but she knew it wouldn't be good. These kids might dip them in a vat of acid.

For a moment, she focused on some of the faces and cringed at what she saw. Mouths open so wide in shouts that teeth were visible. They were frantic beasts, an angry mob, the crowd at the Roman Coliseum witnessing the bloody gladiator games. One boy beat his chest like *King Kong*. Another looked at her, winked, and humped the air. Some of them shook clenched fists in the air and screamed up at the sky like they were possessed.

Are they possessed?

She'd never considered that possibility before. What if the demon that was James Bender had done something to them? Even after all she'd seen, she couldn't believe that. James hadn't sent monsters from hell into their bodies. This was something that had been there all along. It had been growing. She'd seen flashes of it every year she taught. The book, *The Maddening*, only ignited that fuel bubbling up inside them. They were on fire now and there was no putting it out.

"Lauren, dammit!" Charlie yelled.

She'd zoned out, but she was back. Charlie had tried to pass her the ball, but she hadn't been paying attention. Coach McCall ran at his back and was dangerously close to stealing the ball.

"Charlie!" she yelled.

He noticed the coach heading his way and passed it to her. She caught it and dribbled. She'd played basketball in her youth but hadn't tried the sport in a long time. It showed in the sloppy way she handled the ball, but at least the coach hadn't gotten to it.

"Lauren!" Mr. Lafferty yelled.

She was about to pass him the ball when another shot from the rifle rang out. Nobody was hit, but she flinched and dropped the ball. Mr. Cole, who hadn't been doing anything but standing in one place collecting a giant puddle of blood at his feet, was the closest and picked it up as it bounced his way.

Mr. Lafferty ran at the statuesque old man and stole the ball from him, knocking him down in the process. Mr. Cole cried out in pain and toppled over, but the grammar teacher didn't even look back at him. He was hell-bent on getting the ball into the hoop. He might have succeeded too if it weren't for the next bullet whizzing through the air.

It caught him in the middle of his chest, driving him backward through the air and then sending him skidding across the ground. The old man coughed up blood. The basketball rolled away from the court and into the playground.

"You hit him!" Tom announced proudly.

The crowd cheered.

Mr. Lafferty didn't move. He lay on his back, coughing up blood until even that was too difficult. Then his head fell lifelessly to the side.

"I can't believe you fucking hit him!" Tom yelled. "I knew you still had it in you!"

The double click of the gun being cocked told Lauren to duck, but the shot missed her completely. It went unanswered, but it was enough to get her feet moving again. She hadn't even realized she'd stopped in the first place. She'd been glued in place watching the old man die.

"Keep playing!" Scott yelled.

Charlie ran out to pick up the ball. He was making his way back to the court when Blind Terry pulled the trigger again. The bullet pinged off something metallic. He cocked it and fired again, then again, and again. Lauren looked back and saw that his brother was helping him reload so he could shoot faster.

She didn't see how it happened, but when she looked back toward Charlie, she saw that Joel now had the ball and was running to the opposite hoop.

"Give me it, dammit, you're missing everyone," Lauren heard Tom say.

Joel was racing across the court, so close to tossing up the ball when his right knee exploded.

"Joel!" she screamed.

"You're breaking the rules!" Liz yelled up at Tom who obviously didn't give a shit about the game. He wanted to kill the teachers.

Charlie slammed into Lauren, tackling her to the ground as a bullet flew past her head and blew a chunk of concrete off the ground.

"My leg!" Joel screamed, and it was the last thing he got out before the next bullet struck his skull, blowing through his forehead and out the other side.

Blood showered the ground behind him.

Lauren watched in horror as bullets rained down on them, tearing into each of the teachers around her.

The next bullet hit Mr. Cole who was sitting up, trying to get back to his feet. It opened his neck and threw him back to the ground.

Paula screamed and caught the next round in the gut.

By this point, Scott had stood up with Liz and they were yelling at Tom who'd stopped firing long enough to yell back. It was an all-out verbal war back and forth between the kids. Some sided with Tom and wanted to see all the teachers slaughtered. Others wanted to see the game played out and were upset by the interruption.

"You can't cheat!" Gavin yelled.

"This game is bullshit," Alan, the boy who'd been falsely accused of stabbing Mrs. Lowell's nephew cried. "You want to play a real game, let's go in there and stab 'em all."

"The rules are there for a reason!" Scott yelled.

"Everyone calm down!" Mrs. Grainger demanded.

"Shut the fuck up, bitch," Tom replied.

"Don't talk to her like that," Liz yelled.

"What made you the leader of us all anyway?" Tom asked.

"Let's just kill them all," Kent said.

"You're all acting crazy!" Josie Simmons declared.

Everyone spoke at once and nobody would shut up. They were out of control.

Coach McCall was the only other teacher still standing. He was on all fours crawling toward the darkness of the playground.

"This is it," Charlie whispered to her. "We go now, or we don't make it out of here at all. They're distracted."

She knew he was right. This was their only chance. So, they ran.

26

CHARLIE

Charlie knew they only had half a minute at the most before the kids realized they were making a run for it. Coach McCall had crawled toward the playground, so he knew he and Lauren needed to go the opposite direction, to spread out the teenagers and force them to choose which way to go.

With no chance to scoop up their clothes, and no time to put them on anyway, Charlie and Lauren ran completely naked through the park. Behind him, he heard the teenagers arguing.

"Fuck you!" somebody yelled. It sounded like Tom.

"Fuck me? Fuck you!" another boy replied. Scott.

Then bullets exploded from two different guns, and the screams were almost as loud. Had they turned on each other? Would it be that simple? Would these kids tear each other apart?

"This way," Lauren whispered as she led him toward the boardwalk maze he'd been so terrified of earlier this night.

If he'd only known of the horrors that awaited him where he'd thought he'd be safe. If he'd had any idea what was in store for him, he would have returned to his car and called the cops. If he hadn't been in love with Lauren, he might have listened to Bogdan in the first place and stayed at the *other* party.

The *other* party. It seemed like so long ago that he'd sat across from Rebecca and flirted innocently with her. Dropping her off at her apartment with the promise to return seemed like a whole different night. It couldn't have been earlier this evening.

"We have to get to my car," Charlie told her.

"The gate's locked," she said. "I saw the boys lock it up."

"What boys?" he asked.

"I haven't seen them," she said, "not since... okay be quiet. Jerome and Brandon are around somewhere. We can't go to your car. They'll be watching the exit."

More gunshots sounded off behind them. They were far away.

"Are they killing each other?" he whispered.

"I hope so," she replied. "I hope they destroy each other. I hope they shoot that librarian right between her ugly fucking eyes."

She was so gruesome, and Charlie couldn't blame her. He felt the exact same way. They would make it to his car and drive straight to the police, and he hoped when the cops arrived at the park, there wasn't enough of them left to identify one from the other. They deserved that much. They deserved the worst deaths possible.

He suddenly regretted the amount of time and effort he put into teaching them. Guilt drove through his entire body at the thought of not getting an invitation because he was one of the *good* teachers. Especially when some of the things that made the *bad* teachers deserving of violent deaths were things like keeping a kid with subpar grades from playing on the basketball team or telling a student she had the wrong answer or even explaining to a student's father that he was misbehaving in class.

Over dinner, he'd tried to convince Lauren that their students were good kids and she'd see that eventually. He'd told her they were only going through a phase in life and that they'd eventually realize how shitty they behaved. None of that was true. Not with these kids. He'd been wrong.

This was the way of our world now. Kids were walking into schools armed to the teeth and unleashing hell on their classmates because they'd gotten bullied or weren't invited to parties or felt like an outsider. They felt they were owed something.

Maybe Mrs. Grainger and these kids aren't wrong about this Maddening. It's already happening. This world is losing its fucking mind.

"This way," Lauren said as she tugged his hand and pulled him down a path that led right.

"How do you know where you're going?"

"I used to play here all the time as a kid. It's easy to get lost if you don't know the way."

"Good."

"No, please!" Coach McCall screamed, followed by the blast of a gun so loud it scattered the sleeping birds in the trees.

"They're not fighting anymore," Lauren said.

That meant either some of them, the ones opposing the victors, were dead, or the kids had settled their differences. Charlie hoped it was the former because at least that would mean there were less of them to deal with. Even now, after all he'd endured, he hoped Josie Simmons was among the living. She'd seemed out of place the entire evening. They'd never heard her story. Why was she even here? Who had wronged her to the point she felt the need to have them killed?

"Walk softer," Lauren whispered.

He hadn't realized he'd been stomping, but she was right, he needed to be as quiet as possible.

"Ow, fuck," she swore under her breath as she swatted at her neck.

The bugs were out tonight and with them both stripped bare, they were like a Thanksgiving feast. Seconds after her attack, he felt the familiar sting of a mosquito on his chest. Instinctively, his hand dropped and covered his more delicate parts.

"Where are we going?" he asked.

"I know a way out of here. Or, at least I hope I do. If it still exists."

"Ohhhh Mr. and Mrs. Charlie," Liz's voice sang out to them from somewhere along the boardwalk.

She could have been standing at the entrance to the dark forest maze or only twenty yards away. It was so hard to tell in this place. Everything echoed.

Something rippled the water beneath the boards where they stood, and Charlie jumped. He couldn't see a thing out here, and his mind started messing with him. A splash in the water below them startled him again.

"What is that?" he whispered.

"Don't worry. It's nothing."

"Nothing?"

"Could be a croc. I don't know."

She didn't seem the least bit perturbed by this. As if she was used to spending her evenings walking above monstrous reptiles lurking below her feet.

"Ohhhh Mr. and Mrs. Charlie," Liz called out again. "Where are you?"

"You know you can't escape this way, right?" someone else yelled.

It was a man's voice, but it didn't sound like Scott's. It could have been Tom. Both boys were as wicked as they come, but Charlie felt slightly less threatened by Scott. At least he followed the orders of his girlfriend where Tom seemed to want to kill them all and put an end to this party.

Party. A Grad Night party. You had to seek an invitation. If you hadn't wanted one so bad, you'd be home in bed right now.

And Lauren would be dead. There wasn't a doubt in his mind. He hadn't exactly saved her life, but if he weren't here earlier, she might have gotten dragged onto that stage for the spelling bee. If she'd gotten even one letter wrong, she would have been hanged. Even after that, there were several times he'd reminded her to calm down when it was clear her temper was flaring. Then, on the basketball court, he'd convinced her it was time to make a run for it. She would be dead right now, if it weren't for him. He'd come to this party for a reason, and he needed to make sure she survived the night.

"Shh," Lauren said, putting a hand against his chest and stopping him from moving forward.

They stood in the deep darkness. There was no sound except for their breathing. No bugs chirped. The wind didn't even blow through the trees. All was completely silent. Too quiet.

THUD... THUD... THUD...

Heavy footsteps slammed against the wooden boardwalk as someone raced down a path too close for comfort. For a second, Charlie thought it was coming right at them, but then it faded off in the opposite direction.

Then the heavy running came again, but this time on the other side of them. Charlie didn't know how many paths zipped back and forth across this swamp, but he knew there couldn't be enough to keep them hidden forever.

THUD... THUD... THUD...

Feet slammed against the boardwalk, this time up ahead of them, as if the person had come all the way around from an adjoining trail and would bump right into them at any second.

Lauren's lips touched his ear and she whispered, "We need to get in the water."

Oh, hell no. Fuck that. No fucking way.

Charlie wasn't a pussy, but who knew what was in that water? It could be a crocodile or one of a hundred different kinds of snakes. Venomous or not, he didn't want one anywhere near him. And he'd seen movies where certain underwater creatures could swim right up your dick hole.

"No," he whispered back.

"It's the only way."

Fuck... fuck... fuck...

He knew he had no choice.

27

LAUREN

She'd seen things in these waters as a kid. Usually the local wildlife services would swoop in and escort animals out of the park if and when the need arose, but from the looks of it, the park hadn't been kept in tip-top shape the way it had when she was a child. Anything could be in the water. She wasn't joking with Charlie when she said it could be a croc. This wasn't the time for practical jokes.

But, like she'd told that little girl, Courtney, so long ago, she believed this forest would take care of her. She didn't know why. It was a feeling she'd had since a child. She knew, deep down, that she wasn't in danger from the park or its many different creatures. After all, she'd fed them Goldfish crackers.

You can do this. You're safe. You have to believe you're safe.

More than likely if anything large inhabited this area it would be an alligator since they preferred freshwater environments, and Lauren wasn't sure where this body of water connected. If it connected to anything at all. She'd seen snakes on its muddy banks, but she didn't know if they were poisonous. As a kid, she used to pretend she fed water moccasins so they wouldn't leap out of the water and bite her face whenever she leaned over the boardwalk railings. They were as common to the Florida lakes as barracudas in the Fort Lauderdale intercoastal.

Charlie clearly wasn't going to enter the water first, so she took it upon herself to be the brave one, climbing her naked body over the wooden railing and down the other side. She let the toes of one foot touch the water first. She cupped a hand over her mouth to stop the "whoop" that nearly slipped out of her mouth. The water was freezing.

Footsteps approached slowly from ahead of them, the darkness hiding whoever was heading their way.

With a sudden, terror-filled new sense of urgency, Charlie threw a leg over the banister and climbed down beside her.

"Humph," he said quietly as his feet touched the water.

Slowly, Charlie. Very slowly.

Any loud ripple of water or violent *kerplunk* would key the kids in on their location.

Kids. These aren't kids. They're the Children of the fucking Corn.

Lauren's thighs lowered into the water and she was hesitant to sink any deeper, afraid of what might be beneath that dark pool's surface. Scared of what kind of strange creature might come and nibble at her lady parts, snack on her labia. She imagined Charlie was suffering the same fear. She couldn't help the mental image of a long black snake opening its mouth wide and clamping down on the man's flaccid cock.

Thank God for cold-water shrinkage. Maybe that will save him.

Beside her, Charlie had lowered himself into the water, all the way to his waist. Panic set in and he tried to pull himself out, his arms not strong enough to yank him clear of the water. His head jerked from side to side like a child refusing to take a bath. Something must have touched him beneath the water to illicit this reaction.

She touched the top of his head to calm him down and then pushed firmly against it, telling him nonverbally that he needed to man-up and get in the water. To drive home the point, she lowered herself all the way to neck deep beside him. Her feet touched the muddy ground below, toes sinking into the slimy lake floor.

Her mind played tricks on her. Suddenly, below the water, there were giant cockroach-like creatures combing the floor for food, their antennae brushing the top of her foot, finding exactly what they wanted to eat.

Piranhas with razor-sharp teeth swam around them, trying to figure out what the cockroaches had discovered. Was it meat? They were more interested in the body heat emanating from her core, traveling through the water on an invisible ribbon of warmth coming straight out of her pussy and toward whatever's feelers were in close proximity.

Charlie would piss himself in the water. She was almost certain of this fact. That slowly spreading radius of hot urine would attract new visitors. Snakes of all shapes, sizes, colors, and textures. They were slithering around them right now.

The underwater pressure of something swimming too close for comfort pushed against her nipples and she knew it was a snake.

Dear God. No. Please. We've been through so much.

She whimpered and Charlie reached out to her. Only she wasn't expecting it because she couldn't see beneath the dark water's surface. When his fingers touched her hip, she squealed. Her eyes shot open as she realized what she'd done. She cupped her hand over her mouth and trembled, her shaky breath hot against her clasped fingers.

Charlie's hand reached out to her above the surface and grabbed her free hand.

"Did you hear that?" someone yelled. "I think they're over here!"

With their hands linked, Lauren led him toward the boardwalk and under it. Together in the darkness, Charlie pulled her body close to his. Her breasts pressed against his chest and, even though it wasn't the moment for a romantic encounter, she felt a slight twinge of wanting. If this were happening under any other circumstance, she would kiss him. His forehead leaned forward and touched hers. She placed her toes on top of his shoes to get her feet out of the slimy mud and to raise up to his height.

She was naked. She was with a man she'd secretly wanted for a long time. And she was terrified.

Something under the water nibbled at her leg. Her jaw clenched and she shivered, doing her best to keep her teeth from chattering. The slightest puff of breath seeped from her chest, up her throat, and past her lips. It cut through the silence and was astonishingly loud.

"They're around here somewhere," a male's voice said. "I swear I heard them."

Footsteps made their way toward them overhead. Grains of dirt and pieces of clumped up soil scattered around them with each heavy thud of the boots above. Whoever it was stood right over their heads and Lauren couldn't hold her whimper in anymore. She'd been tucking her breath deep in her chest for too long, so long that she knew when she exhaled it would come out too loud.

Charlie must have sensed her fear. She couldn't see him, but she felt him when he mashed his lips against hers and slid his tongue into her mouth, kissing her with a deep-seated passion that didn't belong in this moment, but that she'd readily accept if it kept her mind off the murderous teenagers looming above. He pulled her body tighter against him and gripped the back of her head the way a real man does when he's claiming his woman.

She knew what this was. She wasn't an idiot.

This was him accepting his fate. He knew there was a good chance they wouldn't get out of this alive, and he wasn't going to let himself die without letting her know how badly he wanted her. She'd sensed it in him lately. She knew he was infatuated with her, but she'd never allowed herself to open up and give in to her own desires. She'd been too afraid of the men from her past. None of them had treated her right.

And now that she'd found one who might be able to pull it off, they were both about to die.

The footsteps continued past them, and their owner sighed in frustration. The whoosh of what could have been a machete blade cutting through the air sounded off, followed by, "Where the fuck are they?" spoken through gritted teeth.

Lauren finally let her breath seep out past Charlie's lips. She was about to pull away when she decided, "fuck it," and kissed him again. If this was going to be her last, she wanted to relish in it a little longer. It wasn't like it was safe for them to go anywhere.

When the moment died down, she rested her head against his

shoulder, and they stayed that way awhile, both lost in a blackwater slow dance to no music. If she'd been able to choose a soundtrack song for right now, she'd pick something too cheesy. It would probably be something the students hunting them would consider a forgotten classic but wasn't much older than they were. Maybe a Mariah Carey ballad or even something from further back in time, like a Firehouse tune or that song by Winger.

"Are we going to die tonight?" she whispered into his ear.

"No," he said. "You're going to show me that way out."

"Maybe we could just stay here. What if we don't move until sunrise?"

It was a safe bet. If they remained hidden in the water that long, the students would undoubtedly believe they'd escaped over the fence.

"I like that idea," he replied.

"Gotcha," a gruff voice said, and then strong fingers gripped her hair, dug all the way to the roots, and pulled her back and away from Charlie.

"Lauren!" he yelled.

"Found 'em!" Tom yelled, and out of the corner of her eye she could see him reaching around from the topside of the boardwalk. He'd sprawled out on his belly and was holding Lauren by her scalp.

"Get them up here," a calm voice said. It sounded like Liz. "We need to hurry up and finish this. The sun will be rising soon, and we have a lot of cleaning up to do. Besides, it's almost time for our last game."

Charlie swatted at the hand holding her, but then Kent leaned over the opposite side with a gun of his own. A pistol like the one Scott was holding earlier. "I wouldn't do that if I were you. Get out of the water, you fucking douche."

28

CHARLIE

She hadn't bothered to wipe her face. Liz's forehead, cheeks, and chin were specked with blood. Her hair was matted with it. Whatever transpired after Charlie and Lauren fled was gruesome. How many of them survived? Only three were here now. Tom, who held them at gunpoint, had his face slathered in what Charlie thought was mud at first, but once he stepped into the moonlight he realized was blood. He wore it proudly, like war paint. Streaks from two fingers decorated his cheeks while a long smear ran across his forehead.

Kent handed his gun to Liz, who passed a baseball bat his way. He was relatively clean, slapping the end of the baseball bat against his empty palm. He was itching to hit them both. The boy seemed to have found his *true* self tonight. He'd never been a particularly violent kid, as far as Charlie knew, but he was now. A switch had been flipped in him the second he killed Mrs. Moreau.

"Keep looking at me like that, fucker," Kent threatened.

"This isn't you, Kent," Charlie replied. "I've taught you. You're a good kid."

"Shut up, Charlie," he warned. "Don't give me a reason to bash in that skull of yours."

He didn't need any more reason than he already had. All the

teachers were dead now. All but Lauren and him. For the first time since running away from the basketball court, Charlie let that sink in. He'd been too afraid before. Only escape seemed important. Now, he imagined Joel's face and all the time they'd spent confiding in each other. He was Charlie's only friend. He was gone now.

"You killed Joel," Charlie whispered.

"Are you done whining now?" Liz asked.

She was as heartless as a person could be, and that wasn't because her dad had cheated on her mom with Mrs. Laymon. It wasn't because her mom drank too much or treated Liz like shit. Plenty of kids grew up with parents who neglected them, and they didn't turn out like this. She was pure evil. Her eyes simmered with it. She was enjoying this. Tom was just as bad.

Kent too. His eyes were blank, and his mouth drooped open. Charlie recognized that look. It was the one Private Pyle wore in the movie *Full Metal Jacket.* That demented, irrational haze that replaced the Marine's simple-minded persona, making him certifiably nuts. This park setting was Kent's latrine scene, and he was more than willing to swing that heavy club. With all his weight behind it, he could do some real damage. The only thing holding him back was Liz, who held a higher position in their degenerate chain of command.

This wasn't the same kid who'd sat in his class and complained about the reading selection with every new book. Even when Charlie tried to introduce something they might actually enjoy like Joseph Conrad's *Heart of Darkness* or Richard Connell's *The Most Dangerous Game,* the boy cringed and asked if they could read something fun. Unwilling to assign these twelfth graders pornography, Charlie had to finally understand that this boy was not going to find joy in reading.

Charlie diverted his stare and thought about his class reading material. He'd tried so hard to please his students. As he considered the list of stories he'd introduced, he couldn't help feeling like perhaps he'd played a part in tonight's monstrosities. Most were about the madness of men and overcoming the obstacles, hardships, and horrors of life.

"The most dangerous game," Charlie said to himself.

They were playing it now. The park was the island, the students were General Zaroff, and the teachers were Rainsford. *He* was partially responsible for tonight. Charlie may have been the one to put this idea into their heads.

No, I'm not responsible. Teachers have been assigning the classics to students for ages and never has something like this occurred.

Students didn't run around killing mockingbirds or taming shrews or flying over cuckoos' nests. They didn't commit couples' suicide after reading *Romeo & Juliet*. They didn't sleep with their mothers and murder their fathers because it happened in *Oedipus Rex*. More novels came to mind, classics with titles that sounded violent: *War and Peace, Crime and Punishment,* and *The Masque of the Red Death*.

No, this has nothing to do with literature. This is insane. It's satanic.

If book titles and book plots could cause kids to alter their train of thought, then what about *Their Eyes Were Watching God* or *A Farewell to Arms*. Two titles that hinted at a higher power and giving up weapons. No, these titles hadn't influenced them any more than any of the others.

Besides, Charlie grew up reading Poe, Lovecraft, Bradbury, and Jackson. It's where he discovered his love for literature. And he hadn't gone mad because of it.

Liz grinned in the minimal moonlight seeping through the trees.

"Thought you'd get away, huh?" she asked.

It was a rhetorical question. Of course, they'd *hoped* to get away. Had Charlie ever really thought it would work? At first, no, but when he heard the students fighting behind him, he had a glimmer of hope that they might reach the fence. Then it would be only a matter of making it back to civilization. He hadn't seen many houses near the park, and he figured the kids probably had lookouts on the road.

If he were alone right now, he would make a run for it. He wasn't fast enough, he knew that, but it didn't matter anymore. Charlie was tired of playing their games. Tom would shoot him in the back if he took off at a sprint. Liz might too. His own life he would risk, but Lauren's was worth more. She needed to make it through this night.

She was a caring teacher, a good woman, and she didn't deserve any of this.

None of us deserves this.

These kids had no idea how good they had it. Historically, school-house discipline was unforgiving, unpleasant, and unchallenged. If a teacher decided they didn't like a student, life would become a living hell for that kid. Students didn't seek revenge. They obeyed the teacher, asked for forgiveness, and hoped their parents believed even a portion of their story. The teacher was always right.

Students now were prone to frenzied fits of violent rage all because their feelings got hurt or they didn't get the grade they felt they deserved or because their cell phone was taken away. When Charlie really stopped to think about it, they were fucking pansies. Crybabies. They had no idea what it meant to show up for school every day and actually put in the work to earn honor roll status. Now, it was more like they felt they were owed a decent grade. They deserved to graduate unless a teacher could prove otherwise. It was the educational equiva-lent to the legal system's probable cause. Unless a teacher could demonstrate through clear and precise evidence that a student didn't deserve to graduate, they would be given that diploma.

Gone were the days of realizing years later they should have performed like a student deserving of a *free* public school education instead of being forced to fight for their GED through night school classes, which oftentimes meant leaving the baby home with Grandma or being exhausted at work the next day. There was no such thing as punishment for being a pussy.

That's it. They're all pussies.

"Hey, Mr. Charlie," Kent said, "you remember that time you made me repeat my speech three days in a row because you knew I hadn't actually read *Of Mice and Men?*" It was like he'd heard Charlie's thoughts. "That was kind of a dick move, don't you think?"

It wasn't an asshole move. The first time he stood up, he told the class he'd read a book about a man trying to survive in a house full of mice. The second time he recited verbatim the movie blurb from the Internet Movie Database website. On his third attempt, he gave a shitty rendition of another summary he'd found online. In the end, he relented and gave the boy a "C" out of pity and out of respect for the other students' time wasted listening to him.

They're pussies. He's a pussy.

The thought nagged at him, urging him to take action. His flight response had failed. His fight hadn't quite kicked in yet, but it was brewing in his gut now. The temperature was set to high and it was nearly ready.

"I should have given you a fourth try," Charlie answered.

Tom laughed. Liz did too. Kent reacted differently with a heavy-handed swat at the back of Charlie's head. It stung and knocked his face forward to the point he almost ran into Lauren. He decided to keep his mouth shut after that. Lauren, however, picked up the slack.

"Where is everyone else?" she asked. "Where's Scott?"

Charlie heard her ask the question, but he couldn't focus on it. His mind was elsewhere. He remembered the last time, before tonight, someone had hit him in the back of the head.

He was twelve years old, back in his old neighborhood. His middle school was practically segregated. Not by the teachers or staff but by the students themselves. That was what sucked most about school district boundaries. At school, he was picked on by the privileged white kids because of where he lived and how he dressed. At home, he was bullied by everyone else. He cursed his ancestors for the hard time he was handed due to their transgressions.

The summer was officially over, and his friend Junior didn't attend his school, so Charlie found himself walking alone all the way through the better part of town, over the railroad tracks, and into his neighborhood. AJ and his gang of hoodlums didn't bother him anymore. An older boy named Levi had picked up the slack. Every single day he followed Charlie home, calling him every cuss word a kid his age knew, and some Charlie was pretty sure he made up.

"Hey, ivory-faced fucktard," Levi called him one day as they neared the tracks.

Charlie ignored him.

Levi yanked back on Charlie's backpack, "Where you goin' cracka?"

A group of Levi's friends formed crescent shapes to both sides of him, escorting him as he walked.

"Home, man," Charlie replied. "I'm just going home. I'm not bothering anybody."

"Hit him, Levi!" somebody yelled.

Why would he need to hit him? He hadn't done anything. He only wanted to go home, do his homework, and play Streetfighter II where he could pretend to be the tough guy he definitely was not.

More than anything, Charlie wanted to run off and hide in an abandoned church, high up on a hill, like Ponyboy Curtis and his friend Johnny in S.E. Hinton's The Outsiders. Books were his only escape. It was how he pretended everything was okay. He wished he could read one as he walked, so he wouldn't hear the names the other kids called him.

"Look at how he walks," Levi teased.

Charlie ignored him, wondering what it was about his walk that bothered the boy.

"Watch him," Levi said, "I bet he fixes his hair in a second."

He definitely wouldn't now.

"I haven't done anything to any of you," Charlie said barely above a whisper.

Levi heard him. "You're botherin' me by walking through here like your shit don't stink."

Charlie's shit definitely stank. In fact, he thought it might stink more than most. His mom always complained about it when she walked into the bathroom after him.

"Where you goin' in such a rush?" Levi continued to pick on him.

When he tried to ignore the boy, Levi pulled on his backpack once more and slapped the back of his head.

This time, Charlie snapped. He spun around the way he'd been taught years ago in karate class. But he never got the chance to throw a punch.

Levi leaned back to avoid a strike, and as he did, his foot stepped *on a rock. The small stone rolled, and with it went Levi. The boy slid back, and both his legs came out from under him.*

Charlie watched in awe as Levi fell onto his head, smacking his skull against the bike pedal of one of his friends. Blood soaked the street and Levi lay unresponsive at Charlie's feet.

"I... I..." Charlie stuttered.

"Holy shit," one of the other kids in the group said. "Did you see that? That cracka knocked Levi out."

Charlie knew the truth. He hadn't touched him.

When he got home from school and told Junior the story, the boy nodded and laughed. It seemed he knew something Charlie didn't.

"What is it?" he asked his friend.

"Nothing," he said. "I told you. You're protected now."

Levi lived, but he couldn't remember much of what happened. A few days later, he approached Charlie and told him he had to respect a boy who could throw a punch like that. It seemed his buddies relayed the story how their childish minds had interpreted it.

Nobody ever attacked Charlie after school again. In fact, he was invited to join one of the neighborhood gangs of boys. They called him Milky because of the color of his skin, and he accepted it with happiness but only on one condition. They had to let Junior join them too. Finally, both boys fit in somewhere.

Snapping back to reality, Charlie remembered why he'd started teaching in the first place. So he could make a difference to kids like him who might be struggling and need someone to look up to. He'd been through a lot of shit in his life.

And this is why they didn't give you an invitation to this party, you jackass.

It didn't matter. These kids were fucked up. They were beyond saving. You could rehabilitate a child who threw temper tantrums, picked his nose, or wet his bed. You could even make a difference in the life of a bully who was more than likely being bullied himself at home. You could fix minor flaws in characters. But this... this was pure evil. What these kids did tonight was beyond reparation. They needed to die, to rot in hell, and Charlie realized he needed to be the one to make sure they did.

"We had a bit of a problem back there," Liz admitted. "You might have noticed the fighting. Scott's dead. Along with some of the others. It's cool though. I was going to dump him anyway."

Charlie laughed under his breath, astonished by the girl's lack of emotion.

Kent smacked the back of his head again, and this time, Charlie snapped. His initial thought was to hit Kent; that seemed like the logical move to make – he was the one who'd hit Charlie after all – but if he was going to attack at all, it needed to surprise them. So, he swung a closed fist in an upward arch and brought two knuckles down hard against the bridge of Tom's nose.

Tom didn't just topple, he flipped over the railing and splashed into the water. Kent hesitated for a second, and it was all the time Charlie needed. He reached out, grabbed Liz's hair, and yanked her head back as Kent swung the bat around. She screamed, but it was too late. The top of the heavy wooden club pinged off her forehead and Charlie was forced to let her fall. The momentum was *that* strong. Her gun skidded across the boardwalk and then plunged into the water.

"Motherfucker!" Kent yelled.

Charlie clasped his hands together and brought them up hard, clubbing Kent beneath his chin and sending the boy falling backward until his heavy frame hit the old wooden rail and snapped it. He fell through and into the water. For only a split second, Charlie glanced right and watched as Kent flailed before realizing he could stand.

It happened so quickly. Blindingly fast.

Something leapt up out of the water. Something with a giant, long, black snout – Charlie couldn't tell the difference between a gator and a croc in the dark of night. It clamped its teeth around Kent's gut and yanked him back. The teenager screamed and swung his arms, trying to strike at the creature with his bat, but unable to do any damage. His wails filled the night and then faded into the gurgle of white water as the beast twisted beneath the surface, tearing him to bits.

Two thoughts hit Charlie. The first was how the boy deserved every second of agony. Second was how they'd been in that water only a minute ago. Maybe the blood Tom wore on his face had drawn it near and it happened to reach Kent first.

"Get... them..." Liz ordered as she clawed at the wooden board-walk, trying to climb back to her feet.

She had no idea what had happened. Tom did and was paddling for the boardwalk, not even thinking about the gun he still held in his hand.

"Run!" Charlie yelled.

Lauren took off with Charlie hot on her heels. Naked, shivering, and racing down the path, the pair ran toward the parking lot. Charlie's sopping wet shoes slapped the path behind her. It was impossible to be as silent as she was with her bare feet. His only hope was that all the other kids were dead already. If so, they finally stood a chance at getting out of here alive.

"This way!" Lauren said, as she turned left.

Charlie followed her, hoping she knew where she was going. He could have sworn the parking lot was the other direction, but then again, he wasn't sure about anything out here. It all looked the same. Darkness, trees, water, wooden railings, and arrows that all seemed to contradict each other.

He skidded to a halt when she passed a sign that clearly read: Exit to Parking Lot.

"Lauren," he did his best to call out to her in a hushed tone.

She stopped and turned toward him. "Come on."

"No, the sign says the parking lot is this way."

"They'll be waiting for us at the parking lot."

Running on blind faith, he followed her when she turned and dashed away from him. At this point, he didn't have any other option. She was right. If he were in their position, he would assign someone to wait at the parking lot. As they continued to run, zipping left and right at the different forks they encountered, he couldn't imagine she actu-ally knew where she was headed. She had to be lost.

Then the water beneath them disappeared and they were running above a grassy lawn. The path demanded they cut left, but instead,

Lauren threw a naked leg over the railing. Her fear forcing any concern about splinters in undesirable places far from her mind. Charlie was able to lift a foot to the railing and push himself up and over it.

He shoved through bushes, lifted tree branches away from his face, caught the whip of one Lauren had let go of in front of him. It whooshed through the air before smacking him in the cheek. It could have been a leather bull whip for all the pain he felt. His eyes teared up and he clenched his jaw, massaging the spot on his cheek with his fingertips.

"Fuck," he complained.

"Sorry," she replied.

The pain dissipated when he saw their destination. Lauren was absolutely right, there was a back door. About halfway down the rusty fence, someone had cut their way through ages ago and either the city didn't know about it or felt it wasn't worth the time and effort to fix it.

"We did it," she said.

Charlie pulled one edge of the fence to the side to help her crawl through. When she made it to the other side, she returned the favor. They were free. Charlie wasn't sure where they would go, but far from here. They could walk the tracks away from the park until they came across someone who could help. All they needed to do was climb the grassy hill in front of them up to the tracks. Lauren reached out and took his hand as she walked up the hill.

The gravel that ran alongside the tracks came into view first.

Then the shoes. Many pairs of them. Charlie pulled Lauren's hand, but it was too late.

Mrs. Grainger stepped into view, tapping a finger against her watch. "Just on time."

Behind her, James Bender stood with his head down and his hands in his pockets.

There were four others: Roth, Josie, Gavin, and Valerie.

"You made it to the final game," came a voice from behind.

Charlie turned to see Liz pulling herself through the hole in the fence. Her forehead had swollen into a huge lump. Tom was with her, his gun pointed right at Charlie.

29

LAUREN

"You made it to the final game," Liz said.

Lauren nearly collapsed. All her energy was gone, and it was replaced with the sudden pangs of hopelessness. They'd gotten away. They'd been so close to escape and she'd led Charlie right into their trap. It seemed impossible. How could they have known about the backdoor? It was her secret.

Charlie's face said it all. He'd fought to free them and now he looked at each of the kids standing on the tracks and at Mrs. Grainger and back at Liz and Tom. He was giving up, accepting defeat. They were once again at gunpoint and it was Lauren's fault. If she'd only listened to Charlie and ran toward the parking lot.

"What?" Charlie asked. "How?"

He was at a loss for words.

"You must be wondering how we knew you'd come this way," Mrs. Grainger said. She chuckled. "Everyone who's spent any time at this park knows about it, Lauren. It's how we all snuck in so we could drink, smoke weed, and fuck our teenage frustrations away."

Charlie was so disappointed. More than she was afraid, Lauren was heartbroken for having let him down.

"I'm sorry," she said.

"It's not your fault. They would have been at the parking lot too."

What he didn't say was, "They were smarter than us." That's what Lauren was thinking. They'd been beaten by teenagers they thought incapable of such intricate planning.

"He's right," Tom said. "We're everywhere. Brandon and Jerome are at the parking lot right now."

She had been right. Brandon and Jerome, the two boys who'd greeted her in the parking lot, had remained in the shadows, guarding the front gate in case any of them escaped. Lauren remembered her arrival and Brandon asking if she was sure she wanted to be there. Had it been a warning? Had he felt bad about escorting her toward the entrance? She was such an idiot. He'd tried to give her a heads up and she failed to see it, replying with something stupid like, "It's your party so I wouldn't miss it for the world."

Always trying to be the nice teacher, you fucking idiot. He tried to warn you!

If she'd gone home, Charlie might not have come to rescue her. Neither of them would be in this situation right now. She might open the newspaper tomorrow morning to see a haunting headline the likes of: Teachers Slaughtered at Grad Night Party. Of course, she imagined it would mention how only Mrs. Grainger and a handful of students had been able to escape. That would have to be their story. They'd come up with something. Maybe they'd pin it on one of the teachers. Or quite possibly on the janitor.

Only a handful of students will escape.

What would they say to their friends? What would the under-classmen say Monday in class? Their school year ended a few weeks after the graduates'.

They'll have no teachers. Half the staff was here tonight. But the library will be fully operational! Maybe this bitch will even get some kind of PTSD payout. She might be set for life after this!

"You filthy bitch," Lauren said, turning her attention to the librarian.

"Oh," Mrs. Grainger said, throwing her hands up as if she'd been attacked for no reason, "what a dirty mouth you have, Ms. Peony. But, that doesn't surprise me. Nothing does anymore."

Lauren looked at the faces of the students still with her. Of course, there was James Bender, his face still shrouded in the darkness of his hood. She imagined his eyes might start glowing with red embers at any moment. There was a demon inside of him, she knew it. He might be the one really behind all this. It wasn't Mrs. Grainger. She was too weak.

"You see?" Mrs. Grainger asked. "There is no escape. *This is* how your night plays out for you. You pathetic teachers with your constant whining in the teacher's lounge. You piss and moan about the teenagers you teach and yet you act just like them. We have teachers cheating on their spouses while they sneak off to fornicate, teachers gossiping about their students, teachers joking about the mean things they did to the kids in their classes."

Lauren heard her, and *they* did too. The teenagers to her left and right were soaking up her words. She was fueling the fire with slanderous remarks. Of course, there was truth to what she said, yet she made it seem so much more hateful than it was. Teachers talking to each other was no different from workers of any other profession letting off some steam about the day's hardships.

"When educators stop disseminating insightful information and begin regurgitating bullshit lectures found in expired texts, it's time to do away with those professors," Mrs. Grainger spat with so much venom she might as well have had a forked tongue. "Facilitators, that's what you've begun calling yourselves. My husband tried to fight the system, to tell them we needed to adapt with the ever-changing, ever-fluid students, and the school system spit him out because of it. They sent him home, early retirement, where he withered away, searching for ways to make the system see, all while in a drunken stupor. He died of a heart attack because of people like you. You're glorified babysitters. And I have to sit in the library and hear all the hogwash you talk day in and day out."

Lauren didn't know Mrs. Grainger's husband. She'd never heard anything about him. She hadn't even realized the woman was a widow.

Standing beside James Bender was Roth, holding a pistol pointed at Charlie. His blood-stained hands had left a smear across his nose and cheek. Next to him stood Josie Simmons, breathing deep, her chest rising and falling. She was clean. Not a drop of blood on her. Gavin and Valerie Kemper both looked beat to hell. The class clown and the pretty blonde had barely made it out of the fight at the basketball court. It seemed the only member of the alumni group to survive was Tom, the one who'd started the mess in the first place.

Isn't that how it always goes? The person to start the problems is always the one least affected by it?

"Why do you think I stopped visiting the teacher's lounge?" Mrs. Grainger continued. "I'm not one of you. You made that clear from day one."

"What are you talking about?" Lauren asked. "I've always been nothing but nice to you."

"You've been cordial," she admitted. "As is expected by a professional. Yet, I know exactly what you are, Ms. Peony. Have you figured out yet why you're here?"

"I'm here because some deranged lunatic didn't have plans on a Friday night," Lauren replied. "To get her rocks off, she thought she'd get payback against the other teachers."

She knew she was only poking the beast at this point, but she'd already crossed the line and figured she should really shove it in and twist it around a little bit.

"Funny thing is," Lauren continued, "I bet you wouldn't have even gotten an invite to a *real* Grad Night party. You had to go and get these kids all riled up instead." Lauren paused again, "Let's not mention the fact that you *let* your husband fade away into non-existence all by himself, instead of helping him work his way through it the way a real wife would."

There came a quiet still. Everyone's eyes fixed on Mrs. Grainger, waiting to see how she'd react to Lauren's response. At this point, Lauren knew she was going to die. If anything might get her out of it, it would be Mrs. Grainger making a stupid mistake by letting her anger get to her.

"You see?" Mrs. Grainger asked, raising her arms, palms up and turning toward the remaining students. "This is one of your mean-spirited teachers. Listen to how she bullies me. How she's bullied you for years." She turned back to Lauren and jabbed a finger in her direction. "Let me tell you why you're here, Ms. Peony. Do you remember a boy named Justin?"

Lauren thought back. She'd taught for many years and Justin was a fairly common name. There'd been Justin Baxter, Justin Carmichael, Justin Tracks, Justin Leopold, and...

"Justin Gentry," Josie Simmons suddenly said, stepping away from the others to come closer to Lauren. "Do you remember him, Ms. Peony?"

The name rang a bell, but she couldn't remember anything particularly significant that had happened with the boy. She opened her mouth to speak, but there was nothing to say. She couldn't imagine what that boy would have to do with her being brought to a murder party.

"Justin Gentry was my boyfriend," Josie said.

Was her boyfriend?

Lauren couldn't think of any reason she could be blamed for an end to their relationship.

"I'm sorry," she said, "I don't understand."

"Typical," Mrs. Grainger quipped.

"Why don't you shut the fuck up for a second?" Charlie shouted.

"Exhibit B," Mrs. Grainger replied. "Another prime example of your leaders in this day and age."

"Fuck off," Charlie replied. "You all are drinking this woman's Kool-Aid. She has you so consumed with hate."

"I did none of this," Mrs. Grainger defended herself.

"It's The Maddening," Liz said from behind them.

"Charlie," Lauren said, putting a hand on his shoulder.

Josie was crying now. She'd dropped to a knee and was sobbing. This was one of the sweetest girls Lauren had ever taught, and she was having a complete breakdown in front of everyone. "You don't even remember him," she said through violent sobs. "He meant nothing to anyone but me."

Lauren wanted so badly to remember whatever it was that was tormenting Josie right now. She would never in a million years do anything on purpose that would result in someone feeling so much pain. Josie had been quiet all night, more of a bystander than an active participant. She would have been at odds with all of this, Lauren knew, but evidently there was a good reason why she'd joined the others. It seemed Lauren was a part of it. Only she had no idea what it was.

She walked away from Charlie, not giving a shit what anyone else had to say about it and squatted down next to Josie. It must have been a sight for the others. The computer teacher completely naked trying to console a student. "Honey, whatever I've done, you must know it wasn't intentional."

"Fuck you!" Josie yelled. She leapt to her feet and smacked Lauren so hard it sent her sprawling across the gravel.

"Lauren!" Charlie yelled as he ran to her aid.

Josie stormed at them yelling, "Justin did nothing to anyone. He kept to himself. He was only in tenth grade when you told the other teachers you thought there was something wrong with him!"

Lauren rubbed at her head and sat up next to Charlie. She remembered now. Justin was a boy in her class who never answered questions, never completed his work, and didn't talk much to the other kids. He was a quiet, sweet boy, and she'd been worried about his failing grades. She'd had a gut feeling he might be on the autism spectrum. Then Justin wasn't in her class anymore. She'd heard that he'd changed schools. That was all.

"Josie, I... I..." Lauren struggled with the words. "I only said I thought..."

"You thought he was crazy!" Josie yelled.

"No, I thought he was... special."

"Ha," Mrs. Grainger laughed, stepping in at the worst moment, "I think we all know what special means, don't we, Ms. Peony? Stupid, dumb, ignorant, unable to keep up with the others, and in need of some serious help."

"No," Lauren said. "I thought he..."

"Do you know what it can do to someone to be told they're not good enough?" Josie asked. "Do you have any idea what it feels like to know you're different and to be told that a teacher thinks you should be evaluated?"

She had thought that. It was the reason she'd brought it up in the teacher's lounge. She wanted to find out what the other teachers thought, to see if they'd had any of the same experiences with him. She'd mentioned him at that specific moment because Ms. Keen, the school psychology teacher, and Mrs. Laymon, the guidance counselor, were both there at the time. They'd listened to her but hadn't provided much feedback. Then Justin was gone, and Lauren didn't have to wonder about it anymore. Her job was to teach the kids who showed up. Justin was no longer in attendance. But she'd had no idea it might be because of her. Nobody had said anything to her about it.

"They sent him away," Josie cried, wiping at her tears with the back of her hand.

"Here you go, Josie," Roth said, handing his gun to her. "Do you know how to use it? It's locked and loaded, baby. Just pull the trigger."

"Shoot her," Valerie urged. "It'll be fuckin' awesome."

"You'll have a story to tell," Gavin assured her. "You can say you helped kick off The Maddening."

"Do it," James Bender growled.

His voice seemed to come from somewhere else, like it grew inside his gut and emanated through his neck without ever meeting his mouth. It was sewer-water wet and carried the foul odor of vomit and shit. Lauren felt his breath hit her like a gust of hot, humid, and hellish wind. She covered her mouth and nose with the palm of her hand and Charlie shoved his nose into her shoulder to do the same.

He gagged. "Oh, God."

"His parents wanted him to go to a school that would understand him better," Josie cried, ignoring the stench as if it didn't exist at all. "Like I understood him." She looked down at her feet and sniffed, once again wiping at her tears with her free hand. "I understood him. I was in love with him."

"And what happened to him?" Mrs. Grainger asked.

Josie whipped her head to the left and glared at the librarian, then refocused her anger at Lauren. "He jumped in front of a train. Left a note on his dresser saying he was alone. He said he never understood his schoolwork, he felt stupid, and he couldn't keep up. That he'd always be behind everyone else. Just like Ms. Peony said."

Lauren felt like she'd been punched in the stomach. Sharp claws dug into her chest and stabbed into her heart. She would have never wished this on anyone. She had no idea. Her name was in the letter? And they hadn't told her?

"Josie, I never…"

You never what? Never expected a student to jump in front of a train? Never thought of the consequences of your actions?

Far away a train whistle screamed its shrill tune, shrieking its oncoming arrival. Mrs. Grainger clapped her hands together and smiled.

"It's time," she said. "James?"

James reached a long, charcoal black arm out of the sleeve of his hooded sweater. His skin was like a thick, charred tree root extending out. She remembered those dark hands from the graduation ceremony when she thought she'd imagined them. Dangling from his long, bony, clawed fingers was a set of handcuffs.

His eyes glowed, but not red the way Lauren had expected them to. They were yellow orbs, glimmering in the moonlight. His mouth opened and his top lip lifted higher than what should have been possible, revealing a set of sharp, uneven, jagged teeth.

When his head tilted back, Lauren caught a glimpse of the face beneath the hood. It was monstrous, with pieces of skin sewn together from a variety of ethnicities. Almost doll-like. He was a patchwork of what hell might expect a teenager to look like. He was one-part olive skinned, one-part pale. Another part freckled and another a much darker complexion. Blonde hair, ginger, and brunette.

He wasn't a teenage boy at all but more like a multicolored, demonic tapestry. None of his pieces fit quite perfectly, which left tiny gaps between his stitched seams. Some of his patches bulged, some were so old they'd begun to curl at the edges, and all looked glossy, like a layer of lacquer had been painted over him to bring the whole masterpiece to completion.

Lauren didn't need to ask what he was to understand. He was every teenager rolled into one. He was each agonizing heart, every mistreated malcontent, and all of the wishes and curses born from frustration, anger, and hate.

James Bender was an evil creation made up from the minds of so many members of the modern tormented youth.

She found herself recoiling from the sight of him, trying to slide her naked ass backward so she could hide behind Charlie.

"Thank you," Mrs. Grainger said as she reached out and took the handcuffs from James's claw. She handed them to Roth, who gestured for Gavin to come with him. Tom stepped closer and kept his gun aimed at Charlie. "Up on your feet, you two."

"Josie, give the gun to Valerie," Roth said, "I think she's more likely to shoot."

"I can handle it!" she demanded. "And if anyone's going to shoot this bitch, it's going to be me."

This wasn't Josie. She didn't have this kind of anger in her. How could she have gone on for so long, so mad at her teacher, without showing a single sign?

But she had shown signs, hadn't she?

Lauren thought back to the tenth grade, when Justin was still at the school. Josie was always pleasant in class, always a sweetheart, but there had been a different kind of light about her back then. She'd joked more, talked a little more, and definitely smiled more. There'd been that pep in her step. She was a young lady in love. Lauren had taken that away from her and since then she'd become a sullen shadow of the girl she'd once been.

"I'm sorry," Lauren repeated. "I'm so sorry, Josie."

She felt herself being lifted up from underneath her arm. She allowed her feet to assist, too overwhelmed by the news of Justin's death to put up a fight. Even as Roth slapped a cuff on her wrist and stretched out the long chain so the other cuff would meet Charlie's, she didn't struggle.

30

CHARLIE

Charlie loved her. It was an odd thing to consider right now, but when he saw the hurt in Lauren's eyes, the pain she felt from hearing about Justin's death, he sensed so much in that moment. She cared beyond what most other people he knew were capable of. She'd forgotten about her own well-being as she'd watched Josie bawl in front of her.

Of course, Lauren hadn't tried to exile the boy. She only did what a million other teachers do every day. She tried to help her student. She didn't want him to fail, so she'd asked about him with the intention of possibly getting him some help.

Josie had seen the situation through the eyes of a distraught, love-struck young woman in a great deal of pain. To her, loss overpowered every other feeling. Mrs. Grainger had used the girl's agony and twisted it into a tool for destruction.

Now that Lauren knew the truth, she'd given up fighting.

Does she think she deserves to be hit by this train?

If she did, she was wrong. She was cuffed to Charlie with at least six feet of chain between them. He pulled at the cuff on his wrist, yanked on the chain, and it was clear there was no getting free of this thing.

"Over there," Roth ordered him. "Tom, shoot this fucker if he doesn't listen. I'm tired and ready to go home."

"Me too, man," Tom replied. "This shit is exhausting."

"I said over there, you dumb fuck," Roth said as he pushed Charlie.

They were being forced to stand side-by-side with Charlie on the park side of the tracks and Lauren on the other with Mrs. Grainger, James, Roth, Josie, Gavin and Valerie.

Charlie had only Tom and Liz for neighbors.

The chain stretched between them, dangling over the tracks.

"Be careful, Roth," Tom said. "Kent got too close and this asshole knocked him into the water for the gator to eat."

"Yeah, be careful, Roth," Charlie warned him.

He wanted so badly to haul his wannabe gangster ass back to the boardwalk and toss him into the water too. As far as Charlie was concerned, he and that gator were on the same team.

Lauren moved and the chain brushed the tracks with a clang.

"Liz, would you like to explain the rules of this game?" Mrs. Grainger asked.

"It has changed a bit," Liz said with a giggle. "The plan was to keep Lauren around and cuff one of her arms to one of her legs and see if she could hop out of harm's way with only a few seconds to spare, but, and this is kind of funny, Ms. Peony, I'm going to use my creativity again. Remember that creativity you said I don't have? That. I'm going to use *that* and change the game to better fit the occasion."

"Just get on with it," Charlie said.

He was done with the theatrics. If he didn't have two guns pointed at him right now, he would launch himself at one of the students and beat him to a pulp. They might kill him, but at least he would breathe his last breath by taking someone else's.

"It's a tragic love story," Liz said, "just like Josie and Justin's. There are two of you. The chain is long enough to stretch out between the two of you, but you've probably noticed you can't go far. When the train comes, if it hits that chain, it's definitely going to drag you under. If it doesn't kill you, it'll definitely cripple you. My guess is it'll kill you both."

"Damn, that's fucked up," Roth said.

"Or, one of you can choose life and pull the other one into the train's path," Liz continued, "and maybe if you pull hard enough you won't get dragged under the train. Can't be sure though. You're probably gonna die either way."

"Or!" Gavin shouted, "They can have a good old-fashioned tug-o-war. My money would be on Mr. Charlie though. He's kind of tougher."

"Ms. Peony's a little bigger though, don't you think?" Valerie asked.

Charlie looked left at each kid as they continued cracking jokes. The train's horn blew again. It was getting closer.

James Bender had his face down again, but Charlie had seen him a few minutes ago. The monster had revealed himself for only a moment, but it had been long enough for Charlie to catch a glimpse of the boy's mask.

It was a mask, wasn't it?

The black arms and hands seemed so real.

Charlie looked once more at the two students on his side of the tracks. He'd fared well against them so far. Tom would shoot him. He had no doubts about that. He was far more likely to pull the trigger than anyone else in this twisted, fucked-up group of graduates.

The train blew its horn again. Charlie could feel the ground shaking beneath his feet. He'd walked enough railroad tracks to know this thing was close and it was speeding toward him, even if his back was to the train.

"You can turn around and wait if you want," Liz said. "Might be more fun if you can see the train coming."

Charlie wanted to grab hold of Liz, hug her tight, and leap in front of this metallic beast barreling its way toward them. If Lauren weren't attached to his wrist, he might seriously consider it.

"I don't want to see," Lauren whispered to him.

"Then we won't," he replied. "Hey." She looked up at him. "I was too nervous to say this. I always have been, but I've always wanted you. You're it for me. I'm in love with you."

She smiled.

"You're a beautiful person, Lauren," he added. "Don't let them take that away from you. You've done nothing wrong. Even knowing how this would end, I would come to this party to save you a hundred times."

"It might be too late for this," Lauren replied, "but I kinda like you too. I guess if there's anyone I'd want to be chained to naked on some train tracks…"

The fact she could find humor at this moment wasn't lost on him. It was another reason she deserved to live. He'd already made up his mind. At the last second, he would jump at her, knock her out of harm's way, and he would take the hit from the train.

"I love you, Lauren Peony," he said.

He looked at Tom with his gun pointed at him. Then, he looked at Josie who also wielded one. Neither flinched. They were both ready to pull the trigger if he moved. One on each side of the tracks. Tom could plug him full of bullet holes while Josie shot Lauren. It would be that easy for these two.

Who would they shoot first? If it was Lauren, this would be for nothing. His only hope was the train would give him enough of a distraction.

"Go ahead and try something," Tom warned him, his gun hand steady. "I hope you do."

Josie's hand trembled, the aim of her gun rising and falling with her breath.

The ground shook even harder. The train whistled. He glanced over his shoulder and saw its bright light headed their way. They had maybe thirty seconds left. Their shadows stretched out in front of them, reaching out for what seemed like eternity until they rejoined the darkness a mile ahead. Or perhaps they never would. The train's light would keep going, obliterating the shadows.

Light always wins at some point. If not now, it will win later.

Then, as he peered once more over at Tom and Liz on his side of the tracks, he saw that perhaps the light *would* win this time. Crouched down in the darkness at the side of the fence, were people. Who they were, Charlie couldn't quite tell, but it was clear they were staying hidden from sight. It looked like the one in front had a gun and some of the others held other random objects.

Knives, bats, and even what looked like a broomstick and an iron.

The shadowy figure in front, the one with the gun, nodded at him.

Tom and Liz didn't see it because they were focused on him.

Nobody else saw them either.

The train was twenty seconds away.

Ten.

Five.

Charlie tugged the chain with all his might. Lauren's wrist snapped from the pressure, but her body flew his way. He threw the chain over his back and shoulder and ran from the tracks, yanking her violently across to his side.

As he made his move, the strangers in the shadow ran out with their guns and other weapons pointed at Tom and Liz, causing the two to take their eyes off him in the process.

Josie didn't react. The train was suddenly there, in the way, blocking her.

The train clipped Lauren's foot and she screamed in agony as the force threw her into the air and into Charlie. They toppled and rolled until they finally unfolded from each other's bodies in a cloud of dust.

Lauren clung to consciousness, crying out as her eyes rolled back and she curled up into a ball, clutching her injured foot with her good hand. The other wrist dangled from the cuff Charlie pulled along as he threw himself on top of her to stop the volley of bullets he expected to come their way.

As he held onto her, he reached for her foot, hating that he'd hurt her, but thanking God she was alive. Blood spurted from it, and it was hard to tell for sure, but it seemed the two biggest toes were ripped completely off.

Lauren lay screaming beneath him, but the bullets he expected never came. The train continued to whoosh by, screeching its metallic rage as it shot by at a tremendous speed. The others were stuck on the opposite side.

Tom and Liz had their hands raised over their heads. Tom's gun was on the ground. Standing in front of them, leading the charge of this new group of teenagers, and armed with a gun, was Bogdan. The rest were all the *good* kids. The ones Charlie never expected to see again. It was everyone, or at least most of the people, from the *other* party.

Rita was right behind Bogdan. She marched toward Liz.

"Came to join the party?" Liz called out over the noise of the passing train. "I'm sorry, but you weren't invited."

"Really, bitch?" Rita replied as she threw a punch at Liz that knocked her head back.

Liz fell to the ground with Rita on top of her.

"I've never liked you," Rita yelled, dropping more punches at Liz's already beaten and swollen head and face.

"Bog?" Charlie said questioningly as if the boy might vanish if his name were spoken aloud.

"You're naked, Mr. Charlie," Bogdan replied.

Charlie glanced down and saw what the teenagers saw. He was naked and leaning over Lauren's bare body. She still lay crying beneath him.

"We need to get her help," Charlie said. "She's hurt bad."

"We will," Bogdan promised. "The cops are on their way."

"There's others on the other side of the train," Charlie warned them.

"We know."

"How did you know?" Charlie asked.

The train chose that moment to finish its racket as it sailed past and out of view as quickly as it had arrived. Standing on the other side of the train was the rest of the evil bastards.

But, Josie had her gun pointed at them all and had them huddled together. Roth, Gavin, and Valerie lay prone on their bellies, their fingers interlaced behind their heads. Mrs. Grainger was on her knees. James Bender stood tall, facing Josie with only five feet between them.

"I can't do this," she yelled at all of them, keeping her eyes on James Bender. "I *won't* do it. I didn't want to at all."

"Josie called me," Bogdan informed Charlie. "She said there was a big fight and she snuck away to use a payphone somewhere in the park. Called the cops too, but they didn't take her seriously. We were already talking about coming to the park before she called. We knew something bad had to be going on here."

"You fucking bitch!" Liz yelled at Josie, blood gurgling from her lips as she lay on her back with Rita still straddling her.

"Josie said she'd made a mistake and needed help," Bogdan continued over Liz's yelling. "She told me about the train and what time it was scheduled to pass through here. We tried to get here sooner, but—"

"You sneaky bitch!" Liz went on screaming at Josie. "I knew we shouldn't have let you into our circle!"

"I'm not like you," Josie said to James Bender. She peered around him to yell at the others. "I'm not like any of you!"

Charlie stretched the chain between his wrist and Lauren's and snatched Tom's gun up off the ground.

Tom took a step forward and yelled, "I'll fucking kill—"

Charlie pulled the trigger and the gun's roar silenced Tom with a bullet straight through his forehead. When his body hit the ground, the teacher stood there for a second, considering doing the same to Liz, but he wanted her to live long enough to see her plan fail. With ice cold veins, he pointed the gun at Roth.

"Don't shoot me, Mr. Charlie," the boy begged.

"Uncuff me," Charlie ordered.

Roth looked up at Josie, afraid she'd shoot him if he moved. She nodded, and he scampered over to Charlie, dug trembling hands into his pocket for the key, and unlocked the teacher.

Charlie shoved the kid toward Lauren. "Her too."

Roth did as he was told and then darted back to his position with the others.

Charlie crossed the tracks and stalked toward the others. "Stay on the ground, all of you," he ordered.

"I did what you asked," Roth whimpered. "I unlocked you. Don't shoot, Mr. Charlie."

"When I do, you'll be the first to know," Charlie promised.

Bogdan followed close behind. Dreading turning his back to Liz, Charlie left his trust with Rita and the rest of the good kids. They'd been put through so much hell at the hands of these little pieces of shit, that Charlie had no doubt they would keep control of the situation.

The truth was Charlie wanted to shoot every one of these kids in Liz's camp. They'd stolen from him the one thing he held dear. His overall belief in the good of his students. Liz and her evil misfits had stripped that from him, and without it, he felt lost. He was duped, deceived, and now, slightly deranged. They needed to pay for what they'd done.

He could still hear Lauren crying as he pointed the gun at Gavin, Valerie, Roth, and Mrs. Grainger, one at a time, considering shooting each of them.

James Bender halted and looked his way. Josie didn't take her gun off the hooded demon.

When James lifted his head and peered at Charlie, the teacher's mind went numb. He couldn't move. He couldn't shoot. He was no longer on the railroad tracks at all. This was that kind of darkness that gripped you, that kept you frozen. This was the kind you should run from.

He was twelve years old again. He sat in that patch of grass behind his apartment building, with his back against the wall, reading. He was alone and in the dark with only an overhead porch light illuminating his book.

A page tore free from his paperback and swirled through the air in front of him. He watched it dance for a moment with innocent fascination. It seemed it would never hit the ground. But then it stopped and hovered in front of his eyes, perfectly still, lying flat on the breeze, so thin he almost couldn't make it out at all.

He leaned closer to see it better.

It shot forward and whipped across the bridge of his nose, a thin paper razorblade slicing him wide open.

He screamed and another page leapt from his book.

It crossed his forehead and nicked his skin.

Page after page took to the air, each one assaulting him, criss-crossing his face.

He tried to block them with his hands, and they cut open the skin of his palms and fingers. One ran right up the middle of his thumb and index fingers to split open the webbing between them.

Beyond the pages, stood AJ and the other boys from the young bully's group. Levi and his gang joined them, and they all yelled at him, circling around him and shaking angry fists in the air as they riddled him with vocal ammunition.

"Cracka muthafucka!"

"White milk piece of shit!"

"Pasty pussy!"

"White bread bastard!"

And the pages kept coming. One slid up the side of his face and sawed back and forth, lobbing off his ear.

Pressing his palm against the grass, he tried to stand but his paper assailants slashed the backs of both knees, sending him crashing back onto his ass.

He screamed in agony and a page slit the space between his lips, cutting the corners of his mouth.

As if that was all that kept his jaw connected to the rest of his face, the bottom portion of his mouth elongated with intense, burning pressure and then ripped free and landed in his lap. Charlie stared down at his blood-soaked shorts and saw his teeth and chin.

Charlie picked up that portion of his jaw and tried once more to stand, fighting through the pain at the back of his knees. The boys surrounding him continued to yell obscenities at him, but where words failed them, they decided rocks wouldn't.

Each was armed with one, and as they flung them his way, what left their hands as simple stones transformed in midair. They went from cool brown and grey to fiery red-hot embers launched from catapults. They careened at him with the whistle of bottle rockets.

The first slammed into his right forearm, snapping it in half like a frail twig. He screamed in agony and tried to lift his left arm to block his face, but a ball of fire shattered his shoulder, and he dropped the piece of mangled jaw onto the grass.

Smoldering stones plummeted through his chest and stomach, singing right in as they carved giant gorges in his upper body, like hot lava easily melting everything in its path. Charlie could do nothing but fall to the grass and stare in horror at the caverns forged in his ripped-open ribcage and stomach.

He couldn't stare for long before searing pain hit his right eye in the form of a paper blade slicing his pupil. Another nicked the other one. His vision blurred and the boys' images became shadows. Darkness with firelight launching seemingly from within them.

And they never stopped their chants.

Unable to sit up any longer, Charlie let his back slide down the wall until he lay on the lawn in the fetal position, his jaw on the ground next to him.

A gash at the back of his neck caused him to raise his head, and that was all the time it took for the next page to slide across his throat, opening him up so quickly he couldn't even form a whimper.

Blood ran warm down to the grass beneath him and he fought to clamp the torn skin closed with his hands. His blood was so slippery he couldn't keep a tight grip, and his life drained quickly from all the wounds in his body. Frigid cold replaced it.

His only company as he lay dying was the shadows of his tormenters.

"No," Charlie said, his voice gurgling through the hole in his throat. The rest of it escaped from the gaping pit where the bottom half of his jaw should have been.

His voice was stronger inside his head. It was louder there. So, he yelled a mental, "No!"

The boys kept shouting at him and the papers continued to whip across his body. Fireballs hit the arches of his feet and the wall beside his head, raining chunks of brick down on him. But he was numb to the pain by this point. He was dying.

"I can't die like this!" he yelled.

A new figure emerged through the darkness, pushing past the

blurry shadow figures. An orange, warm glow illuminated the head and shoulders of a being that radiated warmth and love. As it neared, the darker forms scattered, like they were afraid of it.

The glowing figure moved closer to Charlie and spoke to him with a familiar voice.

Junior said, "I asked my auntie to perform a safety ritual for you. That is what you saw that night. She made sure they won't bother you anymore. You're protected now."

It was the words his friend had spoken to him so long ago.

Junior repeated, "I told you. You are protected now."

And Charlie was no longer afraid.

"Mr. Charlie!" Bogdan yelled, snapping Charlie out of his momentary stupor.

James Bender was a foot away from him and had reached out to grab the gun. A black, tar-like arm reached out of the sleeves of his sweatshirt. His fingers were much longer than any man's and the nails were long and chipped, jagged. His face was dark, and when the moonlight hit it, Charlie saw a patchwork of stitches like a kid's old stuffed animal brought back to life many times over the years. His eyes lit up, glowing like yellow high beams on a car.

"Look at him," Mrs. Grainger said, "Isn't he magnificent?"

"What the fuck are you?" Charlie asked.

"I am the loss," he spoke with a guttural sound, like his voice shot out from the depths of hell and raked across his throat, tearing holes into it and seeping out from various places, "the pain, the torture, the hatred, the chaos, the destruction, the evil that men do in the body of the innocent. I am every misshaped youth burning in the fiery pits of hell. I am the shattered, the broken... all of them here as one."

"Beautiful," Mrs. Grainger said. "Let The Maddening begin."

"Enough of your shit," Charlie said, turning his gaze away from James Bender's demonic form. He pointed the gun at Mrs. Grainger.

She smiled up at him and said, "You wouldn't da—"

Charlie shot her in the face, right between the eyes.

"I am—" James Bender began again, but Charlie interrupted him.

"—I don't care what you are," he said, "I'm protected now. And you can go back to hell."

He pointed the gun right at the center of his grotesque-grandmother-quilt-like face and pulled the trigger. The pistol cracked and he fired again and again just in case.

Bullets slammed into the face of the demon boy. Yellow light exploded from where they struck him. The screams of a thousand teenagers rang out, shrieking so loudly Charlie nearly dropped the gun in his attempt to cover his ears.

James Bender fell to his knees. His fingers grasped at the bullet holes, feeling them out, trying to cram into them like its claws might plug them. One long talon reached into his forehead, curled around inside the hole, and cranked back on it so hard it tore the skin and bone free. More yellow light shot out, illuminating the night.

"Charlie!" Lauren yelled.

The demon kept raking at its face, trying to pull more holes open. Light emitted through the stitched-up seams, and his mouth dropped open, stretching out a full twelve inches, light bursting forth and blasting Charlie in the face.

Charlie fell onto his ass and scooted away from the boy who was still pulling pieces of his face open, digging his sharp nails into his scalp, cheeks, and eye sockets. Squeals and multi-voiced cries evacuated him on rays of light. Charlie shielded his eyes and looked over at Roth, Gavin, and Valerie who all watched in horror as the evil creature they'd followed exploded in a blast of light.

The final boom was deafening. Charlie's hair blew back as James Bender's body exploded into a hundred pieces and disappeared into the night air. Only the echoes of his wails remained for a second or two longer.

Valerie whimpered from her spot on the ground, like she was the victim in all this.

Charlie regarded them all as terrified children, but they weren't innocent. They had too much blood on their hands. Yet, Charlie felt no desire to kill them. He despised Roth, hated the boy, but he felt no need to shoot him. All three of them, and especially Liz – if her connected father didn't somehow get her out of this mess – deserved to sit in prison for the rest of their lives. They needed to spend their adulthoods thinking about the mistakes they made as teenagers. For the first time ever, they would be held accountable for their actions.

There, in the dying light of their false god, Charlie saw them shrivel up and become nothing more than hollowed out kids containing an unbelievable amount of self-righteousness. This new world of theirs had them believing they were owed something. Now, in the wake of their murder spree, they'd find out what they truly deserved.

Bogdan came through for him the way only one other person in life had, and, like Junior, Charlie owed him his life. This young boy was twice the man he should have been at this age. He was a good kid, a good young man, and Charlie imagined they'd be lifelong friends.

The cops arrived shortly after. They did what cops did. Reporters did what they did too. Paramedics provided Charlie and Lauren with blankets to cover their naked bodies. Once Lauren was loaded into the back of an ambulance, Charlie finally found himself alone with Bogdan.

"You saved my life tonight, Bog. Mine and Lauren's," he said.

"I didn't want you to come to this party, Mr. Charlie."

"I know you didn't."

"And then when you left, I couldn't stop thinking about what they might do to you. I never knew it was going to be anything like *this*. I only knew that I and my friends weren't invited and that it had some-thing to do with a special treat for the teachers. I knew it was going to be a trick of some kind and that it would be bad."

"It was bad all right."

"Mr. Charlie, you believe me that I didn't know, right?"

"Of course, I do, Bog. But none of that's important. What's impor-tant is how it ended. You showed up when I needed you. When I thought it was all over."

"You told me to," he said.

Charlie raised his eyebrows, wondering what the boy meant by that.

"Remember the conversation we had the other day in the hallway?

In front of your class?" he asked. "The one where you told me I needed to stick up for myself more? You said there were three things I always needed to stand up for... my family, myself, and the things I believed in."

"I remember," Charlie said.

"Well, I believe in you, Mr. Charlie."

Bogdan's words cut straight to his heart and Charlie felt his eyes well up with tears. No matter what these rotten kids had taken from him. No matter what they'd done to Lauren and all the other teachers. They *did not* represent all of today's youth. There was hope for this generation yet. Bogdan showed him that.

"When Josie called me and told me what was happening, I knew I needed to come. And the others did too," he added.

"You're a good man, Bog," Charlie said.

"Takes one to know one, Sir."

Bogdan put out his hand for Charlie to shake, but the teacher swatted it away and wrapped the boy up in a hug.

31

LAUREN

The aftermath of violent crime scenes was the same in all the movies. The surrounding trees always blinked in the revolving red and blue glow of police codes. Twenty or so cops would busy themselves inside yellow caution tape while reporters did their best to steal secrets from the other side. Witnesses gave statements to detectives while injured survivors were hauled off on gurneys. Lauren supposed that was how things went at the train tracks that night too, but she couldn't remember much after James Bender exploded.

Only an incredible amount of pain.

In the weeks that followed, Lauren struggled with nearly every aspect of her life. Her wrist would heal, and she'd get by with less toes than the average joe, but mentally she'd never be the same. She'd spent her entire adult life building a career she no longer believed in. In truth, she'd lost that spark, that personal drive to really excel at her job, a long time ago. Now, she found herself starting over from scratch. Her college degree and all of her on-the-job experience related to education. Now that she had no desire to pass on that knowledge, she felt lost.

The nightmares were the worst part. Nearly every single night she woke up with her sheets soaked with sweat. In them, she often saw

James Bender watching her from his perch atop the jungle gym. She could still hear that low growl that floated on the wind that night in the park. That odd rhythmic groan that seemed to remain on the breeze through the entire ordeal. She heard it in her dreams and sometimes she swore she even heard it while awake.

Her therapist thought it might be a good idea for her to visit the park again at some point in the future. She considered it, but right now was too soon. If she ever did return, she'd go with Charlie by her side.

They were planning to move in together. They might as well since he'd spent every night since Grad Night at her apartment. She couldn't go through life alone right now. Every time she walked into her living room or dining room, she thought she might find an invitation waiting for her. Of course, she never did.

Charlie wasn't ready to give up teaching entirely. He was too good at it to stop altogether. Instead, he got a job teaching overseas children English as a second language. Using an online platform kept him out of the actual classroom, and that was all that really mattered. She didn't want him to be anywhere around teenagers again.

She often wondered how DS High got back on its feet with half the staff dead or gone. What did the students and parents think now that they knew the truth?

Every talk show in the surrounding area invited Charlie and her on to discuss the events of that night. She couldn't do it. At some point, she might be able to, but she didn't see how getting on TV and reciting the incident would change anything. The kids nowadays were broken. Even their parents were too late to fix this.

Liz, Roth, Valerie, and Gavin did go onto a talk show where they tried to pin the entire thing on Mrs. Grainger and James Bender. Of course, their interviews were conducted live via satellite since each was serving a prison sentence. They were all over the age of eighteen by the time the trials wrapped up, meaning the Dustin Hertz law did nothing to protect them. They would serve hard time for the rest of their lives. Not even Liz's father could protect her this time.

The Graduate Four, as the surviving villains of the story became known, all insisted that Josie Simmons should have been considered a part of their group. That she made it the Graduate Five. They were the only ones telling *that* story. Charlie, Lauren, Bogdan, and the others all insisted there was no truth to that rumor.

Josie wasn't like the rest of them. She had been a girl dealing with great pain. What she did was unthinkable and unrepairable. She wasn't innocent, but in the end, if she hadn't helped them, things might have ended badly. Her bravery and refusal to see two of her favorite teachers get killed had won out. So, they decided to protect her the same way she'd protected them. They supported her claim that she had accidentally stumbled into the wrong party and had witnessed such atrocities she'd been momentarily frozen with fear.

That girl would have to live the rest of her life knowing what she'd been involved with. She'd have to look at herself in the mirror every day and know she'd sat back and watched the murder of her teachers. That would be torment enough.

Unsurprisingly, nobody had ever heard of James Bender. According to the school, a boy with that name had never been enrolled, despite all of the teachers having known the name and having mentioned at some point that the boy creeped them out. He wasn't a boy at all. Lauren knew that now. He was the embodiment of all that was wrong with today's youth. Their black hearts had conjured up a demon and he walked the halls of DS High like one of the students. The teachers had known no different, each assuming he just wasn't in their class. It turned out he wasn't in any class at all.

Now, six months later, Lauren was glad to have the whole situation behind her. She and Charlie completely moved cities. They were enjoying a much more relaxed lifestyle in a small undisclosed town that afforded them a lifestyle together they would have never been able to support back home. It was a stress-free lifestyle. Charlie continued his online teaching and also got a job teaching part time at a community college. Lauren wasn't happy about that at first, but they needed the extra income.

Besides, they had a baby on the way, and her job working at a mall fashion boutique wasn't exactly paying top dollar. It did allow her to go home at the end of the day and completely forget about her job. She didn't have to take work home with her like she did every single day at the school.

Life was perfect until time for senior prom rolled around at the end of the school year. Working in a place that specialized in dresses and high-priced fashion accessories, she came face to face with seventeen and eighteen-year-olds preparing for their graduation parties. She did her best to focus on the job and not think about her own experience.

It worked. She was finally getting a grasp on reality and understanding the events that transpired back home weren't typical. Her students hadn't dealt with life the same way every other kid did.

That was what she thought, until a girl named Fiona plopped her backpack down onto the counter and pulled out her wallet to fork over three-hundred dollars for the dress she'd decided on for prom.

"You ready to finish school?" Lauren asked the girl as she rang up her purchase.

Fiona rolled her eyes and smacked her bubble gum. "Yeah, whatevs. Just ready to get out of this lame-ass school and move on to the easy world."

"The easy world?" Lauren asked.

"Yeah, real life," the girl replied. "Where I don't have to get up early and go sit in classes all day. Where I don't have to listen to people talk all day long. The real world. The easy one."

The girl's card came back declined.

"Dammit," the girl swore as Lauren relayed the bad news. "It's my fuckin' dad. He's always cutting me off. Here, try this one."

She fished into her backpack again, and as she searched for a different credit card, a book slid out and thumped against the countertop. Lauren leaned closer to get a look at the book's cover. She'd seen it before.

"*The Maddening*," she read out loud and fought to control her breathing.

"Huh?" Fiona asked.

Lauren slapped a hand against the book. She was going into a full-blown panic attack.

"Jeez, what's your deal, lady?" Fiona asked.

Lauren couldn't breathe. She slapped the book again and reached for the phone. She needed to call Charlie. Only he could calm her down when she got all worked up like this. Fiona looked down to see what Lauren was slapping at and saw the book.

"Oh, it's fucking great," Fiona replied. "Totally changing the way I view the world."

She was about to faint, and this teenager was standing there grinning at her.

"You okay?" the girl asked.

"No, don't read that book," Lauren managed to say.

"Hurry up already!" the girl's friend called out from behind her.

"Hold your fuckin' horses!" the teenager yelled at her friend. She turned back to Lauren and handed over a second credit card. "Here, try this card."

Lauren took the card but could barely hold it in her trembling hand. "Please don't read that book."

"I've already read it," Fiona replied. "Twice."

"Where did you get it?"

"A friend," she said cheerfully. "Can you please ring up the dress?"

Lauren went through the motions, putting the credit card through. This one worked. She was numb as the girl signed the receipt and said, "Thanks. I might come back for my Grad Night dress."

"Grad Night?" Lauren asked.

"Yep, it's gonna be the party of the century."

"Hurry up, Fiona," the friend called again, this time from the door. "James wants to get out of here."

"James?" Lauren asked.

Fiona took her dress and walked toward the door, calling out over her shoulder, "Yeah, my prom date."

Lauren rushed to the door and made it there just in time to see the two girls walk away with a young boy between them. He wore dirty sneakers, filthy jeans, and a black hooded sweater. His head was down, his face hidden in the shadows, and as Lauren stared at them, he glanced over at her. His eyes glowed yellow.

The End.

If you liked what you read and want to find out more about the book mentioned in this story: *The Maddening* by T.K. Tantrum, make sure you read the books in my Diablo Snuff series so you can get a handle on all that. This, of course, was a stand-alone book, but it's kind of fun when you know the inside scoop, so go pick up a copy of *A Foreign Evil*, *The Grindhouse*, and soon to be published, *The Maddening*… books 1-3 by Carver Pike. Be advised, unlike this story, those have very graphic sexual content.

ABOUT THE AUTHOR

My name is Carver Pike. Since as far back as I can remember, I've been fascinated by everything horror. I'd sit cross-legged in front of the TV and watch The Texas Chainsaw Massacre while devouring a bowl of Kaboom cereal. I always wished the ghost at the end of each episode of Scooby-Doo wouldn't be just another man behind the mask. I wanted real ghastly ghouls, dastardly demons, and malevolent monsters.

At some point, I knew I couldn't sit back and keep watching this horror world from the stands. I wanted to be in the game. So, now I wield this virtual pen and sling ink onto this page with the hopes of someday being a major player. I want to create those worlds you visit, feed that fear that keeps you up late at night, and entertain you in ways only the greatest storytellers can.

I'm currently living in Central America with my wife and four kids. When I'm not writing, you can find me watching horror movies with my family or interacting with readers on social media.

Hopefully, we'll form a great author-reader relationship and you'll come to trust that Carver Pike will always keep you entertained.

Check out http://www.CarverPike.com for more info.

ALSO BY CARVER PIKE

www.ingramcontent.com/pod-product-compliance
Lightning Source LLC
Chambersburg PA
CBHW020945260626
47169CB00006B/1826